INHERITANCE

CONFLUENCE BOOK 3

JENNIFER FOEHNER WELLS

Blue Bedlam
SCIENCE FICTION

Jennifer Foehner Wells
Blue Bedlam Science Fiction
www.jenthulhu.com
jen@jenthulhu.com

Cover art © 2016 Galen Dara
Book Layout © 2017 Vellum

Inheritance/ Jennifer Foehner Wells. — 2nd ed.
ISBN 9781973381884 (paperback edition)

For Geoff

"Oh," said the general, "it supplies me with the most exciting hunting in the world. No other hunting compares with it for an instant. Every day I hunt, and I never grow bored now, for I have a quarry with which I can match my wits."

RICHARD CONNELL
THE MOST DANGEROUS GAME

PROLOGUE

DRUDII CODEX ENTRY 432.24

The following excerpt is taken from correspondence originally intended for Barl Tinumun, a highly decorated admiral and leader of the drudii fleet fighting for Inaricaa at the end of the inaricaan-rewquian war in the Hesteau system.

The messages were sent by Commander Yern Iubem, one of many drudii scouts sent by Admiral Tinumun in search of Terra, the isolated, far-flung world the Cunabula wrote of cryptically in ancient digital texts. The Cunabula reputedly interbred several strains of their most aggressive hominid species on this world, planning to create a warrior species to protect their galactic genetic legacy in the difficult millennia to come. The drudii hoped to find refuge and allies on this world—if they could locate it in time.

However, by the time the messages reached the Hesteau system, Tinumun was already dead, betrayed by the drudii's inaricaan siblings, who had created the drudii subspecies from their own people in time of war. It was at this time that the government of Inaricaa hired a lovek mercenary fleet to destroy the drudii fleet and then hunt down whoever had escaped.

Barl,

I hope this dispatch finds you having successfully navigated the diplomatic negotiations for our rights at home. That is optimistic of me, I think, given that I haven't received any reply to my previous seven missives as well as the hostility with which we were received upon returning home. I've routed each successive communique through different relay points in hopes that there is a simple mechanical explanation for your reticence, but as time goes on I worry for you...and for all of us.

This will be my final message. Simply put, our technology is failing. We were never meant to be colonists. Had we known we would be here for such a duration we certainly would have been outfitted differently. The time is long since past when we had enough fuel for a return trip, and the natives of this world do not have any industry that could recreate such complex compounds even in their crudest forms. But we are soldiers, not scientists, and so here we are.

I believe we are occupying the world we sought. As we had hoped, the terrans are a genetically compatible species. We proved this first via rudimentary genetic testing and then by virtue of physical trials.

The indigenous people are socially hierarchical in nature, competitive, patriarchal, tribal, jingoistic, and belligerent, for the most part. They are certainly more aggressive than any species we have ever encountered. This is a generality, of course. Exceptions abound, but I don't think I mischaracterize the majority.

Culturally these people have divided themselves into

factions, mainly by continent. These factions have become so entrenched that significant cosmetic traits have evolved to differentiate between them, further fueling their divisiveness, though our genetic tests show no significant difference between them. These factions frequently fight each other for resources and land. Within factions, familial subfactions have formed which do the same. Alliances between groups tend to be short-lived and abandoned when convenient.

We have found the terrans in a primitive preindustrial state, and the planet itself in a glacial geological epoch. Long-range communication on the ground does not exist. Travel is undertaken on the backs of large animals. Life is hard and primitive. Moving ahead without any technology will be a challenge. Record keeping will be difficult, but we shall persevere.

When we did not receive any reply to our third communique, we decided upon a contingency plan. I have separated the crew geographically, placing each crewmember on a different continent in close proximity to a geoelectromagnetic source. Marking those sources with durable monuments is a high priority so that you can find us when you arrive, since communication will no longer be possible.

We have perforce learned many skills the locals find useful, and I believe my crewmembers will prosper in this trade economy. Each individual is commissioned with the task of creating their own breeding program. We went over, at length, all materials we could find in the *Reveles*'s archive on maintaining genetic viability and how to pass down our mission from generation to generation as a secret oral tradition. This puts myself and the two other female crewmembers at a disadvantage, given the prevalent patriarchal cultural norms worldwide, but we are undaunted. We will keep our breeding groups close-knit and we will be ready for you, if you come.

I, myself, have produced nine offspring by nine different

male terrans. All nine display full druidic traits. I selected suitable terran mates for the two eldest, who have now come to reproductive viability. The second generation also displays full druidic traits. We test and train each child. If, in time, the traits become diluted, we will migrate to join another enclave for interbreeding. We will strive to keep our culture and knowledge intact. We have found the terrans to be quite flexible and curious about such things.

As a precaution we have sunk our ship in an ocean to prevent its detection. It raised too many questions among the natives, and leaving it visible on the planet's surface only left us vulnerable to incidental discovery from outsiders.

This is the state of things.

I continue to hope that you are safe and will come to us here with the resources needed for our people to thrive out of harm's way on this isolated world.

With respect,
Yern Iubem

Commander of the *Reveles*
Truth, Honor, Victory

1

IT WAS a good thing she loved him.

Darcy Eberhardt wanted nothing more than to plant her butt in the red, dusty gravel and refuse to go a step farther, but she plodded on in Adam's wake anyway. Eventually, he'd stop. She'd learned long ago that unpleasant things like this interminable hike and the academic part of medical school felt Sisyphean, but everything, everything, everything had an end.

She'd keep going until she dropped, if necessary. She was nothing if not dogged, but she couldn't refrain from protesting as they passed a flat, level area next to the sketchy trail, yet another perfectly adequate place to set up camp. "Adam! We're going to have to do this again tomorrow, just to get home! This is far enough. It's lovely here. Beautiful, even. Let's stop."

He was twenty paces ahead and just glanced back with a patient smile. "It's not much farther. It'll be so worth it, Darce."

It would have to be monumentally exciting to be worth it at this point, she thought, but she wouldn't say that out loud and ruin his fun. He'd been anticipating this hike for weeks. It seemed to be really important to him—and if it was important to him, it was important to her. So, she would trudge on until he let her stop.

She was too preoccupied by sheer exhaustion—not to mention hunger pangs, painfully blistered feet, and aching calves—to actually care about the scenery anymore. They'd woken before dawn to arrive at the trailhead as the sun came up, so they'd have enough time to do the hike in a single day. To say she was unaccustomed to this level of strenuous exercise would be an understatement.

Though the sky was still intensely blue, the shadows were lengthening and cooler breezes were kicking up. Her bra was still saturated with sweat and she was starting to feel cold and clammy now that the day's heat was subsiding. She'd been drenched and dried a few times over the course of the day, boulder hopping and even wading through creeks to get to this remote location. She was a filthy, bedraggled mess.

Her ponytail had slipped down, plastering her tightly coiled locks, heavy and sweaty, against her neck. She paused to remake it higher on her head, and the cool breeze kissed her neck. She shivered despite the sun still shining on her. Even slathered with SPF 50 she was going to be darker after this excursion. She sighed. At least she was making some vitamin D.

What passed for a trail looked deceptively flat, but her calves knew otherwise. As her pounding heart slowed, she captured the bite valve hovering over her right shoulder between her teeth—gently squeezing to release a flood of plastic-flavored, lukewarm water into her mouth—and took in the scenery.

They'd gained some altitude. The view was breathtaking, with layered, red-limestone rock formations and scrub for miles in every direction. After growing up in the spaces between lush green cornfields in Ohio, the Arizona desert was like a beautiful, alien landscape.

Still...

It wasn't attractive to whine and complain, but she just wanted to lie down, get warm and dry, eat something delicious, and not move for three days.

What a luxury that would be.

She already felt guilty about the break in her routine. She should be studying. Another round of exams was coming up and there just weren't enough hours in the week to do everything. Maybe she shouldn't have let Adam convince her to do this hike. He'd declared that she was too stressed, that she needed time away to refuel, that it would be easier to do the work if she could relax, get closer to nature, and remember what she was working toward. This wasn't the first time they'd done something like this. Camping and hiking trips were his go-to stress relief. Normally she didn't mind so much.

But she didn't see how getting bone-tired on a hike was going to accomplish that. He was trying to help, but he didn't understand. He was already living like an adult. He worked a nine-to-five job and had plenty of free time. He'd already forgotten what cramming for exams felt like. And this was so much more difficult than undergrad had ever been. It was relentless.

But he'd been more than patient for the last year and a half. He didn't complain when she begged off at the last minute or fell asleep mid-date. He didn't ask for much. So here she was. Humoring the guy who brought her breakfast in bed most Sunday mornings and didn't complain that she spent the rest of the day studying instead of hanging out with him.

She shrugged. There was plenty of guilt to go around in medical school. Most relationships couldn't survive this kind of stress. Almost everyone she knew was single or just having fun without commitments. But she thought that the two of them were different. They were stronger than most. They could beat the odds. If they managed to stay together, she'd make it up to him one day.

She shifted her weight. Her knees felt compressed and achy. The backpack should have gotten lighter as she drank the water level down, but it only seemed heavier as the day went on. She paused to stretch and adjust a strap, smiling ruefully as she remembered Adam chuckling at her when he caught her trying to fit her pathology textbook into the pack earlier that morning. She freely admitted now that it was a good thing he had, but she needed to stay within that book's orbit if she was going to pass the class on the first try.

She resolved to break out the notes she'd smuggled into the pack and study for at least an hour when they arrived at the campsite. Microbiology wasn't so bad. She had a good, solid foundation in that, thanks to undergraduate coursework. Pathology, however, was kicking her butt. It fascinated her, but it just didn't seem like there was time to commit all of it to memory in a way that would last the rest of her adult life.

She constantly fretted about it. She was smart and worked hard. She would pass the boards. But could she retain all of these facts she was stuffing into her head, every last gene product, chromosome location, and toxin name? What if one day someone died because of this little hike? How could she ever forgive herself if that were to happen?

Everyone expected so much of her. She was the first to go to college from either side of the family. She hadn't gotten to this point alone. She intended to work in poor underserved minority communities to give back. It was easier for people of color to trust a doctor with brown skin and they both needed and deserved for her to become the best doctor she could possibly be.

She sighed and looked up. Adam was waiting for her, just a few feet away.

"How do you feel, Darce?" he asked as she came up alongside him.

She didn't trust herself to reply. He looked too cheerful, too unaffected by the thirteen-mile ordeal. She hated the feeling that welled up inside her. It was offensive to feel that way about someone she cared about so much.

What was I thinking when I decided to date an exercise nut?

He bussed her forehead and some of her irritation melted away. He was gentle and kind even when she was a total grump. He was definitely a keeper. "This is a very special place. It's used mostly by my people, kept quiet to keep tourists from ruining it. There's no one for miles. We're completely alone."

She grimaced and raised her eyebrows at him. "It's special?"

He looked a little wary. "This isn't like your mom's new-age woo-woo stuff. It's been documented, scientifically."

A crow circled overhead, cawing raucously, the first sound she'd heard aside from their own voices and footsteps for hours. Her lip curled a little as she shielded her eyes to look up at it. Her mother would probably say it was an omen. Would it be bad or good? What would she say it meant? Truth be told she hadn't spent enough time with her mother to absorb much of the nonsense. Her mom was always off somewhere new "finding herself." Thank God her dad was a rock.

"What's been documented?" she asked, trying to keep her skepticism contained.

His mouth screwed up into a mischievous smile. He tugged on her arm and pulled her along. She groaned theatrically and let herself be dragged. Whatever this was, his enthusiasm for it hadn't declined a bit.

As they reached the crest of the outcropping, she slowed and dropped Adam's hand. She could hear rushing water. Then the view opened up. A small, bowl-shaped gorge was nestled on the other side, with a fifty-foot waterfall ending in a pool of sparkling turquoise water.

Adam grinned. "Yeah? See? Not so shabby. And this isn't the half of it." He took off at a brisk pace down the slope.

She felt a little lighter as she followed him, giddily slipping in the loose gravel, moving faster than she had for hours. The trail wound down the shoulder of the ridge with a couple of switchbacks and got far steeper as they got closer to the bottom.

Someone had anchored a heavy chain in the cliff face to hold on to and carved some rough footholds. For the first time that day, Darcy worried a bit for their safety. A fall from that height could certainly be fatal.

She checked her cell. There was no signal and the battery was almost dead. It had been fully charged when they left, though she'd never had a phone that could hold a charge for a whole day, so she wasn't surprised. She had the worst luck with cell phones. The batteries never lasted more than a couple of months.

Finally, they reached a point where the trail simply dropped off. A rickety wooden ladder had been placed there to descend the last twelve feet or so. Her legs felt wobbly as she climbed down, but they got to the bottom without incident.

Adam stripped, discarding his clothes on a pile of limestone fallen from the cliff face, and waded into the pool. Darcy glanced around, reassuring herself that they were truly alone, and quickly followed suit. The water was cool and shallow. Her weariness melted away as she submerged herself, washing away the sweat and grit of the day. She floated easily on the surface for a few minutes before she started to feel chilled and rose, refreshed, to dress and give Adam a hand setting up camp.

They pitched the tent some distance from the spray on a high spot jutting out from the canyon wall like a shelf. Adam assembled a lightweight camp stove and pulled out a package of dehydrated soup. Darcy arranged his bedroll inside the tent then came to join him, wrapping her own sleeping bag around herself and turning on their small LED lantern. Darkness was settling quickly inside the canyon. Temperatures could range by as much as forty to fifty degrees in the desert between day and night. Despite the growing chill, she was surprised to notice she really didn't feel as terrible as she'd thought she would.

Adam handed her a baggie of whole-grain crackers. "Some carbs will help you warm up quickly, Darce."

She took them gratefully and smiled at him. "So, okay. This is pretty amazing. Sorry I complained."

He looked pleased with himself and handed her a packet of almond butter. She squeezed its contents into her mouth while the soup heated up. It was sticky, rich and satisfying. She resisted asking for his.

"You mentioned the People use this place? What for?" Adam was multiracial—part black, part Asian, part Native American. One of his grandfathers was a member of the White Mountain Apache Tribe. Adam had never made much of that during their college days in Ohio. He just sort of passed as an ambiguously brown guy, with people always asking him where he was from. Since moving back to Phoenix after graduation, he'd been exploring the Native aspect of his heritage more. She envied that to some degree though she worried about him getting involved with what she could only call mysticism, something she was excruciatingly sensitive to because of her own upbringing.

But at least he was connecting with that group better than she'd ever connected with either of her own. She acted "too white" for most African Americans she knew and she would never be anything more than the token black friend for most whites. Neither group could truly understand her experiences. They were too far out of both of their comfort zones. Darcy lived in the space between two cultures, legitimately belonging to both, but never fully accepted by either. She was a piece without a puzzle. A minority within a minority.

But Adam understood only too well. It was a common bond they shared.

Adam rose carefully so he wouldn't knock over the precariously balanced stove and took her hand. He led her across the gorge to an open place where someone had left several tall, narrow stacks of flat stones. There was a gnarled and twisted shrub nearby, covered in waxy blue berries and emanating the woodsy, pungent scent of juniper.

"Do you feel it, Darcy?"

Her eyebrows drew together. He was being uncharacteristically cryptic. She wasn't sure where this was going and she was getting uncomfortable. "Feel what?"

"The energy of this place."

She blinked slowly and dropped his hand. She didn't want to hurt his feelings, but if he was starting down some shamanistic path...she couldn't go there with him. He knew that.

She stood there, staring blankly at a stack of stones, probably placed there with some kind of religious intent. She couldn't decide how to remind him that she had spent her childhood powerlessly watching her mother become sequentially obsessed with a multitude of gurus and belief systems, each time declaring it was the one true path, trusting, being drawn in, and often scammed. Before Darcy had moved in with her dad, there'd been many months of not eating much besides ramen, peanut butter, and government cheese, because her mother had given all her hard-earned money to another cybercriminal preying on those who desperately needed something to believe in outside themselves.

He knew her well enough to interpret her silence correctly. "Hey, no! No, no, no. It's not like that."

She searched his earnest face. "What's it like, Adam?"

"No one completely understands it, but they've documented some weird stuff. Even the government has done some kind of geological survey, here and at other places like this. All this red rock is full of iron oxide. There are large quartz deposits under the rock and that's got something to do with it. Also, there's some kind of mineral called magnetite. It has to do with geology and magnetism. It's like a hot spot of geomagnetic energy."

"A hot spot? Like for Wi-Fi?" She tried to keep the amusement from her voice, but wasn't very successful.

"Look, birds navigate by sensing geomagnetism, right? So, who says we can't sense it? Especially if there are places where it's concentrated? What if it affects our brain waves? Our mental state? Gives us a feeling of well-being or enhances our ability to heal?"

"Adam, birds have specialized anatomical structures. They evolved to detect that stuff. We aren't birds. We're human. We learned to migrate using environmental cues and maps and things. And besides, if that's really true, why aren't birds dive-bombing this place?"

He frowned and shook his head and she felt kind of bad for making light of something he cared about. "I shouldn't have said anything."

"If people feel something here, it's just because the landscape is breathtaking. It's so beautiful, it brings tears to my eyes. That might feel like something spiritual to some people."

"Yeah, probably. I should check the soup, see if it's ready."

She couldn't stop herself from asking, "Is someone making money off this site?"

He didn't answer and his stride was stiff as he walked back to the campsite. She'd offended him and she'd have to apologize, but maybe it would be better if she left him alone for a few minutes, so she lingered. She found a large circle of stacked stones nearby, divided into four quadrants, very precisely laid out.

The wind made an eerie, mournful sound, sweeping through the gorge. It blew wisps of unruly hair that had escaped her pony-tail around her face as she squatted to examine the stacked stones. She picked up a flat rock lying nearby, about the size of a paperback book, and placed it on top of the pile. As she did so, slowly and deliberately, she felt a tingling sensation in her fingertips.

She gasped like she'd been burned, jerked her arm back, and scrambled away. The stack of stones swayed a little, but did not fall. She glanced toward the campsite to see if Adam had seen her. He looked thoughtful, slightly turned away, stirring the soup. He hadn't noticed.

She stared at the stones, her mind boiling with flummoxed consternation. A powerful instinct told her she should walk away and never think of that moment again. That was the part of her that was always on guard against anything that reminded her of her mother's foolishness.

But she couldn't do it. Something equally potent, the part of her that had to *understand*, commanded she investigate further. She stepped to the edge of the circle.

Tentatively, she laid her hand flat atop the stack. This time her whole hand tingled and the sensation began to slowly ascend her arm, pulling her. She shuffled closer, now inside the circle.

She could no longer take her hand away.

The hair on her arm stood on end. She gaped as a faint blue light began to glow around her hand where it touched the stone. Streaks of the light surged up her arm, under the skin. She realized with detached fascination that they traced the paths of the major nerves.

Her body ached with a sudden onset of leaden fatigue. She rocked back, hard, onto her back, feet slipping out from under her, right hand still held fast to the stones.

Her low-rise shorts had slipped down, leaving her lower back exposed. She was horrified to realize a similar tingling sensation was emanating from that point of contact with the limestone floor of the gorge, traveling simultaneously up her spine and down her legs. She looked down to see the blue light outlining the nerves inside her thighs, heading steadily toward her feet.

Her limbs were no longer under her control. Her legs went rigid, straightening and flattening against the exposed rock under her.

Her left hand crossed her body of its own accord, pinning itself to the stone floor, and began to glow in the same way. She arched, struggling to keep the rest of her body from being drawn down. It was futile. As the tingling blue light crawled up her arm, it drew that limb down to the stone and then her shoulder too. The stack of stones fell on top of her with a soft clatter, but she barely felt it as her body stretched over the dusty canyon floor, shuddering with pins and needles.

It never occurred to her to scream. She felt as though she were trapped in a dream where anything could happen to her body while she remained motionless, observing herself under-going some kind of transformation.

Something was clearly affecting her central nervous system. The glowing lines along her nerves... It felt like that light was being drawn into her. But how? From where? And what would it do to her?

She closed her eyes to shut it out, but behind her lids, there was nothing but blue fire.

2

SHE HAD TO BE HALLUCINATING. Maybe she'd brushed up against the wrong plant on the hike or accidentally consumed some kind of psychoactive substance and was tripping. Or it was a stroke, an aneurism, a seizure, or—holy shit—she might actually be dying.

Her head swam. It felt like she was spinning. She was hyperventilating and couldn't stop. Her vision darkened, spiraling down to a pinpoint.

She was paralyzed, glowing *blue* like a neon beer sign. Why hadn't Adam seen her? Why hadn't he come to help her? Had he known this would happen? Was that why he'd brought her out here, speaking of special energy like some hippie?

Her lips pulled back in a rictus. How could something like this even happen?

She was alone. So alone.

Her body vibrated like a tuning fork, grew hot, and she felt sweat bead up all over. Something was building inside her, pouring into her. She was pinioned in the eye of a vortex. It swirled around her, through her, slowly reaching a rumbling crescendo. Her heart pounded so hard it felt like it could burst from her chest.

It was unbearable. It would never stop.

And then, all at once, it did.

The blue aura was gone. She trembled violently. Her body still felt thick and heavy, but she could move again. The sweat on her skin cooled quickly and she began to shiver. She tried to call to Adam, but all that came out of her mouth was a mewl. She gasped for breath and tried again, gaining some strength with each new attempt.

Then he was there, pulling the rocks off of her, cradling her in his arms.

"What happened? Did you fall?"

She sobbed, clutching at him weakly, saying, "I don't know," over and over.

"You're so cold. I need to warm you up. Can you walk? Is anything broken?"

His warm, brown eyes were so worried, searching. It helped to ground her. She stared into them and worked to match his breathing, to calm down so she could think more clearly. "I don't think I broke anything when I fell. I should be able to walk."

He stood, pulling her with him. She swayed on her feet, grateful for his support. They stepped outside the stone circle and a weird feeling came over her. She stopped moving.

"Okay?"

"Yes." She forced herself to take another step. It felt like she'd just disconnected from something powerful, like an appliance being unplugged.

He helped her back to the campsite and wrapped her up in her sleeping bag. He put a blue metal coffee mug, half-filled with steaming soup, in her hands. Then he settled behind her, wrapping his arms around her as though he could still her violent shivering with a tight hug.

She slumped against him, completely enervated. "I think I just had a seizure," she whispered.

"Have you ever had one before?"

"No. I can't think what else it could be." The mug was too hot. She loosened her sleeves and pulled them over her hands so she could grip it more comfortably.

"I should never have left you alone. I'm so sorry, Darcy." He buried his face in the nape of her neck. "I pushed you too hard when I knew you were stressed."

"Adam, this isn't your fault. Things like this just happen." She was feeling much warmer now. The shivering was slowing. She could feel the weakness subsiding.

"I should hike back until I can get a cell signal so I can call for help, but I don't want to leave you." He sounded anguished.

"No...that's not...don't go. I'm okay now."

"But you need medical attention—"

"No, they can't do anything for me tonight. I wouldn't even see a neurologist if I went to a hospital right now. Only twenty-five percent of seizures are caused by epilepsy. This was more likely from sleep deprivation, dehydration or...meningitis or something." It felt good to turn off the feelings and just be analytical about it. That was what she did best.

"Meningitis? Jesus! Darcy—"

She leaned back to look at him. His eyes were wide. She was freaking him out. "Oh—no—it's definitely not meningitis. I don't have any other symptoms of that. It's probably just dehydration. I tried to keep drinking all day, but maybe I didn't drink enough. My electrolytes must be off."

She blew on the soup to give herself something to do and sipped at it, guiltily. She was saying all this stuff to make sense of it, to reassure him. And herself. She was trying to explain away the experience, rewriting her own memory to make it less strange.

She was lying to both of them. That scared her because that

wasn't something she did. That hadn't been a seizure. Something had just happened to her, something beyond current medical explanation. She just didn't want to believe it.

She knew that and yet she couldn't stop. She didn't want to be that person—the one who had a bizarre experience and squandered a lifetime catechizing about it, searching for meaning, living for the sole purpose of telling the story to others, with people like her mom as devout followers, believing themselves chosen for some special purpose.

She wasn't special. Not that way. No one was.

She couldn't explain what had happened, but that didn't mean some scientist someday wouldn't. Adam had said there was geomagnetic energy documented in the gorge. Maybe it was a rare phenomenon, a discharge of energy of some kind, something like lightning. It had scrambled her neurochemistry. It had made her hallucinate the blue glow and the lines under her skin. She was lucky to be alive.

If she told someone, they'd think she was sick or insane or explain it away like she was already doing. She was probably fine, so there was no logical point in telling anyone, no matter how badly she wanted to. Adam might even believe her. Her mother certainly would. But everything would change. She didn't want it to.

Maybe some people would curl up in a ball and brood over what had just happened. That was not how she operated. She ignored things she didn't want to deal with. She moved on.

Her father had taught her that. He was black. He'd helped her see that it was the only way to deal with the slights and microaggressions she dealt with every day as a person of color, something her mother, as a white woman, didn't understand. Ignoring some things was the only way to stay sane.

Though it had seemed like hours at the time, that strange episode with the stones had probably only lasted five minutes.

How could she let five minutes of weirdness change the course of her life?

She turned, straightened, and smiled at Adam. She needed to act normal, to feel normal—and fast. "Well, that was sure weird. Sorry."

His eyebrows drew together and he leaned in, touching his forehead to hers. His breath came out in a rush against her cheek and he cupped his hand at the back of her head, holding her close. "Damn. You scared me, Darcy. Are you sure you're okay?"

"Yup. I'm fine. Soup's good. It's really warming me up."

He pulled her pack closer and poked the bite valve near her face. "Drink up, girl."

She complied and he produced a plastic spoon for her to slurp up the soup's noodles with. He kept fussing over her until she complained about it. She had to admit though, it was nice to be the one someone else took care of, for a change. Usually she was the one who cared for him, her friends, even her parents. It was just a part of being female and being strong. It was also the path she'd chosen for her career. She liked taking care of people. It felt good. But in this moment, it was nice to be on the receiving end.

When Adam was satisfied she'd had enough to eat and drink, he cocooned them together, wrapping her sleeping bag around them both, and produced her favorite chocolate bar—dark chocolate with crunchy, caramel bits. It was still warm from the heat of the day, despite the chill that had descended on the desert. By the time they'd devoured it, his fingers bringing soft, gooey morsels to her lips, she'd almost forgotten anything had happened. She felt normal—better than normal, actually—giddy, happy, and warm.

She kissed him—a delicious, sweet kiss—and licked at a dark smudge of chocolate trailing from the corner of his mouth. He kissed her back, reverently, holding his sticky fingers away from her.

"My gentleman," she whispered huskily, and she captured his hand in her own to bring it to her mouth. She licked and sucked his fingers clean, avidly watching his expression.

It was nearly fully dark now. In the pale light of the small LED lantern, his gaze darkened. "Hey, I don't think this is such a good…"

She silenced him with another kiss, shoving him down flat against the stone. "I think it's a very good idea."

"But you just…"

She bit his neck near the collarbone and gave it a long, slow lick. He sucked in a breath through his teeth.

He pushed on her gently, "Darcy—"

She narrowed her eyes. "Come on, Adam."

After all, she could feel his interest through their clothes—and there were too many of those in the way. She persisted with the kisses—his neck, his earlobe—all the while wriggling to divest herself of her own clothing.

It didn't take much to convince him to help. She savored the feeling of his large, warm hands gliding over her back, flicking at the fastening of her bra.

He knew her pattern of desire well. When her gasping cries reached a point that only he recognized, he gave her what she begged for.

She held her breath, clutching at him. When her bubble of pleasure burst, she cried out. As the sound of her voice echoed through the canyon, she came back to her senses to find Adam hovering over her, a stricken look on his face.

"Oh, shit. Darcy, what's happening?"

"What?" she mumbled.

Her eyes focused and she caught a glimpse of what he had seen, just as it faded away.

Lines under her skin had been glowing blue.

3

THERE WAS A SMUDGED, transparent yellow dot slowly bouncing in the Lovek's peripheral vision. It pissed him off for two reasons. First and foremost, he hated being reminded this was only a simulation. Second, after several cycles of tracking, he had the gildrut's scent. His prey was close at hand. The scent was fresh, lingering in the reeds. It couldn't be far off. He had to stay vigilant or he'd lose it in this watery environment.

The vasdasz had risen within him, rare from just a simulation. Every nerve ending tingled, every sense heightened. His circulatory system pounded a primal tattoo. His body flushed a dusky violet, seething with energy and the pleasure of the hunt. He wasn't about to stop now, no matter who thought they needed his attention.

He turned slowly, feet sinking into the marshy soil. He could virtually taste the alkaline tang as molecules of muck seeped into his sensate skin. His nostrils flared and his exposed body hair stood on end, analyzing the breeze in their respective manners. His vision swept the waterlogged plain, slightly unfocused. He allowed his brain to take in all the data, then let his subconscious mind guide him, in the way of old.

Relying on instinct was a riskier strategy. He could use the technology he had to hand, but it was more virtuous to rely solely on his senses. Therein dwelt the richness of the sport. It made the kill far more satisfying.

If he failed to trap the gildrut in time, he'd get a jolt, and that would come soon. His lip curled. That was win-win as far as he was concerned, though he was a minority when it came to such matters. Few found pain invigorating like he did. Many quit a sim just as the countdown reached zero, to avoid it.

The sim designers should have done something about that flaw in the game for those with his proclivities—ideally they'd make it impossible to play for an interval of time as a penalty. But that wouldn't suit the code monkeys' greed. They wanted their players so hooked on sims they'd pass all their free time in them, spending all their credits not only on the sims themselves, but on the intravenous nutrient-delivery systems and appetite suppressants the same corporations hawked to make life simpler for devoted sim-hounds.

He was not of that wastrel type. It wasn't about escape or competition for him. It was about the delicious difficulty of the hunt.

Whoever had created this sim must have been a lovek—or have known one intimately. Every detail was right, completely immersive, and fully integrated with his central nervous system. It was incredibly challenging. Pure pleasure.

But it was still just a sim.

It kept his mind sharp. It took the edge off of his lust for the hunt, helped to keep him sane. And yet, even without the yellow pixel winking at the edge of his sight, he could never completely forget that none of this was real.

One day he'd have a challenge.

His eyes narrowed and focused on a bent stem and he naturally extrapolated from that data. There. The gildrut hid there, quaking, hoping the Lovek couldn't hear its stifled, ragged breathing over the cacophonous cries of the amphibious creatures dwelling in this soggy place.

It would have been far better to keep running than to hide, but gildrut never knew that. They never knew the full extent of lovek abilities. How could they? Lovek were rare enough, even on his homeworld. To most of the galaxy, his species was but a myth to tell children to keep them wary and obedient.

Solitary and territorial, arisen in the harshest, most barren of climates, lovek had evolved more varied and finely honed sensory organs than any other known sentients, all in the name of survival. Their culture had changed drastically long ago when outsiders came, bringing civilization and technology. But those were distractions from a life's purpose, the only honest route to true fulfillment—the hunt. This wasn't a real hunt, but it was damn close and it was necessary to keep his senses sharp because a true challenge in the real world was nearly impossible to find.

He picked up his feet, finally closing in on the cowering sack of meat who had led him on such a merry chase. The stench of its fear was heavy and cloying. It was likely spent, resigned to its end.

He didn't flinch or slow as he disturbed a swarm of clacking insects. The vasdasz reached a crescendo inside his head, a tiny gland in his brain spilling neurotransmitters into his bloodstream at full bore.

The gildrut sprang from its hiding spot and heaved a scoop of muck into the Lovek's face. This one was spirited and still had some fight left in it. The Lovek snarled with glee and took off in pursuit, swiping at eyes and nose as he galloped after it.

The gildrut had longer legs. It could have bested him in a sprint, but this was a marathon of epic proportions and the vasdasz could keep him going well beyond typical hominid endurance.

It had been a foolish gambit to hide in the reeds. Once upright, it would be difficult to find a place to hide again. It was open to the sky as far as the eye could see. The clumps of grassy stalks reached just above his waist. Unless it managed to double back and return to the woods, he had it well in hand.

The gildrut's energy flagged. It slipped in the slime and went down, flailing. It turned over, defiance in its eyes.

"You have performed well. Go with honor into the next realm." The Lovek spoke the traditional words and sank to a knee to deliver the final thrust.

He was flush. Every nerve ending screamed with impending joy. As he reached out a hand, his throat ached to release the roar of completion.

But something held his hand fast in midair. He snarled, pushing and pulling, but it was frozen in place. It, as well as his entire body, was immobile. He realized his vision had gone drab, nearly devoid of color, and the transparent yellow dot that he'd ignored when it was dancing in his peripheral vision had taken up most of his field of view.

Someone wanted his attention badly enough to risk his rage. There was no pausing this kind of simulation. If he left it now, it meant starting over. The gildrut would rest and find new resources. It would learn and be even more challenging to capture, next time.

Frustration seethed in him.

The gildrut stared at him, its terrorized gaze transmuting into a confused stare. Then it scrambled away. He watched it race, slide, and splash over the terrain toward the trees, glancing back at him from time to time in consternation.

"Exit!" he bellowed. Instantly, he was free, grappling at the port embedded deep in his neck and ripping the dark helmet from his face. A quick glance around the low-lit room showed him his target. He hurtled the helmet at the lithe figure, standing ready for that very action. The woody bitch caught it easily and looked unperturbed.

He eyed her malevolently, contemplating putting his claws through *her* throat instead, but quickly discarded that notion. She was the best captain he'd ever employed. It was remarkable to find a scientist with innate leadership skills and few scruples. She was tough and long-lived as long as he provided the right environment for her, which was easy enough to do.

So he curbed his darker urges at some personal cost. He couldn't replace her. Also, he had to admit, it pleased him that they were both equally rare and unknown species in the galaxy. Plant-animal hybrids were completely unknown and she claimed to be the only individual to leave her homeworld for centuries. It put people off-balance when they arrived as a pair, made them unsure where to start with custom or nicety.

He sank onto the sleeping platform behind him, a show of weakness he wouldn't allow anyone but her to witness. His skin was already greening with jaundice as his body broke down hemoglobin and recycled the precious iron, returning it to storage for another hunt on another day. His head was pounding from the incomplete kill. He started to bark, "Bring me a—"

She was already placing a beverage in his hand. A single sniff told him it was palyo tonic. It would ease the hormonal hangover. She knew him too well for one who was not a mate. He almost liked her.

He threw the drink down his gullet and closed his eyes. He cleared his throat and turned it into a growl. "It couldn't wait another moment, Hain?"

She settled herself on a recreational platform, just outside his reach. "By your order."

It was like her to throw his own mandates in his face at a time like this, without apology, without a measure of respect to soften the interruption. He detested insolence. He lunged at her, closing his fist around her narrow, lichen-encrusted throat. She had no lungs. He wasn't blocking her air. But it was still a vulnerable part of her anatomy. Severing her head would be easy enough and quite final. "You would do well to remember your place, weed."

She blinked slowly, unfazed, and stared back at him without a hint of emotion. He released her and sank onto the sleeping platform. "Well?"

She dipped her head, and the ferny fronds decorating her skull waved. "We took samples from the planet according to established protocols, focusing, as usual, on remote locations with geomagnetic intensity. Testing revealed ninety-seven percent of the samples of the dominant species to be unremarkable anthropoid bipedal hominids. Most of the specimens are soft, the product of an overabundance of resources and little nutritional sense, not atypical for cultures at a midindustrial, prototechnological stage of development."

He opened one eye a fraction. There had to be more to it than this. None of this was unexpected. The only surprise had been finding a habitable planet so far from any known trade route. It was completely off the star map. That suited him well.

She straightened slightly under his gimlet glare and he felt a measure of satisfaction at this minute evidence of her discomfiture. She knew who called the shots.

"One specimen had a markedly different profile. I noted distinctive characteristics during the pickup and rushed the primary genetic sequencing. More-extensive testing will be necessary and that will take a great deal of time, but I just processed the preliminary results. You need to see them immediately."

It was her typically dispassionate delivery, yet there was some breath of intensity in her voice or manner. His hair stood on end, almost against his will. He felt his senses sharpening despite the post-vasdaszian haze.

Hain almost vibrated with excitement, watching his reaction with dilated pupils. Her stomata emitted more ozone than usual. Every chemoreceptor on his body took notice. He could hear her weak, dual-chambered heart flutter. He sat up, forgetting his fatigue.

She continued, "I've never seen genetics like this. It is the stuff of legend."

His breath caught. "Do not play with me, Hain. What kind of genetics are we speaking of?"

"Sir, it is drudii. The most complete genome we've ever found. As close to full-drudii as is statistically possible, though the odds were greatly against it. Shall I ready your personal shuttle and begin the search for a suitable planet?"

He stood. "No. We will not be rash. This is a once-in-a-lifetime occasion. We will evaluate before taking any action."

He sent a small prayer of gratitude to the Cunabula.

Finally.

4

"YOU...DARCY...JESUS!"

Adam rolled to his feet, pulling up his pants. He stood over her, staring at her with a frightened look on his face.

A rush of conflicting emotions surged inside her. Fear, confusion—even anger that her body had just done something that she hadn't been able to control. She felt exposed and raw. She whipped the sleeping bag back over herself and stayed still, staring numbly at the sky, trying to figure out what had just happened.

He'd seen the blue lines under her skin.

Okay. She hadn't hallucinated them. They were real. Two people don't hallucinate the same thing.

She wanted to burrow down under the sleeping bag and pretend this wasn't happening.

She noticed for the first time that the sky was very different out here, so far from the cities' light pollution. The sky wasn't black with just a few glowing pinpricks like back home in the Midwest. It was a breathtaking, cobalt canopy of glowing glitter.

"What was that?" he whispered, forcing her to stay present, instead of escaping inside her mind.

Her voice came out weaker than she wanted. She found herself repeating the same words she'd been saying earlier, right after the event. "I don't know." She cleared her throat and felt for her clothes so she could slip them back on.

"Darcy, you're freaking me out!"

She huffed, and it was almost a sob. Almost. She fought to hold back a second wave of tears, her face stretching tight with the effort. She could barely get words out. "I'm freaking out too."

He eased down next to her. He didn't touch her though. Was he afraid of her? "Come on, baby. You've got to talk to me."

She darted a look at him. He was worried.

She pulled a sweatshirt over her head. "Something happened to me that I can't explain. Over there." She shifted her gaze toward the stacks of stones, now obscured by the dark outside the circle of light from the lantern.

"What? Just now?"

She wanted to crumple. She wanted him to protect her from this, whatever it was. But she knew he couldn't. It was too late.

An accusing tone crept into her voice. "What did they tell you about this place? Why did you bring me here?"

He spread his hands and looked hurt and bewildered. "They told me it was romantic. They told me it was a spiritual place, filled with good energy. I brought you here to make a beautiful memory with you."

There was only an inch of air between them, but it felt like miles.

"I touched one of those stacks of stones with my bare hand." Her voice sounded brittle and distant to her own ears. She didn't want to confess but there wasn't any choice left to her now. She forced herself to continue, "It wouldn't let go of me. My hand started to tingle...and glow. It felt like something...something like light, or energy, or something, was pouring into me." She looked at her hand, which seemed so normal now, and tried to decide if the words she was using were even adequate to describe what had happened. "It pulled me down to the ground until I was stuck there and my whole body was glowing, like you just saw."

She glanced at him. His brows were drawn together and he stared at the stone floor between his knees.

She kept going because she didn't know what else to do. "I thought...I didn't know what to think. I thought maybe it was a hallucination, or a seizure, like I said. I was hoping it was over, that I'd never have to think about it again. But you saw it too, which means...it is something. But I swear to you, on my life, Adam, I don't know what it is and I'm scared shitless!"

Adam stood, peering into the dark in the direction of the stacked stones.

She blabbered to fill the vacuum his silence created. "It's got to be some kind of energy field. I absorbed it or something. It's going to fade away. I'm going to be fine."

She suddenly started thinking about radiation exposure and wondering if she should be worried that her DNA was being scrambled by it. Was this going to significantly shorten her lifespan? Was she going to be able to have children? Was she going to spend the rest of her life in hospitals, fading away in excruciating pain because of this hike?

This was exactly why she didn't want to think about it. Because once she started worrying, it would be so hard to stop. It was better to stay numb, always pushing forward to the next thing.

Why wasn't he saying anything? Why wasn't he comforting her? It hurt that he was silent and brooding. What was he thinking? Was he considering breaking up with her? Maybe she should save him the trouble. After all, why would he want to stay with a freak?

All her life she'd been avoiding anything spiritual or mystical in nature because of the way she'd seen her mother submit to those things and lose herself in them. She'd filled her life with school and studying and science projects—concrete things, real things that she could touch and understand, even if it was hard. And now this. Some unnatural force had toyed with her and ruined the life she'd worked so hard to build.

Her eye kept being drawn to the ladder and the trail above, leading the way home. She'd always had an excellent sense of direction. She could find her way back to the car, even in the dark, she was sure of it. At least it would be cooler tonight than tomorrow. She wanted to get away from this place. It felt like the walls were closing in and she needed to escape.

She would make it easy for Adam. He'd struggle with breaking up with her. It would be painful for him. She'd just go. It would save both of them the agony of a protracted nice-guy breakup.

Her throat hurt and her breath was coming too fast. She recognized the sensation. She was on the verge of a panic attack. She hadn't had one in years, not since high school. Adam had never seen that weakness, in fact. She couldn't bear to have him see her like this now when she was sure he had to be questioning whether he even wanted to be with her. She had to go. She had to get away from this terrible place.

She finished dressing, silently slipped her feet into her shoes, then knelt to tie them. She found her bra lying nearby and stuffed it into the pack. She rummaged around until she found a flashlight and then shouldered her gear. She looked up to see Adam watching her warily.

"What are you doing?"

"I'm going home." She tried to sound calm, but her voice shook, betraying her. Her emotions were completely out of control and she hated herself for it. She set off for the ladder. Her gait was disjointed as she stumbled over the uneven stone. She knew he was watching her and that made her feel self-conscious, like she was performing in a play. She was being melodramatic, she knew that, and yet she had to do it. She'd been hurt too many times to stand around and wait for him to end it. She sniffed loudly, trying so damn hard not to give in to the pressure of the tears behind her eyes.

They'd been together for three years. But if this was how he handled something serious, by brooding and keeping his distance, then she'd been wasting her time. It didn't matter how good their relationship was in the day-to-day if she couldn't count on him in a crisis.

She should have known. There was no one in the world she could count on aside from her dad. She was better off alone.

She stopped at the ladder, pressed her forehead into it and held on for dear life, trying to breathe evenly, to stop the spiraling thoughts before she completely lost it. She was hyperventilating and it seemed impossible to stop. She felt doomed. The best relationship of her life was over. She was alone again. All she wanted was to curl up in a ball until the pain subsided and she could be numb. But first she had to get out of there.

She stuck the small flashlight between her teeth and put her foot on the first rung, testing the stability of the ladder. She'd just heaved herself up when she felt his hands on her.

They didn't pull on her or demand anything. They were gentle, a warm, comforting weight, instantly quelling her momentum. She pulled the flashlight from her mouth and froze, waiting, desperately wanting it all to be made right.

"Darcy," he said quietly. "If you really want to go now, give me a minute to pack up so I can come with you. It's not safe to go alone after dark."

"Adam—" It was all she could get out. She was turning into his arms without conscious thought. It wasn't giving in, she told herself, it was just giving him a chance. It had been rash to assume she knew what he was thinking, impulsive to walk away because her stupid feelings were hurt. She had to stop doing things like that if she was going to hang on to him—if she was going to be a good doctor. She had to learn to take a minute and think first, to give people the opportunity to explain.

"I'm sorry," he murmured into her hair. "I flipped out. You must be scared. I'm here for you." He held her in a big bear hug. Her feet didn't touch the ground. She wrapped her legs around him, clinging to him for dear life.

She managed to choke out, "I don't know what it is." And she let go of a deep, wracking sob.

"I know, baby." He walked back to the campsite with her in his arms and sat down with her on his lap. He rocked her and listened as she poured out more details about what happened, most of it incoherent, mixed with sobs and tears and snot. It was embarrassing and cathartic. She'd never broken down in front of him like that before. She'd always been as solid as stone.

He gave her the bandana that'd been wrapped around his neck most of the day. It was still moist from his sweat and smelled salty and musky, like him. Somehow, it didn't seem gross at all. It seemed kind of wonderful. When she'd finally let out all of the built-up stress, she used the bandana to mop herself up. She felt limp and exhausted and a little uneasy about being so vulnerable with him. That wasn't her way.

When she was finally able to quiet down, she slipped off his lap with a watery laugh to find somewhere nearby to relieve herself. When she returned, she found he'd brought out the rest of the sleeping gear and laid it out on the ground in front of the tent. He was busily messing with the zippers on both of the sleeping bags, joining his bag to hers to make one larger one.

"I haven't noticed any animal activity down here. I think we'll be safe enough to sleep in the open. It's still early. We can look at the stars for a while before we go to sleep. We can leave at first light, if you want. It'll be safer."

"Okay." She nodded, smiling weakly. "I'd like that."

They curled up together, with her head on his chest and one arm thrown over him, hugging him tight. His heart thumped slow and steady, lulling her into a light doze.

"Do you think you'll tell your mom?"

She inhaled sharply at the sound of his voice. But she didn't have to think about the answer. "Invite all the crazy to come home to roost? No, thank you."

"She might know someone who could help."

Darcy snorted. "Some witch doctor? Or an exorcist?"

He squeezed her arm gently. "What if I asked a tribal elder or the diyin?"

She went rigid. The thought of telling someone else was so scary. But he was right—the People might know more about it. Maybe it had happened before. "It depends on what you say. I guess if you're careful. I don't want to get drawn into something weird."

He rubbed his cheek against hers and kissed the top of her head. "I know. I'll be careful."

He was quiet for a long while. She started to drift, then startled when he spoke again, so quietly she almost didn't hear him. "I'm going to touch those stones in the morning, Darcy."

A surge of panic gripped her. "No, Adam. You're not."

They argued for a while but she couldn't get him to agree to leave the stones alone. Eventually they just stopped talking about it. He cuddled her and murmured against her hair that it would be okay, that he'd help her figure it all out.

She felt safe in his arms. She wasn't alone. He was there for her. This would pass and they would be okay, more than okay. The silence lengthened until she finally relaxed and slept.

5

SOMETHING WOKE Darcy from a deep sleep.

She'd been dreaming about something that seemed important, but she couldn't remember what that was. Possibly it was something frightening after the stress of the day before. Surely that was why her heart was pounding and why she felt frozen, afraid to move or breathe.

She waited, listening. A cool breeze ruffled her hair, bringing with it the fleeting sound of crunching steps over the stone near the top of the gorge, as well as hissing and something rhythmically clacking together. She didn't know what it was and that bothered her. Something told her that the sounds were some kind of large animal vocalizations, but she couldn't put her finger on what kind of animals they might be.

The sounds came and went with the caprice of the wind. They played tricks on her mind. She could almost believe the animals were speaking two different languages to each other, one comprised of low-pitched hissing tones, the other of clicks and clacks.

It was surreal. She felt suddenly cold and more than a little frightened. She shrank down and prayed she was dreaming, though it seemed far too real to be a dream.

Adam had said there was no evidence of any animals in the area and she had trusted that he knew what he was talking about. She was aware that there were plenty of snakes, birds, lizards, and scorpions in the Sonoran Desert, but she sensed that these things that she was listening to, whatever they were, were much larger than that.

They were coming closer. It almost seemed like they were arguing. She would hear the low hiss, it would rise in volume—its tone becoming more belligerent—and then it would be cut off by the staccato clacking. Perhaps the two animals were having some kind of territorial dispute.

She went through a mental checklist of all the kinds of desert wildlife she knew of, trying to pinpoint what it might be. She needed to figure out if it was a threat or if it could be ignored.

It wasn't a bobcat or a coyote. They wouldn't make those kinds of sounds. Predators would be nearly silent and solitary. They certainly wouldn't have a prolonged interaction with another animal. It could be a mule deer or a javelina, just stumbling around up there, looking for food in the scrub, maybe. But somehow that didn't seem plausible either.

She moved slowly, deliberately, until her lips were touching Adam's ear and her hand was on his chest. She jostled him and whispered, "Adam!"

He shifted and turned his head, one eye peering at her. His lips smacked together like there was a bad taste in his mouth. "What?" he asked, full baritone.

She shushed him harshly and then strained to listen for any sign that he'd been heard.

"What's wrong?" he asked, a little more quietly.

"There's something up there. Something big. Listen."

He grunted and rolled onto his back. "I don't hear anything."

She didn't either. Had they gone away or were they listening now, too?

After a few minutes, he sighed and went for the zipper.

"What are you doing?"

"I'm awake. I'm going to pee. Is that okay?"

She felt silly all of a sudden. She was acting like a hysterical person. She didn't need him to protect her. It was probably part wild animals, part distortion of sound on the wind, part dark-night childish fears with a hefty dose of imagination fueling the paranoia she was feeling.

Adam didn't wait for an answer. He peeled back the zipper and crawled out. A rush of cold air snuck into the bag as he staggered away with a flashlight. She patted the bag down around her and huddled on her side with the bag pulled up to her nose.

Then she saw the dark outline of something large skimming the rim of the gorge with its nose pointed toward the center, blotting out the stars. Nearly silent, it seemed bigger than a helicopter, but triangular in shape. She couldn't see a lot of detail in the faint light of just a partial moon, but it didn't look like any kind of vehicle she'd ever seen before.

The nose of the ship swung around and pointed at her. It hesitated for a moment and didn't continue its arc around the top of the canyon. It zipped to a new location, moving like a hummingbird, until it was very close, hovering ten feet above the floor of the gorge near the waterfall's pool, the nose of the ship still pointed in her direction. Then it slowly lowered and touched the stone with only a whisper of sound.

She hadn't made any conscious decision, hadn't even felt herself move, but she had scrambled out of the sleeping bag and found herself standing with her back to the cliff face.

They were trapped. The ship had just landed between them and the ladder that, as far as she knew, was the only way out of the gorge.

She couldn't take her eyes from it. She backed up slowly, her hand gliding over the rough, gritty wall. She realized she was mumbling Adam's name over and over again like a terrorized child and stopped. She turned her head for a second to call for him a little louder.

The light from a flashlight blinded her and she panicked as it was almost certainly revealing their location to whatever was inside that ship. "Turn that off!" she demanded.

Adam emerged from the scrub nearby and sidled up to her. "Oh, sorry. What's up, babe? Did you lose your flashlight?"

"No, we've got a problem. Look." She pointed at the ship and he saw it for the first time.

"Holy shit," he whispered. "What do you think that is? Some kind of secret government airplane?"

"I don't think so. I think it knows we're here. We need to hide or find another way out. Now."

"What? They're probably just doing some kind of military exercise. Maybe they've got a malfunction or something. They might need some help. They probably can't get cell signal out here either."

"No, Adam, no. It was looking for us."

"Darcy, we have permission to be here. This is reservation land. They're the ones that are going to get in trouble."

A section of the ship came away with a white puff of powder that drifted in the moonlight. The section slowly lowered to the stone. It was a ramp. Two figures appeared. In the dim light, it was hard to make out more than silhouettes. One was tall and slim with arms that were disproportionately long and thin. The other was very short, clearly not human. It was some kind of animal.

She felt horror growing inside her, rooting her with disbelief to the spot where she stood, as she fought to understand what she was seeing and hearing. The low hissing tones and the clacks had come from that pair. That was loud and clear now.

The second creature began to descend the ramp, revealing that it was every bit as big as the first, that it just moved low to the ground...on multiple legs. From that distance in the dim light, she couldn't tell how many. It seemed like six or maybe eight.

Adam grabbed her arm and pulled her into the scrub. They ran, fueled by blind terror. Pungent limbs tore at her clothing and hair as she followed Adam around the perimeter of the gorge. He stopped periodically to scan the cliff face for another possible exit route carved into the stone. But there wasn't one. Without rock-climbing equipment, she didn't see any possible way out except for the ladder.

The hisses and clacks grew louder, reverberating off the rock with ominous overtones. Sometimes the strange utterances morphed into angry shouts that sounded bizarrely like Italian, Portuguese, or some other romance language.

Darcy looked to Adam. He spoke Spanish, but he showed no sign of recognizing anything they were saying. They darted through open spaces toward the cover of the scrub until they reached the pool. The dull roar of the waterfall muted most of the sounds that the visitors were making.

Adam sent her a questioning look. She nodded. The waterfall would hide them and muffle any sounds they might make. It was also the last hiding place between them, the ship, and the ladder.

They ducked under the cold sluice, drenched instantly. There was a small hollow behind the falls, but the depression wasn't deep enough to protect them from the constant, chilling spray. Water dripped from her hair and ran down her nose, stealing all her warmth. She was covered in gooseflesh and shivering. Adam wrapped his arms around her and put his chin on top of her head.

He put his mouth to her ear. "Let's wait just another couple of minutes, then make a dash for the ladder. Hopefully they'll be on the other side of the canyon by then and won't even see us."

She met his eyes and nodded once. He held her gaze, a disquieted, perplexed look on his face. She knew what he was thinking. She was thinking the same thing. The world had changed overnight. Reality was far different from what they'd thought. One hike in the desert had just changed their lives forever.

She wondered if the two events were related. Had the blue light under her skin summoned these strangers here? Was this somehow her fault? If she hadn't touched the stack of stones, would they be sleeping peacefully now under the stars? Or was the world just a crazy, surreal place? Once you stepped away from the safety in numbers that civilization provided, were you exposed and vulnerable to any number of insane possibilities?

Or was she just unlucky? Had all her mother's silly new-age stuff marked her as a target? Had a childhood surrounded by too many crystals channeled some kind of negative voodoo energy?

Adam moved, interrupting her increasingly paranoid thoughts. He gripped her, shoving her back in the niche, and edged slowly to the other side of the falls. She could barely see him. Without his warmth, she began to shudder violently. Her fingers and toes were numb and thick like blocks of wood.

He stood in the water. She didn't know how he could see anything, but he must have. He came back for her and they dashed through the falls together, heading for the cover of a desert ironwood tree with saguaro cactus growing up through its limbs. She recoiled as the cactus pricked her shoulder through her sopping-wet clothes. They huddled there for a minute, listening. She couldn't hear anything but the waterfall.

They locked eyes and came to a silent agreement. He jerked his head, indicating she should go first. She took off at a dead sprint, intending to skirt the black, hulking ship and head straight for the ladder and escape.

She pulled up short, almost immediately. Adam barreled into her from behind, knocking her to her knees. She scrambled to her feet, backing into him.

Directly in front of her, moonlight glinted off the carapace of a segmented body. It was reared up on hinged, sticklike hind legs, bristling with hairs. Its forelegs terminated in pincers which held a long, metallic stick, fluidly following Darcy's every movement. It made a chittering, clacking sound. Its eyes were dark, glittering, multifaceted protuberances, completely inhuman in every respect.

She turned, her heart pounding in her throat. The enormous insect's companion had come through the falls behind them and held a similar instrument under its arm. It wasn't human either. It was hard to make out, but it moved unnaturally—its limbs flowed as though it didn't have joints and there was something on its head that looked almost leafy. It was the one making the disturbing low susurrations.

With one alien to each side and the wall of the canyon behind them, there was nowhere to go except into the pool. She turned to grab Adam, but she was too late. The stick the tall alien held made contact with Adam's side. A blinding ray of white light emanated from the device, enveloping him. His eyes rolled back as he crumpled to the ground.

She screamed his name and reached for him to break his fall. Her fingers were glowing.

Something touched her back. All her muscles seized up painfully, and she realized she was engulfed in a similar beam of light from behind.

She was falling, too.

6

DARCY WOKE, bathed in a warm, blinding light. She was too disoriented to discern whether it was the same light that had knocked her out or something new. She had no sense of time passing—a second might have gone by since she fell unconscious in the gorge or it might have been days or weeks.

She blinked and squinted to clear her blurry vision, but that didn't work. There was something thick and waxy coating her eyes, and they weren't doing what she wanted them to. She tried to bring her hands to her face to wipe it away, but couldn't.

A cold wave of panic washed over her. Her body was immobilized and felt numb. A scream rose in her throat, aching to be released, but it was held there—the muscles refused to budge. There was something lodged there. It was impossible to swallow. She wanted to cough, but couldn't. She felt grateful that she could breathe at all.

She was pretty sure she'd been chemically sedated, but that it was wearing off. She was experiencing anesthetic awareness. She wasn't supposed to be awake. Someone was doing something to her, surgically, without her consent.

What was happening to her?

Gradually the panic subsided and she was able to perceive more input from her body. There was a sharp, heavy pressure building in her forehead. Periodically she felt hot little scrambling jolts shooting through her cranium, short-circuiting her thoughts. Each incipient shock created a disquieting sense of deja vu as she re-experienced the trauma of regaining consciousness again and again.

Oh, God, what could they be doing inside her head?

Something smooth and cool lay over her cheeks and the air smelled stale and medicinal. Intermittently she'd catch a whiff of something damp and rich, like compost tinged with cinnamon. It was foreign, strange. She didn't like it.

There was also a soft shushing sound. It was more than that, actually. It was a constant, whisper-soft breath, tickling the curled tendrils of hair around her ear. She focused on that. It was the most calming thing she could perceive. She pretended it was her mother's soothing hush when she was small and hurt or fearful.

In the background, there was something clacking in a mesmerizing way. She had the odd sensation that a translation of the clacking was just there, on the tip of her brain. She could *almost* understand its message. It made her uneasy for some reason, but she couldn't determine why, so she tried to ignore it, tried to stay calm, tried to hold on to sanity.

"Click-click-clack...regaining consciousness, mistress...clack-ity-click-clack-click."

"Shush-hush-hish-hissssssssssss...delicate...shish...here... ssssss...more precisely, this time...hishshshshsh...didn't kill this one...praise the Cunabula."

Darcy drifted away and began to dream of giant bugs flamenco dancing in a grove of frolicking trees, sending her secret messages in Morse code with castanets.

Darcy opened her eyes to a dim room. She felt heavy and weak. Her head ached ferociously.

Something shiny and green was waving around in front of her face. It felt like an invasion. She raised a limp hand to bat it away.

There was a chittering sound. It sounded like an indignant warning. It also sounded like...speech.

She blinked. Her eyes could barely open and were pointing in two different directions. With effort, she focused them.

Looming in her field of vision was an inexpressive insect face, its double-jointed antennae hovering over her, twitching.

She screamed uncontrollably, coming up off the platform she lay on despite bone-deep fatigue.

It slipped down and backed away from her on four hind legs, gleaming emerald thorax and head still upright. Its forelegs folded in a pose that looked astonishingly like human disapproval.

She was so shocked, she went silent.

The insect emitted more clacking sounds. As they registered, some aspect of her brain began to tumble them around, replaying them over and over again like echoes. Words formed out of the disordered noise: "Too loud. Foolish, half-witted anthropoid."

She gasped. Her eyes bulged. "You just...spoke..." But she stopped herself, because that wasn't what she'd actually said. She'd said, "Vuas itust...loquestas..."

Everything was spinning, rotating wildly around this insect that had her full attention. She couldn't take her eyes off it.

Its head inclined in something like acknowledgement. More clacking followed.

She watched, fascinated. Her eye was drawn to small sections of its shell just above the joints of its forelimbs—it was doing something akin to shrugging to make the sounds—and those sounds were consonants somehow.

She reeled, sure she must be dreaming.

Consonants. But there were vowels too, very subtle, between the clacks. She narrowed her eyes, trying to see how it was producing those softer sounds. The mandible, a sort of sideways beak, remained stationary. It did not appear to be producing any sound from its mouth whatsoever. The vowel sounds came from elsewhere.

"The implant is functioning well," it said.

"Didn't anyone ever teach you that it's impolite to stare?" a breathy voice said from the other side of Darcy's bed.

Darcy jumped and whipped around. Then she groaned and clutched her head. Her vision went black for a second. The sudden movement made her brain throb. She didn't have a choice. She had to lie back down.

"Caution. I wouldn't do that if I were you. We probably should have kept you tied down." The owner of this newest voice came into her field of view.

"Oh..." That was all Darcy could say. A person unlike any other she'd ever witnessed stood before her. She instantly made a connection with a small sculpture of a face shrouded in leaves that had hung in her childhood home: the Green Man. It was a symbol of rebirth and renewal that her mother loved.

"Lights."

The lights came up, harsh and bright, making Darcy squint painfully.

The intense white light revealed a willowy, feminine form standing at Darcy's feet. This person swayed slightly and turned her face up to the lights in the ceiling. Her voice came out a breathy monotone, but vibrated somehow with pleasure when she said, "That's better. I am called Hain."

Very little of Hain's skin showed, and what did was a muted

yellow-chartreuse. She wasn't wearing clothing. Rather, her trunk was encrusted with coral-colored, striated medallions of varying size that seemed to grow into each other, in an almost crystalline way, over her skin. Her arms and legs were covered with something organic that looked like aged, golden-yellow paint that had developed a network of fine cracks, like crazing. Even her fingers and toes were covered, those digits being long and fragile looking.

Around her neck sprouted a lush wreath of undulating leafy growth in various shades of waxy greens, some scalloped, others fernlike. Loops of fuzzy, mossy filaments draped over her shoulders and around her hips, flowing with her movements. Atop her head was an airy crown of soft, green branching strands, burgeoning in all directions. Even her face and neck were covered with frilly clusters of green plaques, like lichen, creeping over her features. Her deep, sea-green eyes were incredibly large, expressive, and knowing, but she had the barest suggestion of a nose and just a slit for a mouth. She was otherworldly.

Hain turned to the insect. "They all have so much to say when they speak their insular gibberish, but put a civilized tongue in their mouth and they are reduced to mutes."

The insect chattered a bit. Something told Darcy that sound was laughter. She didn't like it. She didn't like anything that was happening here.

She looked down and was shocked to discover that she was naked, covered only by a gossamer-thin sheet. She scrambled to grab the transparent covering, pulling it up to pool over her more private areas.

With growing horror she realized that all of her skin was reddish and ashy. It felt hot to the touch, stripped of all moisture, painful, as though she'd been burned. What were they doing? Experimenting on her?

In addition, there were thin tubes attached to her body. She groped with clumsy, fumbling fingers along them and found they were inserted directly into her left carotid artery.

Hain had gotten close, was peering at her with intense curiosity. Her monotone voice came out slow and deliberate, like she was speaking to someone with diminished mental faculties. "Do you have a name?"

Darcy ground her teeth before answering. Somewhere between her brain and her tongue, the signals she sent were transformed from English into this other language. She was hearing it for the first time from her own lips, but still understood it. "What have you done to me? Why did you take us? Where am I? Where's Adam?"

Hain's voice continued with little change in pitch or intonation. "Aha! Did you hear this, Chitin47? I had begun to think the Lovek's legends were some kind of ancient galactic joke, mayhap as old as the Cunabula themselves. These anthropoids have been all but reticent until now, but this one has expressed understanding of its past, its current situation, and that of its companion. And umbrage too, a complex emotion. Oh, well done!"

Darcy felt the urge to tug out the tubes and try to fight them somehow. But that would be suicide. If she pulled something that big out of her carotid, she would bleed out in minutes, not to mention that she felt weak as a kitten. "What do you want?"

"I have already requested your name."

Darcy stayed silent.

"You have much to learn about the universe, my provincial little friend. But no matter. You've demonstrated that the device implanted in your brain is functioning properly. That, for now, is all that's needed." Hain turned toward the insect and intoned, "My research shows the closest anatomic analog to be nieblic. Use those protocols for sedation and immune-system stimulation henceforth. Let's get this one healed up and in with the general population. She'll get her answers there. We needn't waste valuable time on explication now."

The insect inclined its head and turned to a console where it began to press buttons and use a touchscreen computer. Hain swept out of the room.

"Wait!" Darcy called weakly, but her eyes were already closing.

7

DARCY HAD COME a long way since the uncontrollable shrieking of her initial waking. She'd worked through several emotional stages since Hain and friends had picked her up in the desert. First, there'd been sheer terror. Next came a period of disbelief and intense feelings of isolation and hopelessness, which had been quickly followed up with outrage, and that was where she'd stayed.

Anger was going to get her and Adam out of here.

She'd arrived at a point where she accepted her current situation but was unwilling to give up hope of escape. She'd been kidnapped for a purpose that wasn't readily apparent. They'd surgically implanted a language chip in her brain, which the insects called a dummy chip whenever Hain wasn't within earshot. It enabled her to communicate with them, which for some reason they found hilarious, and they'd kept her isolated in a recovery room with no contact aside from the insects themselves.

She let out an exasperated sigh and looked down at her itchy, ashy skin. They'd explained that it was standard procedure to strip the topmost layer of epidermis to minimize virulent outbreaks on the ship. That made sense, she supposed, given the history of devastating germs decimating unsuspecting, unexposed populations on Earth. Those kinds of problems would have to be worse within the confines of a ship that kidnapped people regularly from various worlds.

Unfortunately, with that layer of skin went all of her natural bacterial flora as well as her comfort. Her skin had been an itchy, flakey, uncomfortable mess since then, despite the probiotic lotion they'd given her. At least the clothing they gave her to wear wasn't irritating. The fabric skimmed her skin, warming or cooling depending on need, without any weight at all. A shimmery-white jumpsuit, it was made of the most amazing self-healing fabric.

It had been a strange experience to put it on for the first time. One of the insects had stood her up and another held her there. As her head spun, another one of them had poked a hole in a shapeless blob of fabric with a pincer, then pulled that over her head. He'd created holes for Darcy's arms and yanked on the fabric until it covered her. This tugging-and-fitting process had only taken a few minutes before Darcy was dressed in what appeared to be a soft, seamless, form-fitting garment. She had no idea what it was made of, but it was extraordinary.

With nothing much to do during her recovery besides sleep, eavesdrop on the insects, and fret about where Adam was and how to escape, she fiddled with the clothing until she figured it out. She found she could adjust it herself into infinite configurations by clicking a small button imbedded in the fabric of the sleeve. It released the tension in the weave allowing her to manipulate the garment until she was satisfied with the fit. Then she clicked it again to save the setting.

If she kept the sleeves and legs shorter, or the neckline pulled lower, the fabric became denser. Alternately, she could opt to cover more surface area by pulling the fabric up high like a turtle-neck or even farther, into a hood over her hair, which made the fabric become more sheer. She just wished they had let her keep her shoes. It felt weird to be barefoot.

Ultimately, she opted for capri-length pants, three-quarter sleeves, and a scoop neck so that the fabric remained opaque. That was a nod toward modesty. While it wasn't transparent enough to titillate her insect friends with views of her areola and pubic hair, it left little to the imagination, clinging to her like a second skin. She sighed. Who cared if she had back fat or how big her ass was if she was kidnapped on an alien ship in space? As long as the insects didn't mistake her for a grub, she figured she was probably okay.

But she wasn't okay.

She had lots of questions and, so far, very few answers.

Neither Hain nor the insects knew or cared what they'd just done to her medical career, which might very well be over now. No one told her anything about Adam though she asked them about him constantly. She hated that her last night with him had been so strange and volatile. She'd jumped to conclusions about his reaction to the blue light and that hadn't been fair. He deserved better than that. She should have given him more time, a little benefit of the doubt. She'd just been so upset and reacted badly. And now none of that even mattered. She might never know what the hell had happened when she touched those stones.

Hain's offhand commandment had been followed to a T—no one had explained anything to her. They ignored her except to monitor her convalescence from the surgery and ask her general health questions.

But she'd ascertained a few things, just by keeping her eyes and ears open. First of all, she was on a spaceship called the

Vermachten. It boggled her mind. She'd gone from being someone who didn't believe that such things existed, to having a bizarre experience in the desert, to being abducted and experimented on by aliens. The paradigm shift was too great. It was enough to make her think she might have had a psychotic break.

But she'd been treated relatively well. She'd been fed, kept warm. Physically, she felt great. From what she gathered from overhearing snatches of conversation, they now considered her recovery to be complete and were about to put her in some kind of cell.

She dragged her bare feet, trying to take in every detail that she could manage without annoying her escorts so much that they would be tempted to use the knock-out sticks they held. If she and Adam had any hope in hell of escaping this place, she needed to gather as much information about it as possible.

So much of it looked the same. It was a rabbit warren of cramped, dimly lit hallways, coated with a varnish of grime. There was little to differentiate one section of the ship from another, once they left the small infirmary where she'd been kept. She had no idea where Adam was, but now that she was out of the infirmary, she was determined to find him and a way out of this mess.

One of the insects prodded her from behind with the same kind of weapon that had been used to capture her. "Move along, little bigot."

She glanced back, trying to figure out which one of them had made that comment. She'd been cared for by the iridescent green insects throughout her recovery, but she honestly couldn't say if it had been by the same two that were escorting her now or thirty different individuals. They all looked and sounded the same to her. That thought made her uncomfortable. She didn't want him to be right. She'd been trying to pick out some unique characteristic to distinguish between them, but thus far, she hadn't been successful.

She'd become habituated to the sight of their gleaming, oily shells. She no longer shrank from the touch of their pincers or the brush of the hair bristling from their forelegs as they nursed her through the postsurgical recovery.

She'd observed their behavior scrupulously. Yes, they were aliens. And they were giant bugs. They clearly operated under a different set of cultural conventions, but it was equally clear that they had roughly the same set of hierarchical needs that Abraham Maslow had described in his theory of human motivation. So, she could relate to them on a fundamental level. That was a starting point, anyway.

She sensed that this ship had already put a lot of distance between her and her home. She and Adam would need to find an ally on the inside if they were going to escape. Logic dictated that it was more likely they would sneak out, rather than fight their way out, since neither of them had any experience fighting and she doubted that Adam's tai-chi lessons counted. So she kept trying to break through the cultural barriers, to cozy up to her jailers, in hopes of finding someone sympathetic enough to assist an escape attempt.

It was a long shot, but she didn't have a lot of options.

However, her attempts at communicating with her captors were hampered by a few issues. She didn't even bother to try with Hain, who treated her more like a fascinating science project than a person. There was no empathy to be found there.

The insects were taciturn by nature. They seemed to be irritable and quick to take offense. They were focused on their work and disgruntled by distractions. They were annoyed by her naiveté of the universe at large.

And then there was her lifelong aversion to insects. They'd

picked up on that early on, before she'd mastered herself. That hadn't endeared her to them.

But being called a bigot? That was just so damn messed up.

She planted her feet and stopped. She couldn't go another step without being heard. "Look, I'm not a bigot, okay?"

One of them twitched an antenna.

She interpreted that to mean he was annoyed, based on prior experience.

"Really? What's my name?"

She wracked her brain, but had no idea. She'd overheard a few names, but couldn't be sure which name went with which individual. Whatever differences there were between them, she just hadn't figured out yet.

But she would eventually, she was sure.

He folded his forelegs. "I didn't think so."

The other one let out a staccato laugh, and his mandibles worked, an indication of his amusement. "Aw, come on, give the anthropoid a break. Obviously none of them ever leave that rock. You'd be backwards too, if you'd never seen an outsider to your world. She's probably never even heard of the Swarm."

Darcy latched onto the modicum of compassion she'd heard. "Yes! And what if your first exposure to outsiders was being abducted?"

"Not my problem."

A door opened behind Darcy. The less sympathetic of the two insects prodded her to go through the door. She remained focused. "I'm not an anthropoid. I'm human."

"Are you? That distinction means very little here."

"What's the Swarm?"

"You've got a lot of questions."

"I'd have fewer if you'd just answer some of them."

The meaner of the two ignored her quip, backed up a little

bit, and turned slightly. After a moment it chattered to the other one at a rapid-fire pace, too fast for Darcy to understand.

She'd figured out a few days before that they had spiracles on their shoulders through which they forced air to form vowel sounds. It was the concert of these sounds with the consonant sounds made by the joints in their forelimbs that made speech possible for them, since they did not appear to have vocal chords. It was amazing, actually. But when they spoke rapidly, the clipped, forceful consonants were all Darcy could hear.

It was embarrassing that they spoke far slower when speaking to her, just so she could comprehend them. She'd overheard them joking about it, which she was certain was their intent.

They thought she was stupid.

The mean one turned his back and walked away.

The one remaining ducked his head in a gesture of acknowledgement and gently put his foreleg around Darcy, ushering her into a darkened, closet-sized room where just a few dim lights glowed in relief. The door closed behind them.

As soon as they were alone, Darcy appealed to him. Maybe a different tactic would work? So far she'd been unable to get them to tell her why she was there or what they were planning to do with her.

"Please, help me. I just want to survive. I want to know more about your species—how I can tell you apart, what your names are. Please—tell me something about you. Isn't it possible that we could be friends?"

He didn't answer. He didn't move or look at her. He seemed to be deciding. Finally, he gestured at the room. "There is no need for decontamination. You have already undergone the procedure." He paused, and when he spoke again, his clicks came out slow and soft. "No one answered your questions because someone could have been listening."

She held her breath and waited, searching his alien features.

He turned his unblinking, multifaceted eyes to her again, briefly. "My brothers and I are a species called the hymenoptera. We are from a world ten times the size of your world, far distant from here."

She wrinkled her brow. "You're all male?" She had surmised that, but never been certain.

"Yes. Hain is our queen. Her consort, the Lovek, rarely leaves his quarters. He does all his dealings through Hain. I'm told he is like you. An anthropoid species. Apparently he doesn't like us either, because none of us ever sees him."

"Oh." She felt mortified. She wanted to protest, but everything she thought to say sounded crude and insincere.

How could she be blamed for disliking her captors? That only highlighted how alien they really were. There had to be something more to that, a reason why they were so hypersensitive. The whole situation and their reaction to her seemed bizarre. There were so many things she didn't understand.

"We are a hive species. We commonly work interstellar jobs like this. It is work others prefer not to do, but for which we are well suited." He turned away and reached out to the computer interface near the door, pressing a few keys. "Blame is laid at our feet for the wrongdoings of others. These are things you cannot possibly understand."

"But I might—I want to understand."

"You have species like us on your world?"

"Yes." She hesitated. "Similar. But they are smaller. Much... smaller." She was afraid to say anything else, for fear of offending him.

"Ah. Yes. Oxygen is the limiting factor for species like ours. Your world's atmosphere must contain a lower oxygen content. I am called Tesserae71. I am distinguished by the downy black fur around my ocelli."

"I don't know that term..."

"Ocelli? Simple eyes." He tapped a pincer next to the dark spots above his large, compound eyes.

She stared at that part of him, committing his anatomy to memory.

He shifted. "In future, you may not want to stare with such frequency. It may be acceptable within your culture. We find it offensive. It will behoove you to be very cautious once you are inside here."

She looked down at her hands. "Of course. I apologize. I just want to remember you."

"It is unlikely you will see me again."

"What? Why?"

Her stomach flipped over. She'd finally broken through to someone and now she'd never see him again? At least she'd gained some information from him. That was something. Now she knew that Hain pulled the strings for someone else and these guys, the hymenoptera, were merely working joes who punched a card and did what they were told. They weren't the ones behind this. Someone called the Lovek was. She'd heard that name before. From Hain.

"I am an infirmary worker. I am not a guard." He navigated through a few more screens on the control pad, then toggled the switch that opened the next door.

She immediately scanned for Adam's familiar face, but was shocked by the sight she was greeted with.

A cavernous room lay on the other side. Upon the floor, a grid pattern was laid out. Every few feet, a square, circle, or polygon was marked out on the floor in a bright color. Inside each shape, a figure resided.

Darcy balked as Tesserae71 moved forward into the room, sweeping her forcibly along with him. She didn't know why she'd thought that if there were any other prisoners, they'd be human. There wasn't another human in sight.

She gaped. She could never have imagined that there would be so many. There were hundreds of individuals here, maybe thousands, if this wasn't the only room like this.

She couldn't comprehend it. She tried not to stare, but found that almost impossible. Every color of the rainbow was represented as well as fantastical shapes and great range in size. Most of the aliens were clothed to varying degrees in the shimmery white jumpsuits. There were many that, like the hymenoptera, didn't resemble humans at all. Quite a few didn't bear any resemblance to *anything* she recognized.

"It is safe for us to step onto the mat. Your designated space is just down here," Tesserae71 said, forcing her to keep moving down an aisle. The dirty, dark-grey flooring was spongy under her feet. She kept her eyes down, glancing into each colorfully marked out cell as she passed it.

The room buzzed with a cacophony of disparate voices. Some of the individuals were disinterested in her arrival. They lounged on the floor, uncaring, perhaps sleeping. Others were more alert, sitting up or standing. Some appeared to be exercising in place.

Many watched.

Eyes of every imaginable shade and conformation followed them as they walked past dozens of prisoners. She felt like she was on display. Some of them looked as though they wanted to devour her.

"Will you look at the mammaries on that one!" someone hooted behind her.

Her face felt hot.

"Mammals. Always showing off the mammaries."

"Ha! Too true. One of my wives has eight! After her last litter?" Darcy assumed a rude gesture accompanied that comment and the lascivious sound she heard following it.

"Are they that big?"

"Naw. It's about quantity. She goes crazy when you...well, I'm telling you, the more the merrier, friend."

"Not terribly hirsute for an anthropoid. I like that. I do."

Darcy grimaced. That last had come from a provocatively sultry, feminine-sounding voice.

She turned in Tesserae71's grasp and looked down. She wanted to burrow into his prickly, alien embrace. He was the friendliest thing she knew in this place and he was about to leave her there, alone. "Tesserae, please take me back to the infirmary."

He tilted his head to one side, a sure tell that she'd said something stupid. "You address my entire birth cadre when you speak thus. My name is Tesserae71."

"Oh. Sorry."

"The cell you occupied in the infirmary has been filled. Hain is performing the implant on another subject as we speak. Here is your designated space: yellow octagon 194. Step inside, please, and I will activate it."

She hesitated.

"I will use the compliance wand if necessary." He gestured with the rod he held.

Tears pricked the backs of her eyes. "No. You don't have to do that. I'll go." She stepped over the grubby yellow rim into the small octagon, and turned to face him.

He manipulated something on the rod he held and the octagonal boundary lit up briefly. She thought she heard a faint humming sound. "Someone will be along to instruct you about the rules, as well as the schedules for ablutions, nutritive consumption, and voiding. You must stay within your designated area except at the appointed times or the consequences become increasingly dire. I urge you to comply." He turned to leave.

"Wait! Someone was taken with me, at the same time. His name is Adam. I need to find him."

"I know nothing of this. I must return to my post." He skittered away.

She found herself calling after him, "Thank you, Tesserae71! My name is Darcy!"

She wasn't sure why she'd done that, flung her name at him, vainly hoping she'd made an impression on him that could work in her favor. She immediately regretted it. He didn't even turn to acknowledge that she'd spoken. And now all those around her knew her name.

8

DARCY SLOWLY TURNED IN A CIRCLE, forlorn, scanning the sea of prisoners for a glimpse of Adam's dark, curled hair. She couldn't see him anywhere. Either he was the one getting the language chip right now or he was in another room.

"You must be someone very important," an imperious voice lisped from behind her.

She turned to see who had spoken, taking in more fully the individuals closest to her. She managed to hold back from a double take, but only barely.

Inside the next cell was a cobalt-blue slug-like creature that was roughly the size of a plump house cat, though much longer. Crowning its head were two cone-shaped stalks with brilliant orange comblike markings. They undulated bonelessly, moving independently of each other. It had raised lime-green stripes running the length of its body. It held itself up and leaned forward on two stubby tentacles protruding from its single foot. It seemed to be peering at her, but she couldn't detect any eyes.

Darcy looked around, unsure.

"Yes. 'Tis I who speaks at you, mammal."

It *was* the slug who was speaking.

"Um, hello?"

"Who *are* you?" The sound of its voice was haughty and almost...slurpy.

She'd just said her name out loud. Saying it again wasn't going to change anything. "I'm Darcy Eberhardt."

"This tells me nothing. They rearranged every person in this entire section before bringing you out. I want to know why." It turned, its body rippling wavelike over the rubbery floor, leaving a glistening trail in its wake. It presented its backside to her, where a froth of fernlike tendrils sprouted.

She didn't have any idea what it was talking about, so it seemed wiser to stay silent. She watched as the creature took a turn around its cell.

"I can practically taste your fear," the mollusk accused. The stalks on its head pointed at her in condemnation and seemed to vibrate with anger. "There is copious mammalian stress-hormone in the air, and it's all emanating from you. I demand that you stop. It's a form of emotional pollution and I won't have it."

Darcy's eyes widened. She didn't know what to say. It seemed best to placate. "Okay. I'll try."

"Nembrotha is an irritable individual. I find it's best to ignore them when they work themself into this state. I am called Selpis," a rich, feminine voice said gently to Darcy's left.

Darcy stared at the slug for a moment, realizing the person speaking was using a third set of pronouns that Darcy hadn't heard spoken yet—she only knew what they meant because of the chip. They were gender neutral in nature and translated in her mind as the singular "they."

This new voice was the most comprehensible to Darcy's ear of any she'd encountered so far. As Darcy turned to look, she noted satiny, muted-green and brown scales making up Selpis's skin. That, as well as her decidedly nonhuman features, marked her as reptilian in origin—as did the tail that effectively doubled the length of her body.

She was of a comparable size and shape to Darcy, but was leaner, wirier. She moved with a sinewy grace and wore the same white jumpsuit, drawn out into a gauzy, flowing skirted garment. Nembrotha was unclad.

"They? Um, is he...she...?" Darcy asked with a sidelong glance toward Nembrotha, who no longer seemed to be interested, but whom she suspected was listening.

Selpis's large eyes blinked slowly and Darcy thought she detected amusement.

"They are hermaphroditic and I would recommend you take care not to misgender them. They get a little grumpy when people do that. Understandably, I think."

"Oh." Well, that made sense then. Darcy reminded herself not to stare, but she was intrigued by Selpis's anatomy, just as she'd been by the hymenoptera. Selpis's ancestors had clearly learned to walk upright at some point in their distant past, just as humans had. But their tails, flowing to a tapered point directly from their trunks, must have altered the way that their pelvises had evolved. Selpis was bowlegged. Her tail appeared to be prehensile, curling around her body. Perhaps it lent balance to her upright stance.

Selpis's face wasn't the pointy, triangular face you'd expect from a lizard. It came to a softer point, pushed back and rounded, displaying brachycephaly—the same phenomenon that makes the faces of human infants and baby animals appealing. Combined with her large, limpid eyes, it gave her a very youthful appearance.

There was frank understanding in the delicate features of Selpis. She seemed calm and kind as she settled into a tranquil position that reminded Darcy of a yoga pose, her fingers splayed out over her corded knees and her thick tail wrapped around her body. Darcy decided instantly that she liked her.

Silence fell as they regarded each other in furtive glances. Darcy's heart returned to a more normal rhythm as she came to terms with the newest situation she found herself in.

Nembrotha slowed their agitated slithering, though the stalks on their head continued to ripple and twitch. The motion brought to Darcy's mind her childhood dog, scenting the air. Perhaps there were chemoreceptors in those organs.

Darcy tried to relax, but it was very difficult because she felt like she was being watched, assessed. She couldn't stop looking for some sign of Adam in the sea of bodies, and that just meant she continued to catalog exotic faces.

Someone should have told Hollywood a long time ago that aliens weren't anthropomorphized animals. Sure, economics probably dictated that aliens in sci-fi would have to look human with some slightly different defining aspect—scales for a reptilian species overlaid on a human face, for example—because makeup was infinitely less expensive than CG.

But reality was quite different. Hollywood got it right that sentient alien life would take many forms, evolve from many kinds of species, but as it turned out they weren't just human versions of lizards or insects or slugs. They seemed to be lizards or insects or slugs that had developed a certain, almost undefinable type of useful intelligence.

Something in the back of her mind speculated about the conditions under which this type of intelligence might evolve—was a certain brain mass necessary? A requisite body size? Or perhaps it required opposable digits or simply the use of tools. None of that explained Nembrotha. Maybe every species was on the same path to sentience, but took a greater or lesser span of time to achieve it.

It was too much. She sat down on the mat in the center of her yellow octagon, curled her knees up and rested her forehead on them. She wished for Adam to hold her the way he had in the gorge, to help her feel better. She wanted it all to go away.

"Feeling overwhelmed? That's natural. You've just arrived. It's an adjustment," Selpis said gently.

Darcy didn't reply. She just shook her head.

Nembrotha piped up, "You don't know the half of it. Her anatomy's been violated."

Selpis said, "Violated? That's...a bit unusual, even here."

Nembrotha sounded disgusted. "You mean sex. I'm talking about surgery."

Darcy could almost see the reptile's pupils dilate. Selpis leaned forward and her nostrils flared. "Oh? I do believe you are one of the ones all the rumors are about."

Darcy straightened a little. "Rumors?"

The reptile tilted her head to the side and swept Darcy with an evaluating look. "Rumors of a planet without the common language. Full of individuals so unable to communicate that Hain felt it was necessary to implant a specialized language chip in their brains normally used to help those speak who suffer cognitive limitations."

Darcy frowned. "The hymenoptera called it a dummy chip."

Selpis exuded warm understanding. "But you are not a simpleton, are you, love? Your world was simply untouched by the Cunabula. How remarkable."

Darcy frowned. The words Selpis had just spoken echoed in her head. "Wait. There is...a common language?"

Nembrotha harrumphed, came closer to the edge of the yellow square that separated them, and hunched up their body like an accordion. Their wavering stalks extended as far across the divide as they could reach them. They remained outstretched like that until the tips of the stalks began to quiver. Then Nembrotha slipped back in a whoosh and slumped, the stalks gone droopy. "She speaks the truth, as far as I can detect. What strange doings."

Selpis pulled her lips back in an approximation of a smile, and her large eyes gazed at the black ceiling. "I don't believe I've ever explained this to anyone. I've never had a child of my own to share the wonder of the Cunabula with. Everyone just *knows*."

Darcy began to feel impatient. "Knows what?"

The reptile's neck elongated and her head tilted thoughtfully to the side, as though she were preparing to tell a child a story. She blinked slowly. "The Cunabula was a very powerful civilization that existed long ago, so long that very little of them remains extant, except for all of us, of course. Some have called them gods, others geniuses, others intrepid scientists. Whatever we may think they were, all we know of them exists as fragments of digital language, a few literary works, and the histories of the peoples who claimed to know them or at least know of them."

Nembrotha put in, "There are many, many objects attributed to them, but none of them have any provenance. Most of it's just fripperdoodle."

"Fripperdoodle" didn't fully translate for some reason, but based on context, Darcy took it to mean something along the lines of hogwash or crap or nonsense. Nembrotha was either using some kind of colloquialism or had made up a word.

"I've heard this word before—Cunabula," Darcy said slowly. "What did they do that was so important? I don't understand."

Selpis nodded solemnly. "We owe them life." She gestured grandly around the room. "They left the seeds of life on worlds throughout the galaxy, giving rise to all of us. And into each seed they programmed a genetic key that links all of us together, for better or for worse."

Nembrotha made a gurgling sound and drew themself up into a narrower, thinner pose. "That 'key' is Mensententia, the common language."

Selpis leaned forward, curiosity plain on her features. "It normally manifests during puberty or at some other time of great change in a youth's life journey. But not on your world?"

Darcy drew her brows together. "You're saying this language isn't learned? It's innate?"

"Yes."

"No. We have many languages. There is no common language." Her eyes drifted around the room again, taking in the incredible diversity. "All of these people speak the same language?"

"Yes. We are raised with a native tongue, but when we reach an age where we might travel among the stars, the common language emerges to prepare us for the journey. The Cunabula were very wise. They knew it would keep us on a more even footing, minimize catastrophic misunderstandings and wars."

"Too bad they didn't eliminate greed while they were at it," Nembrotha said wetly, their head stalks sweeping the room as though making a point about all of them. They sagged a bit, flattening out.

Selpis gestured at Darcy, her bulbous fingertips splayed. "Your species may have evolved without the Cunabula's interference."

"How would I determine that?" Darcy asked.

Nembrotha shouted over her, outraged, "That's blasphemous!"

Selpis said patiently, "It is not. It is entirely possible. With all of the stars in all the galaxy, you think it's impossible that life could arise independently? I say it's not only possible, it's very probable. The fact that there aren't more encounters like this simply speaks to the notion that independently evolved species may be remote or skittish or so entirely foreign we cannot recognize them."

"I disagree! There are only three possibilities!" Nembrotha

shouted as they resumed their version of agitated pacing. They turned abruptly, a frothy substance oozing from the O of their mouth as they proclaimed, "Either a genetic defect was accidentally introduced early on in their evolution, preventing the expression of Mensententia among her people, which would seem to be almost impossible. *Or,* she comes from a planet of idiots, too stupid to use it yet. *Or,* she comes from the warrior planet that the Cunabula engineered!"

Selpis stared at Nembrotha for a long moment. Her gaze unfocused and her mouth gaped slightly, her eyes shifting back and forth in their orbits before sliding slowly to evaluate Darcy with a questioning look that was slowly transmuting into a hopeful one.

Darcy wanted to shrink inside herself. Every individual in her immediate vicinity had gone silent, waiting for her to remark upon Nembrotha's surprisingly loud declaration. She was in a fishbowl. All around her, the hush rippled out like a wave until the entire room had been silenced, every eye or eyelike organ pointed at her.

"She's not stupid. You can see that plainly in her expression," Selpis breathed.

A gravelly, disdainful sound burbled up out of Nembrotha, and their stalks folded back, their body sagging against the floor as though defeated. Their voice, too, was just a whisper. "She hardly looks like a warrior. She's all round and fleshy. I doubt she could best *me!* Even the cerebral sectilians look scrappier than that girl."

The quiet was almost unbearable. Darcy's mouth went dry. She wasn't sure what they wanted her to say, but it seemed like every person there hoped that her mere presence had generated some kind of opportunity. It was beginning to feel like a bad, quasi-religious experience. Thoughts sifted like snowflakes through her brain. She latched on to one of them.

She blurted out, "It has to be a genetic mutation. Humans can't make their own vitamin C. There are four enzymes required in the liver to manufacture L-ascorbate from glucose, and humans can't make it, though nearly every other animal on Earth can. Our gene for L-gulonolactone oxidase was broken at some point in our early evolutionary history. We have to constantly ingest vitamin C to prevent scurvy."

"Oh, bother." Nembrotha sank even lower to the floor.

A soft titter broke out behind Darcy.

Her face felt hot and she rushed to continue, "I'm just saying. We humans...we may be ignorant of all of—this—going on in the universe, but we aren't stupid. We do, however, seem to be very unlucky, genetically."

Far to her left, a snort rang out. Behind Selpis, someone cackled.

The entire room erupted with discordant laughter.

Darcy wished she could make a hasty exit, wished she could stomp away and hide somewhere. Why did everyone in this place think she was a fool? She was torn between standing defiantly and attempting to stare them all down or curling up in a ball and pretending she wasn't there. She was paralyzed in that moment of indecision, watching the faces around her contorting in hilarity at her expense, when something poked her in the side. She whirled to face a hymenoptera.

"You there. The mistress wants you. Don't try anything funny, anthropoid."

He was not Tesserae71.

9

THE LOVEK LEANED into the wall, palms on either side of his head, drinking in his first sight of the drudii, at long last.

He was tense and salivating. These were moments he'd hoped for over a lifetime. He was going to savor them as much as he would fine food or drink. He'd have the rest of his life to recall them.

He didn't want to miss a microsecond. He didn't want to even blink.

She stood there alone, fidgeting. He was making her wait for Hain. He wanted to see how she was coping with the stress of the confinement. So far, she knew next to nothing about his business. His people had been instructed to keep her in the dark. He wanted to watch her react. He wanted to *smell* her reacting, hear her heart rhythm change, hear the blood thunder through her veins when she learned the details.

Hain said she was well enough for a confrontation now. Her brain had recovered completely from the trauma of the intricate implantation surgery. She'd been well cared for, every need met, kept calm and on the highest-quality regenerative supplementation, though it had hardly been needed. Her recovery time had been remarkably quick. Still, no expense had been spared to get her in the best physical form possible. He'd allowed her to be placed in the cargo bay for a few moments to put her on edge as the reality of her situation here began to clarify, every moment surveilled.

The fact that she didn't have the common language was an interesting puzzle. He didn't put any stock in the maunderings of the disciples of the Cunabula. That species had died out long ago because they were not survivors. Why should any credence be given to the pursuits of evolutionary losers?

The galaxy was at war. It always had been and always would be. No single planet could change that. It was the way of things.

What the girl didn't know was that a small window had been cut out, precisely at his eye level, and replaced with a very special, very expensive material that was perfect for occasions just like this one. With a tap of his finger on the room control, that small span of wall between them had disappeared, leaving just a nanoscale sheet. On his side, it was completely transparent. However, from her point of view, inside the room, it appeared indistinguishable from the rest of the wall.

But he could smell her. She hadn't had a proper cleanse since the hours after they'd picked her up. On her world they would still use water for bathing, would know nothing of an ionic cleanse or a full-body brush-grooming and vacuum.

Though Hain's bugs had sanitized her, they couldn't completely remove the trappings of her culture. Her full, crimped hair reeked of a riot of perfumes—floral, vegetal, synthetic, and animal musk—hinting at the use of a multitude of enhancement products. Vain little beast.

These were subtle compared to her own bodily scents. He wanted nothing more than to bury his nose in her armpits and pubis, inhaling those earthy odors cached in her peculiarly scant body hair, but he couldn't do that. He had to keep his distance. He could smell their alluring aroma, even from the other side of the wall. It was enough.

She turned around and around, nervously plucking at her garment, taking in all the details of the room, her eyes always returning to the door. There was a reclining platform she could make use of, but she chose to remain standing. That was well. She knew the value of remaining alert, even if it wasn't a conscious decision.

She was barely old enough to qualify for adult status. Hopefully that meant she would be canny, resourceful, eager to fight. Sometimes inexperience made for an unpredictable opponent— all to the good.

He felt the moment when her mood shifted from anxiety to boredom and then to annoyance. It was a subtle shift in her demeanor. She was still tense, but now her posture indicated disdain and anger. There were some things that were consistent among anthropoid species.

So, she wasn't a timid rodent. She had some fire. He silently rejoiced.

The Lovek turned to Hain. "It is time."

She nodded and inserted a tiny transmitter into the auditory organ hidden behind one of the lichens that grew slowly across her neck. Then she glided through the door and into the room with the druid girl.

The girl instantly straightened. She watched Hain warily. She didn't trust Hain, that was clear. They faced each other.

He spoke, low and gruff, the microphone on his collar picking up his voice. As long as he didn't speak too loudly, the girl wouldn't hear him through the wall. They'd tested her hearing acumen in the lab before putting her out on the floor with the rest of the cargo. As expected, it was far inferior to his own. "You will tread a fine line now. You must gain her trust while meeting my objectives."

The sharp scent of ozone met his nostrils as Hain mentally readjusted her strategy. He chuckled softly to himself. Hain didn't like surprises, but she was always in command of herself—always the arboreal queen. And always his servant. He made certain of that.

Hain activated the subtle servo-motor that augmented her whisper-soft, reedy voice, made it sound more solid, more mammalian, more like that of an animal that breathed with lungs. She'd been working on a design that would allow her even more volume and fluctuation in tone, but it wasn't ready yet. It was tricky to tap into the brain and make it do things it was not designed to. As a result, her voice still sounded bland, breathy, and unfeeling. That would work against her here. But he had faith she could accomplish his goals no matter how she felt about them personally. Her opinions were inconsequential.

Hain said, "This is a very important interview. Your responses are being recorded and will affect your future more than you can possibly imagine. Take your time and answer thoroughly. I have grown fond of you. I want to see you well placed."

The Lovek smirked. *Well played, Hain.*

The girl's eyes widened. "Please, will you just tell me what you're going to do with me?"

"In time. State your name for the record, please."

The girl's lips twitched in defiance. A moment passed. Finally, she gritted out, "My name is Darcy Eberhardt. I believe you know that."

Hain lowered her gaze to the floor, then raised it slowly to meet the girl's. "Darcy is your gift-name?"

The girl looked confused.

"The one given by your immediate ancestors. I have learned

that it is normally imbued with their hopes and dreams for their offspring. What does yours mean?"

The girl looked reluctant, but answered, "Darcy is...it's my mother's favorite character in a book. It means 'dark.'"

"Dark? How enigmatic you are, Darcy." Hain raised a hand elegantly and swayed in her reedlike way. "Let us begin again, for the sake of your mother's dreams for you. Please state your name for the record."

The girl's eyes looked glossy. Her voice grew soft and husky. "My name is Darcy Eberhardt."

"Good. What is your species?"

She hesitated, looked confused. "I'm human."

"Are you? Are you certain of that?" Hain settled herself on the reclining platform and gestured for the girl to join her.

Darcy sat down nearby, but didn't respond to the query.

"Darcy, do you know what DNA is?"

A cross expression came over the girl's features. "Of course I know what DNA is! I was in medical school when you swiped me—I was going to be a doctor."

Hain smiled patiently. "Good. Then you will understand what I'm about to show you." Hain held out a small multiuse digital processor that she'd outfitted with a durable, rubbery shell and a special screen coating to prevent the girl from frying the electronics. Hain always thought ahead to such contingencies. "You see, Darcy, I am a scientist. I analyzed the DNA of all of the individuals we collected on your world. This is what their genetic profile looks like." Hain handed the tablet to the girl.

The girl took it, held it carefully, and looked as though she was studying it intently. After some time passed, she looked up at Hain questioningly.

Hain leaned in and tapped the tablet. She'd done the same for him. He knew what the girl was seeing on the screen.

"This is how your DNA compares to all of theirs. As you can

see, roughly seventy-five percent of your DNA is human. But there are many loci on your genetic map that are foreign to that species. And there's more, Darcy."

The girl's brows drew together as she scanned the tablet.

Hain tapped the screen. "All of the other humans have twenty-three pairs of chromosomes. This is not an atypical number among sentient anthropoid races. But you have an extra chromosome that is unpaired and much larger than the rest. You have forty-seven chromosomes, total. As I'm sure even you know, something of this nature would normally mark an individual as a genetic aberration, doomed to a short, difficult life with multiple deficiencies and encumbrances. However, this extra chromosome is not harmful to you. It is special."

The girl's hands trembled as they clutched the tablet. "This is my karyotype?"

"Yes, Darcy. I ran it myself three times. You are different, but perhaps you already knew that?"

The girl shook her head. "No, no—you got my DNA mixed up with someone else's. Or there was contamination in the sample. This can't be right."

"I assure you that is not the case."

The girl sprang up and turned, boiling over with anger. "Why are you telling me this? What do you want with me? Where's Adam? Goddamn you to hell! I want to go home!"

Hain looked thoughtful but was unmoved. "When you were very small, you preferred the out-of-doors. You felt at home there, safe in a natural setting. Did you ever play a game—perhaps with a caregiver or another child—a game of hide and find? You were, perhaps, enthralled with the game and hid well—so well that no one could find you? Did you become giddy as they searched for you until they were frantic? Did you look down upon your small body and believe yourself invisible?"

The girl gasped. Her heart rate spiked and her chemistry went haywire.

Ah, Hain. Such a masterful bitch.

"That was not a juvenile flight of fancy. It was not your imagination. You were invisible, to them."

The Lovek whispered to Hain, "You've triggered a memory. Keep pushing."

"On many worlds there are sea creatures that are capable of changing the textures and color patterns of their skins to blend in with their surroundings."

The girl sank to her knees.

"I believe you know of what I speak. Millennia ago an inaricaan scientist co-opted these kinds of genes and incorporated them into a special strand of DNA which was given to your ancestors for a very specific purpose. These genes function more like a bacterial plasmid than an autosomal chromosome. You have this ability, among others."

The girl looked terrified. "Others? There's more?"

"You are a descendant of a powerful subspecies, Darcy. At least one member of it lived on your world and interbred with your ancestors. Your lineage is clear. My analysis shows that you have inherited every major trait."

"But, I..." The girl slumped against the wall, right under his nose. The nanite film held.

Hain moved to stand directly opposite him, but gave no indication that she knew he was there. "Your ancestors did not pass on any practical information about your abilities or how to use them? You never witnessed any individual in your genetic group demonstrating anything unusual?"

"No. Never. I had no idea."

"That's unfortunate. You are a rare and valuable specimen. It would be helpful if you had some knowledge of this."

"Specimen? I'm not a specimen! What is this? Some kind of zoo?"

The Lovek's lip curled into a satisfied smile.

"No. Not a zoo."

"What, then?"

"Would you like to know what your ancestors were called?"

"You're trying to distract me on purpose. What are you hiding?"

"They called themselves drudii. They are sometimes referred to as druids in the literature."

The girl inhaled sharply. These words meant something to her.

Hain could see it as plainly as he could. "So, you've heard this word."

The girl shook her head. "Yes, but not in this context. It's probably just a coincidence—a similar word in my language."

"Perhaps. The drudii are known to have scattered throughout the galaxy, but often left evidence on the worlds they occupied. They built circular monuments comprised of living plant matter, posts, stone, or carved columns depending upon the technology available to them and how long they wanted such monuments to endure. They must have felt quite safe on your world. We observed a large, stone monolithic circle on an island off one of your most populated continents."

The girl's heart rate picked up. He could smell the sweat evaporating from her skin. She whispered, "You must mean Stonehenge."

"You know this place by name? It is some distance from where we found you. Have you visited this place?"

"No. My mother always wanted to go there."

"Ah. Why did she wish to go?"

The girl's voice was shaky. "It's a spiritual place. It supposedly marks the cycle of the sun throughout the year...the solstices, things like that. An ancient people called druids were thought to use it as a temple. But I...she never said anything about being related to them."

"The name is not a coincidence, then. They were open about who they were, because the name meant nothing on a nonspace-faring world. The true purpose of these locations is unknown to the general populace, then?"

The girl just stared blankly.

"The circles mark strong, localized fields of electromagnetic force. These exist randomly throughout empty space, but when they coexist with the strong gravitational force of a large plane-tary body, they permit the drudii to funnel photons into them-selves and store them for later use in specialized cellular organelles."

The girl stared at Hain, dumbfounded.

"These organelles are called apochondria. To the untrained eye, they look very much like mitochondria, but serve a very different purpose. I've isolated them from your blood, Darcy. I wonder if you've ever used them. Perhaps you have, without knowing what was happening?"

The girl sank bonelessly to the floor. "I...oh, my God."

Every hair on the Lovek's body stood on end. His muscles strained. Against his will, the blood lust was rising in him. He breathed evenly to keep it at bay. Now was not the time. The girl was untrained. She needed further assessment.

"Darcy? Can you demonstrate your power?"

The girl still looked dazed. "No...I...don't know how it works."

Hain flowed to the floor, facing the girl, and lightly touched her hand. "Allow me to assist you. We can learn the secrets together."

That was a miscalculation. Perhaps it was too soon, too famil-iar. Or perhaps the cool touch of her woody fingers was too foreign for someone raised on an insular planet. The girl was not willing to accept Hain as a confidant now, possibly not ever. Hain had erred by assuming the girl's youth predisposed her to trusting a firm, but comforting, maternal figure.

The girl snapped, sweeping Hain's hand away. She was on her feet an instant later, seething with anger again. "Don't touch me. I don't want your help. I want to see Adam and I want to go home."

"That is wishful thinking. We must live in the present, always. I think you know that will not happen."

The girl narrowed her eyes. He could see her undeveloped muscles tense under her bald skin. She was holding herself back and that was delicious. Her voice, full of conviction, was equally so. "I'm not saying another word until you tell me why I'm here."

Hain unfolded herself. When she was fully erect again, she met the girl's gaze without flinching. "We are simple traders."

The girl let out a strangled sound as she realized what Hain meant. "You...traffic...in people?" She advanced on Hain. Hain did not move. "You're going to sell me?"

"Yes. You will fetch a pretty price."

The girl flung herself on Hain in an awkward, unpracticed manner, trying fruitlessly to do Hain some injury. So she was untrained in any sort of fighting technique. A blank canvas. He would have to make sure she was trained then.

The bugs moved into the room and quickly subdued and removed the girl. Hain ordered that they return her to her holding cell.

He had plans to make.

10

DARCY GROANED and closed her eyes. Her ego and body were bruised, but she was still seething. So much for the strategy of gaining allies on the inside. Hain was unlikely to be her new bestie after that fit of temper.

She turned her head and winced. A couple of hymenoptera had just tossed her into her cell, and they hadn't done it gently. Selpis and Nembrotha watched her curiously as she lay there, recovering from being manhandled so roughly.

She felt shame—that she hadn't fought back sooner, that she'd let herself be led like a lamb to the slaughter, that she'd trusted even the slightest bit. She'd always been an independent thinker. She'd never acted like a sheep before in her life.

After being abducted by aliens was not a good time to start.

There was no turning back now. She'd leapt on Hain, all of the frustration pouring out of her. She couldn't think of a time in her life when she'd seen red quite like that, so angry that she wanted to hurt someone.

Hain must have had guards just outside the door, because the hymenoptera had come in and pulled her off Hain before she could do any damage—not that she'd be capable of doing much of that. She hadn't even tried to hit anyone since elementary school, defending herself from the bullies shoving her around on the playground. Neither Hain nor the hymenoptera had been surprised by her behavior, though. No, that was clear. They'd expected it.

After keeping her in the dark all this time, Hain had suddenly decided to become a font of information. And it was so messed up. Darcy had dealt with being biracial. She'd been fighting that fight her entire life, but she knew its borders well. She knew what to expect, how to cope. And here comes some alien tree lady in a spaceship—and now she had to add part-alien to the mix and redefine herself all over again. With crazy organelles, extra DNA, freaky powers, and stone circles.

She didn't know if she should laugh or cry. What the hell was she? Human? Druid? She was both biracial and bispecies? Was that even a word? What did it all mean?

But the worst part was to be sold because of it...it was too damn much. It was just too much! What would her grandma Harriet think of this situation? What would she tell her to do?

Grandma Harriet had lived through Jim Crow and though she was a quiet woman, she occasionally spoke of what it had been like. Darcy would never forget the day she came home from school crying and curled up on her grandmother's lap because a white child had teased her, gleefully saying Darcy's grandparents had been slaves and what that meant. She'd been so small. She hadn't believed it. How could people make other people do things just because of the color of their skin?

Grandma Harriet had stroked her cheek and softly told her the truth. The horrible history. The civil war. The continuing struggle to be represented as equal and worthy. She'd been too young to understand all of it. But there were a few things that grandma Harriet had said then that she continued to say again and again. "But we can bear it with the good Lord's help," she'd said. "You're smart. You're strong. You've got to be your own woman, Darcy. Whatever that means to you. Be that."

Those words had always brought comfort. She evoked that again now, clutching it like a talisman against the fear of the unknown and the anger erupting at the mere thought of being sold. She *was* strong. She could bear this and she could find a way out.

She dragged herself into a sitting position. "So, neither one of you thought it was important to tell me that we're all merchandise?"

"Are you joking?" Nembrotha sputtered wetly.

"Joking?" Darcy let loose a string of curses, most of which the implant didn't bother to translate. She leaned forward and pointed at Nembrotha accusingly. "You thought it was so hilarious that I'm from such a backwards planet that I can't even speak properly without a chip in my brain, and it never even occurred to you that I wouldn't have a clue why I was here? Well, I just found out."

Selpis said patiently, "Darcy, we had no way of knowing what you did and did not know. We hardly spoke before they took you away. We are not who you're actually angry with. Direct that anger elsewhere, if you please."

Darcy huffed like a locomotive, nostrils flaring, and rocked back onto her rump. She hated that kind of patient logic. It was the way her mother spoke to her.

Even worse—she hated that Selpis was right. She wasn't mad at them, the hymenoptera, or even Hain. She was furious with herself for being so slow on the uptake when it was obvious what was going on here.

Nembrotha scooted a little closer to their border with Selpis's cell. "The strong emotional reaction she is displaying could go a long way to mitigate her lack of physical robustness.

If she is a member of the warrior species, strong emotional response could be a better asset than being physically imposing."

The tip of Selpis's tail swished and she turned her gaze on Darcy. "Are all humans this fiery?"

Darcy just stared at her. They didn't understand. Maybe they didn't have racial divisions on their worlds. They didn't have the history that made this so disgusting on such a personal level. In another mood, she might have explained. She might have asked more questions about where they came from. But not now. She couldn't. She just could not patiently explain racism to them. Wasn't being held prisoner, the thought of being sold enough to evoke rage in them too?

"Who will they sell us to?" she choked out, trying to swallow some of the anger without it turning into tears.

Nembrotha faced her and spoke quietly. "We know little more than you. The vessel makes stops regularly. Customers and brokers come aboard and make selections. If an individual isn't chosen in a timely manner, rumor has it that they're offered at deep discount to a wholesaler, to free up the space for more-valuable cargo."

People, sold wholesale? Her head was spinning. "That's it? That's how they make a living? They come to a planet, swoop in and steal people away—from their lives, their families, everything they know—and then just sell them to the highest bidder? What kind of...? This is the state of the universe? Aren't there laws against this?"

Selpis looked pained. "Certainly there are. No civilized society condones slavery. But where there are laws, there are always those who live on the fringes, eager to benefit from breaking them. It's likely some of us will be discovered and freed in our lifetimes. You hear of these things in the news reports from time to time."

Just another statistic on the intergalactic nightly news. What a sickening thought. "What will happen to us?"

"The unlucky—" Nembrotha gurgled, a juicy, throat-clearing sound, and their stalks pointed briefly at a hulking brute of an orange-tinged woman scrunched up inside her red hexagon nearby, "—will be laborers, doing some kind of lethal work that would be best left to machines, often in environments where machines cannot function. Or, they may be plunked into one of the many secretive and highly illegal entertainment wars that the rabble can't get enough of. The two of *you* will do well to obtain positions as handmaidens to some aristocratic family, whilst *I* will likely become a sex slave in some two-bit whorehouse catering to a whole host of distasteful fetishes."

Selpis frowned and tsked at Nembrotha. "You're letting your imagination carry you away. We don't have any idea what will happen to us. It is best to accept whatever does with grace, have faith that we will be delivered from this untoward circumstance."

"That's fine for you!" Nembrotha exclaimed. "Your species has a life span fourfold the length of my own. I can't afford to be so patient."

Selpis looked uncomfortable.

Darcy stood and scanned the room. She set her jaw. "I refuse to accept any of this. I'm not a statistic. And I'm not going to be a..." She couldn't even say the word. She was vibrating with anger. "I'm not going to be any of that. No way. I'm going to fight for my freedom. No matter what it takes."

"Oh, sit down," Nembrotha muttered. "Do you think you're the first one to think that? Everyone goes through that phase. Those who actually act on those feelings are all dead."

Selpis extended her hand, an almost maternal gesture, as though she wished to reach across the barrier and soothe Darcy's angst. Then she closed her hand into a limp fist, the long, spindly fingers curling in. Her voice was hushed and barely traveled the distance to Darcy's ear. "Nembrotha is quite right, unfortunately. That kind of attitude is suicidal. We've observed it more than once. If you create too much trouble, you won't be worth keeping around. They can always take another. That is less risk than an uprising."

Darcy shook her head, refusing to submit to the caution they were urging. She had to be her own woman. She raised her voice. "I have a feeling that's not true for me. They aren't going to kill me. If it's an uprising that will get me off this ship, then I guess I'll have to start an uprising."

"Shshshshshshsh!" Selpis hissed at her, her eyes wide, her pupils constricted to narrow slits.

Nembrotha backed up a bit. "Don't be a fool!"

The others around her began to take notice and looked at her curiously.

"Who's with me?" Darcy called out to them nervously. She lifted her chin and injected more force into her voice. "Are we just going to sit here and take this? Together we have power! Let's take back our freedom!"

No one responded. There were some grunts, a few shrugs, and then one by one they all turned their backs on her, even Selpis and Nembrotha. Every individual within a twenty-five-foot radius huddled within their geometric outline as far from Darcy as they could manage without touching the perimeter.

Her heart pounded. She started to feel silly. She didn't actually know what happened to a person who tried to breach the confines of the cell. It just looked like an outline on the floor.

She channeled every inspirational movie speech she could summon. "There are more of us than there are of them! Let's bring these bastards to justice and get our lives back!"

She was panting. She truly believed that if she could motivate them to join her, they could earn their freedom and take over the ship.

Tesserae71 had cautioned her to stay inside the confines of the cell, "or the consequences would become increasingly dire." That had to mean that she would survive a single escape attempt, but that it would be unpleasant. Couldn't they see that? How bad could it be? If she showed them she could take it, they'd join her. They would storm the corridors and take control. That thought bolstered her resolve.

She stood tall, and swept her arms dramatically. "There's no way they can control all of us if we just step out of our cages as one."

No one budged. She saw a few hymenoptera with shock sticks enter the room some distance away. She was running out of time.

She decided to try another tactic. "What are you people? Chicken?"

That didn't translate well. There were a few amused glances over shoulders, a few guffaws.

Right. No one would take her seriously unless she showed them she was willing to go all the way. She just had to be brave, and surely they would see that she was right.

She backed to the edge of the cell, inhaled a deep, steadying breath, and lowered her body into a runner's crouch. She pushed that breath out through clenched teeth and pursed her lips as she launched herself over the low curb the marked the outline of her cell.

And crumpled to the floor in agony. She'd passed through some kind of invisible barrier that had given her an electrical shock, like cattle fencing.

Her nose and teeth dug into the spongy flooring, flooding her senses with industrial scents and foul, organic odors. Hot bile rose in her throat as every nerve ending twitched and every muscle contracted.

"Aughpfgh," she groaned, and struggled to regain command

of herself. She pushed her head up and gulped for air. "Come on!" she coughed. "All of us together."

She looked down at herself as she shoved up on her hands and knees. Translucent blue lines glowed under her skin. She didn't have time to think about that. She stood unsteadily.

The entire room had gone silent.

The hymenoptera were heading for her. She took off, stumbling in the opposite direction, every eye in the room on her. She began to feel ridiculous and impatient. "Get up off your asses and fight with me!"

There was no reply to her outcry.

Crickets didn't chirp, but the hymenoptera did.

More of them funneled into the room. She was picking up speed when she saw hymenoptera coming her way and scrambled to turn and dart down another row. At least no one was laughing at her now.

She continued in this manner until there were few options left. They were gaining on her and not another soul had left their cell to join her. Either they were completely beaten down and had given up all hope or they knew something she didn't. She couldn't believe it hadn't worked. She felt a terrible sense of betrayal and loss. She'd been stupid to act so rashly.

Two hymenoptera were headed straight for her. There was one coming up behind her and several were moving in from adjacent rows. She had to buy more time by acting unpredictably. What was the worst that could happen at this point? It was unlikely they'd kill or maim her if they expected her to fetch a high price.

As long as she was alive, there was hope.

She slowed down and spun, digging her toes into the spongy flooring as she turned and charged in the opposite direction, head down, teeth locked. She ducked low and plowed into the single hymenoptera that had come up behind her, catching him off guard and knocking him to the floor, the shock stick flying from his pincer before he could use it on her. She didn't allow the crash to slow her momentum. She vaulted over him and kept going, darting like a rat in a maze off in another direction.

She couldn't keep up the farce for long. They were getting wise to her, spreading out like a net and funneling her into a corner. Her freedom was shrinking before her eyes.

They came in pairs now, so she wouldn't be able to get by them again. She grunted and turned, meeting the eyes of another prisoner who just looked back at her sadly. It seemed like sadness, anyway. It was hard to tell because the individual was almost completely concealed by dark brown shaggy hair so dense all she could see were eyes. She couldn't even guess their gender, if they even had a gender.

Were they all lost? Had they all given up hope? Then she saw that individual's eyes travel down to her hands and widen, his or her apathy transforming into surprise.

In that split second Darcy looked down too, and felt the same way. Her fingertips were alight and crackling with blue flame.

It wasn't over. Hain had just told her she had powers of some sort. She should be able to use them somehow, right? Desperate times...

No more time to think. They were closing in. There was nowhere left to run.

She switched gears and changed direction again, heading straight for the hymenoptera in direct line with the nearest door. Instinct hurtled her into them, hands palm-out before her, energy surging through her. As she closed the gap, blue sparks jumped from her fingertips and arced across the distance between her and the hymenoptera. It felt like slow motion as she watched their shiny green bodies seize up and fall in a heap.

She darted around them, but her feet fell heavily and were difficult to pick up again. Her energy flagged. Momentum kept her going, but her limbs were too leaden to lift and her muscles felt like rubber bands. It was like she'd been swimming too long and was emerging, exhausted, from a pool. All buoyancy gone, the weight of the world was pulling her down.

She tumbled like a rag doll. She tried ineffectually to bring her hands up to protect her head as she body-slammed the second hymenoptera. He creaked under her weight. There was little give there. His chitinous exoskeleton was dense and tough. She rolled into a limp heap on the other side, panting.

Some energy returned to her limbs and she forced herself up on hands and knees, turning toward the door. She gritted her teeth and struggled to her feet.

But she had taken too long to get back up. She felt a pincer close around her arm and froze before it clamped down hard enough to rip her flesh. She turned toward her captor and tried to summon the energy again. Her fingers tingled with it.

Then she felt the shock stick poke into her ribs and everything went white.

11

IT HAD to have been days since they'd shut her up in a box only slightly bigger than a coffin. It was dark and soundproof like a sensory-deprivation chamber. She didn't bother to scream for help. She knew there was no help coming.

Logically, she could see their dilemma. They couldn't leave her in the same room with the others and they wouldn't kill her because she was worth something. So, clearly, they'd attempt to break her spirit.

Let them try.

At first she'd just huddled at one end to keep warm, shifting and moving as parts of her got painful or went numb, dozing and trying not to think too much. She spent a fair amount of time talking herself out of going nuts from claustrophobia, sometimes out loud.

The interior of the box was smooth. It felt like it was made from plastic-coated metal. It was cool to the touch and seemed to steal her warmth wherever it made contact with her bare skin, though the ambient air temperature was just shy of comfortable.

After a number of hours she clicked the button on her

garment and loosened it until it was as big as she could make it and then cocooned herself in it to keep warmer. It didn't make the hard floor of the box any softer, but being warmer was a significant improvement and she grew accustomed to sleeping curled up in the corner with her head against the wall.

She felt every square inch of the box several times with her fingers, looking for any kind of weak point. There were a couple of places where holes had been cut out and covered with plates. She pressed on those, leveraged her whole body against them, tried kicking them in so hard that she was afraid she'd broken a toe, but they weren't giving. She never even made a dent.

She spent hours doing isometric exercises, isolating and naming each muscle group, working it to the point of quivering cramps to keep her mind busy and her body from seizing up from inactivity. She'd move on from there to other systems, reciting all the facts she'd been cramming into her brain for the past two-plus years.

She was afraid to think about the power she'd manifested before they locked her up, and did whatever she could to distract herself from thoughts of it. It was difficult, though, not to replay that moment over and over in her mind while clenching her hands into fists as if that could prevent the tingly sensation in her fingertips from ever returning.

Once she felt something very strange. She didn't know what it was, but it seemed to shudder through her body in a wave. She couldn't be sure she wasn't imagining it.

Occasionally someone shoved food in and shut the door before she could react, and she ate the tasteless food silently in the inky blackness because there was no other choice.

She considered different strategies she might try and ultimately settled on pretending to have learned a lesson in hopes that they'd put her back on the floor with the other prisoners.

That would afford a greater chance of maintaining her sanity and the best opportunity for another escape attempt.

Darcy heard something and opened her eyes, blinking against a sudden influx of dazzling light. The door had swung open and, unexpectedly, stayed that way.

"What?" Her voice croaked from disuse. She cleared her throat.

"Well, come on, now." The voice sounded impatient, but the individual had stepped back from the door and she couldn't see who was speaking yet. It wasn't one of the hymenoptera. This was someone new. The voice was low-pitched, with an accent she hadn't heard before. It sounded male, but she was afraid to assume anything. "Do I have to ask twice?"

"No!" She scooted quickly toward the opening.

The voice drawled on, lazily, "There's no point in zapping me, by the way. I'm locked in here with you. I'm a prisoner too."

She got to the point where her feet were sticking out of the door and hesitated. Prior to this moment, she'd never even gotten a glimpse out that door. She had no idea how far she was from the floor, and she couldn't sit up to look because there wasn't any clearance. If she went out feetfirst, she could break an ankle. She started to pull them back in so she could ease around and see what she was heading for.

"Hold on. I've got you." The voice sounded exasperated. She flinched as large, cool hands slapped her legs and got a firm grip on them.

"I—okay." If this person was letting her out of that hellhole, then she'd just have to trust.

"Slide down. You won't fall." The voice sounded dry and slightly annoyed.

She slid down and found herself in the embrace of a large and extremely hirsute individual. He smelled strongly of musk and his body was hard with corded musculature. He set her feet on the floor and she took a couple of steps back from him, wrapping her loose garment around her like a robe, seeing all of him for the first time.

"Oh, you—you are—you—"

"Yes?" He shrugged listlessly, eyeing her lazily with cobalt blue eyes.

"Your anatomy is like mine—similar, at least, I think." He wasn't human, that was for sure, but very close—certainly he was the most human-looking individual she'd seen since this nightmare began.

She cataloged their similarities and differences. His face was masculine with a square jawline and a sandy-brown complexion. He was a lot taller than her and solidly built. He wore a white jumpsuit like most of the other captives. An almost-leonine mane topped his head like some kind of eighties guitar hero. It, as well as the downy hair covering most of the rest of his exposed body, was the same dusky tan shade as his skin. Most notable was his eye color—such a vivid shade of blue, they stood out starkly against his otherwise monochromatic features.

He frowned. "It's unlikely that we could breed."

Her mouth opened for a few seconds before she could even speak. "Oh, I—no, no, no, no, no. That's not what I meant."

He eyed her skeptically.

As she looked closer at his face, she realized his skin had a blue undertone that also colored his lips and the whites of his eyes. She remembered he had been cool to the touch as he helped her down. She began to wonder if he was ill, perhaps needed treatment. "Are you cold? I mean, your lips are blue."

"Your lips are red. What does that signify?"

"I—"

He looked bored. "We may have similar lineages, but my people evolved on a colder world than yours, with low oxygen pressure and little environmental iron. My blood primarily carries oxygen on hemocyanin. So most of the time it's blue. Yours is red."

Most of the time? She blinked. "Oh, that's fascinating."

"If you say so."

She had to stop staring. She turned to take in the rest of the space. It was long and narrow, basically a hallway with a door on each end. The side walls were punctuated with openings in rows and columns. Each led to a cell like she'd just emerged from.

Hers was the only one with a door, and it seemed clear that the door had been added as an afterthought, to imprison her. The rest of the pods were open to the hallway. It reminded her of pictures she'd seen of Japanese capsule hotels. She stepped closer to inspect one at eye level. There was something in there coating the inside that rounded the interior out. Was it some kind of insulating material? She furrowed her brow and touched the dark-grey lining. It crumbled under her touch, releasing an earthy scent. It was a claylike substance.

She turned back to the man, who was standing there with a questioning look. "What is this place?"

"These are overflow hymenoptera quarters. The cell they stuck you in was the only one that hadn't been used yet. They didn't want you stinking up one of their chambers. There is a cell down there incubating eggs." He gestured toward the end of the short hallway.

Her eyes widened. "Eggs? Hymenoptera eggs?"

He didn't answer. She assumed that was confirmation.

"Can I see them?"

"You are a curious little thing, aren't you?" he said with a slight crook of his lips. "That could get you in a lot of trouble."

"My name is Darcy."

"I know." He folded his arms and watched her with half-lidded detachment.

"Do you have a name?"

He sighed like the formality was a waste of time. Finally, he shrugged and said, "The name given to the juvenile I once was, was Raub."

That's a weird way to tell someone your name. She continued to look at him expectantly, but he wasn't forthcoming with more information.

She wandered down the hall, peeking into every cell until she found the eggs. They were slightly larger than footballs, mostly opaque, and to her surprise they weren't completely stationary. She could see dark, amorphous shapes in there. The little critters twitched occasionally, causing the entire mass of eggs to vibrate sporadically.

"When do they hatch?"

"Not for a few spins."

"Spins?"

"Standard days."

"Then what happens to them?"

"You seem to be more curious about their fate than your own, Leebska."

Leebska? The word didn't translate. Everything he said seemed to be loaded with a sneer. She probably didn't want to know what it meant, but she asked anyway. "Leebska?"

He screwed his mouth up and eyed her thoughtfully. It seemed like there was a hint of humor in his gaze. "It's a term for a youth, a student, in my native language."

She frowned. His assessment wasn't inaccurate, so she didn't have a foundation for any kind of retort. "What is to be my fate?"

"A question for the ages. I'm not a philosopher. In the short term, I can offer you sustenance, cleanliness, and sanitary relief."

He took her by the arm and led her to one end of the hallway. She followed gratefully. She'd been holding it for what felt like days and she was extremely uncomfortable. The door opened and they went through. This was a hub with several doors. He tapped another door control next to one of them and gestured toward it. "Relieve yourself, clean up, and then I'll meet you back here for a meal."

She stepped toward the open door, then turned. "Why have they sent you, instead of a hymenoptera, to tend to me?"

He narrowed his eyes. "You really don't know?"

"No."

"There's a reason you don't see many hymenoptera electricians, Leebska. Their primitive central nervous systems can't handle even minor electrical discharges."

She stopped breathing. She felt the blood drain from her head. "What?"

"You killed three hymenoptera in your escape attempt."

She stumbled into the washroom until she felt the wall at her back.

His voice was cold. She barely registered it. He said, "Take your time."

The door closed between them.

12

SHE STARED at herself in a mirror mounted to the wall. A look of utter shock was reflected back at her.

I have murdered.

Her hand moved to cover her mouth.

I didn't mean to. I didn't. I just wanted to be free.

A sob escaped from her lips.

I'm a murderer.

A tear trembled on her lashes.

How can I even process this? I'm supposed to do no harm. I'm supposed to help people, heal people.

The tear fell, followed quickly by many more. She watched them and made no move to wipe them away.

It was an accident.

She trembled violently.

Was it? Or was it arrogance? I didn't think it through. I didn't make a plan. I didn't try to practice using this power to see what it was all about. I just leapt with both feet like I always do.

She sank to the floor. She hugged her knees to her chest as tightly as she could.

It was instinct, self-preservation.

She began to rock.

Except I wasn't in any immediate danger. I didn't know where I was going or what I was doing. In that moment, my pride was threatened, not my life.

It all felt so hopeless. In her desperation she'd been so reckless. She just wanted her life back. She wanted to wake up from this nightmare, to find herself in her cozy apartment in Phoenix with her sleep mask over her eyes because the morning sun coming through the east-facing window in the bedroom that she shared with Adam was so relentless.

Oh, God...

The day in the gorge when she'd touched the stones haunted her. She dreamed about that moment incessantly, her body pinned to the stone and something happening that she couldn't understand—still didn't understand. Everything had changed in that moment. It had brought her here somehow to this place. To these circumstances.

She wanted so desperately to go back and refuse to go on that hiking trip.

But the stones hadn't made her impulsive. That was on her. It was the part of herself that she hated most. Now more than ever. She'd never intended to be careless. It just seemed to happen. She got caught up in feelings, in the rush of the moment. How could she stop doing that? How could she change? How could she keep herself from being so rash in the future?

Thoughts churned relentlessly, tumbling over and over themselves as she sought to make sense of what she'd just been told. She twitched violently as a heavy thud sounded on the exterior door. She heard Raub's muffled voice coming through it. "I said take your time, not take an epoch. Delay much longer and I'll come in there and scrub you clean myself."

She scrambled to her feet, swiped her face with her hands,

and smoothed the resultant wetness over her jumpsuit. She slipped the jumpsuit off and threw it in one of the purifying tumblers that resembled a front-loading washing machine. It was exactly the same as the one she'd used in the infirmary. By the time she was done bathing, it would be clean.

She used the facility, then pressed the button that would produce the thing she'd come to think of as a yellow cleaning cube. It was dense, spongelike, and moist. She wiped herself down with it from head to toe, parting her hair carefully with her fingers and daubing it over her scalp, then she threw it down a recycling chute in the wall. Some of its moisture was left on her hair and skin, but primarily it left her with a mild static charge. All her hair prickled on end uncomfortably until she stepped onto the grate inside the ionic sanitizing enclosure. It sensed her weight and warm, ionized air whirled around her naked body, leaving her feeling clean and refreshed.

She shook her head. These ablutions, which had once felt so foreign and strange, were beginning to feel routine. Normally they induced a short-lived, nearly euphoric state. Not today, though. Today, her stomach churned and her heart thudded heavily as she removed her jumpsuit from the tumbler and settled it back into place. If she could no longer live with her thoughts, at least she could stand her own scent again. She'd gotten very ripe during the confinement. She felt much better in body, if not in spirit.

She avoided looking in the full-length mirror again, running her fingers through her hair absently, feeling for tangles, then pulling it back into its ponytail and going to the door to let herself back into the hub.

Raub lounged against the wall with his eye on the door. When she appeared, he straightened and turned without a word to open another door. There, a long, narrow counter-height bench occupied a room. At one end lay a pile of food cubes, a pair of squat plastic cups, and a couple of stools that were a bit short for the table. Raub sidled up to it and stood there, as though waiting for her to approach and join him.

His eyes bored into her. "There's no need to be rude. Is there something amiss with the meal? I thought perhaps you'd like to eat like a civilized person. Was I wrong?"

She came forward, feeling numb and wooden. She didn't know what he expected of her, but surely he wouldn't drop a bomb like that and think she'd be unaffected. She sat down and Raub immediately sat as well, watching her expectantly.

She couldn't meet his gaze for long. She kept looking up to the ceiling, hoping the tears she was fighting would drain away before they spilled over her cheeks.

"How long will you keep me waiting, Leebska? Is this some custom on your world—to delay consuming nourishment until your table partner is ready to consume you?"

"I—no. I don't know your social customs. The...the...ah..." She darted a glance at him. His brow was raised.

She tried again. "The hymenoptera."

She noticed for the first time that his eyelids were so thin as to be somewhat transparent. She could see a network of blue veins through his skin.

She felt a hot, fat tear slide down her cheek. Her lip quivered and she fought to tighten her lips. "I've always eaten alone until now."

He stood suddenly, his stool clattering noisily to the floor. He grabbed her face, jerking it up and tilting it one way and then another, roughly. "What's this?" he growled.

She pulled at his fingers, but he was strong and they wouldn't budge. "What?"

"Your eyes are running sores." He dropped her face and turned away, swearing soft and low. He turned back to her. "Hain will not be pleased if you aren't kept in optimal condition. She will want to see this, run some cultures." He grabbed her arm and moved stiffly toward the door.

"Wait!" She tried to pry his thick fingers from her arm. "I'm not sick."

He turned and cocked a fuzzy brow at her.

"You've never seen tears before?" The word "tears" didn't translate. It came out in English.

"Tiersz?" He looked skeptical. "Is this some kind of druidic self-abasement ritual before meals?"

She felt weary. "No, it's a human expression of emotion."

He steered her back to the table and stood there, aloof. "Human? They told me you were drudii."

She sank back down onto the stool, shaking her head. "I guess I'm that, too. It's complicated. I don't really know who or what I am...or what I'm capable of." *I'm black. I'm white. I'm human. I'm druid. What else am I?*

He sat down and frowned at her. "Most individuals are capable of far more than they imagine." He pushed a food cube at her. "Eat and then tell me of this human 'tiersz' emotion, if you must."

She ignored the food. "I'm not hungry."

He heaved a sigh that turned into something like a growl toward the end. "Can you at least take one bite, Leebska? I'm not permitted to eat unless you do."

"Oh. I didn't realize." She broke off a small corner of the food cube and put it in her mouth. It tasted like sawdust. She chewed out of habit and let her hands fall to her lap.

"Finally," he grumbled, tearing a chunk off of a dense cube and shoving it in his mouth. He eyed her malevolently for a moment, then said, "You're like an adolescent, off your rock for the first time. I'll try to remember that, though I have little experience with adolescents and less patience."

She squirmed uncomfortably. After days of solitude, she

finally had some freedom and company, but now she wanted nothing more than to grieve privately. "Why did they put you in charge of watching me?"

"That seems fairly obvious. You're valuable, but can't be left on the floor to stir up the stock. Normally they'd have either spaced you or confined you here under the care of hymenoptera, but Hain doesn't want you killing the crew left and right and wreaking havoc all over the ship. I'm strong enough to keep you under control and more resistant to your...impulses than the bugs."

She furrowed her brow. "But you said you're a prisoner, too. Why do they trust you?"

"They don't. They're watching us, Leebska." He gestured vaguely at the walls, as though they had eyes. "I've been on the ship a long time. They haven't found a buyer yet that wants to pay what Hain has decided I'm worth. Like you, they couldn't keep me on the floor with the rest." He raised an eyebrow at her. "I killed a few more of the bugs than you did. But we've come to an accord. I remain docile as long as I receive certain perks. All bets are off when they find a buyer."

A lump formed in her throat. She eyed him furtively. Every instinct she had from the moment she'd laid eyes on him told her to be wary of him. He moved with menacing catlike grace and a vaguely predatory air. His words had just confirmed that. He was a killer by choice.

She felt compelled to draw a distinction between them, to let him know that they were not the same. "That was an accident. I didn't know what would happen when I...I...didn't think it would kill them. I didn't *want* to kill them. I just wanted to be free." More hot tears escaped.

His eyes narrowed on her. "That was your first kill?"

She whispered, "Yes," and buried her face in her hands.

His voice was cynical. "This emotion that makes your eyes leak, this is regret?"

She didn't know why, but that made her laugh—a dry, humorless guffaw. It was just so ridiculous. "Yes. Regret. Sadness. Anger. Lots of emotions. Too many."

He looked perturbed. "I see. This washes the emotions away?"

"Not exactly, but to a degree, I suppose that's accurate. It's more of a release." She tilted her head at him. "How do your people cope with strong emotion?"

"Strenuous physical exercise is the preferred method to clear the mind and refocus. Some escape into sims. Others use drugs to alter the mind. I prefer to hit someone or kill something."

She looked down at her hands to conceal her expression. He was disturbing.

He seemed to sense her thoughts and pressed on them, like a finger gouging into a tender spot, with his next words. "Death comes to all."

"I know that!" she said hotly, then softened her tone. "I was training to keep death at bay. I was supposed to be a medical doctor, not a murderer."

"When one agrees to be complicit in pursuits such as slavery, one accepts that life may be capricious."

She frowned. That made sense, but didn't make her feel any better. "I suppose."

"And they were just bugs, after all." The way he said "bugs" made her think it was a slur. She'd heard that tone before and she didn't like it. He watched her steadily.

Her head snapped up. "I don't believe that. Different doesn't mean inferior."

It was so disappointing to find out the rest of the universe was just as full of greedy, amoral, bigoted bastards as Earth. Apparently achieving interstellar travel did not automatically mean that a species was morally evolved.

"Interesting. It seems their perception of you is skewed." He popped a bite of food cube into his mouth.

His comment only confirmed what she'd suspected. The hymenoptera gossiped about her—and they all thought she was one of those bigoted bastards. It also told her something else. Raub was in their inner circle. She shook her head emphatically. "I—we got off on the wrong foot."

"I don't know about feet, but your legs are certainly as prickly as theirs." His lips twitched. Was he suppressing a smile?

"What?" The fingers of her right hand slid down to her outer calf and she cringed. "I can't shave them here like I normally do."

He looked surprised. "You remove your body hair? For what purpose? For speed gain in sport?"

Her eye was drawn to the velvety hair covering his beefy arms and the strange juxtaposition of that. "No, it's a cultural thing. For beauty."

"Beauty? How is such a contrivance beautiful? Nature is beautiful. Why alter yourself in such a manner? Do all of your people do this?"

She absently brought a crumb to her lips. "No. Just the women."

"Adult females only? Does this signal estrus to the males?"

She accidentally inhaled the crumb and started coughing. He watched her with narrowed eyes and shoved one of the cups filled with water closer to her. She took it gratefully and sipped carefully between coughs.

Her face felt hot. "No. It doesn't signal anything. It's just expected. If a grown woman doesn't shave her legs, it's considered odd. We begin to do it around puberty and never stop."

"This is a consequence of oppression, of patriarchy?"

She wanted to say no, but she found herself nonplussed.

She'd never questioned it. It was just how things were done. Now she was free of bras and shaving, but she was in a far worse situation. She'd gladly embrace both of them, if she could just be home again.

She decided to ignore his uncomfortable question and ask her own instead. "Is your culture a patriarchy?"

He nodded as if she'd answered him in the affirmative and was slow to reply, taking his time chewing another bite of food. "No. It is not. Within my species, the genders are of comparable size and equally fierce fighters, though fighting style may vary greatly. There's virtually no dimorphism between the sexes. Females need no protection during gestation, nor assistance rearing young, though one may form a cooperative if that is her inclination. There's equal representation among our leadership, such as it is."

That sounded amazing, except for the fighting part. She couldn't help but wonder what a female of his species looked like. She tried to imagine him with a slightly more feminine appearance. Perhaps, she mused, the females simply looked more feline. She shouldn't have been staring so hard, but it was hard not to. Her thoughts raced with questions about his anatomy and physiology, his culture, his world, and how he had come to be on the ship.

"We are not a vain people. Individuals are judged capable not on appearance, but on merit. Skills are valued above all else."

He'd noticed her staring. "Oh, that's awesome, I mean—I—" She sputtered until she just gave up.

He leaned in, clearly reveling in her discomfort. "Does my appearance please you or repulse you, Leebska? Or have you decided?"

She put her palms flat on the table in an attempt to ground herself. "No—I mean—I'm just curious. You..." She sighed. "I'm not trained in interplanetary relations, can you tell?"

"No matter. We are companions, confined together to these rooms, for now. You are free to do as you wish, within reason. You'll not be confined to the sleeping cell unless you cause more problems. But, be forewarned that if you do decide to do anything foolish, I will not be gentle in suppressing you. I am not eager to give up what little freedom I have." He waved his fingers and turned all his attention to his food and drink.

She lingered for a moment until she was certain that had been a dismissal, and then she left the room to be alone with her thoughts.

13

THE DAYS STRETCHED OUT, long and lonely. Darcy spent a lot of time sitting on the floor opposite the egg cell with her knees drawn up to her chin, watching them squirm and tremble inside their tiny, fluid worlds. They were completely innocent and knew nothing of the ugliness of the universe on the other side of their rubbery, ovoid membranes. She ruminated on that, and her guilt, as she observed them day after day.

She thought about Adam often. She still didn't know what had happened to him, if he was okay, or where he was being kept. She appealed to Raub to help her find out, but he usually just grunted when she brought it up. He said that no one on the ship cared to keep track of who was who. He had no way of knowing which human was the one she described because there were many of them aboard.

Today she was remembering the quirky way Adam had introduced himself to her in the college library. She'd been immersed in studying when he'd sidled up to her table, unburdened himself of his backpack, sat down, and opened a book.

He hadn't said a word or even met her gaze, but it had gotten her attention. The library had been virtually empty. There'd been dozens of study carrels and open tables he could have used. When dinnertime rolled around and she'd gotten up to leave, he'd simply smiled, making eye contact for the first time, and extended a hand. "I'm Adam," he'd said shyly, and he'd gone back to studying. He'd showed up frequently after that, always quiet, never bugging her.

She couldn't decide for the longest time if it was cute or creepy. Finally one day she'd had enough. She'd started out accusatory, threatening to call campus security or even the dean. Truth be told, she'd been in a pretty grumpy mood. She'd had a physics test the next day. He'd frowned and admitted that what he had been doing was pretty weird, but once he'd started on the path he hadn't known how to stop and he was too shy to know how to do it properly. He'd gotten up to leave, promising not to bother her anymore. He'd been so earnest and what he'd said had rung true. She'd noticed him around campus since his visits had started, always just as alone as she was. So she told him to wait and asked him what his major was. They'd started talking. Then they'd had dinner together in the caf that evening. And that was it. They were inseparable. They just clicked. They had a lot in common—both biracial, both outsiders in all the groups everyone else felt they intrinsically belonged to, both serious students. They quickly fell into an easy friendship that eventually led to more. That time in her memory seemed almost magical.

Darcy sighed and returned her focus to the eggs. She found herself feeling protective of them and checked on them often. She rearranged them frequently so that they all had equal exposure to air and none of them were crushed under another's weight. The creatures moved so much that the eggs shifted and often managed to rearrange themselves. She wanted to be sure they'd all survive. When she asked for more information about them, Raub said he knew nothing about bug young and told her she was being ridiculous, that they didn't need any care.

They grew quickly, filling the volume of the eggs. They'd soon hatch as larvae and then the hymenoptera would take them away to another chamber, Raub said. She wasn't sure how she felt about that. On one hand, super-sized larvae sounded disgusting. On the other, she was exceedingly curious to find out what they would look like and how they'd be cared for. She wasn't afraid of the sight of human blood or internal organs. She was going to be a doctor—she needed to let go of this insect-related squeamishness. These new individuals' lives were just as important as her own. Handling them daily reinforced that. It helped, somehow, even if her efforts were meaningless to anyone but herself.

She thought the hymenoptera might object to her touching the eggs, but despite the fact that Raub said they were being watched at all times, no one tried to stop her. She made a point to be very deliberate and open about her actions. She touched them carefully and spoke aloud, describing what she was doing and why she thought it might need to be done.

She never interacted with anyone but him, and even that was infrequent. Raub was let out of the rooms several times a day to retrieve food and water, but no one ever came in. A couple of hymenoptera would stand outside with shock sticks, their pincers on the door controls, and then they'd escort him away and lock her in. She kept her distance.

She talked to the eggs, told them about her life before the abduction. How hard medical school was. What living in the Arizona heat was like compared to Ohio. How good Adam was to her, bringing home her favorite chocolate milkshake on particularly rough days, just hanging with her when she was too tired to go out, or giving her random extra-squeezy hugs to cheer her up. The monologues tended to make her feel sad.

Sometimes she sang to them, whatever she could think of—

lullabies, nursery rhymes, Beatles songs. She wasn't much of a singer and it all came out of her in a weird mishmash of English and the language from the chip in her brain. The rhymes didn't rhyme anymore, and sometimes that made her giggle at the absurdity of her situation—singing to insect eggs because it seemed like a good thing to do and she had nothing better to fill her time with. At least it felt sort of therapeutic.

Raub rolled his eyes whenever he caught her singing. He spent most of his time either exercising or meditating. They rarely spent time together except for meals. She got the distinct impression that he tolerated her because he had to.

An egg wriggled atop its pile with such force that it rolled off over the edge of the cell and onto the floor. Darcy picked it up, examined it for any visible injury, and when she didn't find any, balanced it on her knee, peering through its murky membrane at the developing individual inside.

She heard the door open between the rooms and broke off midsong.

Raub came in and leaned against the wall, frowning. "You should do something more productive to pass the time. You squawk like a seabird."

She shrugged. "There's nothing to do. I'm just waiting to be sold." Saying those words made it feel so real. She focused on the egg on her knee so she wouldn't think about it.

"There's plenty to do, Leebska. Your physical condition is appalling. Let's start with that."

She considered her options. As an only child she had long ago learned to entertain herself, but without anyone to talk to or books to read, games or anything else to occupy her mind aside from fiddling with these larvae, the loneliness and boredom were beginning to eat at her. Raub's demeanor reminded her of a bully's, but if there was no one else in the schoolyard and the bully wanted to play, even the bully could begin to look fun.

She couldn't stop her eyes from lighting up at the prospect of doing something different, even though what he was hinting at seemed to be exercise. "What did you have in mind?"

"I'll teach you to make the most of your time within this limited space and with few tools."

He would teach her something, huh? She'd gotten the impression he wouldn't do anything without getting something in return. She felt somewhat suspicious despite the eagerness welling up inside. "Why?"

He grunted and an amused half sneer pushed up one side of his mouth. "Call it charity, Leebska."

She snorted. There didn't seem to be a quid pro quo.

"Besides, I can't take another minute of your incessant warble. It's a form of aural torture."

She rolled her eyes. He was always complaining about something, like an irascible old dude.

"You will be quiet and focused. You will do as I say. It will serve you well."

She stood, stooping to lay the egg among the others. She didn't like being ordered around, nor was exercise something she enjoyed, but something to do to pass the time? Yes. She'd agree to following his orders if there was something, anything, to distract her from her tortured thoughts. Reluctantly she said, "Okay."

He turned, went into the dining chamber, and pushed the table out of the way. She followed, feeling like an eager puppy. He pointed to an area of open floor in front of him and she quickly moved to occupy it. "First, we quiet the body with a measure of fatigue. Pay attention to detail. This is a short sequence, called the Sahventahl. I expect you to learn it quickly and to execute it flawlessly. It works every muscle group, improves circulation, and moves lymph."

He spread his feet shoulder width apart and pressed his hands to his sides. She did the same. He slowly lifted one foot and placed it deliberately one step in front of him, balancing his weight, while turning at the hip to face forty-five degrees away, sweeping both arms over his abs in front of his body and pushing out in that direction without extending his torso. She watched him closely and mimicked him, careful to execute her movements in a mirror image to his. He continued at a very slow pace, moving fluidly through pose after pose that bent and twisted her body in ways that felt surprisingly good.

Raub was possessed of a feral grace. He seemed to have gone inside himself. His expression was more tranquil than she'd ever seen it.

It reminded her of Adam's tai chi chuan group. She used to sit under a tree in the quad and study while he practiced with them. Just watching the fluid, graceful, synchronous movements had been peaceful. He'd taught her a little bit, but never very seriously because she hadn't shown much interest and she didn't have the free time. Now she wished she could have that time back with him. It was something they should have done together. There were so many things she would have done differently if she'd known what was going to happen to them.

This routine consisted of slow punches, extensions, stretches, and kicks. At first they seemed simple, easy, but many of the maneuvers took so long to execute that after a few repetitions she was feeling a burn. As she began to get a feel for the sequence, she watched less and focused more on her own position and stance.

His focus shifted as well, to a more watchful attitude. More than once he barked at her, "Hold!" and she forced herself to maintain the position without drooping as they arced through a movement at a snail's pace—when all she wanted to do was drop her arms and legs and sprawl on the floor. She wouldn't do that, though. She'd always been stubborn like this. It was her competitive nature, she supposed, or a lifetime of allowing herself to show no weakness in front of whites or blacks. She would go until she dropped, or he finished, whichever came first.

He completed a sequence, lowered his arms, and ordered, "Continue."

She flowed back into the first movement and kept going. Sweat ran down her forehead, around the curve of her brow and down the side of her face to drip on the floor as she reached over and extended her neck to one side. Raub sidled up to her, so close she could smell his alien, musky scent. He lifted her arm a bit higher, closed his fingers over hers to adjust them into a slightly different position.

He circled around her. As she bent at the waist and swiveled, he leaned in over her shoulder and raised her chin with a finger as he whispered in her ear, growling, "I cannot control who they sell you to, Leebska, but I can give you a fighting chance once they possess you. Accept me as your instructor and I will teach you to fight—for your life, for the freedom you desire so strongly, and for control of this power you wield."

Her muscles trembled and her abs burned from the strain of holding the position so long. "But, why—?"

He came around in front of her and supported her leg with a hand as he pushed her center of gravity back through the slow kick. "Like this," he said. Then quietly, "We will not speak of this. We must use caution or they'll separate us. They must think we only endeavor to keep our minds and bodies healthy. They already observe my own exercise regime daily and do not question it. Do you accept my offer, Leebska?"

She frowned. She wondered what he might expect in return for this training. He'd mentioned charity, but she couldn't be sure what that meant to him. She also was unclear about how he could possibly teach her to fight when Hain and the hymenoptera were surely watching them.

Right now she was hating Raub more than a little for baiting her to continue well past the point where she'd wanted to quit. But the idea of being more physically fit, the chance to learn to defend herself, the possibility of escaping, to control her own destiny—all of that was worthy of some effort, some risk.

Except he wasn't answering her question. That galled. She turned her face slowly until it was near the tan tufts of hair covering the place where she assumed his ears would be. "What do you have to gain from helping me?"

His expression stayed blank. He adjusted her posture again. "An ally who is prepared to act should an opportunity present itself."

What does that mean?

A muscle in her leg trembled. She gritted her teeth and continued the movement at the excruciating pace he set. She was pretty sure it was more than that. There was too much calculation lurking behind those freaky dark-blue eyes. But what else did she have to do?

"Yes, I accept," she whispered.

14

THE DAYS BEGAN to speed by. Raub kept her busy. Upon waking there was a short stretching routine and Raub's daily ritual of drinking a large amount of water. That was followed by bathing and a small meal to break the fast. Then she checked on the hymenoptera eggs while he left their rooms for an hour or two. She'd asked what he did during those outings, but he only raised an eyebrow in response. To say he was taciturn would be an understatement.

The afternoons were filled with longer exercise sessions when he taught her lengthier movement sequences, then another short break for a bigger meal. The evening was for meditation and reflection. She was familiar with that sort of stuff, but he wouldn't let her doze off like her mother had.

She mastered several sequences of movements and committed them to muscle memory through sheer repetition. She employed the same kind of diligence while learning the exercise that she'd always applied to studying. If she was going to learn something, she was going to do it properly. She felt herself growing stronger and he increased the difficulty to match that.

She was always challenged and always stubbornly pushing herself to meet those challenges no matter how impossible it felt.

It was important to be practical at this point. If she was stronger and more resilient, she was more likely to survive and find Adam. Once she'd done that, they could work together to get home somehow. She wasn't going to be a damsel in distress waiting for him to rescue her. And if he managed to, she didn't want to be dead weight.

She had to be proactive. She had to be ready for anything. Getting stronger was part of that.

She was shocked the first time she woke to the feeling of Raub's hand on her foot in the middle of the night. She kicked it away and scrambled deeper into the sleeping cell, stifling a scream.

He whispered hoarsely, "Calmly, Leebska. We're going to practice now. Come down."

It was completely black, not a jot of light. Her heart started to slow and she remembered his cryptic remark earlier in the evening when she'd climbed up into her bunk. He'd actually said something when he normally just nodded in reply to her well-wishes for a good night's sleep.

He'd murmured, "I'll wake you soon." She'd thought he meant for morning exercises, because she was always fatigued from all the exercise, slept hard, and had to be woken. It usually felt like no time had passed. But no—he'd meant what he'd said, quite literally.

She was groggy but awake enough to realize that she didn't dare speak in the case they were being monitored, so she scooted to the edge of the cell, turned over on her stomach, and climbed down, her feet finding purchase in the cells below hers.

He was close. She could feel his subtle warmth as her bare feet set down on the floor, though he didn't touch her.

"We'll train here at night. They've stopped watching us now, assuming we're having a sleep cycle. We won't open another door. That would alert them that we're awake."

She rubbed her face like a small child. "Raub—we just trained all day long. I want to sleep."

"You may sleep all you desire when you're dead. Will that be sooner or later, Leebska?"

She sighed.

"Now the real training begins."

Her brain was starting to work again. She felt a surge of grumpiness and disbelief. Up until now she'd been too sleepy to argue. She kept her voice low. "What? In the dark?"

He put his hands on her shoulders and pushed her toward the center of the long, narrow room. "Enough talk. Begin the Sahventahl to warm up."

It was pointless to argue with him. He always won, usually by getting mean and reminding her of her situation and everything she had to lose by not being prepared for any possible type of slave master. That was all it took to rev her up and get her going. She began the sequence, sleepily. Her limbs were still stiff and sore from the previous day's work.

Raub growled, a low rumble in his chest, and she adjusted her stance so that it was less sloppy.

"Can you *see* me?" she whispered. She neared completion of the sequence. She sensed him hovering nearby, but couldn't make out anything in the dark.

"Double the speed of execution. Maintain proper form."

She frowned, but complied. As she finished, he murmured, "Double that, now."

Her heart pounded. This felt more like aerobic exercise. Each time she came to the closing move, he prodded her faster yet, until she flew through the forms in seconds and she began to see what he was after. She was executing a series of punches, kicks and blocking movements—this was a martial art, hidden in the guise of meditative exercise. She channeled her anger, putting more force into each punch and kick. The fatigue disappeared. There was a feeling of exhilaration in performing the sequences at a faster rate and with purpose.

"Maintain this rate and move into the Minestra sequence." He had to be able to see her. Every so often he smoothly darted in and tapped her arm, her hip—to remind her to maintain form whenever she sagged a bit.

He pushed her through every sequence until she begged off for a break just to breathe, hands on knees, gasping for air. Her hair was saturated with sweat. Luckily the garment she wore was made to shed moisture, so she still felt comfortable wherever it touched her skin. As her breathing slowed, she sat down with her back against the wall. Raub slid down next to her and handed her a cup of water.

"Your eyesight is remarkable," she breathed after gulping down most of the contents of the cup.

"Yours is lacking. You're blind unless it's midday." He sounded disapproving.

"You must see more than the standard light spectrum—into ultraviolet and maybe even infrared."

"That *is* the standard light spectrum," he said dryly.

She huffed, smiling. "Yes. I suppose that would depend on your point of view."

"It's remarkable that your species survived. There must not be many large predators on your world."

It was an interesting point. "I don't have any idea how Earth compares to other worlds."

"Obviously."

After that he let her cool down and get some rest, but woke her at the usual time the next morning, presumably so that those watching wouldn't note any change in routine. She was accustomed to getting by on less sleep than most because of medical school, so she didn't complain.

Weeks went by. She began to marvel at the muscles rippling under her skin, how effortless movement began to seem, how she didn't feel like she'd begun her day until she broke a sweat. It cleared out the cobwebs and sharpened her thoughts. She felt like she was building toward a goal. She frequently wished Adam could see her. He'd always told her exercise could do this for her and she'd always resisted, not really believing it was worth the sacrifice of study time. Now she wished she could go back and let him show her.

The nighttime sessions grew more intense. Raub began by feinting jabs at her and blocking her punches and kicks softly. Because she couldn't see him, she had to learn to react instantaneously and be excruciatingly aware of every other sense—the slight wind of his oncoming punch or kick, his breath, every subtle sound he made moving over the floor.

She began to see what some of the more unusual moves were intended to do. If she didn't understand immediately, he'd whisper a quick instruction and it would click into place. Some of the sequences were more like wrestling moves, once she knew their purpose. He taught her various choke holds and how to get her opponent to the floor and pin him, using his momentum as leverage since her body was smaller. He taught her that being smart and quick was just as important as being strong.

These sessions gradually escalated until they were outright sparring. He began to land light blows when her defenses weren't fast enough. They rarely left bruises, but they stung—mostly her pride. That made her work even harder.

The only noises that broke these silent sessions were her soft grunts of effort and the subtle sound of skin slapping skin as she began to mix up the forms instinctively, instead of following a predictable sequence. That kept him more at arm's length and less likely to get in close to strike. He always broke through her defenses eventually, but she took some pride in the fact that she was gradually extending the time that took.

Her tendency toward competitiveness pushed her to do more than just learn to block his blows or thwart his efforts at pinning her. She strove to catch him off guard, to push him back, to get in a few stinging blows of her own. He would always be bigger, stronger, more experienced, and she took that as a challenge. She worked hard at being unpredictable, at trying new ideas, at using her medical knowledge to her advantage as much as she could—a punch to his nose, kidney, or throat, a kick to his outer thigh or abdomen—all the places that she knew were vulnerable on a human. She was gratified when some of it even seemed to work.

She wanted to win.

One thing bothered her, though. Raub was looking at her differently now. He was pleased with her progress, that was clear, but sometimes...it almost seemed like there was a watchful, predatory evaluation in his eye, or even a lustfulness that she didn't like. It was unnerving and made her feel self-conscious and uncomfortable. He didn't try to hide it, which made her think she had to be misinterpreting it.

They were from different planets, so she could never be sure she was deciphering his expressions accurately. But, still, something in the back of her mind reminded her to be wary. He was a prisoner too. He was ruthless. He'd admitted to being a murderer. She decided to stay out of his way as much as possible when they weren't training, though that would be hard.

15

TWO HYMENOPTERA WAITED for Raub on the other side
of the door. The girl hung back with watchful eyes as it closed
behind him. She was intensely curious—always asking questions,
always watching, always noting differences. He'd never spent
such a vast amount of time with someone so inquisitive. She was
like an eager child, completely undeterred by his reticence.

One of the bugs took the lead, and the other came up behind,
as they moved without a word toward Hain's lab. He didn't
acknowledge their presence and they didn't expect him to. It was
routine. They believed what they were told—that he was a
dangerous prisoner like the druid girl. The life span of the bugs
was so short, turnover so great, that none of them had even
glimpsed him before now. It suited his purpose well. They
wouldn't tip the girl off.

Hain stood at a bench, studying something in a tube before
placing it inside one of her analytic instruments. She raised her
eyes from her work briefly to acknowledge his arrival. The bugs
left the room to wait outside and he relaxed a little bit. Now he

could be fully himself for the first time in days. He cleared a spot and perched on one of her workbenches.

"Judging by the infrared surveillance, the training is progressing as planned," she said as she picked up another sample, eyed it carefully, and loaded it.

"It's proceeding on schedule, yes. The girl learns quickly. The diet you've formulated is working well. She's building muscle and strength."

The truth was she was exceeding his initial estimation of her potential. She had a natural acuity for this fighting style and it showed in her enthusiastic execution. Her body was responding well to the activity. It was refining itself. She didn't seem to be fully conscious of the change, but she had begun to move with a new power and grace. Yes, she was coming along nicely.

"Excellent," Hain murmured. Her voice was reedy as usual, but had slightly more modulation.

He raised a brow. "And on your end?"

"The engineers have almost completed the modifications to the tern. Being from such an isolated planet, she should have no notion of the fail-safes that would be in place to prevent the plan from working. From her point of view, it will appear to be good luck that everything falls into place."

He'd come to the same conclusion. "I agree." Her naiveté about the universe at large continued to surprise him. She had no idea how things were normally done, so any deviation from that wouldn't be remarkable to her. She didn't even try to pretend to understand what was going on around her. She was unashamed simply to ask. He wasn't sure if that was a wise strategy or a liability. Regardless, she was open and honest and some part of him found that disturbingly refreshing.

"And psychologically? What is her state? Will she take the bait? Will she perform as hoped?"

He nodded. "I've no doubt she will. She's well adjusted to her situation, but eager to be free. I believe she'll take advantage of any opportunity that presents itself."

"She trusts you. You've grown close. Does that change anything for you?" Hain raised a culture to eye level, but her focus was on him.

He tensed a little. He was sure Hain knew he would find that question insulting, that he didn't like being queried like that. He was not getting attached to the girl. "No," he said coldly. "Don't start getting haughty. This is just a play. You are not in charge here."

Hain had misunderstood his strategy in humoring the girl to create a sense of camaraderie. That strategy was working well. The girl did trust him and was working hard to please him. He wasn't going to change tactics now.

Hain's expression didn't change. She moved to another bench and picked up a tablet processor. She absently tapped it, then handed it to him. "This is the proposed timetable and route through the ship. All safety and security measures on this route will be neutralized at that time to make your passage smooth and simple."

He took it without a word and looked it over, quickly committing it to memory. "This looks adequate. You've selected a planet?"

She took the processor from him and tapped it some more before handing it back. "We're en route now."

The door opened behind him. He stiffened. A hymenoptera stood outside, clacking nervously. "Mistress? Please forgive the interruption, but...a word, please?"

Hain's eyes flashed, but otherwise she looked outwardly calm. "Enter. State your business quickly and be gone."

"Of course, mistress."

Raub sensed the bug coming up behind him uneasily.

"Sensors have detected a spike of genoflaphan hormone in the egg-incubation chamber. The newest batch of young may hatch at any moment and must be tended to promptly."

Hain's hand squeezed her pipette a bit tighter. She didn't look up. "This does not concern me."

He could hear the hymenoptera skitter back a few steps. "No. No. Quite right, mistress. But the female prisoner seems to be aware of the impending emergence and is handling the eggs. I'm sure you understand that this could create many problems with these individuals in the future."

Raub smelled the sharp scent of ozone.

"Retrieve the eggs, then, and bring them within my proximity."

Raub smiled as it dawned on him what the insect actually wanted. She had to imprint on the newborns for them to recognize her as queen. Apparently it was not a chore she relished.

"Yes, mistress, of course. I would have done this already, except for..." The clacking trailed off softly.

Hain's slash of a mouth tilted down. "Oh, the girl. You're afraid of her." She clicked the pipette angrily.

It must be so hard being queen. He held back, just barely, from sniggering at her reaction to their sniveling requests for assistance.

The insect didn't argue with her. They *were* afraid of the girl. And rightly so. She was growing more lethal by the day. It was a pleasure to watch this unfold.

He didn't understand the girl's preoccupation with the eggs. She felt guilt over her first kills, which wasn't entirely out of the realm of normalcy. There was value to life. It shouldn't be taken indiscriminately. But focusing on these new individuals wouldn't bring back the dead. Perhaps her culture was one that believed souls were recycled. He wasn't curious enough to ask. It did highlight her obsessive nature, however, which he considered a positive character trait. She was stubborn and persistent, attributes that would serve her well in the days to come. And him.

He looked up. Hain had turned to him expectantly.

Raub raised his eyebrows, pretending to be ignorant of her wishes. He was relishing this. Yes, he was going to make her ask.

After another beat, she said, "Would you be so kind as to lock the prisoner up so the hymenoptera can retrieve their eggs from that chamber?"

He inclined his head in a courtly manner and hopped down from his perch. "I'm happy to serve, as always, mistress."

She nodded slightly, then returned to her work, stabbing a box of sterile tips with her pipette.

Raub started to go, then turned around. "Have you decided on a name for this cadre?" he asked her lightly.

"No, I have not." She didn't sound perturbed. She couldn't. But there was an agitation in her demeanor that he enjoyed.

"Might I suggest a name?"

Hain's mouth parted to reveal a hint of its brilliant interior— her version of a surprised look and something she rarely let slip. As a ginnan, she had no teeth or tongue. Instead, yellow markings shaped like petals whorled down her throat in a golden spiral, so that when her mouth was held open wide, it resembled a flower in bloom. Her ancestors had evolved the stunning pattern, as well as a sweet woodsy odor, to lure nectar-seeking prey close. Trapped by a caustic, sticky resin, they had become slowly digested meals for Hain's stationary antecedents. The pattern was now a vestigial artifact of evolution. "Yes," she said finally, her eyes wary.

"Call them Darcy." He smirked and, without acknowledging the hymenoptera, left the chamber, heading back to the quarters he shared with the girl. He strolled, taking his time and enjoying the distress that caused his "guards." There were few things more farcical than watching a grown bug squirm. With so little to entertain him, he had to steal these moments when he could.

16

DARCY WAS SITTING against the wall across from the hymenoptera eggs, dozing, when something woke her. She yawned and shifted her stiff limbs. Then she noticed something had changed. She perked up and eased closer to the eggs. They weren't jiggling the way they normally did. They vibrated with a different kind of intensity.

She picked up one of the more active ones cautiously. There was definitely something happening inside there. One of the ends of the egg had grown more transparent, and, as she watched, she could see a mouth gnawing on the membrane, attempting to free itself.

Her heart pounded against her rib cage. For the first time, it occurred to her that when these things hatched they were going to be hungry—and she had nothing to feed them except half a food cube.

She'd expected Raub or the hymenoptera to be there when they hatched. She wondered fleetingly if the hymenoptera had planned this to happen this way. Was she meant to be the first food these critters consumed? Was this their revenge for killing their brethren?

She recognized those first few moments of anxiety as potentially triggering a panic attack and forced herself to breathe slowly—in through her mouth, out through her nose, just like she did when she meditated. The jangly feeling started to recede, her tension eased, and she was able to think logically rather than emotionally.

These things were smaller than her forearm. She could step on them if she had to. She wouldn't, of course. But she wasn't about to be eaten alive. She could leave the room or hide in her own sleeping cell if she felt threatened.

Nevertheless, when the rasping mouth finally did break through, she set the egg down and edged away. But she couldn't stop watching as a translucent creature emerged. It appeared to be eyeless and bristled with sparse, white hairs. Its body was long and segmented. It had a mouth at one end, but tapered and curled into itself at the other. Its skin was so transparent she could see the dark blobs of internal organs at its core. It undulated and twisted, its mouth contracting rhythmically, searching for food, but it didn't make a move toward her.

She was surprised no one had come to care for them. Perhaps she wasn't watched as closely as she'd presumed. She began to feel sorry for it as it blindly and fruitlessly searched for sustenance on the dirty floor. She took a small hunk of the food cube and crumbled it in the palm of her hand, then poured a little water in with it. She mashed it around to make a watery paste, then hesitantly extended her hand to the larva.

Instantly, it dove at her hand. She gasped and pulled back, her heart racing. But she was fine. She hadn't even felt the graze of teeth.

Cautiously, she proffered her hand again. It slurped at the slurry in the hollow of her palm. It was actually quite gentle. It tickled. She broke into a smile and relaxed a little bit. She could see the mixture sliding through the creature's alimentary canal in pulses of peristalsis. It delicately sucked her hand clean.

The larva moved less restlessly now, more like it was simply exploring its environment. She felt a warm, maternal surge of satisfaction at having cared for the infant. Then she looked up and realized several more had hatched while she was paying attention to the first one. They were rooting around frantically amongst the intact eggs and the discarded rubbery shells.

She didn't know if the food was suitable for them or not, but she assumed it was some kind of universal chow. So she mixed some more with water and held out her hand to the newest hatchlings.

"There you go," she said, and giggled as they formed a ring around her hand, pushing and shoving at each other and sucking up the mixture as fast as she could make it. She touched a fingertip to one of them. Its skin was cool and moist and smooth, not gross or slimy like she expected. The white hairs that stood straight out were soft, like kitten whiskers. She was so entranced by watching them eat that she didn't hear the door slide open behind her.

"Halt!" a voice clacked loudly in her ear. "Move away from the young!"

She froze, her shoulders hunching, expecting the paralyzing feeling of the shock stick to descend on her at any moment. But it didn't come. Instead she heard rapid-fire clicks and clacks that sounded distressed. She made out a few phrases here and there, like, "This is disastrous," and "What will we tell the queen?" and "We may have to fertilize another cadre."

Darcy slowly stood and turned, confused. "They're hungry." She looked down. Seven larvae crowded at her feet, craning up at her, bobbing and weaving and caroming into each other, looking for more food.

Raub stood there smirking, with four hymenoptera behind him, all gesticulating nervously and clacking nonstop.

"You had no right!" one of them said.

"They needed care! If you're so concerned, why did you leave them without anyone to watch over them?"

More consternated pops and clacks. "This is the way of things. It's not your concern. You interfered."

She sneered at them. "I—you—I—that's rich."

"Back away from the young," someone ordered.

Another gestured toward Raub. "This one will escort you away now, so we may tend to the young."

Raub came forward and led her through the door into the hub. "Come, Leebska. Let them retrieve their little grubworms and begone."

She looked over her shoulder to see the hymenoptera gathering the eggs and hatchlings and tossing them carelessly into a crude container. She wished they'd treat them gently. "What are they going to do with them?" she asked Raub fearfully. "Will they kill them just because I touched them? I was trying to help!"

He frowned at her then gestured for the hymenoptera's attention. "Your mistress is in the foulest of moods. It'll not be in your best interests to reveal this oversight. I'll not say a word to her about it, and I'd advise all of you to do the same. The human female only handled a small percentage of the grubs and did not cause any harm to them. It should not affect the psychology of the cadre."

The adult hymenoptera stopped what they were doing and looked at each other skeptically. One of them turned to him and said, "Why would you do this? What do you want in return?"

"I want nothing—from you. I've been campaigning for more freedom and more-comfortable living quarters. If you anger Hain further, I doubt she'll feel generous enough to grant my request."

There was a general grumbling among the insects as they

moved into a tight circle to discuss the issue. They came to a decision quickly and turned as one. "We agree with your assessment. We will not tax the mistress's patience with this petty mishap. It will be well."

Darcy breathed a little easier. The insects resumed gathering the eggs and larvae and then left, shutting the door between them, locking them in.

17

WHEN RAUB CAME for Darcy that night, she was ready for him. Instead of catching up on sleep, she'd spent the dark time planning a strategy. They were unevenly matched and she was tired of always coming out on the bottom. In the past she'd managed to gain the upper hand for a while, and a few times she'd even thrown him, but she was rarely able to pin him, unless they were practicing a specific pinning technique. It was time to turn the tables and the only way to do that was with the element of surprise.

She lay there, breathing slowly and deeply as though she were asleep. When his hand reached in to tap her foot to wake her, she grabbed it and yanked hard to throw him off-balance. Then she swooped her feet out and down, making contact with his head and neck and knocking him out of the way as she slid down to her feet.

She followed the sound of his movement. He hadn't vocalized yet, but she could hear his footfalls as he staggered away. She moved in, alternating punches and kicks, and made contact with his midsection. She heard the satisfying hiss of the air being knocked out of him, but she knew that wasn't enough. She had to keep pressing the advantage. It wouldn't last long. He'd recover from that blow quickly.

She kept moving, building momentum. She crouched low and swept her leg with all her strength. She managed to get the timing right and he fell on his ass. Now she knew for certain where his body was, but not any of his limbs. She wasn't sure if he was sprawled out on his back or sitting. She kicked low, finding only air, and crouched into a low side kick where she hoped his head or chest might be.

It was a miscalculation. He grabbed her leg and twisted her off her feet. She rolled and slammed into the wall. Bright white stars dotted her field of vision. She heard his grunt of satisfaction and didn't let herself stop to feel the pain. She followed the sound he'd made and launched herself at him with a roundhouse kick, then hopped back out of range. She seemed to have caught him just as he was getting to his feet.

He growled, soft and low, and she braced herself in a defensive stance, ears straining. He was coming. All her advantage was gone and he was pissed.

She realized she was smiling. It was weird how much she'd grown to enjoy these sessions. The fact that she'd actually caught him off guard and even knocked him down felt like such a victory. She'd enjoy it while she could, because she was about to get her ass kicked.

She was expecting punitive punches and kicks, but he'd decided to mix it up too, because he barreled into her, pinning her to the wall. All the breath went out of her in a whoosh. As she struggled to breathe and worm her way out of his tenacious grip, she realized something was very different about the hold he was using.

She squirmed, trying to suck in air, and he held her even tighter. She'd naively triggered something in him, something she didn't really want to experience. "Raub?" she uttered in a strangled whisper.

He was bigger and heavier. He leveraged that weight at an angle, his upper body pressing into her chest, his hands pinioning her wrists on either side of her head. He crushed her. She could only breathe in shallow gasps.

She waited for him to release her and give her a harsh lecture. He didn't.

She wrenched and twisted, but his grasp was relentless. At some point during the fight her loose ponytail had slipped out, leaving her hair hanging over her shoulders. Raub's face was pressed against the base of her neck, his breath fanning over her skin.

Something wasn't right. He didn't normally get winded just from sparring with her.

His tongue, cool and moist, licked her from collarbone to earlobe in one long, slow motion. She shuddered and a strange, cold sensation spread through her body.

Pins and needles rippled through her extremities. She saw a faint blue glow in her peripheral vision. She opened her mouth, but no words would come out, just a startled wheeze.

She wondered for a second if she should scream. If the hymenoptera came, would that be better or worse?

Should she struggle harder or just go limp? If she shocked him, would she kill him, as she had the hymenoptera? Should she reason with him? What would make this end?

She'd read once that anxious people actually do better in times of crisis than most because they've imagined bad things happening so many times that they instinctively know how to act when shit gets real. She'd felt reassured about choosing medicine as a career after reading that and never doubted that she could handle anything thrown her way, even if she ultimately chose a path that led her to work in the ER or the surgical suite.

Her heart was pounding out of her chest, but her head was cooling and she forced herself to stop struggling. As calmer thoughts prevailed, the blue glow in the margins of her vision receded. That was good. She was gaining control over it. She could call it back if she needed to. She hoped she wouldn't have to.

It was the fight that had brought this on. She wouldn't give him any more fight.

She should have known. He liked the fight too much. She'd been aware of an increasing sexual tension between them, especially as her skills had improved, but she'd dismissed it because he seemed to dislike her so much and they were different species, after all. That had been naive. She couldn't really say she knew him or what he was capable of.

His mouth was open wide against her neck, sharp teeth pressing into her skin, tongue lapping at the curve where her neck met her shoulder. He vibrated with a low growl that rumbled through her upper body.

She was acutely aware that if he simply clamped down his jaw and pulled back, he could rip open her jugular vein and her life would drain away within minutes. She wondered if he knew that, if that was an implicit threat to keep her quiet.

His skin was cool to the touch, like always, but there was something pulsing and twitching rhythmically against her thigh. She'd never seen him naked, but knew instinctively that he could use that unseen appendage against her. She didn't want to find out how that would work. She shoved that repulsive thought aside and focused.

She pushed away the paralyzed feeling and let her body sag, forcing him to hold her up against gravity as dead weight. She swallowed convulsively and worked spittle into her mouth so she could speak. "I don't want this," she croaked. Then she cleared her throat to try again. She couldn't sound the slightest bit hysterical. "No. It's time to stop." She sounded stronger the second time, matter-of-fact, dispassionate.

He barely loosened his jaw and spoke around his mouthful of her neck. "Come now, Leebska. I won't hurt you. Much." She couldn't see his face, couldn't read his intention. She sensed there was some humor there. Maybe he hadn't completely gone off the deep end.

Possible options spun through her brain. She kept her limbs slack, though she longed to tense up and fight. He'd slowed down. Maybe it was finally sinking in that she wasn't fighting anymore.

He pushed her arms up, extending them straight over her head until they touched. He ground her wrists together with one hand while the other clicked the button to loosen the jumpsuit and slipped over her, pulling her garment away until it stretched open to her groin.

"No!" she commanded. "Don't do this."

Her shoulders ached and her arms burned with the strain of holding all her weight, though dangling her aloft by her wrists seemed to be effortless for him. He eased his upper body back slightly and she breathed deeply, to get enough oxygen, to be ready to fight again.

It no longer seemed likely he'd set her loose and lecture her on her dreadful tactics. She refused to be his victim. She would not allow him to violate her.

He groped her.

She brought her knee straight up in a sudden, forceful jab, point-blank into his throbbing junk.

His teeth tightened on her neck and for a terrible moment she thought that was the end. She squeezed her eyes closed and tensed up, waiting for it. But it didn't come.

"No means no," she grated out. Her voice sounded raspy and she berated herself. She didn't know for sure what he would find sexy. Clearly, he was hot for aggression from females.

His breathing was ragged. He pulled his hand away from her groin. His growl quieted. But his teeth were still set into her neck and he kept her suspended there.

He laughed, a quiet wheezing sound, and she felt his teeth release their grip on her skin.

A fat tear rolled down her cheek. She sniffed and looked up into the dark overhead in a vain attempt to control her emotions.

She could feel his breath on her face, knew that he was examining her, though she had no idea how much detail he could see in such pitch-black conditions.

Without warning, he released her and she fell to the floor, limbs flailing. The sound was so loud in the absolute stillness that it felt like a bomb had gone off. Instantly, she pulled her garment up over her breasts and simultaneously down over her knees. She huddled against the wall, knees drawn to her chest, tears flowing freely. She covered her mouth with her hand so she wouldn't sob aloud, her body shuddering as the adrenaline subsided.

She felt him brush against her arm as he settled down next to her. She froze. There was nowhere to run or hide from him. If he made another move, she'd scream bloody murder and bring the hymenoptera running to separate them while she fought him off with every dirty trick she could conceive of.

If that didn't work, she'd use the blue light before she'd submit to him, no matter the cost. She wasn't going to keep being a victim.

"Your offensive was strong, initially, but that single blunder cost you dearly. Had I been a real predator, you'd have been raped and murdered five times over by now, Leebska," he murmured into her ear, calmly, thoughtfully. Then he continued more urgently, "You must know your opponent, anticipate every possible approach. You cannot hold back. Once you lost the advantage, your defense crumbled, utterly. You knew what needed to be done. Why did you wait so long to change your strategy?"

She reeled at his sudden rational turn, as if he hadn't just been mauling her like a rutting bear moments before.

"I—you can't touch me that way!" she retorted with quiet venom.

"Can't I? I think I just did. Do you think a slaver will be different? How will you stop it from happening? I think you liked it."

She smacked his face, hard. The sound echoed against all the surfaces of the room. She didn't question how she'd managed to strike him so squarely in the dark. She didn't care about the consequences. She stood over him and spoke aloud, each word grated through clenched teeth. "If you ever touch me like that again, I'll rip off whatever you've got growing between your legs and feed it to the hymenoptera larvae."

He chuckled softly, and she heard him mutter as she stalked back to her sleeping cell, "I do believe you would."

18

DARCY no longer slept as easily as she once had. Though their routine stayed the same, and Raub acted as though nothing had happened between them—for her, things had changed. She'd always known he was dangerous, but at some point she'd grown too familiar, become too habituated to his gruff manner, and had lost some of her wariness. That had been a mistake.

She had to be more vigilant, less quiescent. Raub was clearly an opportunist. She didn't know what he had to gain from training her, but there was a reason and she needed to know what that was. It could very well make the difference in her survival.

She lay awake on her back in her cell, hands cradled beneath her head, elbows akimbo, thinking. Raub was quiet, but she didn't hear his deep, measured breathing from one of the other cells. He wasn't sleeping either. She had no idea what the time was, but it felt like it was still a few hours before they would rise for the day.

She breathed in a way that she hoped was indistinguishable from her normal sleep sounds. She wasn't sure why she did it. It just seemed like the thing to do.

She heard a rustling sound and strained her ears to try to

distinguish his activity. Raub was getting up. Perhaps it was later than she thought. She waited for him to tap her foot and bark at her to rise, but that didn't happen.

Instead, she heard the door open and shut. Raub had left the rooms they were imprisoned in. That was a distinct change in routine. Now she was curious.

Darcy slipped from her cell, raced to the door, and put her ear against it, in hopes of catching some remnant of conversation as they walked away. She was in the habit of doing this whenever he left the rooms, though normally she heard nothing beyond a few curt words.

This time, she was in luck. They hadn't yet moved. Raub and at least one hymenoptera spoke, just on the other side of the door. She couldn't make out the vowel sounds the hymenoptera made. They were too soft to be heard through the door. But she could hear the clacks of the consonants he spoke and Raub's voice was audible. She was able to piece together most of the conversation, though she didn't understand all of it. They were using plenty of terminology that was unfamiliar. Those words translated inside her head, but they didn't mean anything to her.

At first they were talking a lot of numbers and how they related to stars and planets. It took her a few moments to realize that the insect was explaining to Raub their current position in relation to other worlds. Then he described their trajectory, rate of speed, and the seven planets that lay within reach of that route. Then they discussed timing, duty schedules of various ship personnel, and routes within the ship to a short-range vehicle bay.

Raub was planning an escape attempt.

She stiffened and her nails dug into her skin. She wondered if she fit into this developing plan in some way. He'd said he was training her so she would be a competent ally. But how had he gotten the hymenoptera's loyalty? What did he have to offer him?

The conversation concluded abruptly. She didn't have time

to do more than back away from the door a couple of steps before it opened. Raub strode through swiftly and switched on the lights. She couldn't even disguise her reaction to what she'd heard. Her fingertips tingled. She didn't need to look down to know that the nerves under her skin were glowing faintly. Any kind of strong emotion seemed to bring on this state.

Raub looked mildly surprised. Then he blinked slowly and drawled, "Have you broken the fast yet, Leebska?"

He knew the answer to that question, but it helped her remember to hold her tongue, that the walls had eyes and ears. She took a few shallow breaths, her chest heaving, and shook her head. She closed her eyes for a second and focused on calming herself. When the blue blaze behind her lids dimmed she opened them again to find Raub watching her approvingly.

"Let us begin," he said, and launched into the stretching routine they always performed first thing in the morning.

She stared at him for a few seconds, wishing she had a window into his thoughts or at least the ability to speak freely with him. He was so frustratingly opaque, and there was never an opportunity to question him the way she really wanted to. That would have to end. She needed answers and he was the only one who could provide them.

She began the sequence with him, but her heart wasn't in the forms. She was sloppy about it and she didn't care. She stared him down as though daring him to correct her.

When he moved in to adjust her stance, he whispered into her ear, "Your eyes are on fire, Leebska."

He pulled back and she hated his smug smile. She didn't think. She lunged at him, throwing a quick punch and whirling into a turning kick. He blocked them both, easily, as if he expected them. In fact, he caught her leg in midair. She hopped in place and fought to get her balance back.

Her knee twisted painfully from over-rotation as her

momentum carried her through the kick. She hoped she hadn't torn the meniscus in that knee. That would lead to a lot of pain and wouldn't heal well under these conditions.

His lip quirked up into a feral leer, and he leaned in. "I believe you're angry." He released her leg and resumed the stretching sequence. Darcy put a few more paces of distance between them and tested her leg carefully before returning to the sequence herself.

She wanted desperately to confront him, but she might ruin all his plans if she said anything out loud. And what if by some chance those plans included her? She couldn't risk blowing an opportunity to escape. So she bit her tongue and bided her time.

Raub acted as though it were any other day. Meals were the same gruff affairs. Exercise was just as rigorous as ever. The only difference was her simmering temper and his knowing smirk.

Finally, the time for rest came. The lights went out. She passed the time recalling some of the last things she'd been studying before she was taken—toxic proteins and their effects on neurochemistry. Enough time had passed that it was getting harder and harder to remember this stuff without the reinforcement of flash cards or notes. If she ever got back to Earth, she'd be so behind she didn't want to think about it.

When she heard Raub's telltale rustle, she rose, making as little sound as possible. She wasn't sure what to expect from him, so she maintained a defensive posture and moved to where she thought he might be. He was stealthy like a cat, barely making a sound. When she bumped into him, he pounced.

He knocked her back into a bank of cells and attempted to gain control of her flailing limbs. She struggled to keep panic at bay. This felt too much like that other, dangerous time. She hissed a single word as she broke out of his grip: "No."

But he followed on her heels, stalking her. She fended him

off, time after time. Whenever they got close enough to talk quietly, he was on her, and she was barely keeping him at bay.

He'd never give her a chance to talk. He was relishing this. He knew she'd overheard, that she wanted to know more about his plan, but he would draw this out and enjoy every moment of her discomfort and uncertainty.

He was toying with her, and she had no choice but to let him. He was bigger, stronger, and a better fighter. But if she kept thinking like that, she'd never find out what he was up to. He'd keep her guessing forever. He never volunteered anything important, even when directly questioned.

She threw a punch and he blocked it by shoving her arm up so the swing went over his head. She grunted and pushed herself harder. She had to change her strategy.

She didn't hold back. She delivered heavy power slaps in a random pattern to his head—hoping to reduce his visual acuity. He'd told her that landing open-handed hits was better for her size than punching, especially against a larger opponent, but he'd given her little more than an hour of training on that technique. Well, she was getting in some practice now. She found that she liked it. She was rewarded when he took a step back.

With this technique she could deliver stinging blows without as much risk of hand injury, which was always on her mind when jabbing and punching. She could move quickly and dart into his defensive zone, slapping his offensive moves away while moving in with the other arm. Raub was bulky and lumbering compared to her—no wonder he'd let her discover the power of this technique on her own. At least for now, it was leveling their playing field.

Her fingertips stung. She felt sure she was leaving marks on him and that felt good. She pushed him back until he was the one pressed into the wall of sleeping cells and the sound of the slaps she rained on him echoed back eerily from them.

He threw a heavy punch. She slapped it off course, then dove low and jerked his arm down hard, letting his momentum carry him over her shoulder. He tumbled. Before he could regain his feet, she swiveled, landing a kick to his head to disorient him. He tried to rise, but she landed her full body weight on one knee, square on his chest, just as he'd showed her, and grappled with him until she held him immobile.

He wheezed until he caught his breath, then rumbled with soft laughter. She couldn't help but smile. She'd done it. She'd finally pinned him.

"Fine work, Leebska. You'll be an asset when we leave this cesspool."

"We?" He sounded completely normal, but nevertheless she released him slowly, carefully. She was worried that she might have unleashed his dark side again.

"Would I leave you behind after investing so much time in your development?"

"Okay. Good." She remained in a fighter's crouch, her brow furrowed. "Raub, we're not going to..."

"What?" She sensed, more than saw, him lumber to his feet and take a step to steady himself. He sounded amused. He stayed close enough to speak quietly, but didn't move to engage her again.

"What happened before. That wasn't okay."

"Yes?" He was being obtuse on purpose.

"Quit it. You know what I'm talking about. We are not having sex, you and me."

"Hm. No." He sounded unimpressed and like that was the farthest thing from his mind.

She heaved a sigh of relief that she'd finally said those words to him. "Okay, then. Tell me how this is going to happen. What's the plan?"

19

I CAN DO THIS.

Darcy had been avoiding her own reflection, averting her eyes when she hurried through bathing and grooming. She hadn't wanted to see a murderer's eyes looking back at her, bleak and accusing.

She'd done a lot of thinking, though, over the time she'd been held captive in these rooms with Raub. There was little else to do but think.

How long had it been? She didn't know. She hadn't scratched hash marks into the walls of her sleep cell to mark the passage of time. It was less painful to just succumb to the monotony and try not to think about how every single day there were more light-years of space stretching between her and her home and all the people there that she cared about.

But she had put that time to good use, learning new skills that might help to change her fate, and now she'd come to a conclusion. She couldn't ignore the power she had. She hated that she'd hurt anyone with it, but that couldn't be helped. All she could do now was learn to master it, the same way that she was becoming master over the rest of her body.

Nothing worthwhile came easily. She could forgive herself for fighting for her life and flailing. She would not forget—she would just learn to be more careful.

And that meant practice.

The first step was to see if she could manifest the power by thinking about it. She wanted to see what it looked like, to monitor herself as it happened.

She needed to face herself.

Raub had left the rooms on his daily mystery errand. She stood alone in the washroom, nude, hoping that Hain had enough decency that she didn't monitor her there.

She stepped in front of the mirror, her blood racing. Her breath caught. She almost didn't recognize her own reflection. Her hair, normally so carefully arranged in twists, straightened, or at least pulled back in a puffy ponytail, was a thick, glossy mass of wild curls that stood on end. But that wasn't what surprised her.

She was toned. She looked strong. Muscles moved under her skin. She was like an athlete in her prime.

Never in her life had she seen herself this way. She turned and flexed a leg and saw muscles pop out in stark relief. As her gaze travelled up she saw that her stomach was now flat. The little pillow of flab that Adam used to rest his head on was gone, replaced by a taut six-pack.

She'd come a long way from the girl Adam had to coax into going for a bike ride or a hike. She'd transformed herself. He'd be proud of her.

Adam. Despite her protestations, Raub refused to include Adam in the escape plan. He'd told her, in no uncertain terms, that if she wanted to survive she had to give up childish notions like love. Adam's fate was separate from hers, he'd said, and she had to accept that.

She'd pretended to acquiesce, but she was her own woman. When the time came, the route to the place where the tern was berthed would pass by those cavernous rooms where the prisoners were held. Whether Raub liked it or not, she was going to try to find him because that was who she was. If that cost her a chance at freedom, she could bear it. She couldn't live with herself if she didn't try.

She centered herself in front of the mirror, as though she were preparing to meditate, and focused on the memory of how the energy had felt before, when it had come without being summoned by her conscious mind. She remembered how she had tingled, how she had felt so alive, how she had felt it building inside her.

She didn't know if there was any energy left in her, or even what percentage of it she'd discharged on the hymenoptera. It seemed odd that she didn't know, but she reasoned that she never knew what her O_2 sats were, or her blood-alcohol content, though she always had a general idea, just based on how she felt. There was no such sensation attached to this energy—that she'd noticed so far, anyway. Hopefully that would come someday.

She sat there for a long time trying to summon it, but nothing happened. Her sit-bones hurt, her jaw ached from clenching it, and she began to doubt that she could succeed without something pushing her into a highly emotional state.

Her mind wandered. She thought of Adam, knew he was thinking of finding her and escaping too. She contemplated her father, his strong face a mask of worry, the search parties he must have waited fruitlessly for. Her mother and the gurus she'd probably paid every penny of her savings to, hoping for some clue as to what had happened to her only child. Her friends and professors, for whom by now she was only a memory, a mystery in the past.

She was alone, more alone than anyone ever should be, with only herself to rely on, and she had some special attribute that she couldn't even use.

A tear fled down her cheek. She watched it fall, her brown eyes brimming with more, her reflection swimming in a blurry haze. She remembered the night she'd been captured, how helpless she'd felt, even with Adam there with her. Then there was the moment when Raub had held her against the wall and nearly taken her last shred of dignity.

She could fight some, now. She was stronger, but against a more skilled opponent or a gun or shock stick, she had nothing. Would she ever regain control of her life? Was she doomed to be a victim until the end?

She blinked. Her eyes emptied over her cheeks and she leaned forward. There was a faint glow just above her right breast, a mirror to her heart. She knew instinctively that was the core of her power. She focused on it, breathed into that place, moved her consciousness there and felt it grow, felt her body warm and strengthen in response.

She watched the blue lines radiate out until her fingertips crackled. She laughed out loud. She was alight with blue fire. It was exhilarating.

Slowly, she stood and turned, to see the energy from every angle. As she concentrated on rising, the light dimmed somewhat, but it blazed again when she refocused her thoughts. She attempted to dim it on purpose and was rewarded when the blue light quickly reversed itself, flowing back to the centering point opposite her heart.

She banked the flame close to her heart, then stoked it again, over and over, panting with the effort of controlling it, waves of heat rolling off her and sweat trickling from every pore. She shut out every other thought and committed the sensations to memory. She was mesmerized by how it looked, racing along those mysterious pathways under her skin, some kind of secondary central nervous system.

Something made her look up. She turned.

Raub stood in the doorway, watching. "This is very good. What else can you do?"

20

DARCY MADE it a daily habit to slip into the washroom whenever Raub left. She concentrated primarily on calling up and controlling the intensity of her energy. It became a meditative practice. She could keep it low and smoldering for long periods, then, on a moment's notice, whip it up to a crackle.

She was unsure of how to explore it further. Discharging it would likely be noticed and she felt a strong need to conserve it, to hold it in reserve for when it was needed. She had no idea how much was stored within her.

Once she felt she had that well in hand, she turned her attention to the other ability Hain had mentioned—camouflage. She found she had only to think hard about hiding and to press herself against something. Some element in her skin or nervous system searched for input on a level that her brain didn't consciously comprehend. It was some kind of extra sense that sought data about her surroundings—color and texture—then did its best to mimic what it found.

It didn't exactly work the way it was meant to in a stainless-steel-plated bathroom on an alien ship—it smudged her skin a dappled, sooty grey. Only her hair remained unchanged. The process was exhausting, but she could see that it could be very useful under more natural conditions.

In quiet moments, the childhood memory of being invisible repeated in her mind. She'd been playing hide and seek, just as Hain had said. She'd always thought that she had somehow confused the memory of a childhood dream with reality. But now she knew she hadn't—as a child she'd used the ability instinctively, and never realized its significance. By the time she was old enough to know that it might be important, she'd already labeled the memory as fantasy.

Today, instead of leaving her alone, Raub motioned at her impatiently. She'd been summoned to Hain's quarters. It was the first time Darcy had been allowed to leave since the day she woke up inside the sleeping cell.

The hymenoptera kept well back and chattered nervously when she and Raub emerged. They insisted Raub keep one of his meaty hands around Darcy's arm while they brandished their shock sticks at arm's length in front of themselves. There were eight of them to escort her and Raub to Hain's quarters. They seemed to be expecting her to cause trouble.

She started to reassure them that she meant no harm, but Raub shushed her. Reluctantly, she complied. She guessed the threat of her power might serve them well during the upcoming escape attempt.

Darcy recoiled as Raub led her into Hain's quarters. A horrible smell, like sour, composted onions, hit her in a wave and the room was lit up brighter than noon on a midsummer day. She squinted, averting her gaze from the dazzling source of the light. Raub pulled her forward into the room as though leading a blind person, his hand on her arm clenched so hard, her fingers were going numb.

Darcy peeped through her lashes to see Hain lying on her

back inside a clear container studded on all sides with brilliant white lights. She was partially submerged in a glowing, cloudy, green liquid that bubbled and frothed around her body.

"Mistress," Raub said dryly.

"Ah, yes. Good," Hain said in her strange, breathy voice. She lifted the lid and the light switched off.

The room instantly seemed dark by comparison. Darcy looked around owlishly as her eyes adjusted. She realized that this was a laboratory and noted the hymenoptera were lined up in front of the only door, still waving their shock sticks warily.

Hain sat up, the murky liquid sheeting off of her. She nimbly hopped out of the acrylic container, sending droplets flying in all directions. She stood there, dripping all over the floor as though that was normal, and eyed Raub and Darcy appraisingly.

Darcy couldn't help but gawk at the container Hain had just vacated. The liquid inside continued to churn, as though it were alive. She wondered if there was a gas being pumped through it or if it was undergoing a fermentation process, or both. It seemed to be the source of the powerful odor.

Hain spoke again. "You are a fortunate individual, Darcy Eberhardt."

Darcy turned her attention to Hain and didn't hide her contempt. "Really? It sure doesn't feel like it."

Hain's eyes narrowed. "Despite all the trouble you've caused, you still live. I would have spaced a less valuable commodity. Are you ready to cooperate? It's in your best interests, I assure you."

Raub squeezed her arm harder, almost possessively. She didn't like that. She glared at him, not that he noticed.

Darcy gritted her jaw tightly so she wouldn't yelp. He'd warned her to go along with whatever Hain wanted from her. If they were separated now, their plan would be blown and they might not get another chance before one of them was sold. He'd reminded her that working together, they were stronger than either of them was alone. She had to act as though Raub was keeping her in line so Hain would leave them be for just a little bit longer.

Under ideal circumstances she'd never have allied herself with someone like Raub, but in the name of survival, she'd settle for uncharacteristic measures.

Hain gestured to some instruments laid out on the bench in front of her. "It's time to quantify the scope of your genetic gifts, don't you think?"

"I—" Darcy glanced at Raub.

He nodded almost imperceptibly, his expression grim.

She had to admit to being curious, herself. It was patently wrong that Hain knew more about her genetics and heritage than she did. The knowledge could be useful in the days to come, especially if Hain had more information than she'd offered up so far. Raub hadn't given her any hint of what to expect from this interview, but Darcy wasn't surprised that it had taken this tack.

"Yes. I'll cooperate."

Raub's fingers loosened on her arm a fraction, then he shoved her forward and let go. Inarticulate but distressed clacking sounds came from near the door. Darcy picked her way around the puddles and droplets Hain was leaving all over the floor. She wasn't about to slip and fall in front of this audience, nor did she like the idea of getting the mystery substance on her bare skin. She had never been given any shoes, after all.

Hain turned to gesture at a boxy instrument on the bench and a tray of small metallic discs. "If you'll allow me to place sensors on your body," she said. "I've cobbled together a rudimentary bioelectric meter that will measure your electromagnetic output, efficiency, and, of course, heat generated as waste."

Darcy nodded. Hain picked up a tray from the bench and began to press the tiny metal dots into Darcy's skin, starting with each of her fingertips, her palms, the back of her hands, her wrists, then a spiral configuration up her arm.

Hain's touch was moist and cool and she had a graceful way of swaying from task to task that reminded Darcy of foxtail grass moving in the wind. "I thought you were a geneticist?"

"Biology is my area of specialty. However, my work often demands a broad base of knowledge."

"What else will you test?" Darcy asked, bringing her hand to her face to examine one of the thin metallic discs. It was roughly the size and shape of a watch battery, clearly an electrode, like something used on an ECG or EEG, but it was wireless.

"I'll document the extent of your senses and abilities as they are present at this stage, though they will surely require continued monitoring as they develop."

Darcy frowned. That hadn't told her anything, really. "Such as?"

Hain kept working. "Oh, the energy you store is but a small part of it, Darcy. Based on the research I've done, you have the potential to be a formidable combatant, nearly impossible to defeat."

Darcy frowned. "I don't want to be a combatant."

Raub leaned forward, his voice low and gravelly. "You'll *be* whatever your master desires you to *be*."

Darcy choked on her own spit. It shouldn't matter. She and Adam and Raub would be leaving all of this behind soon and she could try to find her way back to Earth somehow. "You're advertising me as a weapon?"

Hain didn't look up. Cool air blew from her mouth and nose in a constant flow, bringing with it the noxious odor of her bizarre bathing fluid tinged with a sickly sweet undertone. While in one of his rare loquacious moods, Raub had told Darcy that Hain didn't have lungs, that her diminutive nose had been carved surgically to make her appear more like other sentient species. He'd said that it was surprising how important a nose was. Without one, people were treated as "other" and never commanded any respect.

Hain crossed the room and slid what looked like a rolled-up sheet of rubbery black plastic out of a compartment under a workbench. She unrolled it and slapped it against the wall near Darcy and Raub. She fiddled with her tablet then tapped it against the dark sheet as she turned away. Instantly, the sheet lit up.

Darcy stepped up to the sheet, now a screen, and stared. A painfully thin female face looked back blankly, her angular cheekbones standing out in geometric relief. Her skin was a warm brown, contrasting with a cream-colored garment festooned with swathes of fabric and ties. Her hair was light brown and pulled away from her face severely in complex braids. She was poised, unmoving. When she finally began to speak, Darcy jumped.

"Greetings. I am your host, Elorpha. This Sectilius Scientific Moment concerns the subspecies drudii, known on some worlds as druids, scientific designation *Inaricaaria hominidae,* subspecies: *drudii.*"

Text appeared at the bottom of the screen, spelling out the scientific name, which Darcy was surprised to realize she could comprehend. Her heart skipped a beat. What did that mean to her? Was she human or druid or both? Was she a footnote in someone's reference book, like a mule or a liger? Darcy barely registered that Hain was kneeling before her, resuming placement of the electrodes on her feet and lower legs.

A planet came on-screen. It was beautiful and blue-green with wispy white clouds like Earth. Darcy swallowed hard. Then she noticed it had three moons. The planet rotated slowly, revealing a large land mass very different from Earth's as well as another moon. Four moons? Was this her druid ancestors' home?

"This novel, anthropoid subspecies hails from Inaricaa,

fourth planet in the Hesteau system. Genetically engineered and enhanced with heritable nanocytotech in an effort to protect its homeworld, it was later reviled by its progenitor species and hunted to virtual extinction by the predatory race, *Lovekitus quamut*. To learn more about the complex and dramatic history of these two species, click on the entry notes." The presenter paused, as if to give the viewer an opportunity to do just that.

Darcy took an involuntary step back. Hain clucked and followed her. Heritable nanocytotech? Reviled? Hunted to virtual extinction? The presentation seemed to be some kind of documentary, but it sounded like this alien woman was reading an entry from a zoology textbook. That felt incredibly weird. The hair on the back of her neck stood on end as the woman took a breath and continued.

"For legal reasons, it must be noted that the knowledge and technology used to give rise to the drudii was destroyed long ago. Any attempt to revive the experiment is forbidden by law on every member planet of the Alliance of Unified Sentient Races. If you believe you have come in contact with an individual of druidic heritage, it is best to keep your distance and alert local authorities, wherever applicable."

What the hell? Alert authorities for what? For being alive? Darcy looked to Raub and Hain in confusion. This smacked of separate water fountains and segregated buses. What kind of bullshit was this?

Hain remained busy, placing the electrodes. Raub watched her with steely eyes.

Elorpha hadn't stopped speaking. "As the war the drudii were engineered to wage concluded, the inaricaans demanded mandatory sterilization of the surviving drudii before allowing them to return to their home planet."

The parallel rocked her. Eugenics laws of the early- to mid-twentieth century led to thousands of women of color in the

United States undergoing forced sterilization, sometimes without their knowledge or consent. It was just one among many reasons that blacks didn't trust doctors. How could this happen in a society that was capable of creating these kinds of abilities? Were people everywhere just inherently evil?

Elorpha continued, "The drudii fled and scattered throughout the galaxy, interbreeding with compatible species of anthropoid origin, leaving a secret legacy behind on many worlds."

Like Earth.

They'd lost the only home they'd ever known.

Like me.

"Within most anthropological circles, it is commonly believed that there are no longer any full-blooded drudii remaining. Hybrids are discovered from time to time. Depending upon the presence of a range of possible genes, some, or all, of the following traits may be present in drudii-hybrid progeny."

Darcy leaned forward, straining to absorb every scrap of information that Elorpha would give her.

"These include the capacity to absorb energy from loci of electromagnetic density on high-gravity planetary bodies and to store this energy in nanocytotech called apochondria—engineered organelles disguised as mitochondria and passed down from mother to offspring in the same manner. This energy can be utilized in various ways."

Darcy's hands clenched. Her nails dug into her palms painfully.

Elorpha continued to speak. "When fully charged in this manner, drudii hybrids experience increased speed, endurance, and agility, accelerated wound regeneration, rumored—but unconfirmed—limb regeneration, and camouflage, via metachrosis. For more information about metachrosis, the process of altering skin color and texture via chromatophores, please click on the entry notes." Elorpha smiled enthusiastically as she spoke about metachrosis, something Darcy had once relegated only to the octopus, an animal that could not be farther removed from her own experience of existence.

She forced herself to focus and not go down a rabbit hole of crazy just yet.

"Drudii hybrids are capable of producing bursts of light to distract an enemy and of creating electromagnetic pulses to disrupt electronics. They may possess the ability to manipulate magnetic fields around a ferromagnetic object. It is also reported they may be able to detect and possibly perceive broadcasts on many wavelengths and frequencies on the EM spectrum. One anecdote claims a subject with some druidic traits was capable of identifying known individuals by brain-wave signatures when prevented from sensing them by standard means. That same individual was suspected of interfacing with binary processors via wireless radio waves. These claims were never substantiated."

Darcy's brows pulled together. She was feeling a little dizzy.

But, still, Elorpha carried on. "There are unverified accounts of drudii creating tremors or even small earthquakes, theoretically disrupting gravity at a particle level. Unconfirmed reports suggest that some drudii may possess the ability to manipulate both gas and liquids, mechanism unknown."

Darcy couldn't help herself. She yelled, "Oh, come on!"

"Some of the first recorded references to drudii concern the earliest specimens, who enacted suicide missions against other worlds, blending into the populace and releasing massive shockwaves of ionizing radiation, resulting in their own deaths as well as the deaths of millions of innocent victims." Elorpha smiled as though pleased with herself. "This concludes the Sectilius Science Moment on the subject of the drudii." Elorpha dipped her head slightly and the screen went blank.

Darcy looked at Hain, who continued to painstakingly place

electrodes on Darcy's skin. It seemed preposterous. She felt strange and lightheaded. She laughed, a single lame guffaw. It was like a tabloid article, a spoof, a science-fiction parody, not something that was real. "Surely you don't believe all of that is true?"

It couldn't be. Could it?

"I do."

A residual drop of moisture glistened on the point of Hain's artificial nose. Darcy watched it, waiting for it to fall, as Hain brusquely clicked the button on the sleeve of her garment and began to remove it in one swift movement.

Darcy wrenched away and backed up, pulling the jumpsuit back up over herself. "What do you think you're doing?" she spit out angrily.

"Nudity is shameful in her culture," Hain said in monotone. A look passed between Hain and Raub. Raub grunted and continued to watch them, looking bored.

Hain reached for the garment again and Darcy slapped her hand away. "You can't just strip me. Tell me where they go and I—"

Raub sighed and said, "The garment is comprised of linked molecular machines and generates its own electromagnetic field that would interfere with the test."

Hain picked up another electrode and stood before her as though waiting. "Our interest is purely scientific."

Darcy huffed and shook her head. "Fine." She slipped the jumpsuit off and laid it on the bench next to her.

Hain continued to place the electrodes in an equally spaced pattern over her chest, back, stomach, and even her inner thighs.

"Is that really necessary?" Darcy asked through clenched teeth.

Hain finished placing the electrodes and stepped back, turning her attention to tapping on a tablet with her long, thin fingers. The crusty growths that extended over her hands still glistened with moisture from the strange bath she'd been taking.

Darcy stood there feeling raw and exposed, waiting for her next instruction. They were keeping her off-balance on purpose. She didn't want to give them the satisfaction of achieving that goal. It took every ounce of willpower not to cover herself with her hands. Finally, she asked, "What happens next?"

Hain's face twisted into a smile. "Very little, until you show me your light. We've established a baseline reading. Let's begin."

Darcy hesitated. She wasn't sure what Hain knew or had seen. But another glance at Raub's glowering face reminded her to just play along. She centered herself and called up the power. She didn't have to look down to know that her chest glowed. Hain's mouth opened slightly as she glanced back and forth between the tablet in her hand and Darcy's body. Darcy caught glimpses of a bright yellow pattern inside her mouth, though she couldn't make out details.

Soft, agitated clacking sounded again from near the door.

"More," Hain commanded in her thin voice.

"I want to see what you're seeing," Darcy replied.

Hain tapped absently on the tablet, not making eye contact.

Darcy extinguished her light.

The slit of Hain's mouth pulled down into an angry gash. Jerkily, she turned and tapped the screen with her tablet again.

The display shifted. Now it said things like Female Drudii Subject and Preliminary Bioelectric Assessment, with a rendering of the electrode dots Hain had placed on her in three dimensions, sketching a rough outline of Darcy's body. Next to each electrode was a numerical value.

"What unit of measurement is this?" Darcy asked.

"Let's continue," Hain enunciated slowly.

Darcy turned to face her with an expectant expression.

Raub interjected, his voice sounding like a warning, "It will be meaningless to you, Leebska."

That was probably true. She didn't care. She kept staring at Hain.

Hain's gash of a mouth was turned down on one side. "They're cipa units. Do I really need to teach you a lesson in basic electronics just now?"

Darcy turned back to the screen and let the light flare in her chest, watching as the numbers skyrocketed and colors bloomed across the display. Her body warmed. She focused and pushed the light outward slowly, down her arms. She could control it inch by inch, if she wanted.

She lifted her arms away from her body so that she wouldn't create static arcs that could disorient her. Her fingers tingled as the energy flared inside them.

Hain watched, mouth opening again, revealing what looked like a yellow flower. "Astonishing. I had no idea." She seemed to come to herself. "This is so very rare. I must document all of this. Is this your maximum potential?"

Darcy came to a decision. "No, I can do more."

Hain tapped on her tablet furiously. "Go ahead."

Darcy brought her energy back down to an ember. Based on their reactions, it was clear that both Hain and Raub lusted to know more about the extent of her abilities. That gave her a small amount of leverage and she was going to use it. "Not until you bring Adam Benally here, so that I can see him. I need to know that he's okay."

Hain's gaze flashed at Raub. His jaw clenched. His eyes were hard and angry, but he didn't speak.

Darcy felt tense. She glanced from Hain to Raub and back again. There was some unspoken conversation going on there.

Hain put some distance between herself and Darcy, but her body language was suddenly more relaxed. She glided across the floor, her fingers dragging languidly over the workbench. "This Adam Benally was the male we found you with on your homeworld?"

Darcy didn't like the sudden shift in Hain's mood, and it wasn't lost on her that Hain had just put a very large object between them. Fear stabbed at her heart. "Yes."

"He was your mate?" Hain blinked slowly and folded her willowy arms like she was speaking to a small child.

Darcy's mouth went dry. Her eyes blurred. There was a roaring in her ears. "Was?" Energy swept through her. She burned.

Faintly, she heard Raub command, "Control yourself, Leebska, before I do it for you."

"Stay back!" she warned him. To Hain, she said, "What did you do to him?"

Hain tilted her head to one side. "I sold him, Darcy. Many, many standard solar days ago."

21

"DID SHE GIVE YOU ANY TROUBLE?" Hain asked, her expression innocent.

"You pushed the girl too hard." Raub slammed his fist into the bench top. It cracked with a satisfying splinter.

She flinched.

He pulled back his fist, flexing it. He'd just come back from escorting Darcy to their quarters, where he'd taken the precaution of locking her in her sleeping cell, just in case she got any crazy ideas now that Hain had let slip what she was capable of. He didn't dare leave her alone for long. She'd gone strangely silent and those disquieting, watery "tiersz" were dripping out of her eyes again.

Shedding light on her abilities had been the plan—to empower her, ready her for what was ahead, allow her time to think, to experiment, to become resourceful while still relying on him, for now, anyway. The recent conversation had accomplished the polar opposite.

Hain raised her chin and stared him down. "You miscalculated her attachment to the male."

She was getting too independent. It was time to remind her of what was at stake. "I miscalculated? You would do well to remember our contract, Hain. Do not forget that I own you. I know the location of your homeworld. If you do not value your own life, value the life of the Mother. Think of the money I could make on all that furniture, harvested from all that lovely, sentient wood."

Hain did not answer. She stared at him blankly, then turned back to her samples, though she did not work. The stink of ozone offended his nose. He'd gotten through to her.

He continued. "She agreed his destiny was separate from hers. There was no need to create this little drama, Hain. Do not second-guess me. From here on, you will stick to the script."

Hain fluttered her fingers to dismiss what he'd said. "Apparently she lied to appease you. What was I to do? I couldn't produce the male."

He glowered at her. "Reinforcing my message to her would have sufficed."

Hain turned back, her mouth puckered slightly in a way that he'd come to know as defiance. "I'm not her progenitor. It cannot be wise to coddle an adult with platitudes. Besides, that wouldn't have worked. She's queried various individuals about this Adam Benally on dozens of occasions. I've made you aware of this. This species is not as logical or opportunistic as one would expect. We must take care not to make assumptions about her behavior. All of the humans were giving us trouble. That's why I sold them off as quickly as possible." She paused, the only way she could give her words emphasis. "We must be realistic if this is to work."

He growled. She made logical points. He didn't like conceding that Hain might be right. She was too clever for her own good.

Hain sidled a little closer, probably sensing that he was calmer. "She will recover quickly from this, just as she has from every other incident. This was a good time to discover she's not as transparent as we had thought. She'll be able to let thoughts of the male go now, be fully engaged in the present. This was fortuitous." She looked ruefully at the bench, then turned, placing her palms together. "Now, as to those plans, I have—"

The deck rocked under their feet and a call to arms blared over the communication system. Hain's face went blank as she mentally connected with the telepathic network created by the kuboderan navigator. Instantly she turned to Raub, her expression grave. "Local system border-patrol net. We, of course, have not filed trajectories with the local authorities nor paid any fees to pass through local space." Her mouth parted a fraction. "It's Level Seven."

Raub swore viciously. He raged, "I would have expected more care to be taken to avoid such inconveniences. You know how important this undertaking is."

She lifted her head a fraction and met his gaze. "It must be new. It's not on any of our maps. We've heard no reports from our associates. We cannot avoid what we are unaware of."

Logic. He curled one hand into a fist, barely holding back from delivering a punch to her face.

If it were a Level Four net or less, they'd have no trouble breaking free. A Level Seven would be dicey. Hain might lose everything, including the ship, and end up in custody herself. Perhaps that was where she belonged. He was beginning to wonder if she was as loyal as he'd thought.

Some things on the ship could be easily hidden or camouflaged. These backwater constables usually had plenty of ballistic tech, but little in the way of sophisticated detection. There was no way to hide the thousands of individuals in the cargo hold, however. That would be a substantial loss, unless the officials could be bought.

There was a chance all the merchandise might be freed on

the spot—and a fairly equal chance that they'd be moved through a less-than-savory sales venue to make a quick chit for some corrupt local authority. This far from a trade hub or busy port, there was little more than a semblance of law. The net might have been put in place by the government of a planet in the nearby system or by a neighborhood magnate looking to expand their wealth. Out in the fringes it was every individual for themself. No one was above reproach. They were all out here for a reason.

And if they found the girl and realized what she was...

He wouldn't let that happen.

His nostrils flared and he didn't bother to quell a roar of frustration. "All this planning ruined by some greedy pless. I'd like to get my hands on them."

"It's salvageable," Hain stated as she opened a drawer and pulled out a handful of laser-deflecting shield generators as well as a small CO_2 cartridge, efficiently attaching them to premade slots in the dense encrustations upon her skin. The tough, symbiotic lichens served as body armor in hand-to-hand combat, but weren't enough to protect her in a firefight. The CO_2 was in anticipation of a possible loss of atmosphere in the short term. It was a precaution most wouldn't have thought of. Hain always planned three moves ahead. "The tern is ready. It's outfitted with plenty of weapons, fuel, and food for a long excursion. We prepared for any contingency. You just have to find the right planet. The onboard computer is capable of giving you all the options in local territories in any direction. There will be something you can use."

She tested the shield generators. They hummed to life. "They aren't wasting any time. There are three vessels en route, closing fast."

"She's not ready," he growled.

"Wherever you decide to go, you'll have plenty of time to

finish the training during the journey. I'll find you before you put your boots on the ground and wait for your signal."

He would have to adapt to the circumstance or risk losing the prize. He picked up an instrument and threw it.

Hain didn't flinch this time. "They're hailing. I must respond quickly or they'll get suspicious."

"You'll fight?"

"If they attempt to board? Yes. We're only partially disabled. They don't know the full extent of our capabilities. We look like a cracker hauler to them. We have all the proper codes. They should let us pass."

That was true. It was a clever disguise. But there wouldn't be many food-supply ships this far off the main routes. "Tell them you're lost to buy time. You've had a bad jump with a sick kuboderan. That's believable."

She nodded and started for the door, then turned, listening intently to the hymenoptera chattering over the kuboderan network. "The aft hangar is clear. Go immediately." With that, she turned on her heel and left, motioning for the two hymenoptera in the hall to join her as she headed for the command deck.

Raub strode swiftly in the opposite direction. The timing couldn't be worse. The girl had just suffered an emotional blow and would likely be skittish.

Now, he'd see what she was really made of.

22

DARCY HELD BACK A SOB, her mouth open in a silent scream. She lay curled on her side, pressing her face into the cold, hard surface of the sleeping cell as if that could push back the raw despair. Tears and drool pooled under her cheek.

How could she ever have let herself hope that she and Adam would escape, get back home, and live out a normal life? How childish that had been. A fantasy.

The truth was, she didn't even know how to begin to accept this new reality. It felt like a living nightmare. The rules kept changing before she could adjust. Nothing was what it seemed to be.

If Hain was telling the truth, then Adam was gone, possibly forever. Her rock. Her biggest cheerleader. Her heart. That knowledge tore at her. What could she do? How could she begin to know what to do next?

She had all this power stored inside her, and she hadn't been able to save him. She'd failed him and probably was incapable of saving herself.

She had two choices now. She could put her head down and

accept that she was going to be sold as a weapon, and that she would possibly be forced to kill people by her new master, who would most likely turn out to be some kind of terrorist or dictator. Or she could put her trust in Raub, who was probably a criminal, and definitely dangerous and unpredictable, in order to attempt to escape the ship.

There were no good choices.

She turned it all over and over in her mind. But she couldn't really think clearly. Her thoughts kept snarling in pain and despair and couldn't get much farther than that.

She didn't want to think anymore. She wanted the oblivion of sleep. She'd think about it all tomorrow. Maybe it wouldn't seem so bad by then.

But she couldn't turn her brain off.

There was one thing that always put her to sleep. She closed her eyes and thought through the sequence of the citric-acid cycle, so necessary for aerobic metabolism. She visualized each molecule and its enzymatic conversion into the next step in the metabolic chain, careful not to forget the three points at which NADH was formed, or how that molecule would later contribute to the production of ATP—the powerhouse of cellular energy— all of this taking place inside the mitochondria of every cell of her body.

She tried not to think about the apochondria Hain had told her about. Or wonder how they processed and stored energy.

If she forgot her place, she just remembered the mnemonic, "Can (cis-Aconitate) I (D-isocitrate) Keep (alpha-ketoglutarate) Selling (Succinyl-CoA) Sex (Succinate) For (Fumarate) Money (Malate), Officer (Oxaloacetate)?" It was a stupid, misogynistic memory device, but she'd never forget it, ever.

She was just drifting into that twilight space between sleep and wakefulness when a loud buzzing sound startled her back to alertness. She'd never heard that sound on the ship before. It sent a frisson down her spine.

Something was wrong.

She got up awkwardly on her knees, hunching to stay upright, her head bumping into the ceiling of her tiny cubicle. She scrubbed at her face with her hands, sniffing deeply to clear her airway of the congestion the tears had generated. Then she scooted forward and pressed on the door. It wouldn't budge. That asshole Raub had locked her in.

She sat back on her heels and frowned. The raucous buzzing silenced itself. Her ears rang with echoes of it. She was sure something was happening. She didn't want to be trapped inside the sleeping cell any longer. Who knew what was going on out there?

If everything Hain had just told her was true, she shouldn't accept any kind of unfavorable circumstance. She had the power to change things. She shouldn't just sit back and wait for something to happen to her anymore.

She had to do something.

She possessed abilities. Surely one of them could get her through this door. She sorted through all the traits the woman in the video had described. Speed, endurance, agility...no. Bursts of light, manipulating magnetic fields, camouflage, electromagnetic pulses. No. Dammit. It was a mechanical lock. None of that stuff was going to do anything to it, even if she'd known how to do any of it.

She put her hand to the door. Someone like Raub might be able to use brute force to break it, but she could too easily hurt herself attempting something like that and still remain trapped. There had to be a way.

Wait a minute. The byproduct of energy production was heat. Whenever she practiced using her energy she got so warm sweat would stream off of her, and afterward she had to drink large volumes of water to slake her thirst. Heat might actually get her out.

She decided to try something she'd never tried before. She called up her energy, focusing it on the tip of her index finger, and slowly slid that finger along the crack of the door where she'd seen the lock from the outside, allowing her pent-up energy to blaze, but not be released. Her finger grew hot, but she didn't let up.

The heat became painful. She didn't falter, even as she smelled the scents of cooking flesh, a hot metallic tang, and smoke. She drew her finger to the bottom of the lock and shoved her shoulder into the door hard.

It gave way, springing open and banging with a loud clang against the other cubicles. She almost lost her balance and tumbled out. She scrabbled to push herself back and change her center of gravity before she fell, then hopped down and hit the lights. They didn't come on at full power, just a dim glow. She looked at her hand. It was darkly discolored and hurt like hell. There wasn't enough light to see the extent of the damage she'd done to herself.

She slipped into the small room that served as their mess hall. She clicked the button on her sleeve and shoved a hand into the fabric of her malleable garment, sculpting a large pocket into the side, then filled it with the small amount of leftover food cubes. It seemed like a good idea to be ready for anything.

She turned and nearly jumped out of her skin. Raub was standing there, silently watching her fill the pocket. His expression was inscrutable.

"It's time," he said.

She wondered if he'd done something that set off the alarm. She eyed him warily. "Time for what?"

Then she looked over his shoulder and down the long, wide hallway lined with sleeping cubicles. The door that led out to the rest of the ship was still open from his arrival. There were no hymenoptera in sight. She turned back to him, confused by their absence. "What did you do?"

"There isn't time to explain. We'll take advantage of the chaos to get away."

So her suspicions were correct. Something was happening. "What chaos? What's going on?" What terrible thing had he done?

"This ship is under attack."

That was not what she'd imagined. She'd thought maybe Raub had killed Hain or some of the hymenoptera or something.

He grabbed her arm and pulled her toward the door.

She resisted. She needed to know more before she just followed him. But it was like trying to stop a semitruck with a feather. He was determined to go and take her with him. She was already uneasy. There was an urgency about his manner that was freaking her out. She dug in her heels and pulled at the hand that held her arm. "Quit keeping me in the dark. If you want my cooperation, you have to tell me more! If the ship is under attack, someone could be trying to rescue us!"

He snarled. "That's naive. We're out on the edge of nowhere. People don't live out here unless they're outlaws. Whoever wants this ship doesn't have good intentions, Leebska. They're pirates, even if they represent a local government. If we stay, conditions will only get worse for us—if we survive their assault on the ship."

"But Hain is a pirate. The Lovek is a pirate," she protested.

"Hain is a biologist. She's a pet."

The deck vibrated under their feet. The sensation built in intensity. There was a loud sound like something large shuttling at high speed through a tube, accompanied by the whine of a giant bottle rocket shooting off. The vibration and sound ceased abruptly. Complete silence followed.

She gulped. A wave of fear washed over her. Something really weird was going on.

Raub's eyes bored into her. "That was the sound of this ship releasing ordnance. The reprisal will be swift. Do you really want to have a conference right now? Or do you want to live?"

She nodded and let his momentum carry her forward. Whatever this ship had just unleashed—someone else was probably going to shoot back. That wasn't good. Not good at all. Ships with holes in them leaked air. People couldn't breathe in vacuum. "Where are we going?"

He released her arm and took off, not bothering to answer. She watched him lope ahead of her without looking back. She hesitated. She was following a man who had been very close to raping her once. But there was a chance for freedom. She ran after him.

23

RAUB SWIFTLY MOVED through the labyrinth of corridors with purpose and stealth, pausing momentarily at every intersection to check for traffic before barreling forward. He clearly knew where he was going. It all looked the same to Darcy. They could be running in circles for all she knew.

He entered a small hexagonal room with six doors. It was the first place that seemed at all familiar to her. She'd been in a similar room the day that the hymenoptera called Tesserae71 had escorted her to her holding cell in the vast room full of prisoners, but she couldn't be sure it was the same place. The only light in the room glowed from panels, alight with displays, keypads, and buttons, that bridged the gaps between the exits. Darcy was careful not to bump into anything.

Raub moved to one of the panels and tapped screens and buttons so rapidly Darcy's eye could barely follow his movements, much less make any sense of them. That didn't stop her from trying to. "What are you doing?" she whispered.

He didn't reply or even deign to look her way. He was completely absorbed in his task. Was this how one got access to another part of the ship that was normally inaccessible? She furrowed her brow. Were they near the holds where the prisoners were kept? If that was the case, how would Raub have that kind of access? And where were the hymenoptera that normally kept Raub under surveillance?

The ship rumbled ominously. She reached out an arm instinctively to Raub to steady herself through the quake and flinched away as soon as it stopped. His feet were planted wide in a stable stance. He'd been expecting that. "What was that?" she hissed.

"A direct hit," he gritted out in a low voice just as the door next to him slid open. "It's a shooting match now." He leaned forward to peer out the opening, then straightened and cursed under his breath. He slapped at a switch that made the door slide shut again.

"What is it?" she whispered.

"There's only one route between here and the berth where the tern I intend to take is racked," he said, through tight lips.

A tern was a short-range vehicle, meant for going planetside, as he put it, from high orbit. It could go longer distances, if necessary, but would be insanely slow and inefficient for such tasks.

He rubbed his hands over his hairy face and tapped some controls. One of the screens lit up, displaying the hallway just outside. He watched it intently.

Darcy stepped closer so she could see what had him so frustrated. They *were* near the prisoner hold. The long corridor he wanted to traverse came to a T adjacent to where she'd been held for that brief time before...before the accident. It was also contiguous to the washrooms and toilets that the prisoners were cycled through on schedules. At the moment there were a bunch of prisoners milling around in that hallway with no hymenoptera in sight supervising them. Normally there would be dozens. She couldn't stop herself from scanning for Adam's profile among them.

Standing some distance apart from the others, in the middle of the corridor, limbs loose in a relaxed pose, was Selpis. As Darcy watched, Nembrotha glided around Selpis and came to rest behind her. Nembrotha's small body flexed and contorted around Selpis's legs, the stalks on their head stretching out impossibly thin in front of them. Something about the slug's body language told her they were anxious. Darcy heard shouting, but couldn't make out words through the closed door.

Selpis's gaze swept appraisingly down the hallway toward the door that hid Darcy and Raub. Her large eyes seemed worried—or was that just Darcy's imagination?

Beyond Selpis and Nembrotha, at the top of the T, a blur of movement caught Darcy's attention. A large, hairy creature and a hymenoptera tumbled in a tangle of limbs across the intersection at that end of the corridor.

Nembrotha and Selpis inched closer to the closed door that she and Raub stood behind as more individuals piled into the fray and the fighting got wilder.

Raub growled a colorful epithet that Darcy didn't understand. Before she could ask what they were going to do next, a door behind them opened. Raub whirled and crouched into a fighting stance. A hymenoptera stood there clacking in surprise, a shock stick held loosely in one pincer.

His mandibles worked. Then he moved around Raub and tapped the control that opened the door leading to the corridor they'd just been watching.

Darcy gaped at the hymenoptera as he passed and belatedly noticed that he was fuzzy on the top of his head around the simple eyes just above his large compound eyes.

"He just ignored us. Why would he do that?" Darcy asked.

"He's the first to arrive. His primary objective is to subdue the fight and get the prisoners back under control. He just communicated our location to the others who are on the way. *They* won't ignore us. We have to move now." Raub slipped out into the corridor like a coiled cat, ready to pounce.

Darcy stood in the doorway. She was at a loss. The prisoners before her were doing exactly what she'd begged them to do when she'd tried to rally them around her months before. But the threat of explosive decompression as the ship that housed them went to war with some unseen entity had roused in them a desperation that mere words could never provoke. Maybe the number of guards had been reduced because of the threat outside. Maybe they'd tumbled outside their holding pens when the ship began to rock and vibrate. Whatever the reason, they were fighting for their lives inside while some unknown threat hammered the ship from the outside.

What made her life more valuable than any of theirs? She was probably going to get away, just by virtue of being in the company of someone as wily and resourceful as Raub who had made this plan in advance. What was their fate going to be?

Darcy watched as the hymenoptera she was fairly certain was Tesserae71 was overpowered. His shock stick tumbled to the decking and he was brutally pummeled. Her heart wrenched to see him treated so cruelly when he had been the only one to be kind to her. Raub was cutting his way through the mob, which seemed to be growing.

She reached the edge of the crowd, and was starting to worry about losing sight of Raub, when Selpis nimbly darted in front of her into the throng and emerged with Tesserae71's mislaid shock stick. Selpis was in the process of concealing the device in her garment when her eyes met Darcy's.

"Oh!" she said. She looked astonished to see Darcy there.

"She's not dead!" Nembrotha lisped.

"Not yet," Darcy said, and strained to see Raub halfway

through the crowd, slamming people out of his path left and right as he made his way. His gaze met hers briefly. He looked angry to see she wasn't right behind him where he'd expected her to be. She needed to catch up to him quickly.

There were hymenoptera filing into the corridor now from all three directions. She took a step forward, just as a body slid across the floor and slammed into her shins. Her arms shot out, reaching for support before she toppled over.

Selpis grasped her arm and steadied her. "Are you with him?" she asked, nodding her head toward Raub.

"I...yes. I am," Darcy answered.

Translucent membranes slid partway over Selpis's eyes, making her look contemplative. "Then we are with you," she said decisively, and stooped to sweep Nembrotha up in her arms like the hermaphroditic slug was simply a small child, bundled up.

Darcy looked down. A hymenoptera lay at her feet on his back, all six of his limbs curled protectively toward his midline and around his head. She couldn't tell how injured he was. She didn't see any blood, but then she wasn't sure if he had red blood or something else. "Tesserae71?" she said, leaning over to touch his chitinous shoulder joint.

The head turned and one of his forelimbs slid down so he could see who was speaking to him. "Yes?" he clacked, so softly she barely heard it over the roars of anger and the sounds of hand-to-hand fighting.

The deck trembled violently. Someone backed into Tesserae71. He curled up around himself again. Darcy shoved that person away from him before he or she stepped on the injured hymenoptera.

She looked up. Raub had turned and was coming back for her, his eyes burning with displeasure. He clear-cut a path by battering anyone that got in his way. Beyond him, hymenoptera were beginning to corral the edges of the crowd toward them, shock sticks held out defensively. Angry prisoners were waiting to take them on. She saw a few more prisoners slipping into the hall from the holding room, joining the fray as something rattled the deck under their feet, shuttling through a long tunnel on its way to wreak destruction on the ship's external foe.

Darcy held out a hand to Tesserae71. "Let me help you," she said.

His jointed foreleg tentatively stretched out to her. She pulled him upright. He skittered a bit and ultimately steadied himself on only five legs, one of his midlegs held at a bad angle against his thorax.

The crowd surged back into them, giving ground as the hymenoptera pressed from the other side. She would have liked to ask Tesserae71 if there was anything she could do to make him more comfortable, but there wasn't time. More hymenoptera were coming up on their heels. She needed to get into the crowd before she was rendered unconscious by a shock stick from behind.

Darcy tensed and found her center. She glanced over one shoulder at Selpis. Selpis had slung Nembrotha over her back and tucked them into her gown. The two tentacles that protruded from the front of Nembrotha's single foot wrapped around Selpis's slender neck, and their striated stalks peeked around her head. Selpis nodded.

Darcy looked back at Tesserae71, expecting him to have distanced himself from her, to be waiting for his brothers to come to his rescue, to fight his tormentors and bring him aid. But he hadn't. He was close, watching her, waiting, just like Selpis.

"Leebska!" Raub roared over the noise.

She pushed forward, ducking between people wherever possible, blocking blows coming from individuals so frenzied with the need for freedom they were fighting everyone in sight in the mad crush. She shoved some out of the way with side kicks, sending them sprawling into each other like bowling pins.

She quickly realized Selpis was very capable and didn't need help. Selpis sidestepped blows gracefully, parrying and blocking attacks with equanimity, even lashing out with her tail to sweep people out of the way.

Tesserae71 was clearly in a lot of pain, and because he was perceived as the enemy, he was more vulnerable. Darcy wasn't sure why she felt the need to protect him, when he had not done the same for her when she'd begged him to. It was probably foolish, an overcompensation for losing Adam. Or maybe the truth was she just didn't want to be alone with Raub any longer than she had to be. It didn't really matter. She had already committed herself to it.

There wasn't much room to maneuver. The crowd grew tighter as they were pushed back from both sides, as prisoners on each end of the long corridor began to fall to the wicked tips of shock sticks. A few individuals began to panic, scream, and wail, the futility of their situation sinking in. She knew how they felt. She remembered how painful it had been to just cross the threshold of her cell. To go through that and not make it any farther than the corridor just outside that room would be a bitter pill.

Darcy thrust herself between two people, just a few feet from Raub, and glanced back to check on Selpis and Tesserae71. A heavy appendage landed hard on her shoulder, claws or talons raking down her back. The neckline of her jumpsuit came up to choke her. She grunted and whirled, raising a knee tight to her body and jackhammering it into her feathered opponent, who tumbled into several other people violently.

She stood there for a moment, just trying to catch her breath, acutely aware of sweat dripping down the side of her face. Something wet was trickling down her back that she hoped was also sweat, but she knew realistically was probably blood. Everything seemed far away. She blinked and her vision unfocused. Her ears roared with white noise.

Someone smacked her across the face and she came to with a start. It was Raub. His face hovered inches above hers. "Do not go into shock, Leebska," he commanded.

She nodded. It was looking grim. They had nearly waded through all the bodies to the other side of the mob, but that meant that they were closer to the tips of shock sticks as hymenoptera picked their way over the fallen to tap more people into submission. She turned to check on the others behind her.

"Focus!" Raub bellowed. "Don't waste your energy on this pless."

Darcy ignored him and lunged for Tesserae71. A many-armed beast had him in a choke hold and was attempting to twist his head off. Tesserae71 feebly plucked at the arms that held him, his mandibles working soundlessly. Selpis was watching Darcy closely, and when Darcy pulled at the arms stippled with suckers, Selpis moved to assist.

"Leave it!" Raub yelled at her.

"No!" she retorted. "I have an idea. We need him to get out of here!"

"By Glendara, you will be the death of me, chit!" Raub punched someone in the face with the heel of his palm and slid behind the slippery creature to pry it off the hymenoptera. It was hard to get a grip on it. It did not want to let go.

Nembrotha said something to Selpis that Darcy didn't catch, then slid up and over her shoulder and into her outstretched hands. Selpis turned the slug's body so that the ferny fronds on their hindquarters were close to one of the arms of Tesserae71's captor. The fronds quivered and a ring of raised, opalescent dots appeared on one of the arms of the creature. Nembrotha scooted back over Selpis's shoulder, letting out a wet cry, "Get back!"

The creature let Tesserae71 go, piercing the air with a high-pitched shriek of pain. It writhed and whipped its arms around, thwacking anything in its path. Darcy pulled Tesserae71 to his feet and backed away, out of the creature's reach. It had created a new level of chaos—one Darcy hoped they could use as a distraction.

"Come on!" She motioned to the others, working her way to one wall near the edge of the crowd. Tesserae71 stooped but followed her closely. As they moved Darcy asked for the shock stick that Selpis had concealed on her person. Selpis handed it over without comment and Darcy pressed it into one of Tesserae71's pincers. She looked into his faceted compound eyes. She couldn't tell what he was thinking, but she'd just helped him twice, probably saved his life. She asked, "Will you help us?"

His head dipped slightly. "I will do as you wish, my queen."

There wasn't time to exchange any more information. The tentacled creature continued to flail wildly behind them. A circle had cleared in its vicinity. Any minute now someone was going to put an end to the commotion it had created.

"Fall into a heap and pretend to be shocked!" she said to Selpis and Raub. "Tesserae71, stand over us like you just shocked us!"

"I do not lie down and pretend anything," Raub ground out.

"They'll pass by us if they think we're already down. We have nothing that will work against their weapons," she pleaded.

He frowned and studied her for a moment until someone crashed into him. He growled and shoved them away.

She shot him a look that told him he better not suggest she use her power against them. He knew how it had ripped her up before. Fighting was one thing. People could be patched up, could recover from bruises and broken bones. But she didn't want any part of killing anyone. He knew that.

Selpis nodded. "It should work."

"If they see his broken leg, it won't," Raub said angrily.

"I shall keep my body turned away," Tesserae71 clacked.

Darcy motioned to Tesserae71. "We'll go down one at a time. Try to make it look realistic."

"I'll go first," Selpis volunteered, and slumped to the floor, arranging her body artfully so that Nembrotha was protected.

Darcy rushed at Tesserae71 and just before she reached him, she flung herself back and slid down the wall. Through her lashes she could see his mandibles working, and she swore it was almost like applause for her performance. He turned to Raub, tilted his head, and extended the device to within inches of Raub's shoulder. Raub blinked as if to say, "Really?" then crumpled to the floor, his arm flung over his face to hide his expression.

24

DARCY WORRIED that the hymenoptera would notice her as they passed by and would freak out, possibly even poking her to make sure she was unconscious. They all seemed to know who she was, and there was a current of fear and dislike that ran through her every interaction with them. Her hair had conveniently fallen over her face as she fell, and now she peeped through the curls, careful to keep her face slack and her body immobile.

Her back felt jagged and raw. It throbbed in sync with her pounding heart. The ship rocked with the impact of another blast. She slid bonelessly across the floor and watched Tesserae71 skitter around a few steps, tapping a few more individuals with his shock stick while carefully keeping his injured leg out of sight of the other hymenoptera. It worked. The others moved past them without a second glance and then he backed carefully down the hall in the opposite direction, over the fallen stunned bodies littering the floor.

Raub stood as soon as they'd gone by, gesturing impatiently at Darcy. Why did he want her with him when he could have gotten away ten times over on his own already? She was slowing him down.

She rose stiffly. That few seconds of rest had allowed the pain to register more fully. As she came upright, she swayed and her vision narrowed. There was a rushing sound in her ears. She felt someone lean into her, wrapping arms around her to steady her with cool, smooth, pebbled skin. She opened her eyes to see Selpis looking down on her, her large green eyes wide with alarm and Nembrotha's sensory stalks peering over one of Selpis's shoulders. Selpis opened her mouth as though to speak.

Darcy shook her head and brought a finger to her lips. Even though the corridor resounded with screams and warlike cries, she didn't think they should risk making another sound. She lowered her hand and nodded. Selpis loosened her hold on Darcy gradually and then released her when she realized Darcy was steady. Side by side, they headed toward Raub, who stood glowering at them twenty feet down the corridor. As soon as they were in proximity he turned and silently loped ahead, catching up with Tesserae71 and then passing him.

Darcy glanced over her shoulder. The hymenoptera had silenced the many-armed creature and were making significant inroads into quelling the unruly crowd. The number of prisoners fighting was decreasing rapidly.

Raub had reached a point where the corridor changed direction, angling around an obtuse corner. He stopped short and stood there, his hands clenched into fists.

Selpis held back a few paces and flattened herself against the wall. Tesserae71 looked from Darcy to Raub and back again, his mandibles working.

"What is it?" Darcy hissed as quietly as she could.

"A boarding party," Raub growled. "Between us and our berth."

Raub glanced down the corridor. Darcy followed his gaze.

The fighting was all but over and the hymenoptera were beginning to drag the fallen prisoners back into holding cells. It was only a matter of time before their group was noticed.

"Is there any other way around?" Darcy asked.

"Only going back the way we came." Raub gestured behind her, and then his gaze fell on Tesserae71. He pushed away from the wall and approached the hymenoptera. Tesserae71 backed up slightly. Raub swiped the shock stick from the hymenoptera's grasp. "Give me that."

Raub's nostrils flared. He breathed deeply, forcing air in and out quickly until he was chuffing like a locomotive. Darcy straightened. Even in the dim light she could see his blue pallor dissipating as a purple flush swept over his exposed skin, turning it a deeper shade. His expression had gone from menacing to murderous.

His lip curled as he refocused on Darcy. "I expect you to step up now. Our survival depends on it," he said—with no regard for the loudness of his voice.

"I...okay."

He grunted and suddenly broke into a sprint around the corner. Darcy glanced at her three companions. They looked as nonplussed as she felt. Did he expect her to follow him? To fight alongside him? To have his back? She swallowed hard and stepped around the corner. What if Raub was wrong? What if these people were there to liberate them? What if they could help her find Adam or get her home?

The boarding party had left three individuals to guard the passageway that led into the bay where they'd apparently docked or landed. They were wearing grey armor with helmets—she couldn't see faces behind the smoky screens.

Raub barreled down the corridor so fast they were caught off guard. By the time the first one raised a weapon—a gun of some kind—Raub had reached him and used the length of the shock stick to knock the gun out of his hand. He grabbed that guy under his armpits and swiveled, blocking a blast from a second man. He then ran at that man with the first guy still held in his arms, smashing the first one into the second with a deafening crash.

He looked up then and roared, "Leebska!" Fighting hand to hand against the third man, he moved fluidly, anticipating his opponent's moves with grace.

No one was asking questions. No one was trying to discern whether Raub was a member of the crew or a prisoner. Did the boarding party know what this ship was? She could fight them—she had the skills now to do serious damage—but what if they were there to free them from Hain and the Lovek?

"Wait!" she yelled. She jogged toward him. "They might be able to help us! My enemy's enemy is my ally!"

She looked down to step over the crumpled men at her feet and suddenly realized that Raub hadn't just knocked them out—he'd crushed them. There were dark liquids pooling on the decking beneath the armored bodies. The earthy, metallic scent of blood and death reached her nose. He had killed them. She recoiled, backing into Selpis and Tesserae71.

Nembrotha's sensory stalks twisted in the air on either side of Selpis's head. Selpis looked solemn as she leaned forward over the bodies, her eyes darting from the dead men to Raub. He'd just finished off another one of armored men.

Nembrotha lisped, "They won't be allies now. Not when they see this. We're with that lunatic now, whether we like it or not."

Raub swooped, picking up a discarded weapon in each hand, and turned to face them. Purple veins stood out on his neck and cheeks, parting the velvety fuzz. His eyes were dark with anger. He looked like a predator. "Come now, Leebska, or die here." He raised one of the weapons and pointed it at them.

Her heart pounded in her throat. She felt cold and sick. He was a killer.

But she was too, wasn't she? Were they the same?

Boots thundered down the passageway leading to wherever the second ship was docked. And behind her, she heard the clattering steps of approaching hymenoptera.

Selpis's cool fingers wrapped around her arm and pulled her forward over the corpses. Darcy followed, stumbling and slipping in before she got her footing and built some forward momentum.

Raub sidestepped and appeared to be taking aim behind her. A series of brief white flashes reflected off the grimy walls of the corridor but the gun didn't make a sound. She didn't have time to think about why that might be. She heard the crashing sound of chitinous bodies hitting the decking. More death.

Her vision blurred around the edges. She must have lost a lot of blood. She was beginning to feel weak.

Raub gestured impatiently down the hall toward the next door and began to walk backward, training his gun down the corridor. That must lead to the berth he'd spoken of, where the tern he was planning to steal was parked. Selpis pulled her past Raub toward that door with Tesserae71 scuttling right behind them.

She heard shouting coming from the direction of the second ship just as they reached the door. It was locked.

25

SELPIS TURNED DILATED eyes on her. "There must be a code."

If Raub didn't have this code they were going to be in real trouble. Darcy turned to call down the corridor to him, but her voice came out weaker than she intended and she wasn't sure he heard her. He was focused on the figures in grey armor pouring out of the corridor from the other shuttle bay. They were waving around guns, but no one was shooting yet.

Then she noticed that one of those men had a small red dot on his chest—which suddenly burst into flames. There'd been no sound of a weapon firing. What? Had Raub done that?

Tesserae71 pushed her down and reached up for the keypad. She stared at him dully and realized there was a red dot on the back of his head. She lurched for him without thought, pulling him down. As she tumbled backward, a scorched and smoking spot appeared on the wall just below the keypad where Tesserae71's head had been.

Selpis went down with them, hard, into a tangle. Darcy thought she felt something tearing in her back and gritted her teeth as her vision swam in and out of focus. The overwhelming scent of burning plastic filled her nose and lungs, making it hard to breathe.

They floundered for a moment, limbs flailing, as each of them tried to regain their feet. Tesserae71 got his legs under himself first and reached up to the keypad again, tapping on the symbols there. She heard a strange crackling sound and smelled a sickly sweet odor like spoiled meat cooking. The door swooshed open and Tesserae71 collapsed back on top of her.

He was unmoving, dead weight. She shoved at him fruitlessly. He was lighter than he looked, but she didn't have any energy left.

Selpis crawled out from under them through the open doorway and got upright, reaching for Darcy. But before Darcy could grab her outstretched hand, Raub barreled through, pushing Selpis out of the way. He leaned out, aiming his weapon again, then hauled Darcy through by the arm as though she weighed nothing.

Her vision closed in, pain screaming through her back. When she was able to refocus, Raub was stooping and throwing her over his shoulder. She yelped in pain, but he ignored her.

She lifted her head, her vision swimming, trying to stay alert. She gasped when she saw Tesserae71 sprawled prone on the decking just outside the door with a steaming hole in his thorax. "No!" She wriggled and fought Raub's grip. "He might still be alive! We have to give him a chance."

Raub grunted and swatted her rump. "Stay still, Leebska. The bug served its purpose. It's dead." He leaned forward and pressed a symbol to close the door.

She pushed on him and thrashed until he let her down. She mashed on the symbols, trying to trigger the door to reopen, energy surging back into her limbs with her desperation.

"Enough. We're running out of time. Keep this up and I'll

leave you behind." Raub was already striding toward a sleek black vehicle, identical to the one that had been used to abduct her. For all she knew it was the same vehicle. It was the size of a city bus.

"You don't know he's dead!" she yelled at Raub's back.

"Your attachment to stray pets will be your death. It has a broken leg and a ruptured thorax. Its entrails were likely cooked by the laser weapons of the incursion team. When its cadre finds it, they will kill it because it's useless."

"But you don't know—" Darcy spat.

Selpis was at her side. She gently pushed Darcy's hands out of the way and pressed a symbol combination. "I was watching," she murmured.

The door slid open. On the other side, one of the grey-suited individuals knelt over Tesserae71. The figure lifted its head.

Darcy lunged forward without thought and channeled every-thing she had into a powerful scissor kick, sending the figure flying back to crash into the opposite wall. She swept Tesserae71 up into her arms, ignoring the pain searing her back, and spun around, his light, chitinous legs dragging limply behind.

"I've got the door," Selpis said, at her side.

Raub had opened the craft. A ramp was lowering. The second the ramp touched the decking, Raub bounded up it. She was suddenly terrified he'd leave them behind. She was equally afraid of being cooped up with him in such a small vehicle, but what choice was left to her now?

She took off at a run. Selpis kept up with Nembrotha still slung around her neck. They galloped up the ramp as it lifted, scooping them, stumbling, into the vehicle.

Darcy looked around wildly. Raub grunted as he thrust himself into a bucket seat at one end of the craft. The seat had been facing them, but as soon as he was in position it rotated so that his back was to them and he was facing a windshield, surrounded by a console with multiple screens that wrapped around his body one hundred and eighty degrees or more. He began tapping and flicking buttons and switches as though he were an old pro at piloting this vehicle.

There was another, similar, seat next to his, but no others. She and Selpis were standing in the middle of an empty cargo area. "There are only two seats," Darcy murmured, and started to move toward the second bucket seat to secure the hymenoptera.

Selpis moved to the back of the craft, where there were panels on each side draped with cargo netting. She pulled the mesh from the wall. "Put him in here," she said.

"But..." Darcy's instinct was to put him in the safest spot, but Selpis was giving her a quelling look, her large, expressive eyes darting from Raub to Darcy and back again. She was probably right. Raub wouldn't let her put the hymenoptera in the copilot seat if he'd just left him for dead.

"Shouldn't we do something for him?" Darcy lamented, peering at Tesserae71 as she slipped him into the netting and taking in his injuries. He wasn't bleeding. The wound must have been cauterized by the heat of the laser or...maybe he didn't have blood? She felt like she should be administering first aid, but she had no idea what was needed. His anatomy was so different.

Tesserae71's mandibles were slowly opening and closing but he was silent. He raised a foreleg feebly and let it drop.

Raub growled an unintelligible warning.

Selpis was already climbing into the netting on the opposite wall. She pulled Nembrotha off her shoulders and tucked them in beside her.

"Survival first," Nembrotha spluttered, their sensory stalks poking out of the mesh and twirling in the air.

Darcy turned, stumbling as the ship lurched. Her stomach flip-flopped. Through the windshield she could see a large door to the outside of the ship opening, revealing a sea of stars. Her jaw dropped. There were so many, so close together that the sky wasn't black—it glowed a dark silvery grey.

She paused in stunned astonishment for only a moment before dashing for the open seat, grabbing the armrest, and flinging herself down. She grimaced as her back made contact with the seat. The chair pivoted to face front and then lifted up several inches, which was good because otherwise she wouldn't have been able see over the console surrounding her.

Raub side-eyed her then snarled, "You're bleeding on my ship."

She wasn't about to apologize for something that was beyond her control. She huffed as she worked out how to buckle the harness while keeping her hands well away from any button, screen, or switch. There was no way to know what any of them did and she wasn't eager to increase the level of confusion.

"Do not get any blood on the console."

"I wasn't planning on touching it," she snapped. She got the harness together and not a moment too soon. She was crushed back into her seat as the ship leapt into space.

26

DARCY CAUGHT a glimpse of large dark objects against the field of stars and flinched as orange explosions lit them up briefly, illuminating details in small sections. All doubt that she'd actually been on a spaceship this whole time vanished in that instant.

Just as she thought she was getting her bearings, the view outside the ship flipped upside down. Her body jerked against the harness, then was pressed into the seat, then the straps were biting into her shoulders.

Each movement pulled painfully at the wound on her back. She locked her jaw to block the whimpers that her throat wanted to make. Up became down, forward became backward, until she was thoroughly disoriented as they spiraled and twisted in seemingly random patterns.

She considered protesting, then wondered if they'd been hit and were out of control, before it dawned on her that he was flying erratically to evade weapons fire and capture.

Beside her, Raub grunted and his hands moved fluidly over the controls. He was intensely focused. But this wasn't just about fleeing in the chaos of the *Vermachten* being captured and boarded. They weren't running away. No distance grew between them and the other ships. If anything, they were getting closer.

He was clearly strategizing, seeking weakness. She could see it in his gaze. It was the same kind of predatory look he gave her sometimes. In fact, his skin was still cast in that strange purple flush. That thought crystalized. She hadn't misinterpreted that expression.

The sweat on her body went cold.

She caught her first glimpse of the *Vermachten* in the flash of light from an explosion. It was a rounded hexagonal disk and massive. Unlike the other ships, it was black as night. Not a single external light or a lit window to betray its presence.

A huge triangular ship suddenly loomed in front of them, filling the windshield. There was a silent explosion just off-center of the nose of that ship, and then they dived away beneath it. Raub had done that, she was sure. There hadn't been any kind of visible laser line or even a discharging sound of any kind, but she was certain he'd fired on them. The tern must contain a bigger version of those silent weapons she'd seen him discharge in the corridor outside the berth.

"What are you doing?" she cried. "Those ships are huge in comparison to this one! Why are you fighting them?"

"It was clear they'd detected us immediately. The *Vermachten* is caught in a border-patrol net and is disabled. It's not going anywhere. They'll naturally assume that the commanding officer is aboard this ship, attempting to escape, and therefore they'll follow us—that would put us on the defensive. They know the *Vermachten* will still be here when they get back. I will not be quarried like prey. We get away cleanly or die here and now."

Darcy swallowed hard. It was even more dire than she'd thought. "But how can you possibly hope to best them?"

"I will best them because they'll underestimate a ship of this size, assuming it's not adequately armed or piloted by an experienced pilot. Besides, the *Vermachten* has already weakened their defenses. Now quiet your mouth unless you can handle the weapons system."

She blinked. Their very survival was at stake and she had no idea how she could contribute. She looked helplessly at the controls. They meant nothing to her. All she could do was hang on and watch while her life and the lives of her companions hung in the balance, hinging on this insane alien's sense of self-preservation and skill.

Her heart hammered in her throat. She looked over her shoulder to check on Selpis, Nembrotha, and Tesserae71. Selpis was curled in the fetal position around Nembrotha, and Tesserae71 looked unconscious or possibly dead, with his legs poking through the cargo mesh at odd angles.

A loud beeping sounded. Raub's attention refocused and the ship lurched again. When he turned the tern to face the *Vermachten*'s captors, Darcy saw something streaking across the screen, originating from the *Vermachten*. It exploded upon impact against one of the opposition's ships. At least the *Vermachten* didn't seem to be firing on the tern.

Pieces broke off. Fireballs rolled away from it to extinguish in the vacuum. A chain reaction seemed to have started, and the other two ships in the formation were moving away— though, due to their size, they were moving at a lumbering pace. The tern seemed to be a nimble little craft by comparison.

The tern shuddered and an ear-piercing siren sounded. Raub let out a curse, mashing on the console until the siren went silent.

A small screen popped up in front of him. He tapped at symbols until images of one of the two remaining ships appeared. He scrolled through them, then enlarged one image and scribed a line in green over it with his fingertip.

The ship tumbled again. Raub leaned over and slapped at her

console, causing a similar screen to emerge from it. He pointed at it with an open hand.

"Familiarize yourself with this," he snarled. Then the ship spun wildly and she was slung to one side of her harness. The torn muscles in her back shrieked and her vision dimmed for a moment.

"I—"

"A child could do it. We are going to enfilade one ship along that line. I have my hands full here. We were just hit and our maneuverability is compromised by thirty-seven percent. The autotargeting system will do most of it. You'll trigger that system on my mark."

He seemed certain she would do it. This situation was so out of control. She hadn't yet come to terms with the fact that she'd accidentally killed three people—now she was supposed to fire on an entire ship? It was one thing when he did it, but would she? She gulped and looked around wildly.

"Place your hands on the console," he barked.

"We don't know—these could be the good guys! Why are we shooting at them? We should be talking to them—they might give us sanctuary if they know we are escaping prisoners!"

"I've told you it's too late for that. As far as they're concerned we're guilty. They don't care about our circumstances." He spared her an angry look.

She wished she knew if that were true. She wished there were someone else to consult. Was he just a paranoid, delusional psychopath or did he know what he was talking about? Did she have any choice but to trust him? He was a member of this galactic society and she was an outsider.

She grimaced and made her decision. She didn't really have a choice. She wanted to survive. She laid her hands on the console. A bunch of symbols appeared on the screen.

She was starting to decipher them when Raub said, "I'm

authorizing your biometric signature now." The symbols disappeared before she could make any sense of them.

"Now what?" Darcy glanced at Raub. The fine fuzz covering his face and beefy arms had darkened in patches and flattened to his skin, sweat beading on it in places. It made him look more human, though still feral.

"When I say, 'Mark,' you tap this red square and it will start the sequence."

"That's it?"

"That's it."

She was almost getting used to the spinning and plunging. They skirted the wreckage of the ruined ship and came up underneath one of the others. On her screen, the targeting system recognized it as the same ship Raub had marked for his strafing pass. The image wavered then was replaced with a refreshed image in real time from their angle of approach, with the green line still superimposed over the image.

"Get ready..." Raub growled. She glanced at him. He seemed to be fighting the controls.

Darcy braced her hand against the side of the screen so she wouldn't accidentally press the red square too soon, but kept her thumb in range. She felt nauseated. Everything about this was so wrong.

They got impossibly close. Darcy found herself shrinking back into the seat, fearing that impact was inevitable.

"Mark!" Raub yelled.

She tapped her thumb on the screen and the red button disappeared. Time slowed. Or maybe that was the tern.

The viewpoint on the screen changed again to a close view from the underside of the tern. The green line gradually disappeared, to be replaced by a glowing red line scored by the targeting system as they passed by. Fiery orange clouds plumed out of the line from time to time but quickly disappeared.

The fissure they'd created widened, and pieces began to break away in chunks as secondary explosions erupted from the line. When they were almost to the end of their run she started to notice that lights all over the ship were winking out.

She looked up at the windshield in time to see a second missile leave the *Vermachten* and impact the third and final ship. It began to splinter apart in seconds. She panted. Her fingers tingled. She'd never seen so much impersonal death and destruction in her life. How many innocent people had she just killed? She tried not to think about it.

But they'd survived. They'd escaped.

The tern rotated at a more sedate speed and leveled out. The battle was behind them and there was nothing but stars visible through the windshield.

Her brow furrowed. "You aren't going to attack the *Vermachten?*" she asked.

"They're disabled and stuck in a border net. The local authorities will be hunting them if they manage to get away. They won't have time or inclination to follow us."

Could he be right? Would Hain cut her losses and just let them get away? Somehow she doubted it. She remembered the gleam of avarice in Hain's eye when she told Darcy how valuable she was. She wondered if Raub knew that little detail. He'd been present, seen all the stuff about the druids, and knew she was rare. Maybe he didn't think any of that mattered.

"But I would think you'd want to get revenge on Hain and the Lovek for taking you captive," she replied and then clamped her mouth shut. That was a slippery slope. The circumstances she was under were altering her sense of morality. Did she want to fire on the *Vermachten* with all those innocent prisoners inside just to make Hain and the Lovek pay for what they'd done to her? Was she that ruthless? Was she that afraid? What the hell was happening to her?

He was silent for a moment. "Revenge is a petty concept," he said, so low she had to strain to hear him. He eased back in his seat and focused on the controls, ignoring her.

She stared at him. For the first time since she'd met Raub she was sure about something about him. His statement rang false. It was bullshit. He was playing a role, pretending all the zen crap he'd been teaching her was his true philosophy. There were a lot of things she didn't understand about the universe, but one thing she did know for certain was that Raub did not think revenge was beneath him. She knew that like she knew she needed to breathe oxygen.

What else was he lying about?

Who or what had she just allied herself with?

The small screen on her side of the console displayed a view of the ships they'd left behind them. She watched as they became amorphous shapes against a sea of stars, dotted with orange flashes, growing smaller and smaller in the distance.

Her sense of disquiet grew.

27

RAUB WAS ENGROSSED in something on his side of the console, flicking and scrolling and tapping on it. Darcy'd been watching him and wondering what she should do.

Triage. That's what she should be doing.

She reached for the latch on her harness. "Is it safe for me to go check on the others now?"

He grunted. She would take that as a yes.

She unbuckled herself, and her body lifted away from the seat. Panicking, she clutched at the armrests as the chair automatically swiveled to face the back of the ship and then cautiously pushed herself down until the decking was under her feet. It felt strange. She realized her feet were not going to stick when she let go of the armrests and had no idea how to maneuver her body to get where she wanted to go. She felt buoyant, kind of like she was immersed in water, but not quite.

Selpis and Nembrotha were slowly extricating themselves from the cargo netting, which was floating freely from the wall. They seemed a little more competent in this environment than she was. Of course, Selpis had the advantage of a prehensile tail to use in addition to her limbs.

Darcy took a tentative step and drifted away from the floor, arms and legs flailing, until she bumped into the ceiling of the craft. She splayed her hands out to slow herself down and let her elbows bend until she came to rest with head and upper back against the ceiling.

A loud, sloppy sucking sound emanated from below her, followed by a harsh whisper from Selpis: "Quiet!"

Great. The slug was laughing at her.

She'd never given gravity much thought while on the *Vermachten*, but now, in its absence, she realized it was something she'd taken for granted. The slightest push against any surface would send her sailing across the cargo area. She had to concentrate on every movement to maintain a semblance of control and find creative ways to anchor herself. She'd manage. She always did.

She gently pushed on the ceiling and did her best to gracefully float down toward Tesserae71. Selpis was already clinging to the mesh surrounding him and reached out an arm to steady her and pull her in close.

"First time in null g?" Nembrotha slurped, the staccato wet chuckle echoing in their throat as they spoke. Their body was wrapped loosely around Selpis's thin neck like a slimy scarf, their orange-fringed sensory stalks extended and waving in her direction.

Darcy frowned. "Obviously." She grabbed the netting and pulled herself hand over hand closer to Tesserae71. He was very still. Not even a twitch. His shell was dull compared to how it normally looked.

"Not dead yet," Nembrotha said juicily, but with authority.

Darcy darted a look at them. They seemed to have an acute sense of chemical detection. Since she had no idea how to check for signs of life from Tesserae71, she was obliged to believe

Nembrotha knew what they were talking about. "Yet? Is there anything we can do for him?"

Nembrotha gurgled in a way that Darcy interpreted as an exasperated sigh. "Of course there is. The wound is clean. We should pack it with regen gel and seal it to prevent sepsis."

Darcy glanced at Selpis, who blinked back at her blankly. "Nembrotha was a chemist before they were taken. They would know better than I."

Darcy didn't know how a chemist would know about medical care for a hymenoptera, but nevertheless she looked around. There were compartments in the bulkheads lining both sides of the tern. Maybe some of them contained emergency medical supplies. She looked briefly at Raub, who was still intent on looking at screens on the console. She wasn't going to ask his permission because he wouldn't give it. She'd just do what she had to do and deal with the consequences.

She reached for the nearest compartment, feeling all around the door for a trigger mechanism since there wasn't a handle. When she pressed the lower-left corner it sprang open. Behind the door was a mesh barrier. She stared through the mesh, trying to decipher the symbols on the boxes and canisters. The translations came, but not as quickly as reading English would have.

Selpis moved closer. "This is food," she said impatiently. "Let's try another."

They opened every compartment quietly, instinctively knowing that they shouldn't do anything to attract Raub's attention. The compartments mostly contained food, water, and some equipment Darcy didn't recognize, but finally they did find some rudimentary medical supplies.

Under Nembrotha's direction they opened a package of bright-blue gel and squeezed it into the hole in Tesserae71's thorax. The insect didn't move at all. Darcy kept her hand over the wound to keep the gel from floating back out while Selpis fashioned a patch to place over it.

As she worked on Tesserae71, she glanced down for the first time since she'd broken out of her cell to look at the index finger she'd used to break the lock. It was angry red and throbbing. There was black stuff flaking off where her nail had been. It wasn't as bad as she'd thought, actually. The nail would grow back.

Darcy wished she could do more for Tesserae71. He was probably in shock and would have benefited from IV fluids—if she'd had them or known how to administer them—but she didn't. He'd either survive or he wouldn't. Without Nembrotha's help, he probably wouldn't have had a chance.

"Should we try to drip some water in his mouth or something? He might need fluid," Darcy asked quietly.

"No," Nembrotha said firmly. "That would be dangerous. He'll absorb some fluid from the gel. He doesn't require much." The slug seemed to be enjoying playing the expert. She just hoped they were right.

"We should do something for his leg as well," Darcy said. She wasn't sure how this regeneration gel worked, but it said plainly on the wrapper that it worked on all species for a variety of purposes. She squeezed the remainder of the gel pack onto a piece of gauze and wrapped it around the hymenoptera's injured midleg, then took a self-sticking bandage from Selpis and wound it around to hold the cloth in place.

She cast around. "We need something to splint his leg."

"Splint?" Selpis asked.

"To keep it straight and immobile—"

"Nonsense," Nembrotha slurped. "The bandaging material is very strong. Just wrap some more on the leg. If it is possible to heal this injury, that will be sufficient."

Darcy didn't see any other alternative so she did as

prescribed and carefully wrapped the leg with more of the bandaging material. When she was done, she had to concede that the limb was being held firmly, and he wouldn't be putting any weight on it in the absence of gravity anyway. She'd just have to hope that it would work. With five other legs to depend on, he probably wouldn't be significantly handicapped if he survived the burn.

She sighed. Now that the adrenaline was wearing off, exhaustion was setting in.

Selpis gently grabbed her upper arm. "We should tend to your injuries as well, Darcy."

"The anthropoid is healing already," Nembrotha sputtered. "We've no need to waste supplies on her. Some food, one lengthy rest cycle, or some meditation and she'll be hearty as Hirank."

Selpis didn't have eyebrows, but the horny ridges above her eye sockets were mobile and expressive—now they drew together in consternation. "That's not possible."

Darcy allowed Selpis to turn her. She clicked the button on her sleeve to loosen the jumpsuit and let it slide over her shoulder so Selpis could reach the injury. Even as she did, she realized that her back wasn't feeling as raw and painful as it had just a short time before. She held her breath and braced herself against the bulkhead to endure the pain of cleaning the raw wound. She was sure that the creature's claw had not only broken the skin, but torn muscle as well.

Selpis wiped gently with a sponge from the medical kit, murmuring aloud as she did so. "There's a lot of blood..."

Darcy wasn't surprised. The wound was bad. She was sure she'd lost a great deal. She needed stitches—maybe even surgery. Without proper medical care she could be disfigured for life. But there was none of that for her out here. She'd have to hope she could survive without it.

Selpis clucked and began to wipe a little harder.

Darcy flinched at the pressure on her tender skin but knew that Selpis hadn't touched the worst parts yet.

Selpis's voice sounded incredulous. "I wouldn't believe this if I weren't seeing it with my own eyes. I saw this injury just after it was created. It was a deep, jagged gash. But now...the skin is unbroken. It simply looks red and irritated. There may be a permanent scar, but the wound has closed. I've never seen anything heal so fast."

"What?" Darcy asked, reaching up to feel for herself. The muscles in her shoulder and back protested. She was experiencing a lot of pain, but it was nothing at all like the pain she'd felt just an hour before. Her skin was raised, warm and tender to the touch, but it was smooth and unbroken.

"Just as I said it would be," Nembrotha gurgled haughtily.

"The Cunabula gave your species many gifts," Selpis breathed as she continued to wipe the blood from Darcy's back.

"This is why they treated her so differently on the ship. These are unusual traits. She would be valuable on the black market," Nembrotha said.

Darcy turned her head to look at them. Selpis held her at arm's length and something in her expression changed.

"But I—I've never healed like this before," Darcy protested. She thought back to touching the stones. They'd supercharged her body. Then she remembered the video Hain had showed her. It had said she would experience accelerated healing. But at this level?

It was a disturbing reminder that she was not fully human.

She breathed slowly and tried not to let the burst of panic she was feeling show on her face. She glanced back down at her finger. Maybe it had been worse...

"Did Hain experiment on you?" Selpis whispered. "She did perform surgery, you said. Perhaps she did more than implant a chip to allow you to speak Mensententia."

Darcy shook her head. "I don't think so."

In response, Nembrotha's sensory stalks stretched even closer to her and waved around. "You are an unusual specimen for an anthropoid," they said. "But then, so is that one." Nembrotha's head craned back around, and their sensory stalks indicated Raub.

Darcy suddenly felt bone-tired. She didn't like being called a specimen, and she was tempted to snap at Nembrotha, but when it came down to it she was simply too exhausted.

She reached up to try to close the gap on the back of the garment, so no one could see the healing wound anymore. But she couldn't let go of the mesh or she'd drift away, and one-handed she couldn't properly reach.

"Allow me," Selpis said, and gently resealed the clothing.

"Thank you," Darcy mumbled. She clicked the button to save the setting on the jumpsuit.

"We should eat," Nembrotha declared.

Selpis rummaged in the compartments again and doled out a few food cubes and small pouches of water. She handed two sets to Darcy. "Would you?" She indicated Raub at the front of the ship.

Darcy took the food and water, cradling it against her body with one hand, and pushed off for the cockpit. She gave herself a large margin for error and bumped into the wall next to the empty seat. She turned awkwardly, hearing Nembrotha's damp squeaks and chortles over her shoulder.

She managed to maneuver into the seat and hold on while it swiveled to face forward. Raub didn't acknowledge that she'd returned.

She extended the food and water toward him with one hand, drifting out of the seat a little. "Raub?"

He didn't move or speak, just continued to pore over information on his screen.

She spoke louder. "Raub, do you want something to eat or drink?"

He inhaled sharply and turned those cold cobalt eyes on her. The whites of his eyes seemed greenish, as did his skin. She looked at the display for a source of yellow light, but it was mostly white. "Leave it. I've more pressing things to be concerned with." He gestured with an open hand to a storage compartment on the dashboard near the top of his console.

She slipped the food and water into it. "What is it?"

"This craft has a limited range. I must find a planet within reach where we can either refuel or find passage to a larger hub. This sector is not well documented. It is not an easy task."

"Oh." Darcy shrank down into her seat a little. She knew this news should concern her, but she'd just had enough. He seemed to know what he was doing. He could handle it. Her back ached something fierce and her body felt drained. She couldn't process anything else right now.

He turned away. "You should sleep while your body regenerates. It is foolish to remain awake. You're practically catatonic." And with that he was refocused on the screen again.

She slipped her own cubes and pouch into a compartment and snapped the harness into place. She didn't even try to keep her eyes open.

28

DARCY STARTLED AWAKE SEVERAL TIMES, her limbs flailing, with the intense feeling that she was falling due to the lack of gravity. Eventually she found that she could curl up and wedge her upper body sideways in the harness so that she felt more anchored to the seat. That helped and she slept soundly after that.

When she woke, she noted that Raub was no longer in the pilot seat, and she kept hearing a soft thumping sound that she couldn't identify.

She flinched. A spurt of anxiety shot through her. What was Raub doing? She shouldn't have left him alone with her friends. She had to protect them from him.

She unbuckled the harness, triggering the seat to swivel once her weight drifted out of it. As it turned, she heard a soft clucking sound coming from below and to her left. She looked down to find Selpis, Nembrotha, and Tesserae71 crammed into a small hollow just below and to the side of her seat. They were safe.

She set thoughts of Raub aside for the moment. "Tesserae71, how are you feeling?"

Tesserae71 moved slightly and chirped, "Adequate to serve your needs, my queen."

"Your queen?" Nembrotha derided with their usual soggy bluster. "I thought Hain was your queen. Do hymenoptera shift loyalties so easily?"

Movement in the corner of Darcy's eye tugged at her attention, but she kept her focus on the hymenoptera. She wanted to hear his reply.

He opened and shut his mandibles a few times then clacked, "I was dead to Hain and my cadre. Darcy Eberhardt has given me a second life. I will serve her now in whatever capacity she will have me."

Selpis laid a hand lightly on one of the hymenoptera's limbs for a second. "That's lovely, Tesserae71, but I doubt that Darcy will want you to serve in any role other than as her companion."

Darcy was about to chime in when Nembrotha spluttered, "You aren't fit to lift a pincer for yourself, much less anyone else. Save your subservient foolishness for that churl." Nembrotha's sensory stalks swung toward the rear section of the tern.

Darcy followed Nembrotha's gaze, and the reason for the three of them being scrunched up in the front section became clear. Raub was utilizing the entire cargo area of the ship as a gym. He gently bounced off the ceiling, twisting his body through the space until he made contact with the floor and slowly pushed off again, curling into a new configuration. He wasn't bouncing around like popcorn back there; his movements were slow, controlled, graceful even. He was still slightly greenish. She wondered if it was jaundice. His lightly furred body was slick with sweat, making him appear more humanoid. As he spun, droplets flung from the tips of his unruly mane.

"*That*," Nembrotha said, with ire, "is *not* good for the air recycling system."

"He's been at it for hours," Selpis said, blinking rapidly. "He clearly has enviable reserves of energy." Selpis's gaze flicked back to Darcy in an evaluating way that made Darcy feel uncomfortable. "Is he your mate?"

"No!" The very idea made Darcy cringe. "My boyfriend and I were kidnapped at the same time. His name is Adam Benally. Hain sold him. I'm going to find him and buy him back...somehow."

"A hero's quest. How quaint," Nembrotha said with a wet snuffle.

Selpis blinked. "Don't buy him back—just take him and run. Those who traffic in sentients in this way don't deserve any compensation."

"I will assist in any way I can, my queen," Tesserae71 chittered softly.

Darcy almost smiled. "Just call me Darcy."

"As you wish," the hymenoptera said gravely.

"Sickening," Nembrotha gurgled.

Selpis shushed the slug then asked, "Do you know what species Raub is? What planet he's from?"

Darcy shrugged. "No. He never said."

Nembrotha slithered over Selpis's shoulder, down her front, and then up over one of the reptile's knees. Darcy supposed they were able to create suction with their single foot, since they didn't float away. They arched up, close to Darcy's face, their sensory stalks twitching in the air just an inch from her chin. "You did not find that odd?"

"Should I have?"

"It is atypical not to reveal such details upon first meeting," the slug replied.

"Well, I don't know where any of you come from," Darcy said wryly.

"Ah, yes," Selpis said smoothly. "Our first meeting was unusual. And you did indicate that you didn't know anything about the greater galaxy, so it wouldn't have meant much to you, I suppose."

Tesserae71 clacked formally, "My species is from a planet called Giro, but I've never been there, nor has anyone I've ever met. All I've ever known is the *Vermachten* and now this tern."

Nembrotha began to make their way back up to their spot on Selpis's neck. "I am a baryana. My homeworld is Limnuac. And there will be a large reward on offer for anyone who aids me in my return."

Tesserae71 turned slightly toward Selpis. "Is that why you care for them?"

Selpis's eyes lit up with amusement. "Because of a reward? No. Nembrotha prevented my sale to a loathsome slaver. They saved me from an unsavory fate and I owe them a debt because of that."

Darcy pushed herself down closer to them and wedged herself under the copilot's seat. "What happened?"

Selpis looked away, her eyes unfocused. Her tail seemed to curl around her body more tightly. "A merchant was paraded through the holding room, and she selected a group she wanted to inspect more carefully."

"Both Selpis and I were among them," Nembrotha interjected.

"My people are preferred for the most abhorrent positions in the slave trade because...because my world is gone...my people scattered across the galaxy." Selpis took a deep breath and exhaled slowly.

"Gone?" Darcy asked softly. She reached out to touch Selpis's cool hand.

Selpis ducked her head but didn't pull away. "Consumed by the Swarm. Without a central government to appeal to for rescue, we are often stuck in these situations. Someone like Nembrotha might be sold, but if they are able to get word out, then recovery is possible."

"Only if that someone is as important as I am," Nembrotha lisped. "There are many governments that are indifferent to the plight of their citizenry."

Darcy furrowed her brow. She didn't think any governments on Earth were even aware that aliens were visiting their planet, much less going to bat for people when they were abducted in this way. But what if they were? What if someone was looking for her and Adam right now? It seemed unlikely. She was pretty sure she had no one to count on aside from herself. And Adam. He was smart. He might have escaped by now and was trying to find her.

And she was hurtling away from him at unknown speeds.

"We were removed to a private room. The slaver poked and prodded us..." Selpis sighed.

"Humiliating behavior," Nembrotha declared.

Silence stretched out. The only sound was Raub's padding feet and hands against the inside surfaces of the ship as he exercised. Darcy got the feeling that there was a lot being left unsaid because it was too painful to say out loud.

Selpis tilted her head to one side. "A few were selected. I was among them." Her eyes closed. "It would have been a difficult life."

Nembrotha's small blue body rippled. "Hain invited the slaver to inspect my person more closely. Until that moment, I had been present as merely a curiosity. There had been no serious intention to purchase, praise the Cunabula. I secreted a slow-acting central nervous system toxin when she placed her hands upon me. She was dead before the negotiations were complete. No one suspected my part in it, and Selpis was returned to the holding room. Being a largely unknown species has its benefits."

Darcy felt her eyes widen and she looked at Nembrotha with a new level of respect. "Why did you do that?"

"Selpis had been kind to me," they said. "I didn't want that fate for her."

A thin, transparent membrane slid down over Selpis's eyes and her chin lowered, brushing over Nembrotha's back. There was clearly some affection between them.

"You've got quite an arsenal," Darcy mused. She'd definitely underestimated the imperious little slug.

"Size has nothing to do with it," they replied sharply, their slushy speech not diminishing their umbrage. "My people are formidable. More so when challenged en masse, but even singly we are not to be trifled with."

Tesserae71 clacked softly in agreement and seemed to ease away from Nembrotha ever so slightly.

Darcy bit her lip. "People keep mentioning the Swarm like it's something everyone knows about, but..."

Selpis's eyes snapped back open.

Tesserae71 chattered with surprise. "You don't?"

Darcy shook her head. "No. Would you tell me?"

The trio began to talk over each other. She caught bits and pieces of what they were saying.

"—a scourge on the galaxy."

"—and insatiable hunger."

"—simply evil incarnate."

The last comment trailed off and Darcy felt none the wiser. "But what is it?"

"Big bugs," Nembrotha said.

Tesserae71 turned to look at Selpis. "You describe them," he said.

Selpis blinked owlishly. "It is a species of insect—a beetle—that is mammoth in proportion. There are many legends about them, many of which probably aren't true. But what is true is that they devour worlds."

"What?"

Nembrotha craned toward Darcy. "They consume every living thing on land, in air, and living in the sea."

Darcy might have wondered if they were kidding if they hadn't all seemed so serious. "But how?"

"A freakish confluence of evolutionary mutations that first enabled them to grow larger than any other known flying land-based insect species, *then* allowed them to conquer the sea, and *then* to not only survive in the vacuum of space between worlds but to zip around in it. It would be too much to be believed if it were fiction," Nembrotha spat.

"And they're hard to kill," Selpis said.

"Good grief," Darcy mumbled. "And these giant insects destroyed your world?"

"Yes," Selpis replied.

Tesserae71's mandibles worked soundlessly though his head was facing away. She sensed that this talk disturbed him somehow.

Selpis turned to him and patted his thorax. "Insect species in general have a tough time because of the Swarm."

"Why?"

"I think it's natural to want to put taxonomic groups into the same categories—to say that they share traits in common. In some ways these classifications are true. All mammals are warm-blooded. Reptiles like myself are cold-blooded. We can make generalities like this. But to say all primates are aggressive or that all reptiles are subservient is inaccurate."

Darcy nodded vigorously. "Of course. People can be very different depending on a lot of factors."

Selpis went on. "There is a tendency to make other insect species scapegoats for what the Swarm has done."

Tesserae71 clacked in agreement, though his head remained turned away.

That made sense. It put a lot of comments Darcy had over-heard into a new context.

Raub spoke from above and behind her, his baritone voice startling her so much that she lost contact with the bulkhead she was braced against. She bounced up, banging her head against the armrest of the copilot seat, arms and legs scrambling to find purchase and narrowly missing kicking Selpis in the face.

"Your gossip session is over. Time to train."

29

RAUB FINISHED his conditioning session and found a towel to scrub most of the sweat from his body. He was disappointed by how slowly the girl was adapting to null g. All the lessons he'd taught her about proprioception in the dark during her nightly sessions in the hymenoptera quarters seemed to have completely left her. He'd been preparing her to be ready for anything, to mold herself to any circumstance. It was as though he'd taught her nothing.

The mere sound of his voice set off a bout of floundering.

She was still too young, too soft. The flesh wound she'd incurred in the fight to get to the tern had probably been her first serious blooding. Such trifles were common among the children of his people. It wouldn't have slowed him down or stopped him from fighting as a ten-year-old boy. She'd healed fast from the wound and that demonstrated her potential. Now he'd make her live up to it.

There was still much work to do. During the escape, she'd frozen, become ineffectual, like a cornered prey animal. He had to trigger her need to fight and defend—to get on top and stay on top.

These unsuitable companions made her weak. Sitting around and blathering would get her nowhere. She'd have to harden up or all of this would be for naught.

He had many spins to accomplish this goal before they reached their destination, and the tern was stocked with a few methods he could utilize to put his ideas into practice.

Petulance dominated her doughy features. "I haven't eaten anything since I woke up."

"What of it?"

Her confidantes cringed away from him, instinctively making themselves smaller when he came near. He relished the power he held over them. If they had any intelligence at all they'd stay well under his notice. They knew they were only alive because of the girl's whim. He would allow them to remain that way because they might prove useful to manipulate her in the future.

Darcy let out a noisy breath. "I don't want to reopen the wound on my back."

Whining.

Unacceptable.

"It's healed. You just slept for most of two spins like an infant."

He repressed the urge to chuckle at her expression, because it would make her more difficult to motivate.

"Even the worm laughs at how you handle yourself in micro-gravity. Are you going to let that stand?"

"No!" she said defiantly, and her eyeballs rolled around in their sockets. "What am I supposed to do?"

He began by directing her through a series of simple exercises. First, he made her target specific locations within the tern and move toward them at a slow pace with the goal of reaching them without losing control—simple sequences of aim, push, grab, absorb the momentum, maneuver the body toward a new destination, and then repeat.

When she mastered that, he told her to curl into a ball as she moved through the cabin and unfurl fully as she reached her target. He repeated those exercises, the next time requiring that she spin a full rotation en route. Then again, but with a midcabin flip. Subsequently he required that she bounce off two surfaces from front to back of the ship and still reach her target point precisely. He continued to ramp up the complexity until her muscles trembled and sweat flowed freely from her pores. But she didn't complain. She did the work without comment, her teeth clenched in concentration.

It was inconvenient that null g was the least effective place to train. It was difficult to make gains without gravity forcing muscles to adapt. But it would allow him to refocus on the mental aspects of her development. To teach her to be more resourceful and cunning—and adaptable.

When she began to lose accuracy from fatigue, he allowed her to stop. He was satisfied with the ground she'd gained. In only one session she'd learned proficiency in null-g movement.

She rested easily against the tern's ceiling, panting. He threw a towel at her. She caught it without bouncing around violently or grabbing for anything to stabilize her. Yes. She'd gained some ease. Progress.

"Tomorrow we work harder," he told her as he pushed off for the latrine in the rear compartment. "This was just an introduction."

She snorted, but her gaze turned on him sharply. "Why do you care so much about this?"

He narrowed his eyes and turned back to face her. "You are a hilut in a galaxy of drakun. I'm teaching you to survive. Do not question me about it again."

She held his eyes without flinching. Good. That was exactly what he wanted.

30

THERE WASN'T any way to mark time inside the tern. They
ended up following Raub's biorhythm by default, and the days he
set were long. There was punishing exercise for a good portion of
the day. He constantly reminded her that null g would rob her of
muscle tone and bone mass if she didn't work hard to prevent it.
Exercise was followed by what he called mental training and no
downtime. It helped the time pass so she didn't complain.

She still didn't know why he treated her like a protégé. He
said it was his way of preparing her to face the galaxy, but she
knew it was more than that. She watched him more closely than
ever now. There had been some ulterior motive to getting her on
this tern, and she had to figure out what that was.

Sometimes he talked her through very detailed scenarios
and drilled her on how she would react, but more often he put
her in a virtual-reality contraption where she played a hunting
game for hours on end, usually alone against the computer, but
sometimes against him. Then he would critique her performance like he was doing a post-game play-by-play breakdown,
pointing out missed opportunities to thwart the virtual prey, and

times when she wasn't aggressive enough, wary enough, or canny enough. His obsession with the game verged on madness, but it passed many hours that would otherwise have been empty.

She asked once if there were other types of games she could play. He'd barked out a laugh and said, "There is no other game. This is the only one that matters."

The distances between things in space were bigger than she ever could have imagined. Nothing seemed to change outside through the windshield. It was just a never-ending sea of stars. None of them stood out to her. None of them ever seemed to get closer or farther away.

Tesserae71 was healing slowly. She checked his damaged leg and his thorax wound from time to time. It didn't look like his shell was going to close over. Once his insides healed, they'd have to create a permanent patch to cover the wound to keep it from getting infected. He didn't move much, which concerned her. He clearly feared incurring more injuries to his legs, which she agreed was a legitimate concern because they seemed to be brittle. She assumed he was sleeping most of the time, but there was no way to be certain since his eyes were so different and never closed.

The others found ways to occupy themselves, telling each other stories, playing word-association games and logic puzzles. She guessed that they'd been dealing with the issue of boredom since they were taken aboard the *Vermachten* and had already learned how to cope. Selpis and Nembrotha only moved around the cabin when Raub was sleeping, and then only with great stealth. It was strange and painful, but ultimately sensible. At least there would be freedom for them once this journey was complete.

For the most part Raub pretended the others weren't even present. He didn't like her to spend time with them. She didn't know why that was, but was afraid to probe for fear he would stop tolerating them eating and drinking his supplies.

The journey began to feel unending, and she had to remind herself that it wasn't. Eventually a new life would begin. Like many other things in her life, this was something to just get through.

They kept on like this, day after day with little change in routine. Some days she felt angry and trapped. She couldn't help but sulk or lash out at Raub, and then he'd intentionally provoke her into a physical match. On those days she was happy to spar with him, to aggressively work those feelings out until she was spent physically and emotionally and practically blacked out when it was finally time to sleep. It was a small miracle they hadn't broken anything on the little ship, because there were times they got so caught up in these matches that they forgot where they were.

They slammed into the walls of the craft, sometimes hard enough to leave dents in the bulkheads or cause injuries to each other. She was actually causing him some damage now. The lack of gravity leveled the playing field to a degree, making his height and weight less of an issue. They both healed disturbingly quickly, and more than once she wondered if he carried the druid gene and apochondria as well.

Over time, pain came to have less meaning to her. She got used to being battered and kept fighting despite any injuries because she was usually back to normal by the next time they sparred. Raub encouraged that behavior. He certainly never let anything stop him. He was relentless.

These brawls seemed to unnerve her companions, though she reassured them that she was okay. She knew it was messed up. It wasn't normal. But none of this was normal. This had become a new, completely insane, normal.

She held an absorbent pad to her nose to wick away the blood pooling there and crouched down in the little alcove with her friends. Raub had used her momentum to slam her face into the floor shortly before they called it quits for the day. She felt pleasantly drained as the adrenaline wore off, and ignored the throbbing in the center of her face as she checked on how her friends were doing.

Selpis stared at her solemnly, then leaned forward with one hand, wordlessly pulling on Darcy's nose until she was assured it was straight. Selpis often helped her clean up or reset her injuries after these battles.

Selpis's brow ridges drew together in what Darcy had come to realize was her version of a frown. "I don't know what passes for a standard of beauty on your world, but perhaps a crushed nose isn't aesthetically pleasing?"

"Not really."

"Why do you do this?"

Darcy looked away. She didn't know, to be honest. She shrugged. "I might have to fight to get Adam back. It makes sense to learn."

"He must be very important to you. You have changed a great deal since they first put you in that cell and you tried to start an insurrection."

"He is."

Selpis stared at her hard, but didn't say anything.

"It's my fault he was taken," Darcy said very quietly. She was surprised she'd said it aloud. And once she did, a dam seemed to break. Tears flooded her eyes, but because of microgravity, they didn't go anywhere. Her throat ached. "Hain was looking for someone like me. Adam just happened to be with me." She wrapped her arms around herself, hugging herself tight, and tipped her head forward, turning away to hide her face from Selpis's knowing look.

"That is circumstance. Not fault," Selpis said. She wrapped

an arm around Darcy and pulled her closer. It was the first tender contact she'd had with another person since she'd been taken from Earth. She found herself clinging to the reptilian woman. Selpis's skin was pebbled and cool, but it didn't make the hug any less warm. She didn't want to let go. It was so reassuring. It felt so safe.

"Adam is funny and sweet. I could be hard to live with. It wasn't always easy. But he just...he was always positive, always good. He's been there for me, you know? Now I need to be there for him."

Nembrotha slipped down from Selpis's shoulders to glide over Selpis and Darcy's twined arms. It felt strange. The muscles rippling in the slug's single foot tickled as they created suction while traveling over her skin. Nembrotha turned their face up to her, sensory stalks waving. "Is this the kind of life he would want for you?"

"I'm sure he wants me to survive," she replied.

"Survive, yes," Nembrotha lisped. "But would he want you to become a vigilante? Or a sidekick for this beast? It could take a lifetime to track him down. It will be a difficult life."

That was too much reality for Darcy. She squeezed her eyes shut. The tears balled up in the inner corners of her eyes. She couldn't answer.

"Is he capable? Resourceful?" Selpis asked.

"Yes..."

"If he has the same gifts you have, then he is surely just as formidable. No doubt he is also free by now and looking for you," Selpis said.

"But he doesn't. We aren't the same. I'm different."

"A different species?" Nembrotha asked.

"No—yes—I'm not sure." She paused and swallowed. This was awkward. She couldn't tell them she had the druid gene or the apochondria. If they knew what that was, they might not treat her the same way. The video Hain had showed her warned people to be afraid of druid hybrids. She suspected they were commonly represented as unstable and dangerous.

Selpis tilted her head to the side, but then went on. "There were rumors among the other captives that the humans were causing a lot of trouble. They had to be kept separate from each other because they were difficult to keep contained. I heard they were fierce fighters. We assumed they were talking about you, at first, but then we realized there were others."

"That had to be the reason Hain sold all the humans so quickly," Nembrotha mused. They scooted farther up Darcy's arm, lifted one of the two stubby tentacles on the front of their foot, and patted it against the corner of each of Darcy's eyes, absorbing the tears that had collected there. It was an oddly touching gesture. "Your devotion speaks well of you. Or it is supremely foolish. I haven't decided."

Tesserae71 roused and clacked softly, "She saved the three of us, why should we doubt she could find and save her Adam?"

"We shouldn't," Selpis said. "I've no doubt she can."

Nembrotha crawled up over Darcy's shoulder until their mouth was close to her opposite ear. Their wet whisper was barely audible. "What does that one think of this plan?" Their sensory stalks waved toward Raub, who was engaged in cooldown exercises. He would expect her to be back up and into the VR gear soon.

"I haven't talked to him about it," Darcy replied.

"Don't," the baryana said softly, for her ear only.

She turned her head slightly toward Nembrotha, searching their alien expression.

"That one helps no one unless it is to his advantage. Never trust him. Never. He is not what he seems." Nembrotha glided from her shoulders back to Selpis. "He's ready for you."

She looked up at Raub, but he was still holding fast to a bar protruding from the ceiling, doing ab crunches. She opened her mouth to ask Nembrotha to explain.

"Leebska!" Raub bellowed suddenly, and shoved away from the bar.

She pushed herself up and turned to face her friends. Nembrotha was already curled around Selpis's shoulders again, their sensory stalks drooping like they were dozing.

31

DARCY WOKE to find Raub sitting up and focused on the ship's controls. He normally slept in the pilot seat and she'd seen him check their position from time to time, maybe even make course corrections, but she hadn't seen him concentrating like this since the day they stole the tern.

Over the course of the journey, she had occasionally asked him how much longer it would be or questioned him about their destination, but he usually just grunted in response. He wasn't really much of a talker unless he was imparting some kind of strategic fighting wisdom when they were sparring or if he felt the need to correct her form when they were working out.

She righted herself in the copilot seat, rubbing her face, and leaned over to glance down over the side to see her three companions still unmoving. She inhaled deeply, her eyes wandering, and settled her gaze on the windshield to groggily look out at the stars. She gasped and sat up straighter. Her heart started to pound. Instantly she was awake.

There was finally something new to see outside. It was small, clearly still very far away, but— "Is that a planet?" she cried.

Raub didn't answer but reached out to touch the largest screen embedded in his console. He brought up the small ball she was staring at and magnified it until it filled the screen.

She unlatched and pushed herself between the two consoles, brushing against Raub in her eagerness to ogle the image.

It was a planet. It was green and blue and had white clouds. It looked so much like Earth tears sprang to her eyes.

It wasn't Earth. She knew that immediately. The configuration of the continents was all wrong. But it was a planet and it was going to be the place where she started her new life. She didn't know what to expect once they got there, but she'd have to find a way to make money so she could retrace the *Vermachten's* steps and track down Adam's buyer.

"What's it called?"

The others were stirring. She sensed them moving behind her, keeping their distance, but likely hoping for a glimpse of their destination.

"Ulream," Raub said flatly.

"Never heard of it," she heard Nembrotha mutter.

Raub ignored the baryana.

That fact didn't really surprise her. Raub had said they were in a remote part of the galaxy, where inhabited planets were sparsely distributed and not well documented.

"Tell us about it," Darcy said.

"Its atmosphere has a high oxygen content. It's a mining colony. We should be able to book passage on an ore-transport ship with jump capabilities."

"What kind of people live there?" she asked.

"A small population of belastoise. There is no sentient indigenous life."

Nembrotha made a soggy snorting sound and Selpis hushed them.

Darcy frowned and glanced back at her friends. She'd

expected them to be happy, but Selpis looked stricken and she couldn't be sure but it seemed like Nembrotha was sneering with disgust. Their sensory stalks hung limp and their expressive mouth was drawn up like a purse. Tesserae drifted in place, his mandibles working. The trio returned to their corner of the tern.

Something was wrong.

"What are belastoise like?" she asked Raub.

"You'll find out soon enough." His tone was dismissive. He wasn't interested in talking about it.

"How much longer?"

She waited a few minutes, but he didn't reply. She bit back an angry comment and pushed herself into the rear of the cabin, simmering silently, barely resisting the temptation to slam things. She wanted to demand details from him, but it wouldn't make any difference. It would only piss him off, and he'd just be more reticent.

The planet was visible. She'd be able to watch it get closer over time, and it wasn't like they were going to be there in ten minutes. If she was patient he might be more forthcoming. She hoped.

She pulled out some food to break the fast and went to share it with her companions. They took it from her without comment. There was no conversation. None of them seemed to be making eye contact with her. She didn't understand why.

Why wasn't anyone excited about finally getting somewhere? They couldn't stay inside this tiny ship forever. What was going on?

The answer came that night.

She'd been asleep for hours when she started awake with Nembrotha hissing in her ear. It took her a moment to collect herself and realize what was going on. She opened her mouth to ask what they were doing, but they shushed her and told her to go to the lavatory.

It was so odd that she did what she was told. The ship was dark and silent except for the sounds of Raub's deep breathing and the occasional rustle from Tesserae71's restless movements. There was a dim safety light in the back. She unlatched herself from the seat as quietly as she could and pushed off for the back of the ship with Nembrotha clinging to her chest.

Once inside the latrine, she hovered there dumbly for a moment, blinking. "Do you have to go?" she whispered. Selpis handled all of their bathroom breaks. She didn't know what to do for them.

"Turn on the vacuum," they replied, their voice barely audible.

She did. The machine that removed bodily waste whirred softly, creating some white noise.

Nembrotha curled around her neck, their mouth brushing up against her ear, and began to speak. "The belastoise are xenophobes. They don't mix with outsiders because they consider them unclean. They will not so much as speak with any of us."

"But—"

"No. Do not delude yourself. There will be no belastoise jumpship. Once we get there, we will be marooned."

Her mouth hung open. "Why?"

"Why would he choose such a planet? I don't presume to know. But be on your guard. All of this could be an elaborate ruse to sell you to an eccentric buyer."

Her head was spinning. "No, it's probably just the only planet that was in range."

"Possibly. He has created that illusion for you, anyway. He creates many illusions. All of them for you."

She stared at the dull finish on the metal-clad walls of the tiny cubicle, not actually seeing it, her thoughts churning.

"Be wary of what he is turning you into, Darcy." Nembrotha's tone dripped with weight. She was pretty sure that was the first time they'd ever used her actual name when addressing her. She thought of all the times they'd made ridiculous pronouncements that turned out to be true.

"How do you know all of this?"

"I was trained in detecting the biochemical markers of deception across a wide variety of species." Nembrotha waggled their sensory stalks at her. "I was Prime Chemist for the Yamaah Imperial Ambassadorial Synod. It was my job to know things. Now turn off the vacuum, fumble around convincingly for a moment and go back to the cockpit."

She tapped the button to turn off the waste vacuum, woodenly banged around for a minute like someone would if they were sleepily using the facilities, then made her way back to the copilot seat. Nembrotha slipped away without another sound, presumably to rejoin Selpis in the small alcove below.

Raub hadn't stirred. He was still breathing with the same deep cadence. She should have asked Nembrotha more questions. Prime Chemist...biochemical markers of deception...a lot of their statements made more sense now. They were practically a walking, talking mass spectrometer if they could detect the chemicals people made that way. She wondered what they knew about her that they weren't saying.

But then her mind turned to the other things they'd said, the point of the furtive conversation: *What was Raub turning her into?*

She felt cold and hollow inside. As a medical student she'd pledged her life to ease the suffering of others. Since arriving on the *Vermachten*, she'd killed three people...at least. There were also the ships he'd ordered her to fire on when they were escaping. She'd done it. She'd been desperate enough to survive that she'd executed his commands.

It did not sit well with her.

There were too many unanswered questions. Too much she didn't know.

She didn't want this to be her life. The truth was she didn't like the person she was becoming. Something had to change. But all of her options were bad. There didn't seem to be any good choices when you were faced with being a prisoner or fighting your way to freedom.

She didn't sleep any more that night.

32

THEY WERE STILL about a day out of Ulream and Raub wanted to pass the time in the VR game. Darcy floated untethered in the rear compartment and shoved the virtual-reality gear over her head. It was a huge monstrosity, and under Earth's gravity it would probably weigh thirty to forty pounds. It took a few minutes to adjust to her brainwaves. She'd already put on the thin, haptic, formfitting suit over her clothes.

Before her vision switched over to play mode, she watched Raub insert a comparatively small corded contraption into a port on his neck. It wasn't even visible within his dense hair most of the time. Apparently he played these kinds of games often enough that he'd had an elegantly small version of the gear implanted surgically. All he had to do to play was plug in.

And they were there. Every time she played it was a different kind of landscape. Sometimes desert, other times mountains, occasionally a swamp, or even strange cityscapes filled with different species of people. It was interesting because it gave her a glimpse into what other planets might look like, and it was reassuring to know that a lot of them resembled Earth, even if only in some passing way.

This place was foggy and dark. Everything was in shades of grey, like during twilight, nothing colorful at all. She shivered. The haptic suit was chilling her. It was cold here. She gave herself a minute to really absorb the environment. There were crunchy low plants underneath her feet, and as she walked, she stepped into a slushy puddle. Instantly her foot tingled and began to feel numb. Mist flowed over her skin, wetting her hair and her clothes, which seemed inadequate protection. She wondered if this was a moor like in Scotland, or possibly something a bit more northern, like tundra.

"I think I need a coat," she said aloud.

"Nonsense."

"Yeah, I don't have fur," she said wryly.

She turned and he was right behind her. He cuffed her. Her head whipped back. "Do not insult me if you know what's good for you."

"Good grief! I didn't know that was an insult." She rubbed her jaw and swallowed resentment. She'd get some licks in before this was over. "Touchy. Why is it so dark? We usually play during the day."

"This is day. See? There is the sun." He pointed at the sky, where there was a fuzzy pinprick of yellow light that she had already dismissed as a small moon.

"Yikes. That's the sun? It's so small." She didn't even have to shield her eyes to look in its direction. It reminded her of pictures she'd seen taken by the Curiosity Rover on Mars.

"This is a reproduction of my homeworld."

"Oh." She jogged in place, already forgetting that she was weightless inside the tern. It felt so real that it practically was. "I'm cold. Can we get started?"

He grinned a feral grin with menace lurking behind his eyes.

She could tell he was going to be brutal this time. "That's the kind of talk I like to hear. The cold is good for you. It makes you remember you're alive."

She rubbed her hands together and blew on them. "I haven't forgotten. Who's what?"

"You are the gildrut. I am the kappyr."

She rolled her eyes. He preferred to play this way, which wasn't really a surprise. He was practically the living embodiment of a predator. "Fine. Give me a good head start. There isn't anywhere to go. It's all open."

He bowed at the waist, his arms falling forward with a flourish. She jounced a cursory bow in return and took off running. She looked back once before he was obscured by the mist. He'd remained in that position with his face turned away.

She zigzagged frequently over the uneven terrain, trying to throw him off her scent. She couldn't see far, so she ended up crashing through some marshy ground, each footfall breaking a thin crust of ice into a spongy layer below. Soon her feet were so cold she could barely feel them, and there were sharp stinging sensations on her lower calves making her think there might be small cuts there. She didn't stop to find out. She hadn't completely forgotten it was a simulation.

She came to a sudden halt when she glimpsed a large rock in her peripheral vision. She edged over to it, trying to calm her breathing—she was noisily blowing clouds of steam into the air. She needed to pace herself and try to find a place to hunker down and rest until he found her.

It wasn't just a rock. It was a strangely shaped boulder, jutting up into the fog. A cold breeze kicked up, blowing some of the mist away, and she noticed there was another one nearby. She walked over to it. Then she saw another, and another. She walked past each one until she was back at the first. There were six irregularly shaped stones, standing on end, arranged in a ring.

She shivered violently. What would happen if she stepped inside the circle?

She thought she heard a faint footfall and froze, then put her back against the stone, breathing as shallowly as possible.

Another sound. Definitely a footfall. Damn. He'd caught up with her so quickly. She shouldn't have lollygagged around the stupid rocks for so long.

He was coming. He was damn quiet, but she had learned to listen for him. She held her breath and eased down into a fighting crouch.

Crap. Her feet were so cold.

She wished she could use her camouflage ability, but it didn't register with the simulation gear and therefore was useless. She'd tried it before and she just ended up turning the dull grey and white of the inside of the tern.

She heard him sniffing the air. He was inside the circle. Her scent would be all around it, but he'd be able to home in on her soon.

She was ready.

He burst around the corner with his two fists clasped together, hurling his body around to provide thrust. She ducked the blow intended to smash her head into the stone and kicked, pushing him back. He lost his balance and she followed, kicking again, squarely on his chest, to knock him down.

He rolled to his feet in a fluid, practiced movement and came at her again. They began to spar. He threw punches. She blocked them and tried to dart in for a jab or a kick, but it was a losing battle. He was fighting dirty, not holding back at all. She'd never seen him so ferocious, so out of control.

It was hard to land good kicks when your feet were numb from cold. It wasn't a fair fight. He was more suited to this environment.

Soon she was taking a beating, barely keeping him off her.

He was snarling with glee, the skin under his downy hair flushed purple.

"Okay. I'm done. Enough," she said, spitting blood onto the colorless ground as she swayed with fatigue.

But he didn't stop.

He pummeled her some more. She halfheartedly fought back. She was ready for it to be over.

"Fight, damn you!" he roared in her face.

"No! I'm done!" she yelled back.

He threw her onto the ground and began to pace, muttering to himself.

Something was really weird about this session. It had never been like this before.

"I'm out," she called to him. It was lucky this was just a simulation. If this fight had been real she probably would have lost teeth.

She reached for the button on the headgear.

"No!" he bellowed.

But she was already disengaging. The dark, dismal planet faded away. She lifted the helmet from her head and was dizzy for a few seconds as her eyes readjusted to the lighting in the tern. She started peeling off the haptic suit. No bruises or cuts. Nothing bleeding. She always had to see it to believe it after a rough session. She was already starting to warm.

She looked up in time to see Raub jerk the cord out of the port in his neck. He was actually purple in the real world too.

He pushed off toward her.

It took everything she had to meet his eyes and not cringe away.

"Don't," he said quietly, although spittle flew into her face with the enunciation of it. "Ever. Do that. Again."

She kept her mouth shut, though she desperately wanted to sass him. He was not in a good frame of mind. It could get bad if she antagonized him further. She didn't want to know how bad it could get.

He stared at her, his whole body trembling.

She stared back.

Finally he punched the bulkhead next to her head, leaving a deep dent, then turned away and pushed off to buckle himself into the pilot's seat.

He didn't sleep that night. He stayed up, poring over something on his console, the purple cast in his skin fading, replaced with a sallow yellow-green undertone.

She didn't sleep that night either. She hunkered down next to Selpis and watched and waited.

No fight with him was a fair fight. Ever. And all he wanted from her was a fight. Things had been slowly ratcheting up to this confrontation, until all pretense of teacher and master had disappeared.

He'd never turned that shade of purple during a session before. The only time he'd done that was when they were struggling to get off the *Vermachten*—when he was up against people he considered his enemy. She shivered.

He had wanted something from that scenario that she had thwarted.

She was afraid to wonder what that was.

Nembrotha was right. There was something going on that involved her. Maybe he did have a buyer lined up for her. Or maybe it was something else. Whatever it was, it wasn't good.

As soon as they landed on Ulream, she needed to get away from him. She had a terrible feeling that like a bad penny, or a bad boyfriend, he would keep turning up. She chewed on her lip. She might have to fight him or hide from him or something.

Except she couldn't best him hand to hand. That would never work.

She'd have to be wilier than that. He knew what he'd taught

her, how she fought, the way she thought. No, there was no chance of escaping him that way.

If it came down to it, she'd have to dig deep into all the things she was. She'd use her humanity against him—her medical knowledge, her life experience. If necessary, she'd use her druid side against him too—she'd stun him or shock him into cardiac arrest.

Nembrotha waved their sensory stalks at her sleepily. She felt a surge of protectiveness of her friends. All of them. She'd accepted that personhood was not the same as having an anthropomorphic body. She was something other than human, and she had to stop thinking about that as a bad or scary thing. She couldn't go on as a house divided. She had to be something more like an alloy, two metals, that when combined, made the finished product stronger.

Once again she went through the list of things that Elorpha had cataloged in that Sectilius Science Moment about the druids. Which of those abilities would work against him in a meaningful way?

She got up and slipped into the lavatory. Once inside she worked a loose and broken bolt out of an inconspicuous corner and held it in her hand. She called up her light and concentrated. After many frustrated attempts to move it, she banked her light next to her heart and stared at the bolt. She wasn't sure if it was ferromagnetic.

But maybe manipulating magnetism didn't require the light. She didn't know how that ability worked.

She thought about her body's energy like it was water and visualized that part of herself pouring into and around the bolt to lift it. After some time, it rose from her hand. She toyed with it, lifting it, twirling it, and moving it around before her eyes carefully. She was careful not to drop it and make noise.

She resorbed the field, caught the bolt, and created a tiny

pocket inside her jumpsuit to secrete it away. She wished she had more time and space to practice with it, but she couldn't risk being discovered. She'd come back later to try other things. It would be prudent to do as much as she could before they got to Ulream.

She focused on the metal latch on the door of the latrine, pushing a field around it, then sliding it ever so slowly to the right. The door swung open.

She was beginning to see what she could do.

She'd think outside of the box he thought he had her in.

33

DARCY WANTED to close her eyes, but she couldn't. She clutched the armrests of the copilot's seat, watching as the ground came up to meet them at an insane rate.

She'd watched the planet grow larger day by day, anticipation rising steadily, until they were finally close enough to punch through the atmosphere. Ulream was the third planet in a binary system. When they got near enough, she could see the second star except during eclipses. It was essentially one big star with a second, smaller star, orbiting it.

When they transitioned from space to atmosphere and passed through the clouds, it felt exciting, a lot like traveling in an airplane. But at that point Raub became inseparable from the pilot console and his mood was worse than surly. It only degenerated the closer they got.

Apparently the tern had been damaged in the fight to leave the *Vermachten*, and that made it hard to steer during landing. The tern swayed like a swing as Raub fought with the controls. They surged above the treetops, tilted to one side, then swung back down to skim the canopy, the tips of branches scraping noisily over the bottom of the tern. Raub cursed violently in a language the dummy chip couldn't translate as he pulled the craft up again, but only to one side. She had no idea what might be technically wrong, but it seemed bad to her.

When they started crashing through treetops, she wondered whether they'd have been better off on the *Vermachten*.

"Isn't there somewhere safer we can land, like a desert or a meadow or something?" she yelled as her body canted again on her left side and the tern veered in a crazy arc, foliage brushing the side of the craft from time to time.. She'd seen some wide swathes of blackened areas as they'd descended, probably from recent forest fires. That would be preferable to this.

He didn't spare her a glance as he grappled with the controls.

She pushed up to glance back into the cargo area. Her friends were snugged into the cargo nets again. She hoped they'd be safe there.

They dipped lower. Raub seemed to have given up on gaining altitude to get back above the treetops. The screen of his console showed a red line that cut a jagged path through the terrain below.

Branches buffeted the craft, drowning out all other sound.

And then they were lurching and dodging around trunks. Too fast. Limbs and small trees broke off as they crashed through them. Winged creatures took flight in a blur. The ship was going so fast she could barely process what she was seeing. She pressed herself back in her seat.

Narrow miss after narrow miss. She found herself moving her body from one side to the other as if that would help the tern avoid the trees, and the whole time her right foot stomped on an imaginary brake pedal on the floor under the console.

Then they were just feet above the ground. They struck a sapling but it didn't slow them down. Raub continued his brutish litany in another language.

Contact. They spun. They hit green and brown things, hard. Clods of dirt and shrubs with intact roots flew up over the windshield. She slammed forward and jerked to one side painfully. But they stopped.

Raub leapt up immediately and crossed into the cargo area. He was opening compartments, rummaging around, slamming things.

Darcy took a little longer to regain her senses. She called to the back as she reached for the latch on her harness and eased forward. "Everyone okay back there?"

No one answered.

The seat swiveled. Gravity pulled on her hard. The strength of it surprised her. She felt disoriented and lightheaded.

Raub was stuffing supplies into a knapsack. Selpis looked to be sprawled unconscious in the cargo netting with Nembrotha's sensory stalks peeping up from underneath her. Tesserae71 was curled up with his legs tucked close to his body, his mandibles working silently, one pincer clinging to the net.

She got to her feet and swayed. "Anyone hurt?" she asked. Her heart pounded in a slow dull thud and there was a loud rushing in her ears. She took a ponderous step toward Selpis. Raub brushed by her, ignoring her, and nearly knocked her off her feet.

She staggered, caught herself, then continued forward, gaining more stability as she went. She tried to kneel next to Selpis, but she ended up falling to her knees with bruising force.

"Hey." She reached through the mesh, assessing Selpis's vitals. She slipped her hands over the reptile's cool skin, seeking her pulse. It took longer than it would with a human, but she found it and it seemed strong and steady. Selpis was breathing evenly. Darcy looked for injuries, but found none. Selpis didn't seem to be bleeding anywhere and Darcy couldn't find any obviously broken bones.

Nembrotha slid silently up onto Selpis's abdomen. "Just knocked out. She's in good condition. Don't forget what I told you," they said quietly.

"What?"

"It's time to begin," Raub thundered behind her.

Selpis's hand twitched. Darcy leaned forward to look into her face more carefully. Her eyelids fluttered.

Raub wrenched Darcy's arm brutally as he hauled her to her feet and turned her to face him. "Ow! What gives?" she cried out.

"It would be wise not to ignore me. I said it is time to begin."

She raised her eyes to his and blanched. Raub leaned over her, his gaze hard and unblinking, his jaw set, nostrils flaring. His face was a mask of menace. She hadn't seen him like this since their last VR game. He thrust the knapsack he'd just been packing at her.

She stared at him dumbly, a cold lump of fear churned in her stomach.

"Take it," he demanded.

"What's going on?" she asked, keeping her arms at her sides.

He dropped the pack. It landed at her feet with a thud, narrowly missing her bare toes. He pressed a control, causing a door to open in the side of the tern. "Get out."

"What?"

He grabbed her and shoved her toward the opening, then scooped up the pack and threw it at her. She caught it and held it against her stomach. In her peripheral vision she could see Selpis sitting up. She wanted to go to her and make sure she was okay. She needed to check on Tesserae71, who still wasn't moving.

"I'm not telling you again." Raub pulled out one of the weapons he'd used against the boarding party on the *Vermachten* and pointed it at Selpis and Nembrotha.

Darcy backed up a couple of steps. She was reeling. Had he gone insane? "Why are you doing this?"

"I'll give you a three-spin start," he said calmly. "Then the ritual will begin. You would do well to make the most of that time." He advanced on her slowly, with the gun still trained on Selpis.

She backed up until she stood in the doorway. "What are you talking about? What ritual?"

"The ancient ritual of the gildrut. The hunt."

The hunt.

He went on, "Our peoples have been locked in this contest for centuries. I thought perhaps I would not get the chance to complete this ancestral call. But then Hain found you. You are drudii. I am lovek. It will not end until one or both of us is dead."

The memory of the video Hain had played for her aboard the *Vermachten* surfaced. She'd thought about it often, puzzled over the meaning of so much of what had been stated. The host had said, "...hunted to virtual extinction by the predatory race, *Lovek-itus quamut.*"

Lovek...

The Lovek.

And when she'd first been moved to the prisoner hold Tesser-ae71 had told her, "The Lovek is rarely seen. He keeps to himself, does all his dealings through Hain. He is like you. An anthropoid species."

Raub was the Lovek.

He intended to hunt her.

34

DARCY STUMBLED DOWN THE GANGWAY. Raucous forest sounds and a wave of heat and humidity assaulted her, but she barely noticed them.

Raub was the Lovek.

He grunted and made another threatening gesture toward Selpis.

Darcy backed down one more step, landing abruptly with her bare feet on damp soil.

Raub's lips twisted in a brutal smile. He closed the door on the tern and the gangway retracted.

She stood there staring at the silent ship, still clutching the pack. Now her friends were locked inside the cabin with a madman. What was she supposed to do? Her first instinct was to defy him. To refuse to play this game. To find a way to fight him here and rescue her friends. But he had a weapon. A weapon she'd watched him kill people with. And he'd just been pointing it at Selpis and Nembrotha. He might kill them if she didn't do what he said.

She should have known this was what he was going to do. He

was completely obsessed with that hunting game. She should have seen this coming.

Damn it. She'd let herself be manipulated into this situation.

Could he really have abducted her just to create a scenario in which he could turn her loose and hunt her? Could that actually be happening? Had all the rest been nothing more than machinations—a script he and his crew had followed to prepare her for this tableau?

Had the whole thing been carefully orchestrated? The months of intensive training, the narrow escapes from the guards and the boarding party, the harrowing space battle? Was she just a pawn to this guy? To fulfill some kind of fantasy?

What the hell? This was her *life.*

Who else was in on this? Hain, surely. Was Tesserae71 a party to it too? To help make sure she was conveniently in the right place at the right time? Was Selpis? Nembrotha? Had they been placed in the corridor at that moment to serve as sympathetic plants she would grow attached to so he could threaten them in order to get her to do what he wanted?

Was it even possible that all of that could have been mapped out ahead of time? She didn't like the uncertainty she felt when she thought about that. The relationships she'd formed with the three of them had seemed real. But she couldn't know for sure.

Suddenly she felt very heavy. She crumpled to the ground where she'd been standing. The pack fell from nerveless fingers.

Was there any alternative to running for her life? What else could she do?

He was going to kill her.

He'd trained her, telling himself that made it a fair fight. It didn't. She knew that. She couldn't beat him. There was no way.

She didn't want to die fighting him on some alien planet. All she wanted was to find Adam, get home, and forget that any of this had ever happened.

Tears welled up in her eyes. She looked down at her hands. Though her vision was blurred, she could see that her fingers were shaking. She felt so empty inside. So hopeless.

There wasn't any way out.

She felt so small. She was just one person, alone in this terrifying and huge galaxy that she knew nothing about. There was no one to save her from him or even to help her fight him.

She thought about the people she'd left behind on Earth. She'd never see them again. Her mother, such a flake, but basically harmless. She'd never feel another one of her kisses on the forehead, be given another one of her blessings. Her father, who had worked three jobs to help her defray college expenses and avoid taking on so much debt, whose quiet strength had always inspired her. He was so proud of her ambition. He'd never envelop her in another bear hug.

Adam. She'd failed him. What she wouldn't give to be in some wild place with him now, roughing it. She should have enjoyed those times more instead of wishing she was somewhere else.

She closed her eyes, remembering the two-week camping trip they'd taken in northern Minnesota after college graduation. It had been quiet and peaceful, sitting by the side of a river watching the sun set. She'd teased him that he should have brought a fishing pole so they could have fish for dinner instead of the beef jerky they'd just eaten.

He'd stretched and gotten up, picking up short sticks in the area. She'd thought he was gathering more wood for the fire until he'd stripped off shoes and socks, waded into the stream, and started pushing the sticks down into the water.

"When you give a patient a vaccine, what are you doing?" he'd asked her.

"Protecting them from disease," she'd replied.

"Yeah, but how?"

She'd raised her eyebrows. Apparently he was feeling philosophical that evening. She'd been less so, after hiking all day. "I'm giving them a dead virus to trigger their immune system to create antibodies that will protect them if they are exposed to a live virus." She knew he knew this. She didn't know what he was getting at.

He nodded, bending at the waist, pushing another stick deep into the mud beneath the water. "Yep. You use something natural to change the environment to get the result you want. The vaccine makes the environment hostile to the virus. That's what I'm doing. Changing the environment to make it work for me."

"We're going to have hostile sticks for breakfast in the morning?"

The next morning they'd eaten fish. It had been pretty delicious.

"Where on Earth did you learn to do this stuff?" she'd asked, peering at the simple M-shaped corral he'd made out of sticks that had captured an enormous catfish overnight.

"Oh, God. My dad made me go to survival camp three years in a row as a kid." He'd shrugged. "I like to keep practicing this stuff. You never know when it might come in handy."

Darcy sat up straight.

Wait a minute.

It was true that Raub had the upper hand when it came to a physical fight. But that wasn't all she knew. She had life experience that he knew nothing about.

The only time she'd ever bested him was when she'd acted unpredictably and caught him off guard.

She felt for the broken bolt in the hem of her jumpsuit to reassure herself it was still there.

She had more to draw from than even she had realized. He would underestimate her. If she used her head, if she was as ruthless as he was, she might have a chance. Maybe as a human or druid alone she wouldn't. But she was more than that. Much more.

Darcy the medical student might not be able to survive this. Darcy, Raub's martial-arts protégé, might not either. But Darcy the drudii-human hybrid could do this and find Adam too.

She breathed deeply.

Raub had no idea what she was capable of.

35

DARCY SAT THERE FOR A WHILE, deep in thought, cataloging the kinds of things she knew that she could use to outsmart Raub.

If the thing brushing against Darcy's calf hadn't been so persistent she might have ignored it. But it went on and on, a light tickling, sweeping motion. She turned her head like she was waking from a deep sleep.

It was at least six feet long, with dozens of delicate blood-red legs supporting a segmented, yellow-green speckled shell the diameter of a dinner plate. It was ambling across the forest floor, and her leg just happened to be in its path.

It was so unexpected, so foreign, so huge, that she let out a blood-curdling scream and scrambled away from it. The creature paused, lifted the front of its body up and swung its head around to look at her for a moment, then continued on its way.

She scrambled to her feet and grabbed the pack. While she'd been sitting there brooding, the shadows had lengthened. It was going to be dark in a few hours, and she had no idea what was in the surrounding area. That enormous insect could be just the beginning. There could be predators. This was a stupid time and place to sit around. She had to find somewhere safe to pass the night.

First she needed to see what she was facing out here in this alien wilderness. Stepping carefully in her bare feet, she hiked away from the tern along the path of destruction it had made when it landed, so that she could easily find it again if she needed to. She didn't want to get disoriented first thing, before she even had a plan. Keeping her wits about her was going to be key.

It was odd though. She did have a distinct feeling about the direction she'd been traveling in. In fact... She turned slowly in a circle. She had a very strong sense when she faced a certain way, about twenty degrees off from the path she'd been following, that if she went straight and true in that direction, she'd find the tern again without any trouble. She didn't know what to make of that new feeling and was afraid to trust it, though she'd always had a good sense of direction. Maybe that had been enhanced somehow when the apochondria had been charged back on Earth. That hadn't been on the list of druid powers, but maybe the list hadn't been complete.

She scouted into the woods from time to time but always kept the tern's path in sight just in case. For the most part this was very much like a forest on Earth. The trees had green leaves, though the shapes of those leaves were unfamiliar and most of the leaves' coloration seemed to skew toward blue-green rather than a pure green. Fuzzy pale-orange mossy things grew on some of the tree trunks in thick clumps like shag carpeting, sometimes dripping with brown, wet-looking dots.

The noises that filled the air were not like the birdsong or frog calls from back home. They were a creaking chorus of loud and disparate insect sounds, deeper than those of a Midwestern summer night, throbbing in and out in intensity.

There were crimson blobs growing out of the soil all over the place. She accidentally stepped on one and discovered it was crunchy, crumbling into powder under her weight. She worried about being exposed to something toxic and immediately sat down, to use the hem of her jumpsuit to wipe the blood-red powder off her bare heel. She was already grimy with mud and perspiration from head to toe. She wished she had sturdy shoes, but the abducted aboard the *Vermachten* didn't get to have shoes.

Unless she found a lake or stream to bathe in, she was going to have to stay dirty. Maybe that was better. The shimmering stark white of her jumpsuit stood out in this environment. Dirt might act as a kind of camouflage.

She'd been hoping to find some naturally defensible spot, like a cave or something, but even on Earth caves weren't everywhere. She'd only been inside one once on a guided tour. She didn't know how to find one, even if they existed on this planet.

This planet. She was on an alien planet. It was so surreal. She'd had no idea what she'd expected, but it hadn't been this. Trees. A blue sky overhead. During the journey in the tern she'd imagined that everything would be bizarrely different, but it wasn't. It was only marginally different. So far, anyway.

She leaned against a large fallen log, easily five feet in diameter, to catch her breath and just think. It was hot and she was unused to moving around in gravity after so long. She couldn't see the two suns, but the light had the quality of late afternoon to her. She had to make a decision about how she would spend the night. She didn't have a tent.

Adam had obsessively watched a television show called Adventure Man. She'd watched it with him from time to time. The premise was that a man was dropped off in the remote wilderness with just a few tools, alone, to survive for a week. That guy always used whatever was available in the landscape to construct a shelter. It suddenly struck her that the tree trunk she was leaning against might serve that purpose adequately, if she could build a lean-to.

Maybe it was overkill, maybe it would be completely inadequate, but it gave her some purpose and she supposed she needed that more than anything else at the moment. She gathered long sticks that had fallen from the trees and propped them along the log, creating a triangular space underneath. As she ranged through the immediate area looking for more suitably long sticks, she came across some tall plants, taller than her, that had long, four-inch-wide, ribbon-shaped leaves growing in whirls around a central point, like super-sized grass.

She tried breaking one off at the base, then tried pulling it up, but both attempts failed. It was sturdy and rooted firmly. So she settled for pulling leaves off of several of them and carrying them back to her makeshift shelter. She laid them over the sticks like shingles in hopes they would help keep out any rain, but she was doubtful they would be adequate to prevent her from getting wet in a downpour. She quickly worked up a sweat.

It was a really sad job of it, but it was better to attempt to be prepared in any case. She had to start somewhere. Night might be long here, and she wouldn't have much warning if the weather should change. She could only see small patches of sky overhead.

Once she had the makeshift shelter constructed, she climbed on top of one end of the log to sit and think and observe the woods. She took Raub's pack with her to inspect the contents carefully.

Primarily it was stuffed with what Raub had called crackers—a tougher version of the food cubes they had eaten on the *Vermachten*. Crackers were unflavored, dry nutrition bars. He'd said they were cheap and sold at a high markup to the poor in remote colonies that might suffer famine from time to time. They didn't sound very palatable, but they would satisfy hunger and keep her going for a while.

There were only a few other items inside the pack: a sheathed knife with a tiny forked prong at the tip, a flask-shaped contraption that had a label saying it condensed humidity from the air to create drinkable water, and a very thin rectangular piece of brown fabric that was either a tarp or a blanket or both. So she had food, water, something to keep her warm, and something to defend herself with.

She was thirsty from the work, so she examined the water flask carefully. She sighed. It wasn't turned on and there was no water in the small reservoir. She'd been fooled by its weight until she realized it was more than just a canteen. She figured out how to switch it on and set it nearby. She had to keep the air intake uncovered, so it couldn't stay inside the pack. The instructions said the rate of water production was dependent upon the relative humidity. It was very warm, and the air seemed heavy, so she hoped to see some water collecting inside the reservoir soon. It could also be used to siphon and purify water, so if she happened upon a stream she could drink all she wanted. She hadn't seen one today, but she hadn't travelled far.

She was breaking off a corner of a cracker between her molars when movement overhead made her look up. Something with wings was darting around in the treetops. She chewed on the dry, tasteless piece of the bar automatically as she tried to figure out what she was seeing in the failing light.

She saw a second one. Then a third. Maybe they hunted at dusk. Were they birds picking insects out of the trees? They seemed to fly like hummingbirds, though she was certain they were much larger.

The crackers were gross. It was kind of like eating wet cardboard. She managed to get a few bites in her before putting the bar back in the pack. She kept her eyes on the activity in the trees overhead.

The creatures moved erratically but gracefully, swooping up

and down and changing direction quickly. One of them dove to within twenty feet of her and her jaw dropped. It was an insect, and its wingspan was easily three feet.

It drew closer, hovering just above her. A primordial shiver went down her spine. She held her breath and didn't move.

Its translucent wings were beating so fast they were a blur, generating a breeze that stirred the hair around her face. The light had become too poor to see any but the most prominent details. The creature's body was long and narrow, dark in color with glittering green spots. Two huge, bulbous eyes dominated its head, reflecting and bending the light in a wavy pattern. They almost looked like astronaut helmets.

It was assessing her, she felt sure. Her fingertips burned with energy, her power called up without her thinking about it.

The insect jerked to one side and nosedived behind her. She turned to watch it scoop up some wriggling thing with its legs, bringing the prey toward its mandibles as it rose back up in the air. She could just make out an outline of its victim in the dim light. It seemed to be an insect about the size of a guinea pig, but dark and shiny, maybe a beetle. She heard a crunch. The beetle's struggles ceased and the winged creature zipped off out of sight.

So these huge bugs were carnivorous. She couldn't be sure how hungry these things got or whether they might work together in groups to take down larger prey. She didn't want to be something else's dinner, so she gathered her things and quietly slid off the log. She would stay out of sight while they hunted in her vicinity.

She crawled beneath the structure she'd made and was suddenly sure it was woefully inadequate. She and Adam would have made a fire in the wilds back home, but here that might only make things worse. Raub had mentioned it was a high-oxygen world. She knew that patients who used oxygen had to be treated with extra care because even a little more of the gas in the air could turn a spark into an out-of-control fire. Even if that was something she could control, she didn't want to find out what insects on this world might be drawn to a flame, assuming that what she knew about insects generally could be applied here. There was no way to know. Not yet.

The eyes of that insect haunted her. It had been hunting at dusk—it was probably adapted to hunt all night like an owl, catching less visually adept creatures unawares as they went about their business. That was creeping her out, big time.

So far she'd seen only three creatures, and they'd all been super-sized insects. She remembered what Tesserae71 had said about oxygen being the limiting factor that kept insects from getting larger. That proved that Raub hadn't been lying about it being a high-oxygen atmosphere.

She hadn't seen any mammals, amphibians, or lizards, which seemed strange to her. Was it possible those animals didn't exist here?

She'd known all along that the forest was full of life because she could hear it, but she'd either been oblivious to the sight of it or the creatures stayed well hidden most of the time. She would have to pay more attention to her environment and pick things up fast if she was going to survive.

She laid the blanket on the ground and sat down on it, leaning back against the log. She tried to get comfortable as she inspected the water-collecting flask. It had produced a tiny sip. That was better than nothing. At least it wet her mouth.

She fished the broken bolt out of the tiny pocket on her jumpsuit and toyed with it until the light was completely gone and she could no longer see the bolt's glint. She needed rest but she couldn't let her guard down. For now all she could do was curl up against the log with the knife in her hand and analyze every sound she heard, replaying everything that had happened that day in her mind as she waited for dawn.

Her muscles ached from the exertion of the day and her feet were abraded, bruised, and possibly blistered. Morning was a long time coming, but she was getting used to being patient.

This planet felt very big and scary. She felt very small and alone.

36

TOWARD MORNING FATIGUE took over and Darcy dozed. When light began to peep between the leaves on her improvised shelter, though, she came fully awake. Her feet seemed to have recovered from the trek of the day before. The reservoir in the canteen was full and she drank it greedily, grateful for the pure taste of water on her tongue. She was groggy and stiff, but she had a fresh feeling of resolve.

She'd had plenty of time to think about her options, and she had decided she didn't know enough. There was no reason to trust anything anyone had said to her aboard either the *Verma-chten* or the tern. The only person she could have any faith in at this point was herself.

She was going to begin by climbing the tallest tree she could find to get the lay of the land. She could hike for days in this wood and never reach the end of it, especially if she went in the wrong direction. Climbing a hill would certainly be preferable, but she couldn't see any.

She crawled out of the shelter, the pack on her back with the water-generating flask dangling from it. She looked up warily but didn't see any sign of the large, winged creatures from the evening before. The forest was markedly quieter now, though not silent by any means. There was just a lot of discordant, arrhythmic chirping and clacking with an occasional deep droning sound. Nothing moved that she could see in the immediate area.

She took off hiking down the tern's trail. Again, she was struck with the sense that she didn't need to be so cautious. She felt sure she could easily locate the landing site.

She found a small rise in the landscape and focused her search for trees there. One in particular stood out. With a trunk like an ancient redwood, it was stout and tall. It had a few branches low enough to the ground to be accessible. This was the one.

She hadn't been the kind of kid to climb trees. She'd been born into the internet era. There were so many interesting things to do inside, like playing *Ocarina of Time* or blabbing on the phone endlessly about Buffy. Spending time outside had never held much appeal for her. But there was no reason why she couldn't climb one. It couldn't be that hard.

Yeah. It was hard.

She got her right foot firmly onto a knot and pushed herself up, reaching for the lowest branch, which was a few feet out of reach from ground level. Her angle was bad and she slipped back down, scraping the inside of her leg and both arms. She didn't take the time to even look at the scrapes. She knew from her injuries on the tern that they'd be gone in hours. Getting to the top of the tree was more important than some bloody abrasions.

She kept at it until she figured out how to position her body properly. It took more than a few attempts to learn that she had to hug the tree with arms and legs and grip the bark with her left foot as well in order to stay stable for the seconds she needed to get ahold of the branch.

Then it was about sheer strength and lots of scraping against rough bark. She maneuvered her other hand onto the branch and swung her lower body, crunching her abs with everything she had, until she finally got a leg up. When she got herself seated on the branch, she stopped for only a moment to celebrate the achievement, panting, until the burn in her abdomen subsided a bit. Then she was up and going for the next one.

She'd chosen the tree well, despite the difficulty of heaving herself up to the first branch. The branches in this tree had grown in a radial spiral from the trunk, and the distance between them grew shorter the higher she climbed, so the work got easier with each successive branch. Luckily she didn't have much of an issue with heights—a healthy respect, but no phobia or anything. When any doubts entered her head, she reminded herself that plenty of children on Earth had scrambled up and down trees since the beginning of time and lived to play another day.

Several times she startled creatures from their roosts, but it was hard to get a good look at them as they scurried for cover or took flight. They did all seem to be insectoid in nature, and bigger than any insect she'd ever seen on Earth, but harmless enough. They were obviously more afraid of her than she was of them, which was some comfort.

She'd lost the squeamishness she'd had over insects because of spending so much time with Tesserae71, but he was sentient, and they could communicate and understand each other. Raub had said there was no intelligent indigenous life on this planet, but she had no idea if that was the truth, so she began to use the dummy-chip language to greet each insect she disturbed. None of them answered her.

She felt driven to rush to the top, to ignore the need for breaks, food, or water. Only one thing gave her pause. Textbook images of human mutilation from freak accidents flashed through her mind. Clinicals weren't supposed to be until next year, so she didn't have any surgical or ER experience to counter her feeling of urgency, but she'd studied enough of human anatomy to know her body was fragile.

She didn't have any safety equipment to catch her if she made a mistake. No matter how great her regeneration ability was now, she doubted it could fix the damage a cracked skull would leave in her brain or a sharp tree limb would through the heart. So she slowed down and kept anchored securely with three out of four limbs at all times.

She wondered what Adam would think if he could see her now. He would be proud of her, she thought. He'd always wanted her to enjoy more outside activities with him. She wished he were here. But then he'd be in danger too.

The foliage became less dense. She was seeing more and more sky and catching glimpses that spanned greater distances. She reached for a branch and tested its strength. They were thinner up here, and she wasn't sure how much higher she could go before they wouldn't be able to support her weight. Something pricked or stung her hand. She jerked back and swayed precariously for a moment before regaining control.

Several dots of bright red blood welled up on the back of her hand. She instinctively brought it to her mouth and looked more closely at the limb she'd been grabbing for. She stopped the motion to her mouth when she realized what she was looking at.

It was a stick insect so large she'd originally thought it was a small branch coming off the main one. It was hunched up with its hindquarters curled over its head, waving legs that sported wicked-looking spines. She hoped there wasn't some kind of poison secreted from the points of those prickly appendages.

"Hey, I'm a friend," she said to it. "I didn't mean to surprise you. I hope I didn't hurt you or anything."

It kept waving the spiky legs at her and didn't reply.

"Okay, okay, killer. I guess you don't talk. I'll just get out of your way so you can get back to eating leaves or whatever."

She wiped her hand on her clothes and carefully moved away to try another limb, keeping her eye out for similar insects. If she'd just been poisoned she'd know soon enough. Potential treatments went through her mind, though none of them would be available in the treetops of an alien world. Wouldn't it be funny if Raub tracked her down and found her stiff as a board at the bottom of this tree? It would almost be worth it to thwart all his scheming.

Finally she reached a point where she could see in all directions. The view was breathtaking. It confirmed what she remembered of their descent in the tern. The forest went on as far as the eye could see in every direction—except for small blackened patches that forest fires had burned, probably started by lightning.

But there was something. Wait a minute. She leaned forward to push down on an arching branch to lower it out of her field of view.

What the heck was that?

Okay, there were two things. One looked like a big industrial complex that had been carved out of the trees and walled in. She would have to assume that was the belastoise mining operation. It made sense that Raub would land near it. He would need a way off this planet once he was done with her. The compound looked promising. A feeling of hope surged up inside her. Except as her eye traced the circumference of the wall she didn't see any breaks that looked like gates. That could be a problem. If she could find a way inside, she might be granted sanctuary—unless the belastoise were crazy bigots like Nembrotha had told her. She couldn't be sure that was the truth.

But not far from there was...what?

She stared hard, trying to make sense of what she was seeing. She wished she had binoculars so she could make out more detail.

It was some kind of superstructure. Six—or possibly eight... the air was hazy with heat and humidity and it was far away—spindly black legs towered over the trees and supported a rounded, shiny, black platform topped with...clouds? Was that an optical illusion? The stuff on the surface of it was white and fluffy looking and receded into the actual clouded sky. It looked very sculptural, almost organic in nature. Who had made that? The belastoise? It was near their compound, but the two structures didn't share any architectural elements.

Her eyes bulged. Wait...what?

It was moving.

One of the legs lifted in the air and then slowly set back down.

She leaned precariously forward, trying to see better. She slipped and scrambled to regain her footing, bracing herself again. She scanned the horizon in every direction, looking for more of these huge things, but there was just one that she could see.

Was that a spider? If so, what was on its back? And what could a spider that large possibly eat? She shuddered. She wasn't sure she wanted to know.

Could it be mechanical? Some kind of transportation? If so, hitching a ride could be a good way to outsmart Raub. She'd just disappear.

While she watched, the thing lifted another leg and eased

forward another step. What would it do when it got to the mining colony?

She could sit up here and watch that thing all day and still be none the wiser. She had to get moving. Raub had only given her three days. Now she had an idea of which direction to head in, and she wasn't going to waste another minute.

37

GETTING down from the tree was harder than getting up had been. She was fatigued from lack of sleep, and the pack kept catching on branches. Her muscles were cramping from dehydration. She was hungry too, though she was dreading eating more of the crackers Raub had sent with her.

But she made it down. She turned slowly in a circle. That strange sense oriented her. She still knew where the tern had landed, but now she also knew which direction led toward the mining colony. Maybe it was an instinct that her druid ancestors had passed on to her that she'd just never noticed before, like homing pigeons using the Earth's magnetic field. She hoped it wasn't some hysterical delusion that was going to screw everything up. She decided to trust it because she didn't have any other choice. Even if she'd had a compass, she wouldn't know how to use it on an alien world. To be honest, she wouldn't know how to use one on *Earth*.

She drank all her water and choked down some bites of cracker, then decided to do her best to throw Raub off her trail. She went back to the landing path the tern had made and continued down it in the same direction she'd been going in before for about a quarter mile, making sure to leave evidence that she'd been there.

He'd use traditional tracking techniques. She'd learned that from playing the VR hunting game with him. He thought employing anything aside from his own senses was cheating. But he had an advantage in that his senses were more developed than the average human's. Tricking him wouldn't be easy, but she had to try.

She doubled back, stepping carefully so she wouldn't leave footprints or any other telltale sign going toward the tern. She reached a point where a low limb overhung the path, stood on top of a stone, and got herself up on that limb, then maneuvered around to the other side of the tree to a lower-hanging branch going off in another direction. She crawled out on that limb until it bowed down to the ground under her weight and dropped at least fifty feet from where she'd been on the trail.

She landed as lightly as she could and took off at a lope. It was hot and she was sweating freely. Dehydration was going to be her biggest problem if she didn't find a stream soon. The water-making flask couldn't keep up with the amount of water she needed.

Darcy took the bolt out of her pocket and experimented with it whenever she slowed to a walk as a break from running. She could make it plunge and soar if she really concentrated. She attempted to shoot it like a bullet and then called it back. She'd have to practice that a lot more.

She watched the shadows in the forest to keep track of time. When the twin suns were directly overhead the heat had reached its peak and she was slowing down from thirst and fatigue. She forced herself to keep going. Slow movement was better than no movement. She had no idea how long it would take her to reach that compound, but she guessed it would be longer than three days.

She kept up a clumsy plodding jog for what felt like a few more hours. She'd never tried to run this long in her life. She was somewhat surprised that she could keep it up.

She began to see glimpses of orange and yellow through the trees. When she got closer she could see the bright colors came from a small glade carpeted with large flowers with orange centers and floppy yellow petals that were stirring in the gentle breeze. She stopped at the tree line, bending at the waist and clutching the stitch in her side, sucking in gulps of air, to take it in.

This is what makes me human. I can appreciate the beauty in the sight of this.

Would Raub see anything of worth if he looked at this? What did he value aside from this insane hunt? She didn't have a clue. She didn't understand him at all. Everything he'd shown her had been an act.

She sighed wearily and stepped into the clearing. Without warning the glade transformed into a churning yellow mass as hundreds, maybe thousands, of enormous moths or butterflies took flight as a group.

Darcy stumbled back, coughing and waving her hands in front of her face as the air filled with a yellow dust that tasted sharp and bitter. She wasn't sure if it was pollen or something coating their wings. They flitted off into the forest in every direction. Only a few stayed behind to re-alight upon the orange flowers, which she could now see—through a heavy yellow haze—were virtually petal-less.

So much for the glade. She skirted it and then realized why it was there when she began to hear a burbling sound. There was a stream nearby. She dumped her stuff on the bank and jumped in. Her perspiration-slick skin was coated with sticky yellow stuff, and while she suspected that the dust might mask her scent, it was uncomfortable and she wanted it off.

The water was cool and soothing after the long run. She splashed around for a minute, then reached up and grabbed the flask, pulling down the siphon attachment and sticking it into the water. She drank until she started to feel bloated, then filled the flask and set it aside to bathe more thoroughly.

The yellow stuff didn't want to come off. She stripped down and used her jumpsuit to scrub her skin, then rinsed and wrung that out. It mostly worked. Her hair was a mess that was probably going to mat and turn into dreads, but that couldn't be helped without handfuls of conditioner and a Denman brush so she just soaked it, squeezing and finger combing it under the water and rubbing her fingers over her scalp. Her jumpsuit was back to sparkling white again after its bath, which wasn't necessarily a good thing, but at least it dried almost instantly after she put it back on.

She decided to walk in the stream for a while because it meandered in generally the right direction and she had some idea, probably from watching way too much TV as a kid, that walking through running water could throw a tracking dog off one's scent. She didn't know whether that was a real thing or not, but whatever she could do to hinder Raub, she would try.

When her toes got wrinkly she decided it was time to get out. She took another long drink through the canteen and refilled it, then scrambled onto another branch. The trees were denser here and some of the branches interlaced. She moved from tree to tree as far away from the bank as she could get and dropped to the ground, then began to go in the direction she'd come to think of as north. She wasn't sure if compass directions made any sense on this planet, if there were poles and all that, but it made sense to her and led to the mining camp, so she went with it.

She decided it was time to try out some more of the druid

abilities she was supposed to have. Other than the water condenser, there weren't any electronics at hand, and she certainly wasn't going to mess with that, so she settled on attempting to create bright bursts of light that the video had said could distract an opponent.

She had to be careful. She didn't want to generate a spark that might start a fire. She concentrated on calling up the light to a point just short of creating crackling sparks in her fingertips. Then she imagined herself pulsing and flinging light away from her body.

The first attempt generated a bolt of electricity that arced between her hands and feet. She staggered and felt dizzy. The air sizzled but luckily nothing caught fire. She tried again, this time holding her hands and legs tight to her body. That worked. She created a dazzling white flash.

She repeated the process until it felt natural and she could consistently produce a result. She finally stopped when she produced a burst so bright that she blinded herself for a few minutes. It was time to resume her progress toward the belastoise colony.

The hardest part was finding a way through the crowded trees. Sometimes there was nothing she could do but crawl under low branches. She picked up a second wind and made better time through most of the afternoon. The extra water was helping. She forced herself to eat as often as she could. She kept her mind occupied with being alert for predators, thinking of ways to keep safe while she slept, and determining methods to throw Raub off her trail or slow him down.

When the light began to go, she realized she still didn't really have a good plan for how to spend the night and started to feel a little frantic. She had just about decided she'd just dig into the undergrowth in a dense copse when she noticed a tree that was growing at an angle. Curiosity made her hike over to it. It had been tipped by high winds and was being supported by its neighbors, but half of its roots had been pulled from the ground, leaving a small depression underneath. It was the best she could do and was probably better than what she'd managed the night before, because it wouldn't require any energy to make.

She found a dead limb with dry leaves hanging from the ends and used it like a broom to scrape leaf litter into the hole under the roots, hoping to make the spot more comfortable. By the time she finished that task, she was weary and didn't care much anymore. She curled up inside, wrapped in her blanket because it made her feel safer, with the pack as a pillow and the knife in her hand. She was asleep before it was full dark.

38

THE NIGHT HAD GONE by quickly. She'd been so tired she'd slept hard, only waking a couple of times to adjust position and make sure the knife was close at hand.

By her reckoning, she was halfway through her three-day head start, and so far she'd only been acting defensively. That had to change. She had to think in ways he couldn't predict. It was her only advantage. She had to use the environment against him somehow.

The problem was that she wasn't sure what to do or how to do it. If she didn't figure that out fast, she'd be dead in less than a week.

Deep down she didn't want to kill him. Her life goal was to heal people. But he wouldn't let this go. He was a psychopath. Even if she could somehow outsmart him and find a way to escape this planet, he was going to hound her. He knew this galaxy far better than she did. Nowhere would ever be safe.

If she'd been able to finish medical school, she would have vowed to do no harm. But doctors killed things all the time—they worked hard to kill germs, to cut out cancers, to stop the progression of disease. If she wanted to live, she'd have to kill the thing that plagued her.

As soon as first light penetrated the tangled forest, she was up and out of her hidey-hole and on the move. At midday she found herself on a narrow trail with thickets on either side funneling her forward. She couldn't know what kind of insect or animal had made it, so she stayed alert. It wasn't a great place to hang out, but the only other option was to keep struggling through dense woods. That would slow her down too much. So she alternated jogging and running down the trail at a pace she hoped she could maintain for a long time. The druid gene gave her more energy and stamina. She would need every bit of it.

She came to a low branch blocking the path at about chest height. She pushed it up and back as she went by. When she let go, it snapped into place with a vicious slap.

She stopped and turned around.

She pulled on the branch again, farther this time, then released it. It violently crashed back into its natural position.

This was something she could work with.

She began to scavenge for stout sticks, cracking them down until she had eight of them, all about eighteen inches long. Then she kneeled and scraped the tips with her knife until she'd made a sharp point on each one. She also gouged a thick notch in each of them so she could anchor them to the branch. She carefully gathered up the whittled chips and disposed of them in the thickets so they wouldn't be visible.

She sat down and stared at the tree, working through the problem, mapping out a potential diagram of a contraption in her head. She had watched Adam occasionally set traps for game when they were camping—mostly snare traps, but the concept she had in mind was very similar. She needed two lengths of rope, string, or vine and to build a trigger mechanism out of wood

—that could be made with the knife and sticks lying around on the forest floor.

First she had to find something she could use to tie the stakes to the tree and to pull the branch back and hold it taut. She also had to make a trip line that would blend into the background on the trail. She'd seen vines clinging to some trees the day before, but now of course none were in the immediate area. It took some time to find one. She pulled a long piece down from a tree and hoped it wouldn't give her something like poison ivy.

The vine was woody and inflexible. It wouldn't work as rope. She sat down with it and tried scraping it with her knife to see if she could peel away a long, thin section that would be flexible but strong enough to use. Once she got through the tough outer layer, she was able to pull the vine apart, but only in short sections. Wherever it branched, it invariably broke.

She sighed and sat with her hands buried in her hair, trying to think of other solutions. She tried tying the short pieces together into a longer strand, but she didn't know how to tie any knots aside from a shoestring knot or a surgical knot. The surgical knots made the pieces splinter and break. When she tried over-hand knots the pieces slipped apart. She tried braiding the sections together, but that went nowhere. She briefly tried twisting them and that didn't work either. She threw the pieces down in disgust and walked away. Someone might be able to turn this vine into rope, but she couldn't.

She paced back and forth. *Dammit.* She didn't know *anything* useful. How was she supposed to do this?

Her gaze landed on the pack. She grabbed the knife. If she could just take off the top rim in a spiral... But the knife wouldn't puncture the alien fabric no matter what she did to it. She pulled out the blanket Raub had given her, but it was the same.

She started to shake with frustration, then put the knife down carefully and pushed it away from her. She fingered her jumpsuit thoughtfully. Maybe she could take it apart. She pressed the button on the edge of her sleeve that made the garment flexible. Then she stuck the knife through the fabric about an inch from the bottom of the leg portion and sawed at it. A small piece came off. She tugged on it. It elongated and grew thinner. She pulled again and again until it was as thin as a hair. If she tried to make it any thinner, it broke.

She sat there puzzling. How could she make it strong again? She tried laying it over the jumpsuit and clicking the button. But then it was joined to the jumpsuit and couldn't be separated, even by the knife. It was super strong and nearly transparent, perfect for this task. She clicked the button again to separate her new thread and this time held it close to the button when she activated the jumpsuit. That didn't work. She was thwarted again.

She rocked on her heels, forcing herself to be patient and think. Something crackled behind her and she whirled, jumping to her feet. She strained eyes and ears for what had made the sound. Suddenly a very spiderlike creature the size of a small dog burst from the underbrush and skittered away down the trail in the direction she'd been traveling.

Her heart rate slowed as the creature disappeared from sight. It hadn't come anywhere near her. Just as she was easing back down to think some more about the thread, another one ran out of the woods and down the trail. A few minutes later, three more popped out nearby and did the same. None of them gave her a second look.

She peered into the understory, but couldn't see anything. She cautiously squeezed between a prickly shrub and a stout trunk. Her eyes adjusted to the lower light. A few more spiders fled down the trail. One of them had been heading straight for her but veered off at the last second to give her a wide berth. It looked like it was holding something white on its back.

She knew she should probably run far, far away, but she was too intrigued. She took a few more steps. Then she waited, watching as more spiders headed for the trail. She made her way closer. It was brighter where the insects were coming from. Was there an open space? Maybe there was a stream or something. She might be able to find some water. She worked her way closer and squeezed between two trees.

Darcy gasped and covered her mouth. These trees were completely defoliated and swarming with spiders. Thick, heavy webs draped like super-sized lace between every tree from top to bottom. If it weren't so creepy, it would have been beautiful. She noticed some white lumps overhead in the webs. She wrinkled her brow and looked around more, trying to figure out what they were.

Then she saw a wing sticking out of one. She recognized that wing from her first night in the woods. It probably belonged to one of the dragonfly-like insects that had freaked her out. The spiders must be omnivores.

A spider scrambled down the trunk she was leaning against. She started to back away, but it was already turning around and going back up, then over a web and down another tree. They seemed to be avoiding her.

She was about to turn back when she realized she was staring at exactly what she needed. She slid through the gap between the two trees and a spider politely waited for her to pass before darting through.

She made her way to the nearest web. Spiders fled before her. They really were afraid of her or at least keeping their distance. She wondered why.

The webbing felt sticky but heavy, like fishing line. She tried to break it. She couldn't. It had excellent tensile strength. It was perfect. She sawed it from the tree it was attached to and began to collect it in loops, careful not to let it get tangled. The whole time the spiders flipped out, trying to avoid her. Thankfully they didn't seem to mind her taking a bit of their webbing. She made her way back to her project with care, so the sticky web wouldn't get caught on anything.

She worked slowly, knowing she was saving time by not rushing and turning the webbing into a big snarl. She took one end, attached it to the notch on the first sharpened stake with an overhand knot, and began wrapping the web in a crisscross fashion around the crotch of the branch so that the tip would be hidden by leaves. Then she laid the thread along the branch until she reached the next location where she would affix the next stake.

She labored at a painstaking pace, thinking through every move. Wherever possible she anchored each stake at a second point to keep it horizontal and stable. She repeated this process until she had all eight of the stakes attached to the branch, all stuck at abdomen-to-chest height on Raub.

Would this kill him? It was possible. It seemed more likely that he wouldn't be tricked. He would smell or see something that would cue him to be more cautious. Or he might figure out where she was headed and take another route in order to head her off, bypassing this location entirely. Even if he was hot on her trail and it did deploy properly, she'd seen him heal every bit as fast as she did. Unless one of the stakes actually punctured his heart—and she wouldn't put it past him to have two hearts for redundancy's sake—it would just be a short-term inconvenience for him at most.

But it might slow him down and give her more time to get to the mining compound. And it could kill him. That made it worth the effort.

Now she had to fashion the trigger. She carved two stakes of similar size, with points on one end so she could hammer them into the ground with a heavy log. On the other end of each stake, she made horizontal notches on one side. Next she carved tapered ends and squared off edges into a short stick to wedge between those two notches. That little stick would hopefully hold the branch back until Raub walked along this path and triggered the trip wire, pulling one of the two vertical stakes loose and releasing the tension on the branch.

Now that the trigger was ready, she could put it in place. First she pulled back the branch and tethered it temporarily to the brambles next to the tree so she'd be able to reach it. She walked a few feet ahead so the dirt wouldn't be disturbed around the tree where Raub might see it, then crawled on her belly through the brambles and reached up to grab the branch.

She tested it, pulling it back as far as seemed feasible and marking a place in the soil directly beneath that spot, then retethered the branch while she worked. She hammered one stake into the ground and then held her short stick in place between the two stakes so the spacing would be right as she pounded the second down. She measured out the web she needed and cut it at that point with the knife. Then she carefully pulled the branch back again and tied it tightly to the short stick. It held the branch in place. She breathed a sigh of satisfaction. Finally, she was getting somewhere.

She tied the second length of web to the stake closest to the tree and tossed the remaining web back onto the path. It was coated in dust and dirt now, which served to camouflage it. That was good. She crawled back through the brambles and exited, limbs and face scraped by thorns, sticks, and dirt, leaves in her hair.

She draped the web across the narrow path at about shin height. She didn't want it to be too high because he might notice it. Too low and he might trip over it and fall—the branch might miss him in that case. She tied it to a tree on the opposite side of the path, taut.

She had to test it. She took a long stick, stood back, and pushed on the trip wire. Instantly the branch let loose, slamming back into place just past the wire. It worked better than she'd anticipated.

She took a handful of dirt and smoothed it over the webbing to dull it even more. She wanted it to fade into the shadows. Then she reset the trap, making sure everything was perfectly aligned again. She cut a leafy branch from an inconspicuous place on a tree and used it to smooth out the footprints she'd made in the dry soil—except for a single set she would create, right down the center, as she walked down the path, matching the original steps she'd made when she'd happened upon this spot.

She hoped this undertaking was worth the half day she'd spent on it. She hoped it would take him by surprise.

She hoped it would stop him.

Darcy jogged for a while, doubts plaguing her. Some part of her wanted to go back and undo what she'd done. She'd just set up a murder attempt. It was for self-preservation, true, but it still felt wrong.

She forced herself to remember the boarding party on the *Vermachten* whom she'd seen Raub kill, all the prisoners on the ship he bought and sold like commodities, and the look on his face when he'd kicked her out of the tern and declared the commencement of this deadly game.

She also remembered the moment he'd come close to raping her. She'd done what was necessary then to stop him. She'd do what was necessary to bring this to an end as well.

No matter what it took. No matter what it turned her into.

She sped up and didn't look back.

39

DARCY WOKE at first light on the fourth day with a leaden feeling in the pit of her stomach. Raub had either started after her last night when the three full days had technically passed, or he'd given her an additional grace period and was under way this morning. She couldn't know for sure.

What she did know was that he had more stamina, a longer stride, and more muscle mass than she did. He always caught up with her quickly during their VR scenarios. She knew from sparring with him in the dark that his senses were more extensive, and he might have traveled all night without stopping for sleep. He could easily be halfway to her location by now. He might catch up to her at any point today or tomorrow, and she'd be forced to fight him wherever she was.

She worried her chapped upper lip with her teeth. It might be wisest to seek a better place to have that confrontation, rather than to push on fruitlessly toward the mining colony. It could be advantageous to learn the lay of the land and leave some things in place to give her a tactical advantage, since he had the upper hand, physically, between the two of them.

Except that she couldn't stand the thought of biding her time and waiting for him. It felt like giving up hope that she'd possibly find sanctuary with the belastoise. If he stopped to rest she might have time to reach the mining colony.

At any rate, hiding, even with her camouflaging ability, wouldn't help her. Not with him. His sense of smell was far more acute than a human's. She didn't know how to get around that fundamental fact.

She decided to move on and keep on the lookout for some-place that would be more advantageous for a fight. Here on the narrow trail it was too closed in. He could trap her too easily. She wanted to face him in a place where she had somewhere to go if she needed to run, but close enough to the forest that she could melt away and regroup using her camouflage if necessary.

She crawled out from the nest she'd made under a dense, thorny bush with the impervious blanket wrapped around her, the same way she'd crawled into the tight space the night before. It hadn't kept the thorns from poking her, but it had kept them from making direct contact. The night had been long and uncom-fortable. She hadn't slept nearly as much as she'd wanted to. Worry had a tendency to do that to her.

She sat down on the trail to quickly devour an entire nutri-tion bar, following it with a swig of water. She was so hungry it seemed to taste much better this time. She had to remember to eat more.

Her failure to eat enough might have slowed her down some and led to some loss of muscle mass. That was going to change, starting now. If she felt the slightest hunger pang, she would eat an entire bar. When he caught up to her, she needed to be in the best shape possible.

The pack wasn't appreciably lighter because she hadn't eaten much during the first three days. She shoved the blanket into it along with a sharp-edged flat rock she'd found that she was planning to use today if she found a good place.

She couldn't see much of the sky but it must have been cloudy. The forest seemed darker, more sinister, and the light filtering in cast long, bluish shadows. She felt very alone.

Several hours later she came upon a rotting log lying across the trail. The middle was worn down to bare, shiny wood, probably from the spiders crawling over it. She decided to stop and make a second trap.

She'd gathered an armful of straight, stout sticks as she trotted along. Now she sat down on the far side of the log and carved both ends of every one of them down to sharp points with her knife. She laid them in a pile nearby and took the rock that she'd found the day before out of her pack. It was rounded and had one thin, curved end with a hint of concavity. The other end was a bit thicker. She hoped it would work well as a shovel.

She experimented with stepping over the log to see where her foot would naturally hit on the far side. She decided on the most likely spot, got down on her knees with the stone, and began to pound, scrape, and scoop. It took longer than she'd hoped. The topmost layers of soil were dry and friable, but underneath they were hard packed and dense like clay. Soon she was coated in dirt from head to toe but had managed to create a hole roughly ten inches in diameter and well over a foot deep.

Some of the soil she pushed up underneath the log, where it wouldn't be visible. The rest she scooped onto her blanket and carried away to dump farther down the trail, where Raub wouldn't see it until after he'd gone past this spot. The hardest part was shoving the sharpened sticks firmly into the walls of the pit in two concentric circles so that they angled slightly down, leaving only a small opening in the center. The soil was hard and each stick was a struggle. She finished up with bloody hands.

She took her sharp stone and carefully scraped sheets of

fuzzy orange moss off of trees nearby, layered them over the hole, then covered them with loose dirt to camouflage the trap further. She walked back down the path the way she'd come, smoothing out all of the footprints and other disturbances she'd made. She put her feet in two steps left in the dust from her approach and took off.

When she got back to the log she carefully avoided her trap, which she couldn't see from that side. She cleaned up the rest of the area until it was pristine and took off at a run.

This time she didn't feel nearly as guilty.

40

THE LOVEK EMERGED from the tern and breathed deeply. A slow smile curled his lip. This world's atmosphere was atypically oxygen rich, which would enhance his performance as well as the gildrut's and was already imbuing him with a mild sense of euphoria. It also meant that the planet harbored megafauna in the form of insects and arthropods which, despite what one might expect if exposed only to the effete hymenoptera, could be quite ferocious.

It was a fantasy made reality, everything he'd ever desired.

He locked his prisoners inside. He could have disposed of them, but he might yet need them to motivate the girl, and at any rate the sauria and baryana were both still valuable and the hymenoptera was half dead.

When Hain brought the *Vermachten* into orbit, he'd have the two prisoners put back in the general population, separated from each other now that he knew of their filial affection. He might have to punish the baryana for poisoning one of his best trading partners. Or perhaps he'd just eat the slug if he could find someone to prepare it properly. Their flesh was considered a gourmand's delight. That would be adequate compensation for the loss of income. The druska should have known he'd overhear it prattling about the murder.

He began the movements of the Sahventahl as the sun lightened the sky. He was in no rush. He was going to savor every moment of this undertaking. There was no better way to begin than with a limber body and a quiet mind. He reached out with all his senses, letting his subconscious drift while he gathered information with his body.

When he finished he had already picked up her scent, still lightly lingering in the environment. This world was very different from his homeworld. It was damp and green, brightly lit, and rife with a variety of odors, but he could filter them adequately and isolate the ones he wanted. He had developed that discipline over years of hunting. Now he would prove his worth and earn his place among his ancestors as a true kappyr, a predator of the highest order among the lovek.

She had followed the path the tern had taken in the crash landing, but in reverse. It was no coincidence that it led in the direction of the mining colony. So she didn't necessarily believe the baryana's warning. Savvy little bitch.

An excellent start.

He found her scent clinging to a primitive shelter and at the base of a tree some distance away. She'd crashed around without any care for hiding her trail. That disappointed him, but if she'd climbed the tree to scout the terrain, that was a good sign. If he happened to step on her tracks, his sensate feet could taste her signature, mixed with humus and rot and minerals.

And then he lost her trail, briefly. She'd tried to deceive him. He chuckled when he found her path again upon retracing his steps and circling a tree delicately laced with her scent. Here she'd felt some fear. It lingered in places, heavier and more cloying than the rest of her trail had been. Did she really think that tactics like this would throw him off? She'd have to do better than that.

Her efforts in the stream were more effective. It did take him some time to relocate her trail, but it was far from impossible and he was soon under way again, not stopping to eat or sleep. He carried only a self-regenerating water flask and a small communication device with which to signal Hain when this was finished. He could go weeks without food or more than minimal rest. That was what fat storage was for, after all.

He snarled with glee as he felt a trip wire against his shin, even as he dived for cover and one of her wooden spikes penetrated his shoulder, shoving itself still deeper as he hit the ground. He picked himself up and roared as he pulled it free, thin blue blood running in rivulets down his arm and torso.

He held the piece of wood in his hand and inspected her handiwork with the tree. Not bad. He had not anticipated this kind of cunning from her. It was a delightful surprise. He roared a laugh that made insects flee from the trees around him.

He tucked the bloody spike into a deep pocket on his thigh and moved on, a little more wary, shrugging his shoulder to keep his range of motion intact, relishing the pain. It would take far worse than this to stop him.

He was forced to reduce the speed of his pursuit when rain began to fall, adding to the complexity of the aromatic environment, but not by much. She'd picked a very dangerous route by following this spider trail. It was narrow and would offer her no shelter. It was practically a killing chute. Not to mention the hordes of venomous arthropods who used it frequently to forage and return with food for the spider queen and to tend the egg sacs upon her immense back.

In addition to the rain, the secondary sun was eclipsing the primary, which would dim daylight for several spins. It would also hinder communication due to solar flares and coronal mass ejections, common during eclipses because of gravitational fluctuations around the twin stars. This tended to wreak havoc on technology and bathed the planet in deadly ionizing radiation. The local flora and fauna had adapted to this level of radiation but the miners would have elaborate shielding against it, which was only feasible on a small scale, and even then only because of the rare and valuable ore they harvested. It was one of many reasons why this planet, in a galaxy with need of colonizable worlds, could never be a viable place to permanently settle.

By the time he felt his foot sink into her pit trap, his other leg was already raised to stride over the fallen log. He compensated by throwing his weight back to try to prevent his leg from being caught. He landed with his hip on top of the log, flailing as her spikes carved deeply into his calf despite his efforts. The wind was knocked out of him, and multiple tendons in his knee tore in the struggle.

He grunted, reached down and grasped the spikes that impaled his leg, and with considerable effort shoved them deeper into the walls of the pit so he could ease his leg out. He kept a wary eye on his surroundings. She could be lying in wait to ambush him here, or something else might be attracted to the scent of his blood and come looking for an easy meal. He was ready to fight if need be.

He couldn't reach one of the spikes that impaled his calf near the ankle on the far side, so he pierced the soil with the stake that he'd kept in his pocket from her previous trap to dig it out, the whole time snarling curses. She was definitely more clever than he'd reckoned.

She wasn't just a doe-eyed prey animal. She was wily and scheming in fascinating ways. She'd come from a cushy world without want, with plenty of fat rounding out her flesh, and yet she was driven to best him.

An arthropod scuttled out from the tree line. It stopped when it saw him. He continued to work at the soil with the stake. Another appeared and did the same. Then several more. He worked harder at digging his leg out.

Then there were dozens. They encircled him. He removed the knife from his pack, though he knew it would do little good.

They jumped on him all at once, biting and attempting to bind his limbs with sticky silk strings to prevent him from fighting back. He flung them off, tore them to pieces as he wrenched his leg free and rolled away, crushing a few of them with his body weight.

He roared. Blue blood and arthropod guts littered the soil all around him.

The bitch was better than he'd thought.

41

DARCY WAS ON EDGE. Days had passed. She tried to stay calm but alert, to remain focused on her goal while maintaining vigilance, but inside she was panicking. The forest was closing in. She felt an urgency to get off the trail, and find, at minimum, something a little more open like the area where the tern had landed, but she had no idea where something like that was or how to find it.

She climbed another tree to see if the view from above would help and found that she was a lot closer to the mining colony than she'd realized. She'd covered two-thirds of the distance there or more.

The super spider was still nearby. It was chomping on tree-tops, and the evidence that it had been feeding in the general area for a while was readily apparent. The tops of many of the trees in its vicinity had clearly been cropped, and some even showed signs of regrowth. That answered the question of whether or not it was animal or mechanical in nature. The white fluffy stuff on its back was still a mystery, though now that she was closer she thought it resembled mounds of glistening, transparent eggs. She'd never heard of anything like that, but that didn't mean that wasn't what she was seeing.

The canopy was too dense to determine anything about the understory or which direction she should go in to seek more-open woodland. So she climbed back down and kept going.

Sometimes she felt something she couldn't put her finger on, a kind of presence, tingling just behind her eyes, coming and going. She instinctively thought it must be Raub closing in on her, remembering what Hain's video had said about the druids having the ability to detect the unique electromagnetic brain signatures of different individuals. It made her feel even more paranoid than she already was.

She heard ominous sounds everywhere she turned, and she was sure they were Raub ambushing her to punish her for daring to set the traps she'd left for him. Sometimes she found herself running flat out, blindly, until her shins ached, her leg muscles burned, and the stitch in her side wouldn't let her go any farther. She would then fall to her knees, panting so hard that she couldn't hear anything but blood rushing in her ears and her own ragged breathing.

She didn't want this, any of this. She wanted it all to stop.

She practiced calling up her power and tamping it back down. It crackled like blue fire in her fingertips instantly and made every insect in the neighborhood flit away in panic. She felt full of energy, like it was all around her, soaking into her.

That was somewhat reassuring. It would be there when she needed it. Although she still didn't know the full extent of what she could do with it.

In the back of her mind the memory of Raub saying he wasn't as susceptible to her power as the hymenoptera echoed. What if he had some way of negating that power? What if *he* had some kind of power that he hadn't revealed yet?

What little of the sky she could see darkened and occasionally lit up with flashes of lightning. She'd always hated the way lightning made her feel, but now the sensation was stronger than ever—a weird itchiness, tinged with an inexplicable longing. And now, perhaps, she knew the reason.

Rain started to fall. She could hear it pattering high in the canopy, but it took a long time for large, cold drops to coalesce among the leaves and find their way down to her. She thought that the rainfall was probably good. It would obfuscate any traces of her activity around the traps she'd set, and she hoped it would reduce the lingering scent of her humanity in those places, camouflaging them even further.

The trail was now veering off in the wrong direction, and she decided to leave it behind. It had served its purpose, allowing her to travel faster for some time and funneling Raub into a couple of traps, but she couldn't let it steer her too far off course.

She found a break in the brambles and headed into the dense understory, meandering around thickets wherever possible, sometimes crawling underneath the prickly shrubs next to the damp, spongy, leaf-littered soil. That was where she rested when night fell, wrapped in the blanket in an attempt to stay drier, though it just overheated her due to the warmth of the climate. Sleep was difficult to find. She wanted to start a fire but didn't dare. It would help him find her, and it would be impossible to control in a high-oxygen environment.

The rain didn't let up. It kept on at a steady rate, slowly soaking everything. It was difficult to stay dry. She modified the jumpsuit so that she had a deep hood that came up over her hair, shedding water. That helped.

Her feet were constantly wet. Some kind of fungus or bacteria took hold on her feet, starting between her toes. Every night her immune system would fight it and reduce its coverage, but every day it crept back a bit more until her feet were itchy and painful and covered with a sickly yellow-brown fuzz that she could rub off, but still see traces of under her skin. Eventually she fiddled with the jumpsuit until she discovered a way to modify it so that it fit like tight stockings over her feet. It helped but didn't eliminate the problem. And it stretched the garment so much it became sheer and filmy. She didn't care about modesty as long as it kept her drier.

She ignored the discomfort and kept going.

The humidity was so high the water flask no longer had any trouble keeping up with her needs. She was able to stay hydrated and moving, though she was now slowed significantly by the crowded vegetation. The pack got lighter as she gnawed on the nutrition bars to keep her energy up.

She constantly wondered when Raub was finally going to catch up. It frayed her nerves, which were already in shreds.

Her heart never stopped pounding. Her nerves thrummed under her skin, and every sense was on alert. She felt more desperate by the day, sometimes traveling well into the night because she wasn't sleeping well anyway. She experimented with holding out a hand and pushing a small amount of energy into it until she created a soft glow that illuminated her immediate surroundings. She maintained the light until her hand got too hot, then used the other hand. It was enough to walk by, but not to let her run. She couldn't decide whether it made her feel safer or more at risk of being targeted by a hungry bug. It did seem like all of them were generally avoiding her, though. She frequently noted insects of all sizes and types taking flight when she came near, even before she'd noticed them.

Gradually the forest changed in character yet again. She started seeing trees with long, drooping, feathery blue-green needles that were soft to the touch. The ground underneath them was more comfortable for the catnaps that she stole between marathon sessions of running and jogging.

Still Raub didn't come.

He was toying with her, wearing her down.

It was working.

42

IT WAS ABOUT MIDDAY, but the sky had been growing steadily darker instead of lighter for hours as the rainfall grew more intense. Faint flashes of light penetrated into the dank copse. Thunder rolled seconds later, rumbling in Darcy's chest wall.

She could sense Raub. He was near.

Panic rose in her throat and she bolted forward, ignoring everything except putting one foot in front of the other. She saw snatches of pale, reflected light indicating something solid beyond the trees. It had to be the wall around the compound.

The sense of Raub's proximity grew stronger. He had to be right behind her. Her heart whomped against her rib cage and she picked up more speed.

She'd made it. Now she just had to find a way into the belastoise compound before he caught her. She waded through the thick undergrowth at the tree line, barely registering the branches holding her back in her rush to get out, to get free of the forest and to sanctuary. Lightning flashed nearby, searing her retinas.

Her eyes adjusted to the difference in ambient light. She

stopped in her tracks. Her stomach lurched. Raub stood in the clearing between her and a solid wall in the pouring rain.

He was waiting for her. He leaned forward slightly, his expression wolfish. Despite the rain, dark blue wounds stained his jumpsuit on his shoulder and one calf.

Her traps had worked, but they hadn't stopped him.

Her nostrils flared. She shook her head. *Dammit.*

She took out her flask, drank deeply, then let it fall to the ground along with her pack. Energy crackled under her skin. Lightning flashed over the compound, and as the sound of thunder reached her, she felt a wave of energy roll over her. The lightning was calling to her.

Raub strolled forward, a predatory smile slowly quirking his lips.

She tensed and looked around, taking in all the details she could about the lay of the land. She considered darting back into the trees and using her camouflage ability to hide from him.

"I'll find you, Leebska! I'll always find you!" he shouted above the rain, as though he could hear her thoughts. Could he? Or had he guessed based on whatever bleak and desperate expression had passed over her face?

He broke into a run, barreling straight for her.

She put herself in a fighting stance, weighing her options as she watched his long stride lengthening. His intent seemed to be to slam her bodily into the massive tree behind her. He didn't slow, and in the last split second she decided to try to use that against him.

She sidestepped and swooped down to grab his leg to pitch him off-balance and hopefully throw him, but even as she moved he was seizing her hair and twisting. She swung around violently in his wake and they fell into the scrub in a tangle of limbs and branches.

She was arched on her back with something hard and sharp

projecting up into her shoulder blade. The air had been knocked out of her. She struggled to breathe and to right herself.

He recovered faster and rolled on top of her, pressing her down into the brush painfully, a handful of her hair savagely clutched in his hand. One of her arms was pinned beneath her and his weight made it impossible to get it loose.

If she didn't get out from under him she was as good as dead.

It couldn't be over this soon.

She tried to use her free hand to claw at his eyes. She had to do some damage. She had to break free.

"You make it too easy," he growled, grasping her flailing hand and pressing it brutally into a knobby tree root.

She head butted him so hard she saw stars.

He laughed.

She bucked under him with everything she had, pushing him up with her hips, and twisting under him until she could hook and sweep his leg. Once she had wriggled partway from beneath him she viciously stabbed one foot into his groin.

He woofed out air and his hold loosened a fraction.

She closed her eyes, turned her head, and created a flash of blinding light. She thrashed until she got her arm loose and crashed her fist into his mouth, her knuckles grazing his teeth, scraping off a layer of skin. His head rocked back. Her feet finally found purchase on a root or a stone and she pushed off, squirming out from under him.

Darcy got to her feet and landed a kick to his neck, then swung around for a roundhouse kick to his face, knocking him onto his side. Another kick to his chest flattened him on his back. Her legs harbored her most powerful muscle groups, so against a bigger, heavier, stronger opponent, kicking was her best offense. He had taught her that.

He managed to catch her leg as she delivered another kick.

He twisted it and threw her back to the ground. She scrambled away before he could pin her, backing into the clearing.

He rose, cobalt-blue blood flowing freely from his nose. She reached for the bolt in her pocket, but he came at her again too fast for her to do anything with it, so she left it there. This time it was like the sparring they'd done in the dark on the *Vermachten*. She blocked his punches with the open-handed slap-fighting technique and darted in to deliver stinging blows to any part of him she could reach. She kept moving constantly to keep his punches at bay and push him back.

Somehow he wedged a foot in her path and got her off-balance. He latched onto her arm and twisted it behind her back. A cry of pain hissed out of her as she struggled to break free. His other arm came up around her neck, squeezing like a python. She grappled with his arm and pulled, lifting her feet off the ground to use her entire body weight, but she couldn't get his arm to budge. Nor could she breathe.

There had to be a way to dislodge herself. She punched with one hand at his wounded leg, but she couldn't reach low enough to get at the injuries. He pulled her up harder.

She wheezed in. It felt like breathing through a collapsed straw. She aimed a kick with her heel behind and up, aiming for his groin, but missed when he jerked her backward.

Dropping her weight again, she dug her heels into the ground and pushed him farther back, plowing him into a tree. Immediately, she jumped as high as she could, curling her body, then let herself fall forward in an arc, using her weight and momentum to pull him down and flip him over top of her. This time it worked. He lost his grip as he landed. She rolled out of the way.

"Improvisation. I like it," he said with a sneer. "You are a worthy opponent, Leebska."

"My name is Darcy," she grated at him. "Stop this. I don't want to do this."

She hurt all over. She tried not to think about it and dragged ragged breaths into her throat as she rose into a wary crouch. She grabbed the bolt again and launched it at him.

The bolt narrowly missed him, landing in the leaf litter. It was gone.

"But you must." He leered at her, then leapt.

She pushed his punch aside, letting it propel him past her, and elbowed him in the head as he went by. She turned and kicked his kidneys. Then a blow to the spine. She jumped on his back and wrapped her arm around his neck to give him a taste of his own medicine.

"Why are you doing this?" she cried.

"The why is not important," he gasped.

"The why is always important!" she shouted, hanging on stubbornly.

He lurched forward, bending at the waist, and came back up with a heavy branch, striking her with it. She slapped the branch away with her other hand. It slipped from his grasp.

Raub staggered forward, ducking under a branch to scrape her off him. She fell to the ground, the impact of the limb against her skull causing her vision to narrow to a small tunnel.

She had to get up. She had to fight. She rolled to her side.

He kicked her in the stomach. She groaned, writhing in the soil, tasting damp leaves, humus, and blood.

"Can you feel it? It's magnetite, Leebska. This whole area is charged. Your supply of energy is limitless here. I chose this place very carefully."

He went for another kick but she lunged up with her lower body, grabbing his outstretched leg between hers and pulling him off his feet.

Then she was up again, panting. How much longer could she do this? Her apochondria might be full of energy, but her body was tired of this abuse. Her muscles ached. She spat a mouthful of blood on the ground.

The circled each other, warily. The rain came down harder. The thunder was upon them now. Lightning kept flashing in her peripheral vision. There was a charge growing in the air all around her. She felt a tantalizing urge to pull the lightning itself to her.

He was relentless. He attacked again and again. They became coated in leaves, mud, and red and blue blood. It became harder for him to grip her skin because it was slippery from rain and their mixed gore.

She hit and jabbed him with sticks. She hurled a log at him.

He picked her up by her jumpsuit and threw her.

She swung around trees, plowing into him feet first. She swept his legs, his weight dropping him to the forest floor.

He grabbed her neck and rammed her head into a tree, then stood over her as she lay dazed, blue blood mixing with the rain, dripping down from his face onto her as he panted.

No.

Not panting. He was gulping air, working himself up into that state she'd seen on the ship, in the hallway, against the boarding party. Against her in the VR game. He was turning purple.

He was going to be even more dangerous now. How could she fight him like that?

She scrambled back, crablike, and got to her feet, swaying.

She called up her power. It was all she had left. Her hands glowed blue in the gloom. They crackled with fire and light.

"It's the vasdasz," he called after her. "A secondary circulatory system of red blood, like yours."

"I'll have to kill you," she cried, sounding plaintive and weak. She attempted to sound stronger, angrier. "I don't want to. Please don't make me."

He moved toward her without a word.

She stepped back, stumbling over the uneven ground. She reached out and touched a tree to stop from falling. It instantly burst into flame. She backed away, aghast.

"High-oxygen atmosphere. It doesn't take much to start a fire under these conditions. Just a spark. Soon the entire forest will burn. You will have burned it all."

"No, I—"

But he was right. The flame spread quickly, despite the rain, leaping from tree to tree. It didn't seem to matter that everything was soaked. It went up like dry tinder.

She was appalled. She'd forgotten about the oxygen for just a moment. How many of the creatures she'd seen in the woods would die because of her? How big was her body count already?

She tottered away from the searing heat, into the open with Raub stalking her, taking his time, a black shadow against the blazing light of the burning forest.

"Help me!" she screamed, praying that someone inside the compound was listening. "I don't want to do this!"

A raucous, high-pitched screech sounded overhead.

She darted a look up. The mammoth spider loomed above them, moving toward the flames, its massive head split vertically in a deafening shriek. It went on and on over the sound of the blaze. Darcy wanted to cover her ears but she couldn't. She had to fight.

Raub glanced up but was undaunted. He took another step toward her. His face was a maniacal mask of joy in the flickering light.

Behind him, she saw movement—dark shapes pouring through the gap in the trees that marked the opening of a trail like the one she'd been following several days previous. She darted back a few steps, the source of her fear shifting to this new threat. "Oh, shit!"

Raub huffed. He thought it was a misdirection.

A giant black leg stabbed the ground ten feet from where Darcy stood. The screaming pierced her eardrums. Her head felt like it had been plunged underwater. Her ears seemed full, but they continued to ring with the bellows of the massive arachnid.

She was bound to the spot, unsure of where to run. There was a wall at her back. An inferno before her. A towering beast overhead. And still Raub strode straight at her.

He jerked his head to one side as though scenting the air and finally caught sight of the horde of spiders just as they came even with him. Their bodies were the size of water bottles, leg spans the width of frying pans. There were thousands of them, swarming out of the trees in a river of hairy legs and mirrorlike, globe-shaped eyes.

Then they were on him, crawling up his legs faster than he could react. He roared and batted at them fruitlessly. That was a mistake. They dug their fangs into him, either to hold on or in self-defense—she wasn't sure.

As they reached Darcy, she flamed to life, her entire body glowing blue. Lightning struck just a few feet away. She felt it almost like an extension of herself and she...wanted it, needed it. It called to her. The tail end of it arced toward her. She tingled and buzzed as she absorbed some of the discharge.

It felt amazing. She wanted more. As that thought percolated into her conscious mind she felt terrified. What was she doing? What happened if you overcharged a battery? Would she explode?

The spiders parted into two streams around her, avoiding even the pool of pale blue light on the ground surrounding her. She turned and saw the arachnids converging behind her, scrambling up the gargantuan spider's leg. All they wanted was safety from the fire.

Raub continued to howl. Now on his hands and knees, he

seemed to be enduring the punishment as the spiders raced over him. He was simply an obstacle in their way.

The last of the spiders shimmied up and away to safety. The immense leg lifted, and the ground shook as the queen moved away from the blaze with her drones safely riding on her back.

Darcy was burning up, but it wasn't just the heat from the forest fire. It was inside her. She tried to call her energy back down to her core, but she couldn't. She'd drawn in too much. She had to bleed some of it off before she could get it under control.

Raub stood and staggered toward her like a drunk, his face swollen with hideous contorted lumps. All over his body, massive welts rose under the skin where the drone spiders had pumped poison into him. She wondered if he could survive that. It might slow him down. Maybe it was a perfect opportunity to run. The delay could give her time to find a way into the mining compound.

Behind him the forest was a conflagration as far as the eye could see. Were Selpis, Nembrotha and Tesserae71 safe? Were they still inside the tern, waiting for Raub to come back? Were they friends or enemies? Should she even care about their well-being?

She backed up to the wall and edged sideways, keeping her eye on Raub.

"You will never get away from me, gildrut. I will haunt you like a bad stink that you can't get out of your nose." Raub's voice sounded strangled. He barked a choking laugh.

"It's over!" she shouted at him.

"Never."

He charged.

43

DARCY COULDN'T DO it anymore.

There was no one to help her. No one to stop him but her.

She trembled. Her body knew what to do even if her mind didn't. She reached out for the energy in the air. It was fizzing in her brain, funneling into her whether she wanted it or not.

Her arms stretched out over her head as the lightning coalesced above her, through her. She screamed like a wild animal as she lowered her arms, aimed at Raub, and redirected the energy at him.

White-blue plasma shot from her hands.

His face lit up from the burst of electricity, his eyes bulging in their sockets, nostrils flaring, mouth dropping open in a shout she never heard.

It struck him with a force that blew him back nearly to the tree line.

And then she was falling. She writhed on the ground, clutching her hands to her chest. The pain went beyond anything she had ever experienced. Her vision whited out. She thought she might be dying.

She couldn't tell how long she lay there, wracked with unbelievable pain. She held up her hands once and saw in the firelight that they were shriveled, black, and smoking. She'd disfigured herself, possibly killed herself, to be free of him.

Eventually she struggled to her feet. She had to know, had to be sure.

She couldn't walk in a straight line. She stumbled toward him, spent with pain and anguish, though she was already pulling more energy from the ground beneath her.

Raub's body was steaming. His mane smoldered. There was a black hole in his chest. His eyes stared blankly at the dark sky, drops of rain pooling in them like tears.

It didn't seem real. Could she have done this, killed someone on purpose, just a girl from Ohio?

Falling to her knees, she put her ear to what was left of his chest. She heard nothing but the rain and the roar of the fire, and even that seemed far away.

She lingered, not really believing it was over, until the heat from the fire seeped into her, making her realize she was in danger. She stood and started to turn, then noticed something sliding out of a pocket on the thigh of Raub's jumpsuit.

Two things, actually. She prodded the pocket with her foot. A stake slid out, covered in mud and blue blood. So did a small, shiny piece of tech. It had a blinking red light. She scooped it up with the gnarled remains of one hand. It no longer hurt. It was just a dead thing at the end of her arm. She couldn't feel the device at all and nearly dropped it. She handled it carefully, using her claw-shaped hands like scoops and hooks, and slid it into one of her own pockets to worry about later.

She backed away and began to walk along the wall. It was cooler here. The rain felt soothing. She didn't mind it pattering on her.

She walked around the perimeter, leaving the fire at her back, until she couldn't walk anymore. Then she curled up, made herself as small as possible, and blacked out.

44

DARCY WOKE with the twin suns baking her alive. She could see both of them now, the smaller star was just to one side of the larger one, when she peeped through her lashes. The eclipse was over.

Her skin pigmentation had already responded to the exposure. The uncovered skin was somewhat darker, but dry, ashy, and reddened.

Thirst was paramount. Her head throbbed and her heart was palpitating. She was probably suffering from sunstroke.

Her hands were still charred but a little plumper now. Raw flesh was visible between deep cracks on the surface, weeping a thick, clear fluid despite the heat and her thirst. It was difficult to look at them, and she still couldn't move them. The pain had returned to such a degree that her eyes pricked, but no tears came. She wondered how she'd slept through that kind of discomfort. The nerves under the skin must have been regenerating.

So it seemed her hands would heal. She wondered whether they would be fully restored or if she would be impaired, perhaps limited for life. It hardly seemed to matter. She wouldn't live long enough to see them fully healed unless she could get into the compound. She had no idea how to safely forage for food without poisoning herself, and the thought of catching and eating insects was repugnant.

She licked her lips with a dry tongue—they were blistered and flaking from her ordeal. There was nothing to drink or eat. She'd left her flask and the pack at the edge of the forest. They would have burned.

Getting to her feet was difficult without her hands to brace herself. She rose slowly, leaning against the wall for support despite the scorching heat. A wave of nausea and dizziness swept over her. She swayed in place for a few minutes, then set off again to walk the perimeter, hoping to find a gate nearby.

She knew she should go look for a water source, but the compound was right here, if they'd only let her in. Or maybe if she could hold on for a day or two, the forest would cool enough for her to retrace her steps toward the stream she'd seen before, because that was the only sure source of water she knew of. She wanted to lie down in the stream until all the pain and heat washed away.

The forest, at least what she could see of it now, had stopped burning. All that remained were thick blackened sticks poking up into the sky. The smell of wood smoke and soot lingered, ash floating like snowflakes on the breeze. It was eerily quiet without the background cacophony of insect noises.

Her body felt weak. It was pulling in energy in a steady stream, but that energy was being funneled into her worst injuries, and no amount of energy could make up for the fact that she was dangerously dehydrated.

She panted with the effort of plodding around the wall. Her muscles were stiff, her body felt heavy and unstable, and her calves and feet cramped painfully. She kept on until night fell, but no gate was to be found. She gave up and eased down to the hard-packed earth to sleep again, no longer caring if she ever woke.

"Darcy?" Someone jostled her shoulder gently. "Darcy Eberhardt?"

She tried to answer but couldn't. Her tongue was swollen and filled her mouth. Her lips pulled tight against her teeth and were slightly parted. Something was very wrong. Light blazed against her closed eyes. It was too bright. She couldn't open them.

Someone lifted her and carried her a short distance, then laid her down on something cool and hard. She started to shake like she was hypothermic.

A set of hands smeared something cold and wet all over her body, and someone else dribbled water into her mouth, wetting her sandpapery tongue. She swallowed gratefully, her head coming up to try to find more, to gulp greedily, but a voice admonished her to take it slowly or she'd be sick, so she accepted the drops that were offered until she fell asleep again.

When she woke for the second time she felt significantly improved. She opened her eyes and recognized instantly where she was: inside the tern. She gasped and tried to sit up, adrenaline seizing her heart painfully, though nearly every part of her hurt.

"Hold still, foolish girl," Nembrotha spluttered. "She's awake!"

Darcy just stared at him, her mouth gaping.

Clattering steps and soft, padding feet sounded on the decking. Then Selpis and Tesserae71 were staring down at her. Selpis blinked frequently, her brow ridges coming together in that worried way of hers. Tesserae71's antennae waved and his mandibles worked.

Darcy looked down at herself. Her jumpsuit was stretched all out of proportion but was at least modestly draped over her body. Under that, her skin glistened with the same bright-blue regen gel she'd used on Tesserae71 in the tern many days ago, and her hands were swathed in the same kind of bandages she'd used on his leg and thorax.

"Water?" she rasped.

"Rehydration-and-nourishment fluid would be better," Tesserae71 clacked. He lifted a pouch from a nearby compartment between his pincers and held it close to her mouth. Selpis kneeled behind her to brace her head and shoulders. The liquid tasted funky and metallic, with an earthy B-vitamin flavor, but she lifted her head and drank until her stomach was full, leaving a million questions forming on her tongue.

She stayed in that position for a while, Selpis's hands gently draped over her shoulders. She felt unbelievably weak. She needed contact with the planet as much as she'd needed that liquid. In here, she couldn't recover at the same rate, if she could at all.

She was already depleted. The apochondria would help her, if she gave them what they needed. It was strange how she could sense that, when she'd never known what that feeling had been before. She recognized it now—the emptiness, the yearning—it was for the energy the Earth could provide. Was this emptiness what her mother had been trying to fill all her life? Was she the one who had given Darcy the druid gene? Would she ever be in a position to find out?

It didn't feel like the tern was in motion. She looked toward the windscreen and saw green canopy overhead. "Are we still on Ulream?" she croaked, her voice sounding strange to her own ears.

"Yes, mistress," Tesserae71 clacked.

"I need to go outside. I need to sit on the ground."

No one questioned her. Tesserae71 stooped and slid his

forelegs under her while Selpis triggered the door and scooped up Nembrotha. Tesserae71 deposited her gently on a soft mound of dirt against a tree with plenty of spongy orange moss to cushion her back. It was shady and comfortable. She instantly felt the flow of energy return. They were some distance from the strongest source near the compound, but this was enough.

"That's better. Thank you. I...this helps me a lot." Darcy fumbled with the stretched-out jumpsuit in an attempt to cover herself, but gave up. Her fingers still didn't work and her arms felt like lead.

Her three companions seated themselves around her in a semicircle with solemn looks on their faces. No one spoke for a long time.

"Were you working for him?" Darcy wasn't sure if she'd be able to discern whether they were telling the truth or not, but she had to ask.

"For the Lovek?" Nembrotha said incredulously. "That brute? It's not like someone can recognize that dreadful species on sight."

Selpis was nodding earnestly as Nembrotha spoke, her dewy eyes blinking rapidly. "We were as much in the dark as you were. I thought the rumors that there was a lovek aboard were meant to keep us docile. One expects such tactics. That species is the stuff of myth and legend. I honestly thought it was fiction. I never expected to meet one in person. How could we know that it was the truth?"

Darcy couldn't help but look at Tesserae71, though she knew Raub had left him for dead. That wasn't typically how one treated an ally, but Raub was just ruthless enough to do that.

"Not even I knew his true identity. Hain runs the ship for him. I had never seen his face before that day in the corridor when we left the *Vermachten*."

Darcy sighed. She believed them. They were here now,

caring for her, which acquitted them at any rate. She felt a little guilty for ever doubting them.

"Is he dead, Darcy?" Selpis asked quietly.

"Yes." She still had a hard time believing that was true. But it was. The electricity had probably stopped his heart, and the sheer amount of energy she had discharged had done a lot of damage to his torso. He had looked very dead. The fire had probably consumed his body after she left.

Another one of her victims.

"It was necessary," Nembrotha said solemnly. "I would have butchered him five times over if I'd gotten the chance. And tortured him too. And then played a tune on his bones."

"That doesn't change the fact that I'm a killer."

Selpis tilted her head. "It was you or him. He killed for sport. You killed to save your life. There is a difference. And who knows how many others you've saved from a terrible fate by ending his enterprise. You can go on to do good."

Darcy looked down at her hands, now raw and pink. "Thank you for taking care of me. How did you find me? What happened after he kicked me out of the tern?"

Tesserae71's antennae quivered. "It was much the same as before you left. We stayed in the corner. He exercised, ate, and slept."

"We tried once to overpower him," Selpis said, her eyes cast down. "But we failed and he bound us. He said he would have killed us if he didn't need an incentive to force your cooperation."

"Put me in a blasted box!" Nembrotha cried sloppily, flecks of spittle flying from their tiny O-shaped mouth.

"I believe he underestimated our resourcefulness, though he bound us well. It took us days to free ourselves." She rubbed her wrists self-consciously, and Darcy noted that her scaly skin was discolored and raw in places. "We began immediately to search for you, but you were well hidden in the woods," Selpis said.

Darcy drew her brows together in confusion. "The tern can still fly?"

"Apparently," Nembrotha spluttered.

She turned to Selpis. "You can fly the tern?"

But Tesserae71 spoke up. "All hymenoptera are trained at least cursorily in every department. But my skills at flying the craft are rudimentary."

"Very rudimentary," Nembrotha said derisively. They stretched out, their brilliant orange sensor stalks waving, bright spots of color in the deep shade. "Then there were the fires. We assumed you were both dead."

"But we kept looking," Tesserae71 clacked forcefully.

"And we tried in vain to gain entry to the belastoise compound," Selpis said. "The wall is continuous and impervious. No gates. The only way in is from above, and there's some sort of field that keeps ships and flying insects out."

Darcy heaved a deep sigh. The long day of walking had been futile then. Nembrotha had been right about the belastoise all along.

Tesserae71 gestured with a pincer in the direction Darcy assumed led to the compound. "All attempts at communication were met with silence."

"There is just enough fuel left to achieve escape velocity, but no more. Not enough to get anywhere. We wouldn't even be able to maintain orbit for long. We were on the verge of trying out the tern's weapons on the wall—we hoped to steal some fuel if we could manage it—when we spotted you lying out in the open."

Stealing fuel. Could they manage that? How fortified could the mining colony be if this was such a remote world? Surely the defenses were mainly to keep out the giant insects...

"A good thing we did, too," Nembrotha said wetly. "You were nearly dead."

Darcy nodded. She was feeling sleepy again. She closed her

eyes and concentrated on the energy flowing into her. Something vibrated on her leg, rousing her. She blinked, opened her eyes, and was surprised to see the others were resting as well. She must have slept for some time. She fumbled with the pocket on her leg, realizing the buzzing had to be the device she'd taken off Raub's body.

Tesserae71 lifted his head and leaned toward her. "If I may, mistress?"

"Yes, please."

He slipped the tech out of her pocket. Once he had it in his pincer, his mandibles began to work and his antennae to tremble. The red light was still flashing, but now with more frequency and the device kept buzzing. Symbols flashed over a small square screen, but Darcy couldn't read them because of the angle at which Tesserae71 was holding the device.

"What is it?" Darcy asked.

"It is a communication device," the hymenoptera said. "Someone is calling."

45

DARCY URGED Tesserae71 closer so they could look at the device together. A message appeared, and Tesserae71 recognized the code it used. It was from Hain. He said that the *Vermachten* had to be in orbit around Ulream because this sort of device wasn't capable of long-range communication.

Suddenly their future didn't look so dire. Darcy's mind immediately began to race with possibilities.

The message said little more than "Awaiting further instruction."

In the days that followed, Darcy recovered from her injuries quickly by sleeping a lot and never moving far from that spot under the tree. Once she got better, she did do some target shooting with one of the laser blasters Raub had left in the tern.

There was also a lot of time for conversation. The others were curious. They'd heard the things Raub had said. Darcy explained about the druid gene and how she'd actually killed Raub. None of them seemed surprised or disturbed by this news. "So I'm not fully human. I don't know what I am. I guess I'm a bispecies hybrid."

"We have a word for that on Limnuac, though I doubt you can pronounce it," Nembrotha lisped. They said the word several times, and Darcy tried to repeat it, but Nembrotha insisted every time that she hadn't gotten it right. It sounded a bit like the word sojourner. She liked that. She hoped that she was just on a temporary journey away from home and that she'd eventually get back, with Adam.

The four of them spent a lot of time discussing what their options were, how much Hain might know or would be able to detect about what had happened between Raub and Darcy on the surface of the planet, and what Raub might have done next, had he succeeded in his deadly game to catch and kill Darcy.

Soon they had a plan.

The only one who was unhappy with this plan was the one they needed to rely on the most to carry it out. As Darcy built up her strength, she coached Tesserae71 and practiced his script with him over and over again, until he became somewhat comfortable with his role.

"She will know I am fabricating this scenario," he lamented in the minutes before they were due to begin. "My people do not tell falsehoods. It is not in our nature."

"That is precisely why she *will* believe it," muttered Nembrotha.

Tesserae71's antennae quivered.

Darcy leaned forward and captured one of his restless forelegs in her hand. "You can do it. Just keep your statements brief and matter-of-fact, like we practiced." She eased back against the tree. "Let's have silence, everyone. Go ahead, Tesserae71."

He hesitated, then tapped the button to send a transmission. "Ulream to the *Vermachten*, this is Tesserae71 on the surface."

Within seconds Hain's face appeared on the screen. Darcy

stayed out of view of the camera but kept her eyes on Tesserae71, urging him on silently.

"Report," Hain said.

Tesserae71 responded instantly, just as they had rehearsed. "The Lovek is unconscious. I have administered first aid, but he is in need of advanced medical care. I will lift off in moments to return him to the ship and will require your assistance upon arrival."

Was it Darcy's imagination or had Hain's eyes narrowed?

"What of the girl, Darcy Eberhardt?" Hain asked.

"Dead," Tesserae71 replied instantly.

Darcy smiled.

Hain didn't skip a beat. "And the other prisoners?"

"Also dead."

"And how are you still alive when the rest of your cadre has passed on?" Hain's even, breathy voice asked.

Tesserae71's mandibles worked, but he answered a split second later. "Unknown. Darcy Eberhardt applied regen gel to a wound I sustained. It may have extended my life-span."

"Noted. Do not delay."

"Yes, my queen." Tesserae71 clicked the button to end the transmission.

Darcy barely dared to breathe.

They sat quietly, staring at each other, for a long moment.

"It worked!" Nembrotha shouted, sending spittle flying.

Selpis's mouth turned up on one side. She picked up Nembrotha and boarded the tern.

Tesserae71 extended a foreleg to Darcy. She took it gratefully, grunting with effort as she got to her feet. She was mostly healed now, though the muscles and joints in her hands were still stiff. It would take some time to get fine motor control back, she assumed. She was fully charged and ready to move on to the next phase.

"You did it. I'm proud of you," she said.

"Hold on to that pride," Tesserae71 answered. "You haven't seen me fly the tern yet."

She smiled. Tesserae71 seemed to be developing a wry sense of humor. She liked that. She hoped that she had played a role in his personal evolution. Together, they walked toward the small ship. "What was Hain saying about your cadre? What did that mean?"

"Our life-spans are short, mistress. I am the last survivor of my cadre. There will have been a great deal of turnover since we left the *Vermachten*."

She stopped to stare at him searchingly. "You chose to help me in your final days—"

His mandibles worked. "Yes. I would do it again. And perhaps I will serve you for many more. The healing gel is not normally used on my people. We are seen as...disposable, not worth the cost of medical supplies, because there is always another worker hatched to take one's place and we train quite quickly. But the gel seems to have given me a new vitality. Though I was slow to heal, I am now restored to a more youthful vigor. You have saved my life several times over. I hope to return the favor." He lifted his now-healed midleg and waved it around a bit. "I thought this was impossible. I'm glad it was not."

"You are the last Tesserae then?" she asked softly.

"I am, yes."

"You have value to me, Tesserae71. If our plan works, I will do whatever I can to extend your life even further."

"Thank you, mistress."

"Darcy. Call me Darcy," she said, her smile returning.

"As you wish, my queen."

Darcy sighed.

They ascended the ramp and Tesserae71 climbed into the pilot's seat.

They secured themselves and took off.

46

DARCY QUICKLY FOUND that Tesserae71 had not been joking about his skill in flying the tern. The issue with steering that Raub had had during the landing was only a small part of the problem. Tesserae71 also had a bit of a lead foot.

Liftoff was dizzying but the ride soon smoothed out, though the craft tended to list to one side throughout the flight. Once they cleared the atmosphere it wasn't noticeable anymore. The real problem was putting the tern in its berth. *Vermachten* opened the door for them, but Tesserae71 made two passes, aborting each at the last moment because some angle was wrong, before the third pass was successful. Even so, they crashed around a little before coming to rest. He repressurized the berth immediately.

There wasn't time to congratulate him or let her stomach settle after the nauseating ride. As soon as the tern touched down, Darcy leapt from the copilot's seat and retrieved the laser blaster Raub had held on her companions only a week or so before. She was a decent shot despite the stiffness in her fingers. She hoped she wouldn't have to use it, but she would if she had to. This was who she was now.

She sent Selpis and Nembrotha into the lavatory and crouched down next to the copilot seat. She couldn't be seen through the windshield, and she wouldn't be immediately visible to anyone boarding unless they were looking for her. Then they waited.

A thud sounded against the hull, and an exasperated message arrived from Hain a few minutes later. "What is the delay? I'm waiting."

Darcy nodded to Tesserae71.

He nodded in return, his antennae waving in tandem, having adopted the human gesture and made it his own. Behind his back he held the very same shock stick he had used during their escape from the *Vermachten*. He opened the door, extended the ramp, and burst from the tern, declaring with some desperation, "The Lovek is critical and needs immediate attention!"

Hain quickly passed into the ship. Darcy trained the gun on her then rose slowly to close the door again.

Hain swung around. "You," she said in a monotone. She lifted her woody hands from her sides, displaying their emptiness. Darcy supposed it must be a universal sign of submission in response to a show of force, even this far from Earth.

Outside there was a scuffle as Tesserae71 brandished the shock stick to keep the medically trained hymenoptera at bay. She hoped he was okay.

"Yes, me," Darcy said tightly.

"Where is the Lovek?" Hain asked.

"He's dead."

"You made the killing blow?"

"I did."

"I see. Well, that changes things drastically," Hain said, her reedy voice never changing tone.

"Your circumstances have certainly changed," Darcy replied. She called out, "You can come out of the washroom! It's safe!" The others slid out of the lavatory and stood waiting.

"I don't see why my circumstances should change. I can be of use to you. What is it that you want?"

"I don't think so."

"I was just an employee, Darcy. I was paid. I had no loyalty to the Lovek. If you pay me well, I will serve you just as I did him."

Darcy frowned. She hadn't expected this kind of response. "I don't trust you."

"You have no reason to. You would find me useful, however. I know where Adam Benally is, after all. And I command the hymenoptera."

"I'll take that under consideration. Let's go." Darcy motioned with the laser blaster toward the door.

Hain inclined her head, stepped toward the door, then stopped. "As a show of goodwill I will not use my anipraxic link with the kuboderan to order every hymenoptera to descend on this berth with weapons drawn. In fact, I am telling them to accept you now as the new owner of the *Vermachten*."

Darcy scowled. She had no idea what a kuboderan was or what anipraxic meant, and that was just the beginning of a whole slew of questions. "What?"

"It is lovek law. One who kills a lovek inherits their estate. This is your ship now, Darcy Eberhardt. I certainly have no claim on it. And there is more. You own extensive networks of ships. And land on various planets. You are a very wealthy young woman."

Darcy was dumbfounded. She looked over at Selpis, who was blinking rapidly. She looked just as surprised.

Nembrotha waved their sensor stalks to get Darcy's attention. "Having worked for the Yamaah Imperial Ambassadorial Synod,

I can verify this claim quite easily if you give me access to communications."

Darcy nodded numbly. This wasn't going how she'd thought it would. She'd thought there would be fighting. Wasn't that what Raub had been teaching her all along—that nothing she wanted or needed in the galaxy could be gotten without fighting for her life?

When they opened the door and stepped down the ramp into the berth, Tesserae71 stood with the shock stick at his side. The other hymenoptera had stopped resisting and were quietly waiting.

"You see?" Hain asked. "Of course, these wouldn't give you trouble anyway."

"Why not?" Darcy asked suspiciously.

Hain called to the hymenoptera milling around quietly. "Do you recognize this woman?"

"It is our mistress!" one of them clacked.

"She has returned!" said another.

"Our namesake!" said a third.

The rest was lost in a cacophony of clicks and clacks. They crowded around Darcy, getting as close as possible without touching her. Hain watched silently without displaying any emotion.

Darcy frowned. "What...?"

Hain tilted her head to one side, her eyes roving over the insects. "This is the cadre you hatched. They imprinted on you. The Lovek insisted that they be named after you."

"You named them after me? What do you mean?"

One of the hymenoptera piped up, "I am Darcy46, and this is Darcy3, Darcy17, and Darcy91."

Nembrotha coughed out a chortle. "That's not funny at all!" they cried with glee, then proceeded to giggle maniacally on Selpis's shoulder.

47

DARCY COULDN'T HELP but think that they were about to run into some kind of trap Hain had laid in the ship. She kept the laser blaster ready, but nothing happened. She stood by while Tesserae71 put Hain in a holding cell, and they were free to roam without opposition.

She soon learned that "the kuboderan" was a giant sentient squid named Do'Vela who served as the ship's navigator, and after everything that she'd been through, that didn't surprise her in the least. She wondered if anything would ever surprise her again.

It turned out that anipraxia was a telepathic network that this navigator used to communicate with the crew. Of course it was. It didn't take long for Darcy to join this network and to begin asking the navigator a lot of questions.

Luckily Do'Vela seemed happy to cooperate. Whether this was simply in her nature or by Hain's command remained to be seen, but at any rate Hain was currently excluded from this network in the prisoner hold, and her influence on Do'Vela was blocked as long as she remained there.

Through Do'Vela Darcy learned how the *Vermachten* had broken free of the border-patrol net and the route the ship had taken since leaving Earth. Somewhere, on one of the stops along that route, Darcy would find Adam. She asked the kuboderan to plot a course toward the last place Hain had sold prisoners. To her surprise, the kuboderan did so with alacrity.

Darcy paced the cramped bridge, occupied by several Darcy-named hymenoptera, Selpis, and Nembrotha. Darcy98 turned. "Mistress, there is an incoming transmission from Yamaah addressed to Nembrotha."

Nembrotha perked up and urged Selpis forward to the communications station. Darcy stood on the other side of Darcy98 to watch. Another brightly colored baryana came on-screen and confirmed what Hain had stated about lovek law. The ambassador would forward a death certificate, which would have to be digitally signed by an official witness to the body, and the *Vermachten* would be legally hers, along with all of Raub's other legal holdings, once the form was submitted to the proper authorities.

"Well, that's a problem," Darcy stated after the transmission ended.

"What is?" asked Selpis.

"No one saw the body but me," Darcy replied.

"Fripperdoodle. I will witness. I'm important," Nembrotha said with a wet snuffle.

Selpis's brow ridges went up. "You would perjure yourself for Darcy?"

"I will perjure myself to stick it to the Lovek," they answered imperiously. "It's a mild offense, anyway. And it will come to nothing because I'm sure Darcy knows a dead lovek when she sees it. Keeping all his stuff is a fitting end to that barbarian."

"This is surreal," Darcy whispered.

Selpis straightened. "I would tend to agree with you."

Darcy resumed her pacing. "Do'Vela, are there any busy ports along that route where we could stop to safely let our passengers go?"

"Certainly there are. Several, in fact."

"How long will it take to arrive at the nearest one?"

"Not long. Less than one spin would put us in orbit around Legare."

"Okay, I want to do that first."

"As you wish. We will jump shortly. Laying in coordinates now."

Darcy62 confirmed that the course had been calculated and that a jump sequence was under way. On the central viewscreen a transparent, swirling, circular object formed, distorting the space around it. This gyre grew in size until suddenly the mouth of it pulsed and swallowed them up. Darcy gasped as a familiar but strange feeling rippled through her. And then they were somewhere else and Darcy62 was telling her that the remainder of the journey would be through standard space.

Darcy wondered if she would ever get used to this.

The door to the bridge opened, revealing Tesserae71. The hallway beyond was filled with hymenoptera, most of whom were of the slightly smaller, younger Darcy cadre.

"My queen, we await your leisure," Tesserae71 said.

Darcy exhaled noisily. "Okay. Let's go see what happens next."

She made her way down to the prisoner holding chambers with Selpis, Nembrotha and the group Tesserae71 had brought. A hymenoptera pinned a voice-amplification device to her jumpsuit. She hadn't washed yet, slept, or even eaten anything. She was still covered in mud and leaf fragments. Traces of Raub's blood and her own still stained the front of her clothes from their fight in the rain.

She stared at the sea of faces, separated from each other in their tiny cells, each one of them unique in fascinating ways, hailing from a myriad of worlds, in all colors and sizes and shapes. By her reckoning, they all looked confused or alarmed or even hostile. She was about to shock them.

"I am Darcy Eberhardt. Some of you may remember seeing me here, as a captive alongside you. Like you, I was taken from my life and placed for sale. I am here to tell you that you are now free people. This ship is en route to a place called Legare where you will be free to disembark and find your way home."

Complete silence answered her words.

"You have other options as well. You can stay on the ship and work for me. I seem to own it now. If you have loved ones who have been sold by the previous owner of the ship, please bring that to my attention. We will document your cases and do what we can to help you find them."

Someone sniggered.

In the back someone else yelled, "Is this a joke?"

"Not a joke." She turned to Tesserae71 and nodded. He nodded back and turned off the fields around every cell, except for Hain's. Then Darcy stepped into the nearest cell, extended a hand to the feathery person inside it, and gently helped them over the barrier. They stood staring at her, dumbfounded.

"I won't put up with fighting between you. If you pull anything, your freedom will be revoked until we reach Legare. No exceptions. If you don't like someone, stay away from them. The hymenoptera will not be your guards anymore. They will be serving as peacekeepers. Got it?" She'd meant to say police, but the chip reformed the word into something a little different. She liked it better anyway.

No one else left their cell. They didn't believe her.

Darcy held out her hands. "Come on, now. It's all right. We've set out some food in the hallway. You can have as much as you want."

Still no one moved, but a low murmur rose as the prisoners voiced their disbelief to each other.

She crossed another barrier and led another prisoner out. Then another. She motioned for the hymenoptera to do the same. Selpis joined in too. Soon a few individuals took tentative steps outside their geometrically shaped holding cells. More followed. The rooms filled with a roar as the prisoners congratulated each other on their good fortune. And slowly, a few at a time, people began to leave the confines of the room to see if there really was food in the corridor.

Darcy remained on her guard, walking the perimeter of each of the holding rooms, watching the crowds milling about with an eye out for discord. All sorts of people had been held in these cells. Some of them could have been from opposing factions or criminals of just about any flavor. She didn't want anyone to get hurt because she'd let them go.

Nembrotha had told her she shouldn't have released them from the cells until just before she dumped them on Legare, but that seemed heartless to her. She felt they needed some time to get used to the idea before they were forced to face a new challenge. She had no idea how hard it was going to be for some of them to get back home. There were some, like Selpis, who would have no home to go back to. And what would happen to them?

"Why do you look so unhappy, Darcy?" said a soft, toneless voice.

Hain.

Darcy had been lingering in the corner where Hain was being held. Some part of her was afraid the other captives might want to take revenge on Hain, and Darcy had a feeling that Hain might yet be useful. She didn't want violence of any kind, regardless.

Darcy met her eyes. "Do I?"

Hain swayed to one side like a reed. "I would think you'd be jubilant, having set all these people free, and yet your expression seems to reveal that you are distracted, worried. What is it that you worry about?"

Darcy's eyes narrowed. "How do you feel about me setting them free?"

"How I feel makes little difference."

There was something so odd about staring into such an expressionless face, listening to such a bland voice. Hain seemed to cultivate the perception that she existed divorced from any emotion. And maybe she did. "Why not?"

"You seem to think that I was free to choose this life for myself."

"Are you telling me you weren't?" Darcy asked.

"The Lovek found me after I stole this ship and allowed its crew to die a horrible death on my homeworld. He drew up a contract. He agreed not to turn me over to galactic authorities or to hurt my people if I worked for him. I became an indentured servant at that point and would have been for his entire life. There was no sense in refusing to do anything he commanded. He gave me the run of the ship and the illusion of freedom as long as I maintained the charade that I was the one behind every order so that he could maintain his solitude and anonymity. Even if you keep me in this cell, you have freed me. From him."

Darcy frowned. Hain had allowed people to die and stolen a ship. If that crew had worked for Raub though, Darcy could guess they'd been up to no good. This information painted Hain in a new light. "How do I know you aren't just saying this?"

Hain fluttered her hands in a way that Darcy felt was akin to a shrug. "You'll find the contract in his quarters."

"Why didn't you just kill him then? You'd be the one who owned everything."

Hain's eyes drooped a little. She looked back at the circulating crowd of prisoners. "He planned for that. If I were to file a death certificate, a large bounty would be set on my head and terrible injury would come to my people. He would brook no disobedience from those who served him."

Darcy nodded.

She believed Hain. She wouldn't be foolish. She'd check into this, but if Hain's story was true, then Hain was just as much a victim as any of them were. She motioned to three hymenoptera nearby and asked them to release Hain, keep her well guarded, and follow her. Then she rounded up Selpis, Nembrotha, and Tesserae71 and asked them to come along.

Raub's quarters were gross. They were decorated like something out of a hunting lodge crossed with a whore's boudoir from a bad Western film. There were actually furs and skins on the bed, and she didn't doubt that they were authentic.

The documents were on a tablet computer. Nembrotha pored over them and declared that all of the digital seals looked authentic and they could send an inquiry to verify them.

Nembrotha waved their sensory stalks at Hain. "It seems you may not be the vicious sadist we all assumed you to be."

Hain remained poised. "I urge you to investigate the digital seals. And I would like to offer a simple suggestion and my assistance. If you deem that effort worthwhile, I would ask that you confine me out of reach of the other prisoners until after we leave Legare."

Darcy leveled a hard look at Hain. "Go on."

"I suggest that you consider giving each prisoner a small sum as a travel allowance. Without some currency, they will quickly find themselves in a more dire situation on Legare than they ever were in here. As Raub's legal proxy I can transfer some of his considerable wealth to a bank on Legare and have chits made up for each one of them in whatever amount you feel is fair. That will give them a better chance of survival and of getting home."

Darcy conferred with Selpis and Nembrotha and decided on an amount. They watched intently while Hain made the arrangements via the computer console in Raub's quarters. According to her two companions, Hain didn't do anything fishy.

"That was a good idea. I should have thought of it," Darcy said. "I will confine you to your quarters until after Legare. If any of the other prisoners stay behind, they'll be informed about the situation."

Hain bowed her head. "Thank you, Darcy. I hope to be of service to you again soon."

Darcy picked up a tablet and asked Hain to open the file that showed her genetics. Then she had the hymenoptera escort Hain to her quarters and set up a watch outside the door.

She pored over it carefully. She'd been too shocked the first time to fully comprehend it all. The things she wanted to know were there. There were alien genes on both sets of alleles. That was how she'd gotten the full complement. She'd inherited druidic traits from both parents—one more than the other, but they were both carriers.

How common could this be on Earth? How many others were there like her? Were there many? Or was she unique? A freakish coincidence?

Nembrotha stayed on the tabletop, poking at the computer terminal with the two small tentacles on the front of their foot and occasionally one of their sensor stalks, composing another message to inquire about the veracity of Hain's claims.

Selpis sat down on the floor wearily, eschewing the bed and the rest of the gruesomely draped seating. "Who will you send to the bank tomorrow to retrieve the chits?"

Darcy sat down next to Selpis with her back against the bed. "I was hoping to send you and some hymenoptera."

Selpis shook her head. "That won't do. Not with that sum of money."

Darcy turned to look at Selpis. "Why not?"

"Tesserae71 tried to explain it to you. Insect species are treated as less than, Darcy. It wouldn't be safe. They'd be targeted."

Darcy huffed and shook her head in disbelief.

"What is it?" Selpis asked.

Earth was not unique. The rest of the galaxy also found ways to revile individuals for reasons that had nothing to do with their own actions or their character. Out here, the color of her skin no longer mattered, but she'd taken on a far-worse impediment. She was a dangerous druid who would be imprisoned if anyone detected her genetic makeup.

Darcy sighed. "The hymenoptera and I have more in common than I thought."

48

DARCY ENDED up going to Legare herself with Selpis, Nembrotha, and a rather large and fluffy four-eyed prisoner named Balg who was well liked for being congenial but looked pretty menacing. Tesserae71 piloted a tern for them, but he would stay inside and wait to be safe. He seemed grateful for that concession. He did much better flying a ship that was in good condition, though his landing was more than a little rough.

The city was laid out in a grid, with large landing pads in each quadrant. A trolley traveled the center of every narrow street, and a variety of people were walking up and down brightly colored sidewalks.

But that wasn't the strangest thing. Every building was tall and blocky, with rounded edges and a peculiar finish that resembled dripping candle wax.

Darcy hopped out of the tern and onto bright green pavement, the swishy neutral-tone clothing that Selpis had found for her swirling around her. She was wearing shoes again, and they felt strange and ill-fitting, despite their universal configurable state. When she'd channeled the lightning, the heat must have killed the fungus growing on her feet, but the strange markings it had left behind remained under her skin like a tattoo done in a pointillist style. The fungus had also left her feet feeling more sensitive.

Selpis had insisted that wearing anything else—especially the prison jumpsuits they'd been wearing on the *Vermachten*—would stand out as unusual. Selpis herself was decked out in similar flowing garments in various shades of grey, topped with a black robe sort of thing.

The sky was blue with a hint of violet on the horizon. The few treelike plants that she'd seen between buildings during their descent were various shades of yellow to orange. She'd been warned that the gravity here was going to be slightly stronger than what was standard aboard ship or what she'd experienced on Ulream. That was true. She felt sort of heavy and ponderous.

They had to cross a checkpoint before they could exit the landing pad and go out onto the thoroughfare. Nembrotha had had a digital ID made for Darcy using their connections. It identified her as a species called nieblic.

Nembrotha's willingness to forge documents for her was useful, if a little troubling. They had stated imperiously that anything else would just raise a lot of questions she wouldn't want to answer. She had to stay under the radar if she wanted to avoid serious trouble. She didn't disagree.

The attendant didn't bat an eye at their credentials, which they displayed on handheld devices similar to the one she'd found on Raub. Darcy walked next to a purple building and inconspicuously touched it. It felt like plastic to her. Even from this angle it looked like this substance had been poured over the building.

"What is this stuff?" Darcy asked Selpis quietly.

"Mm? What stuff?"

"On the buildings?" Darcy gestured briefly with her thumb.

"Oh, this is very common these days, but you wouldn't know

that, would you? It's a polymer that's impervious to the elements. It's a good structural support and insulator. It allows buildings to be erected quickly and inexpensively and lasts forever."

Darcy leaned toward Selpis. "Is it poured on?"

Selpis smiled. "Why, yes, I believe it is. Here we are!" Selpis stopped in front of a building. Darcy couldn't see what differentiated this building from any other, but maybe Selpis knew something that she didn't. She'd ask later.

"Darcy, I believe you'd better have a look at this," Nembrotha said.

Darcy looked up at the diminutive baryana on Selpis's shoulder and followed their gaze. There was a jumbo screen covering the front of the building on the opposite side of the street. On it was a woman's face.

A human woman's.

She was blonde, wearing an elaborate cream-colored outfit. The look on her face was determined and maybe even angry. She was speaking, but her voice had been muted.

Darcy's heart started to pound. How could there be an image of a human woman on this screen on Legare? Was she nieblic? Did the two peoples really look that similar?

The image changed to display another woman's face. That woman she recognized. It was Ajaya Varma, an astronaut who had been a member of the first mission to Mars, which had launched about a year before she'd been abducted. Varma looked calm and patient.

The broadcast was silent, but there were subtitles. They read: "Members of a species calling themselves terrans have appeared in Terac space in a proscribed sectilian science vessel asking for sanctuary and wanting to meet with the heads of the Unified Sentient Races. Could these be descendants of the ancient race the Cunabula bred and hid so long ago? Who are they and what do they want? Why do they make an appearance now after so long—and why in such a small number?"

The screen flashed, and a very pale, no-necked individual without hair came on. The subtitle stated that he was an expert on terran lore. "This is a hoax! It is as simple as this: terrans are meant to be a warrior race. Do these two women look like warriors to you? I think not. The search continues."

Next on the screen was a blotchy lavender person with large scales covering her head in place of hair. She was a former ambassador to a planet called Sectilia. "This is how desperate the Sectilius are to be free of their quarantine. They will do anything —including surgically mutilate themselves to look like another species—to get our attention. We should blow them out of the sky of Terac!"

Then another scholar was on the screen, this one resembling a hedgehog. Sort of. "Nothing has been released to date that sways my opinion one way or another. I urge the greater sentient population not to jump to any conclusions at this point. It's impossible to know what is happening in Terac until more information is released."

The display cycled back to the blonde woman again, and underneath her face it read: "Freshly emerging news. Terrans Jane Augusta Holloway and Ajaya Varma seek audience with the USR at Terac."

"I can't...I mean...what the actual f—"

"People are starting to take note of Darcy. We should move on," Balg said in a low, gravelly voice.

"Put your hood up," Selpis whispered in her ear, and grabbed her arm.

Darcy dragged her eyes from the screen as Selpis tugged her through the doorway into the bank. Before the door slid closed behind them, Darcy noted at least a dozen people on the street looking up at the jumbo screen and the image of Ajaya Varma, then back at her with expressions of curiosity, surprise, suspicion, and even fear. She pulled up the hood on her flowing cloak and turned away from their probing gazes.

The rest of the exchange in the bank on Legare passed in a fog. She let Selpis handle everything. They soon had the chits and quickly made their way back to the tern. She kept her head down so her face would be hidden by the hood. She felt like a fugitive.

She sat passively in the back of the tern as Tesserae71 launched them up into the atmosphere, worrying her upper lip with her teeth, lost in thought. There were humans at the galaxy center who wanted an audience with the galaxy's most powerful alliance. What did that mean? How had an astronaut destined for the first Mars colony ended up there? The reactions she'd seen to their sudden appearance seemed to be very negative and suspicious. And those misgivings looked as though they might easily transfer to her, despite the nieblic credentials she held.

What would that mean for Adam and the other humans who had been sold?

How would it affect her search for Adam?

She didn't know.

ABOUT THE AUTHOR

 As a child growing up in rural Illinois, Jennifer Foehner Wells had the wild outdoors, a budding imagination, and books for company.

Her interest in science fiction was piqued early on when a family friend loaned her a collection of Ray Bradbury shorts. That was all it took to set her on a course toward a lifelong love of science and science fiction. She earned a degree in biology in 1995.

Jen's first novel, Fluency, was a virally successful best seller. Her second novel, Remanence, was nominated for the Goodreads Choice Awards of 2016.

Jen currently lives in Pennsylvania with two boisterous boys, the geekiest literature professor on the planet, three semi-crazed cats, a floofie and independent Great Pyrenees, and a five pound Pekingese/Chihuahua mix that steals hearts and takes names.

If you enjoyed this book, please consider leaving a review on your favorite online site and tell your friends about it, both in person and via social media. Help other readers find it! Support the authors from whom you crave more stories.

ALSO BY JENNIFER FOEHNER WELLS

Novels

Fluency (Confluence Book 1)

Remanence (Confluence Book 2)

Valence (Confluence Book 4) —publishing November 2017

Short Fiction

The Grove

Symbiont Seeking Symbiont

Anthologies

The Future Chronicles—Special Edition

The Future Chronicles—Alien Chronicles

The Future Chronicles—Z Chronicles

The Future Chronicles—Galaxy Chronicles

Dark Beyond the Stars

At the Helm Vol. 1: A Sci-Fi Bridge Anthology

BE AMONG THE FIRST

TO EXPLORE

THE CONFLUENCE UNIVERSE

SUBSCRIBE AT:

WWW.JENTHULHU.COM

Made in the USA
Lexington, KY
21 January 2018